RED
DEATH

D0743993

RED DEATH

BEING THE FIRST BOOK
IN THE ADVENTURES OF
JONATHAN BARRETT,
GENTLEMAN VAMPIRE

✦ ✦ ✦

AS RELATED TO

P.N. ELROD

BENBELLA BOOKS
Dallas, TX

BenBella Books Edition
Copyright © 1993 by Pat Elrod
Revisions Copyright © 2003 by Pat Elrod

BenBella Books
6440 N. Central Expressway
Suite 508
Dallas, TX 75206

Send feedback to feedback@benbellabooks.com
www.benbellabooks.com

Library of Congress Cataloging-in-Publication Data

Elrod, P. N. (Patricia Nead)
    Red death : being the first book in the adventures of Jonathan
Barrett, gentleman vampire / as related to P.N. Elrod.
        p. cm.
    ISBN 1-932100-19-9
    1. Vampires--Fiction. I. Title.

PS3555.L68R43 2004
813'.54--dc22

                                                            2003024538

Printed in the United States of America
First BenBella Printing: April 2004

10 9 8 7 6 5 4 3 2 1

Cover illustration by Michael Herring
Cover design by Melody Cadongog
Interior designed and composed by John Reinhardt Book Design

Distributed by Independent Publishers Group
To order call (800) 888-4741
www.ipgbook.com

Remembering Ben,
Ursa,
Jake,
Big Mack
and
Mighty Mite.
Miss you.

And special thanks to
special people:
Joe Marie Ledet,
Roxanne Longstreet Conrad,
Louann Qualls Miller
and the REAL Barretts,
Paul, Julie and Chris.

*It has been observed that all people
are doomed to be in love once in their lives.*

—Henry Fielding

As this tale was written to give entertainment, not instruction, I have made no attempt to re-create the language spoken over two hundred years ago. There have been so many shifts in usage, meaning and nuance that I expect a typical conversation of the 18th century would be largely unintelligible to a present-day reader. Since I have had to "shift" myself as well to avoid becoming too anachronistic in a swiftly changing world, modern usage, words and terms have doubtless found their way into the narrative. This inevitable corruption wrought by time will be annoying, perhaps, to the historian, but my goal is to clarify, not confound the more casual student.

Though some fragments of the following have been elsewhere recorded,[*] Mr. Fleming, an otherwise worthy raconteur, misquoted me outrageously on several important points, which have now been corrected. This is a true accounting of the facts. Only certain names and locations have been changed to protect the guilty and their hapless—and usually innocent—relations and descendants.

Jonathan Barrett, esq.

---

[*] *Bloodcircle* by Jack Fleming, as recounted to P.N. Elrod

CHAPTER
ONE

"You are a prideful, willful, ungrateful wretch!"

This was my mother speaking—or rather screeching—to me, her only son.

To be fair, it was not one of her better days, but she had very few of those, and it was difficult to discern any improvement in her temper at the best of times. Good or bad, it was wise to treat her with the unquestioning respect that she demanded, if not openly, then by implication. I had failed to observe that unspoken rule of behavior, and for the next few minutes was treated to a sneering, acid-filled lecture particularizing the apparently numberless negative aspects of my character. Considering that until recently she'd spent fifteen of my seventeen years removed from my company, she had a surprisingly large store of knowledge to draw upon for her invective.

By the time she'd paused for breath I'd flushed red from head to foot and sweat stung under my arms and seeped along my flanks. I was breathing hard from the effort required to contain my own hot emotions.

"And don't you dare glower at your mother like that, Jonathan Fonteyn," she ordered.

What, then, am I to do? I snarled back to her in my mind. And she'd used my middle name, which I hated, which was exactly why she'd used it. It was her maiden name, yet one more tie to her other than blood.

1

With a massive effort, I swallowed and tried to compose my face to more neutral lines. It helped to look down.

"I am sorry, Mother. Please forgive me." The words were clearly forced and wooden, fooling no one. A show of submission was required at this point to prevent her from launching into another tirade.

Unhampered by the obligation of filial respect, the woman was free to glare at me for as long as she pleased. She had it down to a fine art. She also made no acknowledgment of what I'd just said, meaning that she had not accepted my apology. Such gracious gestures of forgiveness were reserved only for those times when a third party was present as a witness to her loving patience with a wayward son. We were alone in Father's library now; not even a servant was within earshot of her honey-on-broken-glass voice.

I continued to study the floor until she moved herself to speak again. "I will hear no more of your nonsense, Jonathan. There's many another young man who would gladly trade places with you."

Find one, I thought. I would just as cheerfully strike a bargain with him on this very spot.

"The arrangements have been made and cannot be unmade. You've no reason to find complaint with any of it."

True, I had to admit that in spite of my anger. The opportunity was fabulous, something I'd have eagerly jumped for had it been presented to me in any other manner, preferably as one adult to another. What was so objectionable was having everything arranged without my knowledge and sprung without warning and with no room for discussion.

I took a deep breath in the hope that it would steady me and tried to push the resentment away. The breath had to be let out slowly and silently, lest she interpret it as some sort of impertinence.

Finally raising my eyes, I said, "I am quite overwhelmed, Mother. This is rather unexpected."

"I hardly think so," she replied. "Your father and I long ago determined that you would go into law."

Liar. I had decided that in the years she'd been living away from us in Philadelphia. If only she had stayed there.

"It is our fondest hope that you not only follow in his footsteps, but surpass him in your success."

My jaw clamped tight at the unmistakable sarcasm in her emphasis of certain words. This time the anger was on Father's behalf, not for myself. How could she think him a failure?

"To do that, you must have the best education possible. Don't think that this is a mere whim of ours. I—we—have studied the choices carefully over the years and determined that Harvard is simply not capable of delivering the best that is available...."

Just after breakfast, she'd sent for me to come to her in the library. I was mildly apprehensive, wondering what the trouble was this time. It was yet too early in the day for me to have done anything to offend her, unless she'd found something to criticize in the way I chewed my food. I'd not discounted it as a possibility.

As with most of our meals now we'd eaten in uncomfortable silence, Mother at her long-empty spot at one end of the table, and my sister Elizabeth across from me in the middle. Father's place at the head of the table was empty, as he was away on a business errand.

Such silence at the morning meal was new to this household. It had settled upon us like a heavy scavenger bird with Mother's return home. Elizabeth and I had learned that it was better to remain quiet indefinitely than to speak before spoken to lest we draw some disapproving sharpness from her.

The servants were not as lucky. Today one of the girls chanced to drop a spoon, and though no harm was done, she received a lengthy rebuke for her clumsiness that left her in tears. Elizabeth exchanged glances with me while Mother's attention was distracted from us. It was going to be a bad day for everyone, then.

Somehow we got through one more meal under this threatening cloud. Weeks earlier, my sister and I had agreed to always finish eating and leave at the same time so that neither had to face such adversity alone. We did so again, asking permission to be excused and getting it, and had just made good our escape when one of the servants caught up to us and delivered the summons. I was to come to the library at seven of the clock precisely.

"Why couldn't she have said something when we'd been right there in the room with her?" I whispered to Elizabeth after the servant was gone. "Is speaking to me directly so difficult?"

"It's her way of doing things, Jonathan," she replied, but not in a manner to indicate approval. "Just agree with whatever she says and we'll sort it out with Father later."

"Do you know what she wants?" I felt justified in my apprehension. Mother was an expert at criticism. She could turn the smallest of errors—real or imagined— into a capital offense.

"Heavens, it could be anything. You know how she is."

"Unfortunately, yes. May I come see you afterward? I might need you to bind up my wounds."

She burst into that radiant smile reserved only for me. "Yes, little brother. I'll go look for some bandages immediately."

I took myself away and knocked on the library door just as the mantle clock within struck seven. She could not criticize me for being too late or too early.

Mother had seated herself in the chair next to Father's desk; it would have been overdoing things to actually take over his chair. She was canny enough to avoid that. The idea was to suggest his invisible presence approving her every action and word. I was sharply aware of this and not at all fooled, but also not about to make mention of it. In the month since her return, I'd had to face her here alone on a dozen minor transgressions; this was starting out no more differently than the others. I'd speculated that she'd noticed the new buckles on my shoes and was going to deliver a scorching opinion of their style and cost. The other lectures had been on a similar level of importance. I was glad to know that Elizabeth was standing by ready to soothe my burns when it was over.

Mother had assumed the demeanor of royalty granting an anxiously awaited audience, studying some letter or other as I walked in, her wide skirts carefully arranged, the tilt of her head just right. She could not have been an actress, though, for she was much too obvious in her method and would have been hooted from the stage in a serious drama. Farce, perhaps. Yes, she might have been perfect at farce, playing the role of the domineering dowager.

Marie Fonteyn Barrett had been very beautiful once: slender, graceful, with eyes as blue as an autumn sky, her skin milk white and milk soft. So she appeared in her portrait above the library fireplace. In the twenty years since its painting the milk had curdled, the grace turned to stiff arrogance. The eyes were the same color, but had gone hard, so that they seemed less real than the ones in the painting. Her hair was different as well. No more were the flowing black curls of a young bride; now it was piled high over her creased brow and thickly powdered. In the last month it had grown out a bit and needed rearranging. Perhaps she would even wash it and begin afresh. I could but hope for it. Her tense stabbings and jabbings at that awful pile of lard caked with rice flour with her ivory scratching stick got on my nerves.

The curtains were open and cold April sunshine, still too immature for warmth, leached through the windows. The wood in the fireplace had not been lighted, so the room was chilly. Mother was a great believer in conserving household supplies unless it concerned her own comfort. The lack of fire gave me hope that our interview would be mercifully short.

"Jonathan," she said, putting aside the paper in her hand. I recognized it as part of the normal litter on Father's desk, something she'd merely grabbed up to use as a prop. Why was the woman so contrived in her deportment?

"Mother." The word was still awkward for me to say.

She smiled with a benevolent satisfaction that raised my apprehensions somewhat. "Your father and I have some wonderful news for you."

If the news was so wonderful, why was Father not here to deliver it with her? "Indeed, Mother? Then I am anxious to hear it."

"You will be very pleased to learn that you will be going to Cambridge for your university education."

That was hardly news to me, but I put on something resembling good cheer for her sake. "Yes, I am very pleased. I have been looking forward to it all year."

Her brows lowered and eyes narrowed with irritation. Perhaps I was not as pleased as had been expected.

"I shall do my absolute best at Harvard to make you and Father proud of me," I added hopefully.

Now her mouth thinned. "You will be going to Cambridge, Jonathan."

"Yes, Mother, I know. Harvard University is located in Cambridge."

Fury, red-faced and frightening to look upon, suddenly distorted her features so she hardly seemed human. Somehow, I had said the wrong thing. I almost stepped backward. Almost. Her rages were common. We'd all seen this side of her many times and learned by trial and error how to avoid them, but this one mystified me. What had I said? Why was she—?

"You dare to mock me, Jonathan? You dare?"

I raised one hand in a calming gesture. "No, Mother, never."

"You dare?" Her voice rose enough to break my ears, enough to reach the servants' hall. Hopefully, they would know better than to come investigate the din.

"No, Mother. I swear to you, I am not mocking you. I sincerely apologize that I have given offense." Such words came easily; she'd given me ample opportunity for practice over the weeks. I finished off with a bow to emphasize my complete earnestness. Yet another occasion to study the floor.

Thank God that this time it worked. Straightening, I saw her color slowly return to normal and the lines in her face abruptly smoothed out. This strange, swift recovery was more disturbing than her instant rage. Since her return, I'd quickly adjusted to the fact that she was not like other people, which was hardly a comfort during those times when her differences from them were so acutely displayed.

Dominance established, she resumed where she'd left off, almost as though nothing had happened. "You are going to Cambridge, Jonathan. Cambridge in England, Jonathan," she repeated, putting a razor edge on each syllable as though to underscore my abysmal ignorance.

It took me some moments to understand, to sort out the mistake. I suppose that she'd been anticipating a torrent of enthusiasm from me. Instead, my face fell and from my lips popped the first words that came to mind. "But I want to go to Harvard."

That's when the explosion truly came and she started calling me names.

You know the rest.

What was she saying now? Something about the virtues of Cambridge. I did not interrupt; it would have been pointless. She wasn't interested in my opinions or plans I might have made. Any and all objections had been drowned in the hot tidal wave of her temper. To resurrect them again now would only aggravate her more. As Elizabeth had reminded me, I could sort it all out with Father later.

Did Father know about this? I couldn't believe that he would not have spoken to me about it before leaving yesterday. Surely he would have said something, for he, too, had planned that I should go to Harvard. That she had waited until he was absent before breaking her news took on a fresh and ominous meaning, but I couldn't quite see the reason behind it yet. It was difficult to think while she talked on and on, pausing only to collect the occasional nodding agreement from me at appropriate points.

Why was she so concerned about my education after fifteen years of blithe neglect? Marie Fonteyn Barrett had been singularly uninterested in either of her children since we were very small. It was a mixed blessing for us; growing up without a mother had left something of a blank spot in our lives. On the other hand, what sort of broken monsters might we have been had she stayed with Father instead of moving to Philadelphia?

She'd made the long journey from there to our home on Long Island because of the turmoil in that city. With the rebels stirring things up at every opportunity, it had become too dangerous to remain, so she had written Father, and he, being a good and decent man, had said her house was there for her, the doors open. Her swift arrival soon after the receipt of her letter caused us to speculate that she had not actually waited for his reply.

She'd just as swiftly assumed the running of the household in her own manner, subtly and not so subtly disrupting every level of life and work for everyone on our estate. Surprisingly, only a few servants left. Most were very loyal to Father and had the understanding that this was to be a brief visit. When things had settled back to normal in Philadelphia, Mother would soon depart from us.

A likely chance, I thought cynically. Surely she was enjoying herself too much to leave.

She paused in her speech; apparently I'd been delinquent in my latest response.

"This is … is marvelous to hear, Mother. I hardly know what to say."

"A 'thank you' would be appropriate."

Yes, of course it would. "Thank you, Mother."

She nodded, comically regal, but not a bit amusing. My stomach was roiling in reaction to the tempest between my ears. I had to get out of here.

"May I be excused, Mother?"

"Excused? I should think you'd want to hear all the rest of the details we have planned."

"Truly I do, but must confess that my brain is whirling so much now I am hardly able to breathe. I beg but a little time to recover so that I may give you my full attention later."

"Very well. I suppose you'll run off to tell Elizabeth everything."

To this, a correct assumption that was really none of her business, I made another courtly bow upon which she could apply her own interpretation.

She sniffed. "You are excused. But remember: no arguments and no more foolishness. Going to Cambridge in England is the greatest opportunity you're ever going to receive to make something of yourself."

"Yes, Mother." I bowed again, inching anxiously toward the door.

"This is, after all, for your own good," she concluded serenely.

Anger rushed through me again as I turned and stalked from the room. How fond she was of *that* idea. God save me from all the hideous people hell-bent on doing things for my own good. So far there'd been only one in my life, my mother, and she was more than enough.

Quietly shutting the door behind me, I slipped down the hall until there was enough distance between us for noise not to matter, then began to run as though the house were afire. Not bothering with a coat or hat, I threw myself outside into the cold April air. The woman was suffocating. I needed to be free of her and all thought of her. My feet carried me straight to the stables. With its mud, muck, and the irreverent company of the lads, this was one place I would be safe.

"Over here, Mr. Jonathan!"

My black servant, Jericho, waved at me. He was just emerging from the darkness of one of the buildings. Though he was primarily my valet and therefore supposed to keep to the house, neither of us paid much attention to such things. He was fairly high up in the household hierarchy and able to bend a rule here and there as long as nobody minded. If he chose to play the part of a groom, he suffered no loss in status, because working with horses was a source of pleasure for him. Right now, he was a godsend, for he'd saddled up Rolly, my favorite hunter, and was leading him out to me.

I couldn't help but laugh at his foresight. "How did you guess? Magic?"

"No magic," he said, smiling at the old joke between us. He used to tease the servant girls about being able to read their deepest thoughts and as a dedicated observer of human nature he was right more often than not. The younger ones were awed, the older ones amused, and one rather guilty-hearted wench accused him of witchcraft. "I'd heard that Mrs. Barrett wanted to speak to you. Every other time that's happened you've come here to ride it off."

"You're uncanny. Thank you, Jericho. Will you join me?"

"I rather assumed you would prefer the solitude."

Right again. Perhaps he did have hidden powers of divination.

He held Rolly's head as I swung up to the saddle and helped with the stirrups. "I'll tell Miss Elizabeth where you are," he said before I could ask him to do exactly that.

I laughed again, at the wonderful normality he represented, and took up the reins. Knowing what was to come next and how eager I was to get started, Rolly danced away and sprang forward with hardly a signal from me. Doing something that Mother would disapprove of was what I needed most, and leaving the stable yard at a full gallop to jump over a wall into the fields beyond was a most satisfying form of rebellion.

Rolly was almost as perceptive as Jericho and seemed to sense that I wanted to fly as fast and as far as possible. The cold wind roaring past us deafened me to the strident echoes of Mother's voice and blinded me to the memory of her distorted face. She shrank to less than nothing and was lost amid the joy I now felt clinging to the back of the best horse in the world as he carried me to the edge of that world—or at least to the cliffs overlooking the Sound.

We slowed at last, though for a moment I thought that if Rolly decided to leap out toward the sea instead of turning to trot parallel to it he would easily sprout the necessary wings to send us soaring into the sky like some latter-day Pegasus and Bellerophon. What a ride that might be, and I would certainly know better than to try flying him to Mount Olympus to seek out the gods. They could wait for their own turn...if I ever let them have one.

The air cutting over us was clean with the sea smell and starting to warm up as the sun climbed higher. I drank it in like a true-born hedonist until my lungs ached and my throat burned. Rolly picked his own path, and I let him, content enough with the privilege of being on his back. We went east, into the wind, him stretching his neck, his ears up with interest, me busy holding my balance over the uneven ground. The trot sped up to a canter and he shook his head once as though to free himself of the bridle as we approached another fence.

The property it marked belonged to a farmer named Finch who kept a few horses of his own. His lands were smaller than Father's, and he could not afford to have riding animals, but the rough look of the mares on that side made no difference to Rolly, aristocrat though he was. In his eyes a female was a female and to the devil with her looks and age as long as she was ready for mounting. Obviously one of them was in season. I barely had time to turn him and keep him from sailing over the fence right into the middle of them all.

Rolly snorted and neighed out a protest. One of the other horses answered and I had to work hard at getting him out of there.

"Sorry, old man," I told him. "You may have an excellent bloodline, but I don't think Mr. Finch would thank you for passing it on through his mares."

He stamped and tried to rear, but I pulled him in, not letting him get away with it.

"If it's any consolation, I know just how you feel," I confided.

I was seventeen and still a virgin...of sorts. I'd long since worked out ways around certain inevitable frustrations that come from being a healthy young man, but instinctively knew they could hardly be as gratifying as actual experience with an equally healthy young woman. Damn. Now, *why* did I have to start thinking along those paths again? An idiotic question; better to frame it as a syllogism of logic. Premise one: I was, indeed, healthy; premise two: I was, indeed, young. Combine those and I rarely failed to come to a pleasurable conclusion when the desire was upon me. However, I was not prepared to come to any such conclusions here in the open while on horseback. That was definitely something guaranteed to garner maternal disapproval … and I'd probably fall out of the saddle.

The true loss of my virginity was another goal in my personal education I'd planned to achieve at Harvard—if I ever got there, since Mother had said that everything was settled about Cambridge. I wondered if they had girls at Cambridge. Oh, God, this wasn't helping at all. I kicked Rolly into a jarring trot, hoping that it would distract me. The last thing I needed was to return home with any telltale stain on my light-colored breeches. Perhaps if I found a quiet spot in the woods ….

I knew just the one.

As children, Elizabeth, Jericho, and I had gone adventuring, or what we called adventuring, for we really knew the area quite well. Usually our games involved a treasure hunt, for everyone on the island knew that Captain Kidd had come here to bury his booty. It didn't matter to us that such riches were more likely to be fifty miles east of us on the south end of the island; the hunting was more important than the finding. But instead of treasure that day, I'd found a kettle, or a sharpish depression gouged into the earth by some ancient glacier, according to my schoolmaster. Trees and other vegetation concealed its edge. My foot slipped on some wet leaves and down I tumbled into a typical specimen of Long Island's geography.

Jericho came pelting after me, fearful that I had broken my neck. Elizabeth, though hampered by her skirts, followed almost as quickly, shouting tear-choked questions after him. I was almost trampled by their combined concern and inability to stop fast enough.

The wind had certainly been knocked from me, but I'd suffered nothing worse than scrapes and bruises. After the initial fright passed we took stock of our surroundings and claimed it for our own. It became our pirate's cave (albeit open to the sky and to any cattle that wandered in to graze), banditti's lair, and general sanctuary from tiresome adults wanting us to do something more constructive with our time.

Now it seemed that it was still a sanctuary, not from adults, but for adults. Just as I'd guided Rolly down to the easy way into the kettle, I noticed two people far ahead near the line of trees marking the entry. A man and woman walked arm in arm there, obviously on the friendliest of terms.

And even at that distance I abruptly recognized my father. What was he doing here ... Oh.

The woman with him was Mrs. Montagu, his mistress for the last dozen years. She was a sweet-faced, sweet-tempered widow who had always been kind to me and Elizabeth, was everything that Mother was not. Mother, thank God, knew nothing about her, or life for all of us would truly become a living hell.

It was a quietly acknowledged fact in our household that most of Father's business errands took him no more than three miles away so he might visit Matilda Montagu. Their relationship was hardly a secret, but not something to bring up in open conversation. They had not asked for this privacy, but got it, anyway, for both were liked and respected hereabouts. They were discreet and that was all that was required for people to turn a blind eye.

I'd pulled Rolly to a stop and now almost urged him in their direction to tell him what had transpired, then changed my mind.

No. Not fair to interrupt them, I thought.

Father had little enough happiness of his own since Mother's return; I would not trespass upon their tryst with my present troubles. We could talk later. Besides, I had no wish to embarrass him by bringing up the disagreeable details of his wife's latest offenses before his mistress.

Father and Mrs. Montagu continued their leisurely morning walk, unaware of me, which was just as well. It was interesting to watch them together, for this was a side of Father that I'd never really seen. I was somewhat uncomfortable with my curiosity, but not so much as to move on. Not that I expected them to suddenly seize each other and start rolling on the cold damp ground in a frenzy of passion. Nor would I have stayed to watch, my curiosity being limited by the discretions of good taste. But between the demands of my preparatory education and all the other distractions of life, I'd had few opportunities to observe the rules of courtship in our polite society. So far it hardly looked different from the servants', for I'd occasionally seen them strolling about with one another making similar displays of affection.

He had one arm around her waist, one hand, rather. Her wide skirts kept him from getting much closer. He also leaned his head down toward her so as to miss nothing of whatever she was saying. And he was laughing. That was good to see. He had not done much of that in the last month. What about his other hand? Occupied with carrying a bundle or basket. Full of food, probably. It was hardly the best weather for eating comfortably out of doors, but they seemed content to ignore it as long as they were together.

Interesting. Now they paused to face each other. Father stooped slightly and kissed her on the lips for a very long time. My own mouth went dry. Perhaps it was time to leave. As I dithered with indecision their kiss ended and they turned to walk into the shadow of the trees. They did not come out again.

Rolly snorted impatiently and dropped his head to snatch a mouthful of new grass just peeping through last year's dead layer. At some point my fleshly cravings had also altered so that carnal leanings had been supplanted by extreme hunger. The sun was high and far over; I'd been out for hours and had long since digested my breakfast. And there was Elizabeth, who would be wondering whether I'd been thrown. She loved horses too, but didn't trust Rolly to behave himself.

I turned him back up the rise leading around the kettle, heading home.

The horse being more valuable than its rider, I took care of Rolly myself when we reached the stables. As a menial job, I could have easily left it for one of the lads to do and no one would have thought twice about it. Especially Mother. I was raised to be a gentleman and clearly imagined her disapproval while going about my caretaking tasks. But where horses were concerned, such work was no work at all for me. Defiance doubled, I thought, humming with pleasure. Jericho wasn't there or he might have willingly helped out—if I'd invited him. I made a fast job of it, though, and before long was marching up to the kitchen to wheedle a meal from the cook.

Then someone hissed from around a corner of the house. Elizabeth stood there, eyes comically wide and lips compressed, urgently waving at me to come over. Curiosity won out over hunger.

"What is it?" I asked, trotting up.

"Not so loud," she insisted, grabbing my arm and dragging me around the corner. She visibly relaxed once we were out of sight from the kitchen.

"What is it?" I repeated, now mimicking her hoarse whisper.

"Mother was furious that you missed lunch."

I gave vent to an exasperated sigh and raised my voice back to normal. "Damnation, but I'm an adult and my time is my own. She's never minded before."

"Yes, but she wanted to talk to you about Cambridge."

"She told you all that nonsense?"

"In extraordinary detail. She seems to have decided how you're to spend your next few years—down to the last minute."

"How very thorough of her."

"She's in the kitchen with Mrs. Nooth planning out meals, and I didn't think you'd want to run into her."

I took one of Elizabeth's hands and solemnly bowed over it. "For that, dear sister, you have my undying gratitude, but I am famished and must eat. A fellow can hardly spend his life going about in fear of his own mother."

"Ha! It's not fear, it's only avoiding a disagreeable encounter."

She was quite right. I really didn't want to face the woman on an empty stomach; some alternative needed to be thought up, but not out here. The day had warmed a little, but Elizabeth's hand was icy. "Let's go inside, you're freezing. Where's your shawl?"

She shrugged, indifferent to the chill. "Upstairs someplace. You should be the one to talk; look at yourself, riding all morning without hat, coat, or even gloves. It will serve you right if you get the rheumatics, God forbid."

I shrugged as well. The ailments of age were still very far away for me. My morning's ride was worth a spot of stiffness in the joints. We went in by the same side door I'd used to escape, and Elizabeth led me to the library. A good fire was blazing there now, and abruptly forgetting our lack of concern about the cool day, we rushed toward it like moths.

"So you think your going to Cambridge is nonsense?" she asked, stretching out her hands and spreading her long fingers against the flames.

"Mmm. The woman's mad. When I see Father I'll sort it out with him as you said."

"She's very sure of herself. What if he's on her side?"

"Why should he be?"

"Because he usually does whatever she wants. It's not as wearing on the soul, you know. Or as noisy."

"I don't think he will for something as important as this. Besides, look at the impracticality of it. Why send me all the way to England to read law? It may garner me some status, but what else?"

"An education?" she suggested.

"There's that, but everyone knows you really go to university to make the kind of friends and acquaintances who will become useful later in life. If I do that in England, they'll be left behind when I return home."

"You've become cynical already, little brother?" She was hardly a year older than me, but had always taken enjoyment from her position as the eldest.

"Realistic. I've spent a lot of time in this very room listening to Father and his cronies while they're sharing a bottle. I can practice law well enough, but I'll be better at it for having a few friends 'round me as he does. Which reminds me…" I quit the fireplace to open a nearby cupboard and poured myself a bit of wine to keep my strength up. My stomach snarled ingratitude at the thoughtful gesture. It wanted real food.

Elizabeth giggled at the noise. She looked remarkably like the portrait above her. Prettier, I thought. Livelier. Certainly saner.

"What is it?" she asked, taking note of my distraction.

"I was just thinking that you could have almost posed for that." I indicated the painting.

She stood away for a better look. "Perhaps, but my face is longer. If it's all the same to you, I would prefer not to be compared to her at all."

"She may have been different back then," I pointed out. "If not, then why did Father ever marry her and have us?"

"That's hardly our business, Jonathan."

"It certainly is since we're the living results of their … affection? … for one another."

"Now you're being crude."

"No I'm not. When I get crude, you'll know it, dear sister. Who do I look like?"

She tilted her head, unknowingly copying Mother's affected mannerism, but in an unaffected way. "Father, of course, but younger and not as heavy."

"Father's not fat," I protested.

"You know what I mean. When men get older they either go to fat or put on another layer of muscle."

"Or both."

"Ugh. But not you. You've put on the muscle and look just like him."

"That's reassuring." We always regarded Father as being a very handsome man.

"Peacock," said Elizabeth, reading my face and thus my thoughts. I grinned and saluted her with my glass. It was empty, but I corrected that. The wine tasted wonderful but it was shooting straight to my head for having nothing in my belly to slow things.

"Mother will burst a blood vessel if you turn up drunk in the kitchen," she observed without rancor. "Or anyplace else for that matter."

"If I really get drunk, then I shan't care. Would you like some?"

"Yes," she said decisively, and got a wineglass. "She'll make drunkards of us all before she's finished. I'm surprised Father isn't..."

"Father has other occupations to distract him from unpleasantries," I said, pouring generously and thinking fondly of Mrs. Montagu.

"I wish I did," she muttered, and drained off half her portion. "Father goes out, you have your riding and studies, but I'm expected to sit here all day and find contentment with needlework, household duties, and numbering out my prospects."

"Prospects?"

Elizabeth's mouth twisted in disgust. "After she finished going on about Cambridge, she started asking me about the unmarried men in the area."

"Uh-oh."

"*All* of them, including old Mr. Cadwallader. He must be seventy if he's a day."

"But very rich."

"Now who's taking sides?"

"Not I. I was thinking the way she would think."

"Please don't." Elizabeth groaned and finished her wine. I made to pour her another, and she did not refuse it. "I hope things settle down quickly in Philadelphia so she can go back. I know that it's wicked, wishing one's mother away, but..."

"She's only our mother by reason of birth," I said. "If it comes to it, Mrs. Montagu's been more of a mother to us. Or even Mrs. Nooth. I wish Father had married her instead. Mrs. Montagu, that is."

"Then neither of us would have been ourselves, and we wouldn't be sitting here getting drunk."

"It's something to think about, isn't it?"

"A most wicked thought, though," she concluded with an unrepentant grimace.

"Yes, I'm born to be hanged for that one."

"God forbid," she added.

As one, we lifted our glasses in a silent toast to many different things. I felt pleasantly muzzy now, with my limbs heavy and glowing from inner warmth. It was too nice a feeling to dispel with the inevitable scolding that awaited me the moment I stepped into the kitchen.

"P'haps," I speculated, "I should leave Mother and Mrs. Nooth to their work. It would be boorish to disturb them."

Elizabeth instantly noted my change of mind and smiled, shaking her head in mock sadness for my lost bravado.

"P'haps," I continued thoughtfully, "I could just borrow a loaf of bread from one of the lads, then pick up a small cheese from the buttery. That would fill me 'til supper. Father should be home by then and Mother will have something else to be bothered about besides me."

"And have one of the servants blamed for the theft of the cheese?"

"I'll leave a note, confessing all," I promised gravely. "Mrs. Nooth will surely forgive..." Then something soured inside and the game lost its charm. "Damnation, this is my own house. Why should I creep around like a thief?"

Someone's shoe heels clacked and clattered hollowly against the wood floor of the hall. Elizabeth and I instantly recognized a familiar step and hastily replaced the glasses and wine bottle in the cupboard. The answer to my plaintive question swung into the doorway just as we shut everything away and turned our innocent faces toward her in polite regard.

Mother.

She wasn't fooled by our pose. "What are you two doing?" she demanded.

"Only talking, Mother," said Elizabeth.

Mother sniffed, either in disbelief or disdain. Fortunately she was too far away to pick up any scent of the wine. She turned an unfriendly eye upon me. "And where were you all day? Mrs. Nooth placed a perfectly good meal on the table and your portion went to waste."

With as many servants as we had, I doubted that. "I'm sorry, Mother."

"You'll tender your apologies to Mrs. Nooth. She was very offended."

And very forgiving. And in the kitchen. With the food. "Indeed, Mother? I shall go to her immediately and make amends."

She'd heard me but had not listened. "Where were you, Jonathan?"

"Inspecting the fields," I answered easily. It was mostly true, but I resented that this woman was turning me into a liar.

"Never mind such things. You've far more important duties before you than farming. From now on leave menial work to those men who have been hired for it."

"Yes, Mother." My head began spinning with that peculiar weighty disorientation that I associated with intoxication. With each passing minute the wine soaked more deeply into me, increasing its effect, but I was careful not to let it show.

"As long as you're here I want to continue our talk about your education. Elizabeth, you are excused."

From where I stood, I clearly saw the flash of anger in my sister's eyes at being dismissed as though she were one of the servants. Her mouth tightened and her chin lifted, but she said nothing, nothing at all, quite loudly, all the way out the door.

Mother did not ignore her so much as simply not notice. Her attention was entirely fixed upon me. She crossed the room to the chair she'd claimed next to Father's desk and arranged herself. I was not invited to sit, nor did I ask to do so. It might unnecessarily prolong our interview. My stomach, presently awash with wine, would provide me with a valid reason to depart soon enough. I was still hungry, but that was outweighed by the need to hear her out and to gain information in order to present a logical argument against it later. To Father. I knew better than to contend with his wife, who was partial to only her own unique logic and no one else's.

She produced her ivory scratching stick from somewhere and tapped it lightly against the palm of one hand. "And now, Jonathan," she announced importantly, "we will plan out what you are going to do once you get to Cambridge." She paused to poke vigorously at a spot above the nape of her neck with the stick. My teeth instantly went on edge.

Never, never in all my life was I so glad to be drunk.

CHAPTER
TWO

SOME TWENTY MINUTES LATER Mother generously excused me, by which time I'd developed a pressing need to rid myself of the wine. A good deal of it remained behind in my head, though, for it was aching badly. The pain so interfered with my thinking that afterward I couldn't decide whether to visit the kitchen or retreat in misery to my room to sleep it away.

Jericho resolved things when he emerged from the hall leading to the kitchen carrying a covered tray.

"Is that for me?" I asked hopefully in response to his smile of greeting.

"Miss Elizabeth suggested it," he said. "Something to see you through until supper."

"Then God bless her for being the dearest, sweetest sister anyone ever had. Where is she?"

"Out taking a ride of her own."

"Yes. Since Mother came back the horses are getting more than their share of exercise. Come, put that down somewhere."

"I would suggest that you take it in your sitting room. To avoid interruptions," he added significantly.

I glanced uneasily back at the library and indicated that he should lead the way upstairs. Somehow I was able to follow, leaning heavily on the rail and gulping frequently. Hot in the face and dizzy, I staggered the last few feet into my room and collapsed in my chair before the big study table. Jericho smoothly moved some books around to make space for my meal. He had the enviable skill of being able to balance the tray with one hand while his other quickly and quite independently made order out of chaos. Between the blink of one eye and the next he put down his burden and whipped off the cloth revealing a plump loaf of bread, some cheese, and a squat jug. From the latter he poured out drink and gave me the cup.

"More wine?" I asked dubiously.

"Barley water. It will thin the wine in your blood."

"Good idea." I drank deeply and felt better for it, looking at the food with more interest than before, falling upon the cheese. "There's too much here for me, have some." Jericho hesitated, looking uncomfortable. "Is something wrong?"

"No, sir, but I do not think it would be quite—"

"Of course it wouldn't, so..." I kicked out another chair for him. "Those fools in Philadelphia are rebelling against the king without a second thought, so I shall rebel against our local queen. It's been a hard day, Jericho, and I need your company. Eat or not as you choose, but do sit with me."

He closed the door to the hall and only then allowed himself the ease of the chair and the comfort of good food.

He was slightly older than I, and his father was my father's valet. After I was born, they decided that he should assume that duty for me once I had outgrown the nursery. Though a servant, Jericho and I had been friends long before the establishment of his place in the household, and this strict deference for convention troubled me.

"Is it Mother?" I asked, reaching to tear off a piece of bread. I made a mess of it, scattering crumbs everywhere.

"In an indirect way," he admitted. "We've all heard that you're to go off to England soon."

"I most certainly am not. She's got this idea lodged in her head, but Father will shake it loose and that will be the end of it."

"My *bomba* isn't too sure of that," he said. Jericho spoke perfect English, but sometimes used a few words his father had brought with him from Africa, the only baggage he'd been allowed by the slavers.

Knowing that Archimedes might be privy to information I didn't have, I said, "Why does he think so?"

"Because your father does what your mother says."

"Now you're sounding like Elizabeth," I complained. "But Father is the head of this house. Mother will have to do what he says and she knows that. She waited and told me only after he was gone. She thought to put me on her side so he would say yes to please me. I've gone along with it, but only until he comes home." I took a vicious bite from the cheese. Damnation. The woman was treating me like a petulant child, and now I was beginning to sound like one.

"But until then nothing is settled," he said.

"You're worried? What is it?"

"I heard some things in the kitchen. She was talking to Mrs. Nooth, and I wasn't supposed to be listening."

"Never mind that. What was said?"

"She wanted Mrs. Nooth to ask around and find a proper English servant to look after you."

For several moments I lost the power of speech. "To … to …?"

"To take my place," he said calmly.

"Impossible. She can't mean it."

"But she does. She plans to sell me."

The blood hit the top of my head so hard that black smoke clouded my vision. Without knowing how I got there, I found myself up and pacing the length of the room. Nothing intelligible came out of me for quite some time and Jericho knew me well enough not to interrupt.

"It's *not* going to happen," I told him finally. "It's absolutely *not* going to happen. It's ridiculous … utterly … stupid." Then a cold thought rushed past. "Unless you want to …?"

Now it was his turn to be upset, though he was so self-disciplined that in no wise was it comparable to my own display. "No. A man must work and if I must work then I would rather work here. I do not wish to be sold. But your father might still do it for the sake of peace in the family."

I shook my head. "Mother can throw whatever sort of fit she pleases, but you are *not* going to be sold."

He looked reassured. "I have hope then. This is a good place to be; I know of no better. When other servants visit with their masters I hear of the most terrible things. Here we are treated well and given good care. No beatings, no starvations."

"That's something the whole world can do without," I added. He seemed to feel better, but I continued to pace. "Suppose Father arranged for your freedom? Then I could hire you. Mother couldn't have anything to do with it then."

"Except dismiss me and engage a replacement. You have no rights of your own until your twenty-first birthday."

"Blast. Well, no matter what, I won't let it happen. I'll run away to sea first and you can come with me."

A smile crossed his dark features. "But then you would be guilty of theft."

"Jericho, you've been hanging about with lawyers too long."

The smile broadened for a moment, then gradually fell in upon itself. I stopped my restless pacing and leaned against a wall and wished Father home immediately. "Why on earth does she want to hire another valet for me? You're the best there ever was."

He nodded regally at the compliment. "It is not a question of finding someone better. It is because Mrs. Barrett is extremely fond of all things English. She wants an English servant."

"No, thank you. He'd only put on airs, correct my speech, and rearrange my clothes so that I couldn't find anything for myself. And who would I have for company? Except for you and old Rapelji, there's no one intelligent to talk to."

His brows pinched together. "But your sister and father—"

"Are my sister and father. You know what I mean. Some of those long conversations we've had with Rapelji would have bored them to death."

He nodded agreement and his brows dropped back into place. "Speaking of him, did he not give you some more Greek to interpret?" He looked at the pile of books on the table before him.

"Doesn't he always?" Greek was not my favorite study. My tutor well knew that and thus emphasized it more than any other. "I'll see to it later tonight. My head hurts too much for the work right now."

"I'll get you some moss snuff," he said, rising.

"Ugh, no. Mrs. Nooth can take it herself. It's never helped any headache I've had and never will. I'll just lie down until the pain's out of me."

Pushing away from the wall, I wandered to the bed on the far side of the long room and almost dropped into its welcome comfort. Almost, because Jericho was instantly at my side to remove my coat. Since a refusal to cooperate would only inspire silent, long-suffering reproach from him, I gave in and gave up. Once started, off came the waistcoat and shoes as well, all to be taken away for brushing or polishing. I managed to retain my breeches and outer shirt; both would be changed before going down to supper so it didn't matter if I napped in them or not.

"When Father comes home . . ."

"I shall inform you in plenty of time," he promised as he started for the door.

Then peevishly, I asked, "What the devil is that row?"

Jericho listened with me. "A coach, I think."

My heart jumped, but only once. Father had left on horseback, not taken the coach. Jericho and I looked at one another in mutual puzzlement, then he gave back my shoes. Curiosity triumphed over my headache. I reached for an especially florid, Oriental-looking dressing gown that Elizabeth had painstakingly made for me, and shrugged it on. "Let's go see," I sighed.

No one was in the upper hall, but as we came downstairs we glimpsed one of the maids haring off to the kitchen, no doubt with fresh news for Mrs. Nooth. Mother emerged from the library like a merchant ship under full sail and stopped the girl with a curt order. The little wench came to heel and hastened to open wide the big front door. Outside stood a battered-looking coach and four, and there was much activity about the baggage and two alighting passengers. With a great smile, Mother went out to greet them.

I shifted uneasily and glanced at Jericho. He shrugged slightly. Having endured an extremely long month of Mother's quirky temperament I was hard-pressed to imagine that anyone or anything could give her joy. Apparently the possibility existed; we'd just never seen it before.

"They must be friends of hers from Philadelphia," I speculated.

Outside, Mother exchanged a kiss on the cheek with a woman and extended her hand to a man, who bowed deeply over it. Rather too deeply, I thought. What sort of people would find Mother's company so agreeable that they would come for a visit?

Past the broad threshold the wind blew in a few stray leaves and other...rubbish. That's the word that occurred to me when I got a good look at them. They swept into the house, surveying it with bright eyes as if they owned the place. They noticed me at the same time and the woman gave a little exclamation of pleased surprise.

"Dearest Marie, is this your good son, Jonathan Fonteyn?" she demanded in a loud, flat, and childishly thin voice.

I winced.

Mother was capable of swift thought and judgment and her conclusion was that now was not the time for introductions; I was not properly dressed to greet guests. "A moment, Deborah, a moment to catch my breath and then I shall ask him to come and meet you."

Deborah, apparently deducing that she'd been importune, turned a beaming face to Mother and ignored me entirely. The man copied her.

Mother issued a sharp order to the maid for tea and biscuits and then invited her guests into the parlor with a graceful gesture. As they proceeded ahead, she swung a livid face in my direction and pointed upstairs meaningfully.

"Good God," I muttered sourly from clenched teeth, masking my annoyance with a cordial smile and a nod of understanding. Jericho followed as I fled to my room.

"You know who they are?" he asked, putting down my clothes and smoothly moving toward the wardrobe.

"Friends of hers from Philadelphia. Deborah Hardinbrook and her brother, Theophilous Beldon. I've heard her talk about them. At length. She's the widow of some captain who drowned at sea, and he's supposed to be a doctor, God help us. Whatever you do, don't mention my headache to anyone lest it get back to him and he offers to cure it."

Jericho removed a claret-colored coat from the wardrobe and shook it out.

"Why this one?" I asked, as he helped me into it. "It's not my best."

"Exactly. To wear anything really nice might tell these two you wish to impress them. This coat declares that you care nothing about their favor, but at the same time informs them that you are the head of this house in your father's absence and it is *their* job to impress *you.*"

"It will?" All that from one coat?

"It does. Trust me on this matter, Mr. Jonathan."

I would, for he was always right on such details. "Elizabeth. She'll have to be warned."

"And so she shall be," he promised, pulling out a pair of shoes and inspecting the silver buckles for tarnish. There was none, of course.

"I have these," I protested, pointing at the ones on my feet.

"New buckles on old shoes," he chided. "It doesn't look right, not for a first meeting."

"We can switch them to another pair."

He firmly held the shoes out for me. "Wear these. They will demand respect. Save the others for Sunday."

I grunted and did as I was told.

He was finished in a very few minutes. "There. Sometimes you cannot avoid going into the lion's den, but when you must, it is better to be well dressed."

"What makes you think this is a lion's den?"

"What makes you think it is not?"

"Excellent point. Go find Elizabeth, will you?"

"Certainly."

In deference to my sober garb and still-buzzing brain, I did not rush downstairs, though it was tempting. Head high and with a serious face, I paced slowly across the hall to the parlor and paused in the doorway, waiting to be noticed.

Mother had her back to me, so it was Deborah Hardinbrook who looked up and stopped her conversation. Her brother, seated next to her, politely stood. Mother turned and assumed an unfamiliar smile.

"Ah, Jonathan. At last. Do come in and meet my very dear friends." She conducted us through formal introductions.

On my best behavior, I bowed low over Mrs. Hardinbrook's hand and expressed my pleasure at meeting her in French. She was about Mother's age, with a hard eye and lines around her mouth that may have been placed there by laughter but not joy. She assessed me quickly, efficiently, and was fulsome with complements to Mother about me. I felt like an over-priced statue on display, not valued for my own merits, but for the enlargement of its owner.

Dr. Beldon was in his thirties, which also made him seem quite old to me. He was wiry and dark, his brown eyes so large and rounded that they seemed to swell from their sockets. They fastened upon me with an assessment similar to his sister's but with a different kind of intensity, though what it was, I could not have guessed. We bowed and exchanged the necessary social pleasantries toward one another.

Mrs. Hardinbrook resumed her talk with Mother, giving her a full account of the harrowing journey from Philadelphia. At first I listened with resentful politeness, then with interest, for despite her exaggerations of manner, she was amusing. Mother actually seemed to be enjoying herself. Beldon smiled at appropriate moments and occasionally added comments. Unlike his sister, he made an effort to include me in the conversation. Smiling. Smiling. Smiling.

Toad-eaters, I thought behind my own twisted lips. Fawning in deference to the family wealth. Father had taught me to recognize their sort and to be 'ware of them.

"They're full of flattery and little else, laddie," he'd told me. "Having no advantage of their own, they try to put themselves ahead by using others. Useless bloodsuckers, the lot of them, always looking out for their own good, but no one else's, and with bottomless stomachs. Don't let them fool you with fair words or use you in any way. No need to waste your time with any of them."

Perhaps Mother had not heard his opinion, or chose to ignore it. "Where will your journey finally take you, Mrs. Hardinbrook?" I asked when an opening presented itself.

Her face was bright with a shortage of understanding. "I beg your pardon, Master Barrett?"

I ignored the little jibe of her address, meant to place me on a level with beardless children. "Your destination, madam. I was inquiring—"

"*This* is their destination, Jonathan," Mother said firmly, indicating the house with the curve of one hand. "Deborah and her brother are my guests."

This was not unexpected, but certainly unpleasant. Mother's guests, not Father's, and absolutely no mention was made of when they would leave.

"How delightful," I told them, my smile entirely genuine.

There'd be the devil to pay when Father came home, and I looked forward to that confrontation.

SUPPER WAS LESS of a disaster than I'd anticipated.

When Elizabeth returned from her ride, Jericho headed her off at the stables and passed on the news. She charged up to the house immediately.

"What are they like?" she demanded, bursting in after a quick thump on my bedroom door to announce herself.

"You'll have to draw your own conclusions." I was at my table, trying to translate more Greek, but with indifferent results.

"Jonathan, you're not a lawyer yet, so tell me."

"Toad-eaters, without a doubt. They seem clever about it, though, so be careful around them. You know what Father says."

She did, and hurried on to her room to change for supper. I waited in mine until it was time, then escorted her downstairs. She looked perfect in a dress of such a pale gray as to be nearly white with touches of dark pink throughout. The latter, I abruptly noticed, complemented my claret-colored coat in some subtle way. We would present a united front against these invaders, if they bothered to notice.

Mrs. Hardinbrook was again effusive in her praise when she and Elizabeth were introduced. Elizabeth returned one of the complements in French. Our guest was astonished that she was able to speak a foreign language so easily.

"It's nothing," Elizabeth demurred. "I understand that even the children in France do so."

This went right over Mrs. Hardinbrook's uncomprehending head;

Mother glowered ineffectively, but Beldon smothered a knowing smile. When his turn came he bowed gravely over Elizabeth's hand and expressed his enchantment with her. She was politely cool and made no reply beyond a civil nod. Even Mother could find no fault with her for that.

We went in to supper, which, oddly enough, was made bearable by the presence of the guests. They distracted Mother, and for the first time in a month the usual heavy silence was lifted from the table. The relief lasted for the whole meal. Elizabeth and I said next to nothing throughout, our ears instinctively open for information on these strangers.

Mrs. Hardinbrook managed to eat and talk at the same time, rolling along at a quick pace and cleaning her plate down to the last crumb. She spoke of this happening or that person, familiar to Mother, but not to us. Now and then she would touch on a general topic for a time and then our listening became less tedious.

Beldon was taciturn compared to his sister, who made enough speech for both of them. We already knew he was a doctor and learned that his practice had been unfairly disrupted by the unpleasantness in Philadelphia. One of the last people he'd been called to treat had been a victim of a mob of rebel ruffians.

"Poor fellow was dragged right from his home and beaten. They said he'd narrowly escaped being tarred and feathered except for the arrival of some of his friends. Then it was canes and clubs, gentlemen against the rowdies, who were soundly beaten themselves and sent away howling like beasts."

"Being beasts, they only got what they deserved," added Mrs. Hardinbrook with a chuckle for her own joke.

"Beasts, indeed," sniffed Mother. "Why was he beaten?"

"He's Tory, which is reason enough for them," answered Beldon. "These rebel louts have nothing better to do with themselves than stay drunk most of the time, and that heats up the brain. Then it only takes the wrong word in the right ear to set them off like tinder. Some of these rebels are men of education, but most seem to be louts of the lowest class with more wind than brains and more willing to blame the king for their woes than apply themselves to wholesome work. If there had been any proper enforcement of the law, they'd be in jail for sedition instead of hailed as heroes by the ignorant. No good will come of it, mark me."

"What about the injured man?" asked Elizabeth.

"Oh, he'll be all right, by and by. He went to live with his daughter and son-in-law on their farm. After tending to the poor fellow I came to realize that dear Deborah and I would no longer be safe ourselves, so we closed up the house and came here to accept the kind invitation your mother extended to us."

"And glad I am that you did," said Mother. "Beatings, tar, and feathers. Why, the two of you might have been murdered in your beds."

Mrs. Hardinbrook shivered appreciatively at her narrow escape.

"The lot of them should be in jail, down to the last cowardly dog, and the rabble-rousers hanged on the common. What do you think, Mr. Barrett?" Beldon turned toward me.

"I agree," I said heartily. Anyone who had the least responsibility for shifting Beldon and his sister from Philadelphia to my home certainly deserved some sort of severe punishment.

After supper, Mother suggested—or rather ordered—us to remove to the music room so Elizabeth could entertain us by playing on her spinet. This was greeted with enthusiasm from Mrs. Hardinbrook and resignation from Elizabeth.

"Do you play an instrument, Mr. Barrett?" asked Beldon.

"Not a note," I said. "I enjoy music, but haven't the ear or hand to reproduce it for myself."

"What a pity," said Mrs. Hardinbrook. "Theophilous is quite good with a fiddle. Perhaps he could play a duet with Miss Barrett." She had a crafty look in her eye, the idea behind it so insufferably transparent that Mother's head jerked warningly. If his sister did not notice it, Beldon certainly did.

"Another time, Deborah, I beg you. I am quite worn out from the journey, and any sounds I might draw from my fiddle would not be worth the hearing." He spread his hands in mock deprecation and a look swiftly passed between them that said more than his words. She burned for the briefest instant and abruptly subsided into a smile of sympathy for him.

"Yes, of course," she said, not quite able to smooth the edge from her voice.

Elizabeth looked relieved and assumed her seat before the spinet. She played well enough but with little enthusiasm. I drifted toward the door and lifted my eyebrows at Jericho, who had made it his business to keep close and listen in.

"No sign of Father?" I whispered from the side of my mouth.

"None," he answered morosely.

"Have one of the lads sit out by the road with a lantern, then. We wouldn't want him to miss the gate."

He knew as well as I that there was little chance of Father losing himself. If nothing else, his horse knew the way home. I suspected that Mrs. Montagu was proving to be more charming than ever and Father had elected to take supper with her followed by Lord knows what else. He might even spend another night with her.

Jericho promised to see to things and disappeared just as Elizabeth finished her piece. I joined in the applause.

Mrs. Hardinbrook gushed forth with more praise. This time it seemed directed less at Mother and more toward Beldon, in an attempt to draw his attention to Elizabeth. His praise was more subdued and disappointingly neutral, at least from his sister's point of view. Then he stood and bowed to all of us.

"You will think me terribly rude, Mrs. Barrett, but I must beg leave to go to my room. I don't know where Deborah gets all her liveliness, but I am absolutely exhausted."

"I quite understand, Dr. Beldon. Pray do not let us keep you. Jonathan, show Dr. Beldon up to the yellow room, if you please."

It hardly pleased me, but I offered my own bow and waited for Beldon to join me in the hall.

"Your mother is a very kind woman to take us in," he said as we trudged up the stairs.

"Yes."

"I fully realize that this must be an imposition. Deborah and I are very grateful and glad to be here."

What a surprise, I thought.

"I would like to take this opportunity to let you know that I am entirely at the service of you and your house should you require it."

"As a doctor?" I asked, somewhat insolently, now that he was away from Mother's protection.

A perceptive man, he decided interpret the light insult as a joke. "I'm afraid so. Doubtless I could make myself useful working in the fields, but I have more talent for doctoring than animal husbandry or farming."

I paused on the landing and looked at him squarely. "You consider yourself a good doctor, then?"

"As good as most. I studied with Dr. Richard Shippen of Philadelphia," he added with some pride.

"Did you really? The smallpox man?"

Beldon was surprised that I'd heard of him and said as much.

"I should think so. Years ago Mother instructed Father by letter to pack Elizabeth and me off to the man for an inoculation against the pox. I still have the scar. Couldn't have been more than nine, but I remember it vividly, worst six weeks of my life. What a horrible thing to do to children."

"Less horrible than dying of the pox," he pointed out.

I was unwilling to relinquish my hostile opinion of the man. "I'd read that they had Shippen up for body-snatching three years back."

Beldon was not to be drawn and only shook his head, amused. "Something that every teaching physician seems doomed to endure. He was accused of taking a woman's body for his dissecting class, but those subjects only ever come from the Potter's Field, never from Christian burial grounds. The whole business was utterly absurd. The woman he supposedly dissected in the winter had died months earlier in the summer—of a putrid fever. No physician would ever find use for such a long-corrupted subject in his classes. Most absurd," he repeated.

"Oh, yes, very."

Letting that one pass as well, he gestured at one of the doors. "Is this my room?"

"This one," I said, taking him farther down the hall.

"I understand that you have a good library here."

"Yes. Downstairs. Any of the servants can show you the way."

"I'll look forward to it. I was unable to bring many books. Perhaps you would like to inspect my own small collection?"

"Another time, Dr. Beldon. I must return to the ladies, you know."

Again the incessant smile, this one tinged with regret and goodwill. "Yes. The ladies can be quite demanding. Good night, then, Mr. Barrett. Thank you once more for your kindness."

The man sounded utterly sincere. A bit nonplussed, I left before he could try drawing me into another conversation. That macabre story about the doctor dissecting a corpse that did not exist *had* been interesting. Not the sort of tale one could relate in genteel company. Well, Mother's company, anyway.

Tempting as it was to retreat to my room, I felt bound to go back to the parlor and look after Elizabeth. She was still grimly playing, missing a note now and then as her thoughts wandered. Mother was employing her scratching stick. Mrs. Hardinbrook looked bored.

At the end of the piece I applauded louder than the others and walked over to the spinet. "Excellent, Elizabeth. You get better every day."

She knew what I was up to and seized upon it smoothly and with both hands. "You are so kind, Jonathan." She stood up and away from the instrument and curtsied to her audience. "Ah, but I am weary myself. In another minute I'm sure I shall fall asleep on my feet."

"You have had a very long day," I agreed. "Mother, may we be excused? I want to see that Elizabeth makes it upstairs without stumbling."

"Poor thing," said Mrs. Hardinbrook, all sympathy. She started to launch into a no doubt pretty speech, but Mother interrupted her, granting us permission to leave. We took it.

Once outside, Elizabeth and I dropped our formal pretenses and marched toward the stairs as equals.

"Thank you for the rescue," she said.

"Always at your service."

"It looks like we're going to be lumbered with them for as long as Mother is here."

"Sadly, yes."

"Or at least until Father throws them out. Did you see how that harpy was trying to push her brother on me?"

"I noticed that he refused."

"Is that supposed to mean—"

"No slight intended toward you, dear sister. I only meant that Beldon is likely aware that such a liaison would incur Mother's extreme displeasure. You have nothing to fear from him regarding unwanted attentions."

"Thank goodness for that," she sighed. "Do you think it would help to write to the king? We could ask him to send soldiers to Philadelphia to restore order there, then Mother and her friends could leave us in peace."

"Oh, I'm sure he would find your suggestion of great influence in forming his policies."

Her good humor and mine restored, I saw Elizabeth to her room and gratefully returned to my own. Jericho had my things set out for the night, and a fire was going. The tray from our small meal was long cleared away, but he'd left a cup of wine and a plate of biscuits on the mantel for later. He'd also lighted the lamp on the table where my studies waited. Well, even Greek was preferable to the company in the parlor. I readied myself for bed, wrapped up warm in the dressing gown, and opened the first book.

My ever optimistic tutor, Mr. Rapelji, had chosen an especially tricky passage for translation, but it took my mind away from present-day conundrums. The only time I looked up was when Mother and Mrs.

Hardinbrook passed by my closed door on the way to their rooms. Their voices increased and faded along with their footsteps. I took the moment to stretch and look out the window.

High clouds obscured the stars and moon, making it very dark. Jericho would have called in the boy and his lantern by now. If Father hadn't turned up at this late an hour, it could only mean that he would be staying out another night. Damnation.

The intricacies of an ancient battle and the warriors that fought it held my attention for another hour, then someone lightly knocked on my door. I knew who it was and, with a sigh of slight annoyance, answered.

Elizabeth stood waiting with a wan look and a drooping eye. "I couldn't sleep," she explained apologetically. My annoyance faded. As small children had been our habit in the past to visit one another for a late-night talk when wakeful. I'd missed those talks without knowing it.

I invited her in and shut the door quietly. "I could give you some of this Greek. Translating it often inspires me toward slumber."

She threw herself facedown across my bed and propped her chin on her fists. "Mother has that woman in her room and they're still yammering away. I had no idea that two people with so little to say could do so for so long."

"Why don't you listen in? It could be entertaining."

"I have, but they don't talk about anything interesting. It's always clothes, food, or people I've never heard of and wouldn't care to meet. Rubbish, the lot of it. What did you say you were doing?"

"Greek. Care to try some?" I threw myself into my chair and offered her the book I was working from.

She considered, but turned it down. "Will you be seeing Mr. Rapelji tomorrow?"

"Yes, if I can get this finished. He'll probably put me over the coals as usual."

"Oh, may I come along and watch?"

"Yes, you may and be very welcome. With you there it won't be so horrible."

"What exaggeration. You know he never even raises his voice."

"It's the way he doesn't raise it that bothers me."

She chuckled a little, which was good to hear. "Perhaps he will find something interesting for me to do as well. I absolutely do not want to be here tomorrow. One thing I did hear through the wall was Mother making plans to visit some of the neighbors to introduce that woman. She said I'd be coming along. Nice of her to let me know about it, don't you think?"

"We can be gone before breakfast," I assured her, putting my feet up on the table. "Rapelji won't mind feeding us."

"Thank goodness. I'll wager that Mother wants to look the men over hereabouts in hopes of matching me up with one. Ugh!"

"Don't you want to get married?"

"Someday, but not to any man that *she* would pick."

"She picked Father, didn't she?"

"Huh. Her tastes have changed if Beldon is anything to go by."

"He's not so bad," I teased. She made a face at me. "He has pretty manners."

"So does my cat."

"The odd thing is that I did get the impression that he would like to be friends."

"Fine. You can be his friend. I'd sooner marry Mr. Rapelji."

"Or your cat?"

She laughed out loud at that one, and I continued with speculation over what her cat would be likely to wear when they went to church.

"Of course, you'll have to have a lot of cream for the wedding breakfast," I went on. "For the cat's side of the family."

She added a comment of her own, but I couldn't make it out for her giggling and asked her to repeat it. She struggled to take in the breath to do so, but in that moment my door was thrown open with such force that it crashed against the inside wall. Elizabeth choked with surprise and pushed upright. I hastily swung my legs from the table, knocking a book to the floor.

Mother stood on the threshold. Her eyes were wide with incredulity, her mouth torn downward with horrified shock. She looked from one to the other of us, unable to decide which deserved her immediate attention. Elizabeth and I stared back at her with shared confusion.

"Is there something wrong, Mother?" I asked, rising.

Her mouth flapped several times. It might have been comical but for the blistering fury contained in her. It did not remain there for long.

"You two ..." she finally gasped out, pointing at each of us.

"What is it?" I stepped forward, thinking she was ill. She looked feverish with those blazing eyes.

"You ... filthy ... *filthy* unnatural *wretches!*"

"What's the matter with her?" Elizabeth asked.

"Mother?" I put my hand out. "Come and sit down, Mother."

She slapped me away. "You miserable, depraved creature. How could you even think—you're sickening, the pair of you!"

Elizabeth shook her head at me, a sign to keep my distance, and to communicate her own puzzlement.

"Mother. ..." I began, but she came at me and this time slapped me right across the mouth with all her strength. My head snapped to one side, my face afire from the stinging blow. I fell back, eyes smarting, gaping at her without comprehension, too startled to move.

She struck me again with her other hand, fairly rattling my head. Tears started from my eyes from the pain. Another strike. I backed away, suddenly aware of the invective flowing from her. None of it was coherent, broken as it was by her hitting me and the intensity of emotion within. Her temper tantrum this morning was but a shower compared to this gale.

Elizabeth was off the bed by now and shouting at her. I put my hands up to guard myself and tried to back around toward the door and escape. Elizabeth got between us and took solid hold of Mother's arm. Now they were both shouting.

Then Mother hit Elizabeth. Not with an open hand, but a closed fist.

Elizabeth cried out and spun away, her hair flying. She fell against the bed, then dropped to the floor. Her next breath was a bewildered, angry sob. Mother loomed over her, shifting her weight to one foot. Before she could deliver what would have been a vicious kick to my sister's face I caught both her arms from behind and dragged her away. Mother screamed and squirmed and her heels flailed against my shins.

"What is it? Oh, dear, what is it? Marie, what is happening?" Mrs. Hardinbrook dithered in the hall, adding her foolishness to the din.

Mother paid her no mind, thrashing madly about. She'd used up her words and much of her breath. Only hideous little animal grunts escaped from her clenched teeth.

I hoarsely shouted Elizabeth's name, breathless myself. She shook herself and found her feet, moving slowly, and holding her face. She was dazed, but had sense enough to keep clear. Stumbling toward the door, she ran into Mrs. Hardinbrook, who didn't quite know what to do.

"Get some help, you fool!" my sister bellowed, pushing her away. The woman squeaked with fear and fled.

"Elizabeth?"

"I'm all right," she stated shakily.

"*Harlot!*" Mother shouted at her. "Filthy, unnatural *harlot!*"

Elizabeth gaped at her, then her eyes darted to my bed, where she had been giggling hardly a minute past. "Oh, my God. She can't mean *that.*"

Busy as I was, the realization of what she was talking about took longer to dawn upon me. When it did, Mother took advantage of my utter shock to twist from my grasp and round upon us. Her carefully made-up hair had shredded into a tangled mess framing her beet red face like Medusa's snakes. Her eyes fairly popped with rage. She looked absolutely and utterly demented.

"You shameless creatures! It was a cursed day that either of you were born—that you should come to this! You dirty, disgusting. ..."

"Mother, you are *wrong!* You don't know what you're saying."

She could have scorched me with those eyes. "I know what I saw, you unnatural monster."

Elizabeth came in to stand next to me. "She's incensed, Jonathan, don't try to argue with her."

"That was ever and always the excuse," Mother snarled. "*I* don't know what I'm talking about! Is that it? Is that what you'll say? This shame is upon you both. You'll be the ones locked away. Dear God, I should have seen this coming and been here to prevent it." She looked past us. "It's your fault, Samuel. You raised them as *you* would and *see* what has become of them. I swear, if any vile bastard get comes of this unholy union I'll drown it myself. Do you hear me? I said, *do you hear me?*"

As one, Elizabeth and I followed her gaze. Standing in my doorway, still wrapped in his traveling cloak, was our tardy father.

CHAPTER
THREE

HE REGARDED HIS WIFE in a calm manner and nodded soberly. "I hear you, Marie," he said in a gentle, well-controlled voice.

Elizabeth and I began to rush toward him, but he swiftly brought up one hand to stay us. He did not look at us but at Mother.

She glared back. "And where have you been while this wickedness has been going on? Or have you been a part of it? *Have you?*"

He declined to answer that one, his glance shifting briefly to me and back to her again. "Library. Both of you."

We fled. In the hall we met Beldon hurrying along with a black case in hand and his sister in tow. He was dressed for bed, but had thrown on a coat and shoved his bare feet into shoes. Neither spared a word for us, though Mrs. Hardinbrook paused as though sorely tempted. But she went on to be with Beldon and thus watch whatever might come next. She was welcome to do so.

Partway down the stairs we encountered the first of the servants roused by the row, a sleep-drugged maid. I ordered her to the kitchen to brew a pot of strong tea. She tottered out of our path, her face coming awake with questions. I ruthlessly confiscated her candle.

The library was cold, but the fireplace had been swept and readied for tomorrow. I knelt and busied myself with the tinder, bringing it to fiery life with the candle flame while Elizabeth sank onto a settee.

"Are you hurt?" I asked.

Silence, and then an eloquent sniff. She rubbed her swelling and now wet cheek with an impatient hand. "Are you? Your face..."

"It's nothing." But I began to tremble. A piece of kindling slipped from my suddenly fumbling fingers and hit the stone hearth. "My God, Elizabeth."

"I know."

"What she did ... what she thinks ... it's monstrous."

"It's impossible. *She's* impossible. We can't live like this." Elizabeth hated crying and I hated watching her fight it. I left the fire and sat next to her, an arm around her slumped shoulders. It was as much for my solace as hers.

With only the one candle and the embryonic fire, the library was overcrowded with shadows. I'd seen it like this many times, foraging down here for a book when the house was asleep, but never with such a heaviness in my heart.

I was afraid. I was in my own house and afraid.

It was not a child's fear of the dark, or even of that time when I'd fallen into the kettle, or of a hundred other times and incidents. Those fears pass quickly and may eventually be laughed at; this was of an altogether different kind. It would not go away so easily, if at all.

"Why did she *ever* have to come home?" I muttered.

Elizabeth had recovered somewhat when the maid turned up with the tea. I let the girl pour; neither of us were steady enough to do it.

"What's going on up there?" I asked her. I'd heard a lot of rushing about and voices.

"They're all taking care of Mrs. Barrett, sir. Mrs. Nooth is with her and so's that Dr. Beldon. Mrs. Nooth said she'd had some kind of a fit." The girl waited, perhaps hoping to glean more information from me. I disappointed her with a nod of thanks and a clear dismissal.

"'Some kind of a fit'?" Elizabeth echoed sarcastically when we were alone.

"That seems to describe it well enough."

She pulled herself straight and reached for one of the teacups. "I can see us describing it like that from now on. What are we going to *do* with her? Lock her in the attic? Or will we build her a little block house and hire someone to feed her through a slot in the door?"

"It won't come to that," I said.

"Better that than to go through this again. I didn't hate her before, Jonathan, but I do now. What she ... what ... oh, I can't bear it. It's unforgivable. It's perverse and horrible. She has to go."

"But—"

"This is more our house than hers. She had no right to come here and do this to us. We were happy until she came."

True. All true.

Elizabeth put down the cup, her tea untouched. "Father will have to do something. After this, he must do something. He must."

We fell silent. I went back to building up the fire. The chill of the room—and of other things—seeped past my skin and into the bones. It was devastating enough that Mother had violently struck us, but for her to have hurled such a revolting accusation was agonizing. Until now I'd not suspected the depth of her lunacy. She'd just shown it to be nigh to bottomless.

Father came in just as the logs began to properly blaze. As one, Elizabeth and I rushed to him for the embrace we'd been denied earlier. It was something we'd done as children and now we instinctively returned to that simple and much-needed comfort. He smiled and opened his arms wide, folding us in close. I felt better for that solid weight around my shoulders. No matter how bad the situation, I knew that he would be able to make it better.

"Is that tea I spy?" he asked after a moment.

We loosened our grip and Elizabeth glided over to pour. He made a side trip to a cabinet and brought out a bottle of brandy, adding some to each cup.

"I think we all need this," he observed.

He'd shed his cloak at some point, but still carried some of the outdoors with him in his manner. His riding boots were smeared with old mud. He'd been wearing them, I remembered, when he'd taken his morning walk with Mrs. Montagu. Such earlier pleasures had clearly been driven away by tonight's pains, for he looked tired. Older, I realized with another chill, but instead of being burdened by age, he was a man aged by a burden. His wife.

"Well?" he asked. "Which of you wants to talk first?"

Elizabeth stepped in. "Where's Mother?"

"In her room. That fellow with the popping eyes gave her a dose of laudanum to calm her down. He and that silly woman are sitting in with her. Said he was a doctor. Would he be Beldon, then?"

"Yes. The woman is his sister, Deborah Hardinbrook."

Father had heard enough about them from Mother to need no further introduction. "Proper little pair of toadies, but they seem to be making themselves useful for the moment. Now, please, tell me what happened."

Between us we managed to garble the narrative enough for him to raise his hand in protest.

"Jonathan, your turn," he said firmly. "Pretend you're in court."

It was his way of reminding me to present all the facts, but as simply as possible and in good order. I did my best. Elizabeth added nothing, but nodded agreement as I spoke. When I'd finished, our brandy-laced tea was gone.

Father sighed and ran a hand through his graying hair. It was his own, tied back with a now-wilted ribbon. He wore a wig only when engaged in court business or seeing a client. "A pretty mess," he concluded. "Are you badly hurt? Elizabeth?"

She shook her head. I did the same, though my cheeks were tender to touch and likely as red as hers.

"But it might have been worse," I said. "If Mother had kicked her as she'd intended...if I'd not been there to pull Mother away..."

Elizabeth dropped her gaze. "We must do something, Father."

"Indeed," he said, neither agreeing nor disputing. He stood and paced the room a few times. On the last round he checked the hallway for any listeners and closed the door before coming to stand before the fireplace. It was unlike him to behave so. I saw it as more evidence of how Mother's presence had changed life for the worse.

"There are more bad tidings, too," I said.

"Out with it."

"She wants me to go to England to study law."

Father only nodded, which was a bit disappointing. I thought he'd show some kind of dismay or denial. "What else?"

"She wants to sell Jericho and hire an English servant to take his place."

This was news to Elizabeth. "That's—no! No, she mustn't!"

"I told Jericho I'd sooner run away to sea and take him with me."

Father gave out with a chuckle just then, but quickly smothered it. I'd sounded foolish, but just then we needed some foolishness. Some of the shadows looming over us seemed to drop back.

"But Jericho said that I'd be arrested for stealing him," I added.

"Jericho is a most level-headed young fellow. Well, you need not worry about him being sold. Since I bought Archimedes with my own money, both he and his son are my property. Your mother can't sell either of them without my permission, and that is something I shall happily withhold. If she wants an English servant for you, she may hire one, but he will have to take his orders from Jericho."

I blinked with surprise, but Father was serious. We knew enough about the household hierarchies to know that no man of the type Mother would be looking for would accept such work under that condition. Elizabeth smiled at me, new hope and cheer blooming on her face.

Father's own smile came and went more quickly. "England." He sighed.

"I don't want to go, but she said that it's all been arranged."

"Then I've no doubt that it has. Cambridge, I suppose. Yes, she's mentioned it before and no, I did not know that she'd pursued it this far."

"Why?" I asked. "What is it she wants? Is Harvard not good enough for her?"

"That and many other reasons, laddie. Tell me everything you know."

I summarized this morning's conversation, leaving in Mother's tantrum, then went on to her lecture in the afternoon. The latter was little more than a sketch because of my muzzy condition at the time.

"She seems to have everything well in hand," was his comment when I'd finished. "It looks like she's been cooking this up with that bloody sister of hers for some goodly time."

"Aunt Theresa?" The name was not unknown to me, but unfamiliar on the tongue. She lived in London and wrote often to Mother. Hardly a week passed without a thick packet of letters arriving by way of whatever ship had made the crossing. It took months for her correspondence to get here and she filled reams of paper with her spiky, precise hand. Mother had several boxes of those letters in her baggage when she'd moved in.

Father went to his desk and shuffled the papers on top, plucking one from the pile and bringing it back to the better light. It was the same one Mother had been studying this morning. "This is it. You've been accepted at Cambridge; according to this, your studies are to begin at the Michaelmas term. How like her to leave it there for me to just 'find.'"

"She also waited until you were away before telling me. She did it on purpose, I think—"

"She does most everything with a purpose," he growled, putting the paper aside.

"But I don't have to go ... do I?"

Father did not answer right away. Elizabeth's hand, resting on mine, tightened.

"Father?"

Always decisive and in control, he hesitated, frowning at the floor. "I'll talk to her," he said.

"Talk to ...? What does that mean?"

His chin snapped up at my tone, and I shrank inside. Father had no patience for whining; I'd forgotten that he'd taught me better than to indulge in it. But his face softened. "It means that both of you need to know what's really beneath all this so you can understand and make the best of things."

That didn't sound too terribly hopeful.

He poured out another swallow of brandy and drained it away, then looked up at his wife's portrait. "Firstly, I married your mother because I loved her. If her father had realized that, then our lives might have been quite different. Whether for good or for ill, I could not say, but different, perhaps.

"All this took place in England. You know that I went to Cambridge myself. I was out and working with old Roylston when I met Judge Fonteyn and his family. He was wealthy but always looking to either increase it or raise his status in society. I did not fit his idea of an ideal son-in-law, and he saw me not as I was, but as he perceived me to be. He put himself in my place and assumed that I was paying court to his daughter for her inheritance.

"Admittedly, the money made your mother that much more attractive to me, but it was never my real goal. We might have eloped, but Marie persuaded him to consent to our marriage. He did so with ill grace but provided her with a generous allowance. He also drew up a paper for me to sign, stipulating that this allowance was hers and hers alone and I was not to touch it."

"But doesn't a wife's property become her husband's?"

"That's the law, but old Fonteyn's paper was a neat bit of work to get around it. The only way I could marry was to agree with his conditions. I signed it readily enough. He was surprised that I did, and at the same time contemptuous. There was no pleasing the old devil."

That sounded familiar, I thought.

"The marriage took place and we were happy for a time, at least we were when there was sufficient distance between your mother and her family. Her father was a terrible tyrant, couldn't and wouldn't abide me, and it was because of him that I decided to leave England altogether. Marie went along with it, because in those days she still loved me. You both know how we came to settle here, but it was your mother's money that bought this place and it still pays for the servants and the taxes."

"The paper you signed…" said Elizabeth, beginning to see. It was like crystal to me.

"Means that I own none of this." He gestured, indicating the house and all the lands around it. "I have Archimedes, Jericho, and whatever I've gleaned from my practice. Now, I *have* made something of a decent living for myself, but as a rule, lawyers enjoy far more social status than they do money. When Fonteyn died, he divided his fortune between his daughters. There was quite a sum involved, but I'd promised to touch none of it and have kept to that promise. It ... has never bothered me before."

"So Mother is paying for my education," I said.

"She always has. It was she who hired Rapelji, for example."

"And mine, too?" asked Elizabeth.

Father smiled with affection and satisfaction. "No, that was my idea. It is a sad and wasteful thing, but the truth is your mother didn't think it worth trying. She's always had the mistaken idea that an educated woman is socially disadvantaged."

"And yet she herself—?" Elizabeth began swiftly sputtering her way towards outrage.

Father waved a cautioning hand. "I must clarify. She thinks a woman has gained sufficient knowledge if she reads and writes enough to maintain her household and be agreeable in polite company."

Elizabeth snorted.

"I never saw it that way, though, so I made sure that Rapelji was well compensated for the time he spent on you. Your mother was under the impression that you were learning no more than the limits she'd set: your numbers, letters, and some French."

"And my music from Mrs. Hornby?"

"Yes."

"Because every girl in polite society must know how to sing and play?" It was not a question so much as a statement of contempt.

"Yes."

"On the other hand, being able to reason and think would place me at a severe disadvantage?"

"In her view, yes."

Elizabeth rose and threw her arms around him. "Then, thank you, Father!"

He laughed at the embrace. "There now. I may not have done you any favors, girl."

"I don't care." She loosened her grip. "But what about Jonathan going away to England?"

His laugh settled into a sigh. "It is her money that runs this place, puts clothes on your backs, and food in your mouths, and because of that she feels entitled to choose where you are to be educated. She appears to have entirely made up her mind, but I will talk with her. There are other reasons for you to go to Harvard than the fact that it is closer than England."

"And if she doesn't listen?" I asked glumly.

"That possibility exists. You may have to face it."

"But after tonight... Mother isn't... well."

"You need not mince your words, Jonathan. We all know she wasn't in her right mind then. Her father was the same. He'd work himself into a ferocious temper until you'd think his brain would burst, then the fit would pass and like as not he'd have forgotten what angered him, even deny he'd been angry. Whatever poisons lurked in his blood are in your mother as well."

"And us?" Elizabeth's eyebrows were climbing.

Father shrugged. "It's in God's hands, girl, but I've tried to raise you two with the love old Fonteyn was incapable of giving. I think it has made all the difference."

"We're nothing like her," she said thankfully.

He touched her chin lightly with one finger and glanced at me. "Perhaps a little, on the outside. I wish you could have known her in those days." He indicated the portrait. "Everything was so different then, but over the years the poisons began to leech out. She changed, bit by bit. She began to expect things of me that I chose not to provide. She wanted me to advance on to the bench, but I never had the inclination to become a judge. She became fixed on that as hard and fast as her father was fixed upon his money. I could have done as she wanted, but it would not have been what I wanted. Eventually, I could see myself turning into her own little dancing puppet. I would not have been my own man, but rather something tied to her and, in turn, tied to her dead father. In her lucid moments, she knew this, but could never hold on to it for long."

"Is that why she moved away?" I asked.

"In part. In the years after you were born, she got worse. Nothing to do with you, laddie. You were as sweet a child as anyone could ask for, but her nerves were bad. She no longer loved me by then and I... Well, there are few things in life so miserable as a marriage gone wrong. I hope you two will make a better job of it than I did. She had some distant cousins in Philadelphia, so off she went. I think she found some happiness there with such friends as she's gathered 'round. I know I have been happy here."

One of the logs popped noisily. Happiness. I'd taken it for granted until now. Looking at Father, I began to see the heaviness of the burden he'd carried without complaint, all these years. He hadn't told us everything, I could sense that, but I wasn't going to presume on him for more. What we'd just learned was sufficient. Because of it I suddenly knew I was not yet a man and able to carry such a weight, but a frightened boy of seventeen.

✦ ✦ ✦

I SLEPT POORLY for what remained of the night and was up to watch the dawn long before its advent. The house was quiet, and I imagined it to be waiting, wondering what was to happen once Mother woke from her own laudanum-soaked slumber. I dressed warmly and crept outside to the stables to saddle two horses. Elizabeth and I had not changed our plan to spend time with Rapelji. Father knew and had encouraged it. He would have his hands full dealing with Mother and her guests and preferred us out of the way.

Rolly poked his head from his box hopefully, but I passed him by for Belle and Satin, two mares out of the same dam who shared a calm temperament as well as a smooth gait. Rolly vocalized his displeasure, waking the lads who slept over the stable. One of them came down to investigate and sleepily stayed on to help with the saddling before wandering off to the kitchen in hope of an early meal.

I led the horses out to wait by one of the side doors, then went to fetch Elizabeth. She was just inside, pulling on her gloves. There was a sodden look about her indicating that she hadn't slept well, either. On her face, where Mother's fist had landed, was a large, evil-looking bruise. She'd made no effort to cover or disguise it.

"We don't have to go," I said. "It's not likely that you'll be called upon to be visiting the neighbors."

"No, but I can't bear to be in this house with her. Besides, *this* was not my fault." She tilted her head to indicate the damage done. "I've nothing to be ashamed of and people may think what they like."

"You don't care if they know about Mother?"

Elizabeth's face grew hard in a way that I did not like. "Not one whit."

"But why?"

"Why not? Sooner or later they'll start their speculations, their gossip about her. They may as well get the truth from us as make it up for themselves."

"But it's none of their bloody business!"

"As you say." She shrugged. "But mark me, they shall make it so, whether we like it or not. We have only to be calm and truthful and let Mother rave on as her fancy takes her. Then we shall see how many friends she has about her."

I was quite confused by this harsh attitude, for it was an alien one in Elizabeth, then I began to see the point of it all. "You're doing this hoping that Mother will…?"

"A word here and there and she will be shunned by what passes for polite company in these parts. That's what she craves and lives for, the puerile attention and approval of her so-called peers. She's welcome to it, if she can find any willing to endure her company after this."

"What if they believe her and not you? What if she repeats her—that awful accusation against us? You know adults are more likely to believe other adults."

"But they *know* us here. They do not know her. And we are Father's children, raised to be honest and truthful. I think that favors us, Jonathan, so you needn't worry."

"Damnation, I will if I want to."

"Please yourself, then, but support me on this and there's a chance that Mother may move out, bag, baggage, and toad-eaters, and leave us all in peace."

That silenced me.

She handed me a leather bundle. "Here, you'd forgotten your books and papers."

"Thank you," I said faintly, my mind busy with all sorts of things. I couldn't choose whether to approve of her plan or not, but knew that she would go through with it, regardless of my objections.

She led the way into the yard and I helped her onto Satin, her favorite. I swung up on Belle and we set off down the lane leading to the main road, turning into the rising sun. It gave no warmth save within the mind, but was still a cheering sight.

Rapelji lived in a fine, solid farmhouse at the eastern edge of our property. The farm was not his—that had been annexed onto our own lands—but he had a good garden plot for himself and found additional support from several other students in the area. Some of them boarded with him for part of the year and helped with the chores to pay for their tutoring.

As early as we were, Rapelji was already up and about, a short, stocky figure in the middle of his troop of students as he led them through a peculiar series of hops and skips for their morning exercise. Though gray of hair, he was as energetic as any of them. At a distance, you could only tell him from the boys by his flashing spectacles, which somehow stayed on no matter how vigorous his actions. As we drew near, he had them all jumping and clapping their hands over their heads in time to shouting the multiplication table at the top of their lungs. It was great fun, and I'd done it myself at their age. He had the view that since boys were prone to making noise, it might as well be for a constructive purpose.

They got as far as four times twelve when he called a breathless halt. Some of the group had noticed our approach and lost the count.

"Concentration, gentlemen," he admonished. "Concentration, discipline, and courtesy. What is required when you see a lady?"

As one, but with grins and playful shoving, the boys pretended to sweep hats from their bare heads and bowed deeply to Elizabeth. From her saddle, she returned their salute gracefully. My turn was next and I doffed my own hat to them. Rapelji said they'd done well and announced it was time to start the chores. The boys scattered like stirred-up ants. Chores first, then breakfast, then studies.

"Good morning, Miss Elizabeth, Mr. Jonathan. Come in, come in. It's a baking day for the girls and the first loaves are just out of the oven." He gestured us inside. There was a rich smell of hot bread in the air, wafting over the yard from the oven behind the house.

We left the horses to the care of the boys and joined him. Along with a varying number of students, he shared the big house with his two housekeepers, Rachel and Sarah, two elderly siblings that he couldn't always tell apart, so he called them "the girls." They weren't much for intellectual conversation, but kindly toward the students and doted on the teacher. Their cooking and herb lore were legendary.

The front room was where he taught lessons. A long table lined with many chairs took up most of the floor. The walls boasted all kinds of books, papers, some stuffed animals and his prize, a mounted skeleton of some type of small ape. He used it to explain anatomy to us. On another shelf he kept his geological finds, including a rather large specimen of a spiral-shaped sea creature, so old that it had turned to stone. He'd dug it up himself miles inland and delighted in speculating about its origins. The thing had always fascinated me and had sparked many a talk and good-natured argument.

Elizabeth took off her cloak and hat, hanging them on the pegs next to the door: This was a second home to us, Rapelji our eccentric uncle, but we hadn't been over together for some time, a point he commented upon.

"Things are a bit hectic at the house," said Elizabeth. "Two of Mother's friends have come to stay with us for a while."

"Ah, that's good. Company always helps pass the time away." Rapelji, as evident by his huge household, liked having people about him.

"Have you ever met Mother?" I asked. He'd never before mentioned her and I was curious to have his side of the story.

He pursed his plump lips to think. "Oh, yes, but it was years ago and only the one time when I answered her advertisement for a tutor. She interviewed me and sent me on to here. I was the only one willing to make the journey, it seemed. Your good father made the rest of the arrangements and that was that. Perhaps since she is here I should stop over and pay my respects."

"No!" we said in unison.

"No?" he questioned, interested by our reluctance. Then he noticed Elizabeth's face for the first time. Until now, she'd been keeping herself slightly turned away. "Good heavens, child, what has happened to you?"

Though his shock must have been in accordance with Elizabeth's hopes and plans to socially oust Mother from the community, it was still difficult for her. She dropped her gaze. "We've had some problems at home," she mumbled.

"Indeed?" Rapelji could see there was more to be learned. "Well, come sit here and rest yourself." He solicitously held a chair for her. He peered closely at me, now, and noted the swelling that I'd seen in my shaving mirror earlier. I felt myself going red and not knowing why. As with Elizabeth, I had nothing of which to be ashamed.

One of the girls came in to set the table—I think it was Rachel—and her sharp eyes suddenly froze onto our faces in that way old women have.

"Goodness, children, have you been quarreling?" she asked.

Elizabeth's hand went to her cheek and she went very red. I kept my hands down, but nodded to the concerned woman. "Yes, ma'am, but not with each other."

"I'll make you a nice poultice of sugar and yellow soap," Rachel promised.

Sarah appeared next to her, squinted at us, and shook her head. "No, dear, that's for boils. What you want is some cotton dipped in molasses."

"That's for earache," said Rachel.

"Really? I could have sworn...."

"Please, ladies," Elizabeth interrupted. "It's nothing to trouble over. I am in no distress. We ... we must get back to our studies."

Dissatisfied as they obviously were and wanting to stay, Rapelji came to her support, and the two ladies eventually removed themselves and their good intentions. He waited until the door to the kitchen was shut, then gently asked for an explanation.

"Mother ... felt the need to discipline us, sir," I said stiffly.

"And your father agreed?" he asked with surprise. "To this?"

"No, sir. He persuaded her to cease."

Elizabeth heaved an impatient sigh, told me not to be such a diplomat, and gave Rapelji the bald truth. She did not, however, mention Mother's obscene accusation, only that she'd thrown an unreasonable fit. She went on to relate that Father had interrupted things in time and mentioned that Beldon's services as a doctor had been employed. I found myself listening with surprising interest. It seemed that Elizabeth had a talent for storytelling.

Rapelji, the poor man, was out of his depth, as I'd expected. He had no heart for violent domestic disputes, preferring his battles to remain in history books; the more ancient the quarrel the better.

"I know I've embarrassed you, sir," she said. "And I do apologize, but I felt that of all people, you needed to know the truth of what has happened."

"Yes, yes. Oh, you poor girl."

"Anyway, I did not think it fair that you should be unaware of our situation. Mother has a horrible temper, and it is liable to get away from her at the least provocation. Father said she'd inherited it. The doctor visiting us seems to have things in hand, though."

Rapelji heaved a sigh of his own. "Well, then, I can promise that your confidence will stay here"—he tapped his temple—"and shall go no farther. I am so sorry that you have this problem. If you are ever in need, I am at your service."

Past him, the ostensibly closed kitchen door moved slightly. Rachel and Sarah had heard everything, of course, and Elizabeth knew it. She'd made a point of speaking clearly and without moderating her tone to a lower level as others might have done while relating a confidence. A very canny girl, my sister.

"Mr. Rapelji, you have already helped, just by being here," she said, patting his hand.

Our tutor smiled broadly. "Why, then, you are very welcome!"

This made Elizabeth smile and he inquired if we had any other problems requiring assistance. That's when I stepped in and told him about the Cambridge business.

"And you *don't* want to go?" he cried. "Why ever not?"

"It's so far away," I answered. "And it was how she presented it." That sounded feeble even to me and Rapelji pounced on it.

"So it is the wrappings you object to, but not the gift."

"Gift?" This was not the sort of reaction I'd been expecting from him.

"Try looking at it as a gift, not a punishment, Mr. Jonathan. What difference is it if you had a rough introduction to the idea? The idea itself is what matters: the chance to attend one of the great and ancient centers of higher learning in the world."

"I had thought of it a bit, sir," I said with very feeble enthusiasm, but the subtlety was lost on my tutor.

"Good! Think on it some more. If your father cannot turn Mrs. Barrett's mind from the idea, then you won't feel so badly about going."

"I should not like to wager, upon that, sir," I muttered. Rapelji thumped my shoulder, still beaming.

The front door swung wide just then as two of his other students arrived for the day's lessons. They were the Finch boys, Roddy and Nathan.

We stood and greeted them and Rapelji put them through the social ritual of giving respects to my sister. Roddy, my age and awkward, blushed his way through his bow. Elizabeth was no doubt very beautiful to him despite her bruise. He gawked with curiosity, but said nothing except for a general inquiry about her health. For that he received a polite, but general reply that she was well enough today, thank you.

Nathan, a sullen-faced boy of fourteen who knew that manners were a waste of his time, barely got through his bow. It was just enough to accomplish the job, but not so little as to draw a reprimand.

"I killed a rabbit today," he announced proudly, eager to introduce a subject more to his liking.

"Did you now?" said Rapelji.

"A good fat one for the pot." From the cloth bag that carried all his things he hauled out a long, limp bundle of brown-and-gray fur. "Caught 'im in a snare and snapped 'is neck m'self. Next year Da said 'e'd teach me 'ow ter shoot 'em."

"That's 'I caught him in a snare,' Nathan," began Rapelji, always the teacher.

The boy scowled. "You did not, I did. If'n you did, an' it were on *our* land, then Da will shoot you dead for a-poachin'."

Roddy gave Nathan a cuff. "Mr. Rapelji didn't say *he* was a-poachin', he was telling you how to talk right."

Nathan glowered and grunted with disapproval. He was one of the more difficult students and would have been happier working the fields or hunting. Rapelji had often recommended it, but their father was determined that they learn their letters and grimly paid for the effort. Roddy had a better head and might have progressed more if he didn't have Nathan to constantly look after and keep in line.

Morning chores finished, the other boys began to wander in for their breakfast along with half a dozen others from neighboring houses. Nathan's rabbit was the subject of much interest and conversation and he was compelled to repeat his story of how he'd snapped the animal's neck.

He was happy enough to demonstrate this to everyone's satisfaction, but his method sparked a debate on the various ways of snapping animal necks of all kinds. Elizabeth was not in the least fainthearted, but after several minutes of gleeful discussion she began to visibly pale. Rapelji noticed and dispatched Nathan off to the kitchen with his prize, as it was part of Finch's payment for his boys' tutoring.

Later, over tea, fresh bread and hot porridge, we talked about all sorts of things that had nothing to do with Mother. Rapelji used these times to teach the boys how to conduct themselves in civilized conversation as he called it. He was popular, but often the boys' natural high spirits got away with them and pandemonium would reign as each student contributed a comment more loudly than his neighbor, and at the same time. When this happened, Rapelji usually restored order, with a gavel kept handy for this purpose.

When lessons began in earnest, Elizabeth lent a hand supervising some of the younger lads while Rapelji took a moment to check my Greek. He pronounced himself satisfied, which surprised me, considering the interruptions my work had suffered.

"Next, we shall try some original composition," he announced jovially, as though it were an event to celebrate. "Something with a rhyme to it. They often hold competitions at the universities on this and you'll want to have the practice."

"Yes, sir," I said, looking toward Elizabeth for sympathy and only getting a smirk for my pains.

Rapelji sketched out my exercise in Greek for the day, then I was privileged to help the others with their work. Our tutor was of the opinion that nothing drove a lesson home so squarely as one that you must teach to another. He was also careful to be sure that the information we used was correct. On one memorable occasion a boy had given his "students" the impression that Columbus had made landfall in 1493, which was cause for much confusion and at least one fistfight when Rapelji's back was turned.

The lively company around us did indeed help pass the time away as Rapelji maintained. The girls emerged from the kitchen to announce the midday meal, which was received with extreme enthusiasm by one and all. Papers and books were cleared away, hands were washed of chalk and charcoal, and the plates were set out once more. Elizabeth and I stayed on until well into the afternoon, enjoying every minute. There was a bit of unease when one of the younger ones unabashedly asked Elizabeth why she had a black eye and cheek. She gently pointed out that it was impolite to ask such questions. She also told him a simple version of the truth: that her mother had struck her.

This did not cause much alarm, as most of the lads had no small experience with corporal punishment. They'd been curious and, once their need was satisfied, went on to other concerns.

"Why didn't you say you'd run into a door?" I asked her afterward, when we were riding home.

"That would have been a lie."

"I know, but if any of them mentions it to their families, it might start up a lot of gossip with no fact behind it. I thought you wanted to make sure people knew the facts."

"I do. But keep in mind what you said about adults more readily believing other adults. I doubt if it will come up in conversation when they return home, anyway. Nathan's rabbit drew far more attention than I."

"Hah! Roddy Finch couldn't keep his eyes off you. This will get around, dear sister, don't you worry."

"You're doing enough for both of us, and what objections do you have to Roddy Finch?"

"None, really, just to his beastly little brother. That Nathan's going to be trouble one day."

Too soon and we were on the lane to our house. Never before had we been reluctant to return home. Neither of us knew what might be waiting there nor did we especially care to find out. After the cheerful noise and activity of Rapelji's everything seemed ominously silent and sinister.

"I hope Father's straightened things out," I said.

Elizabeth quietly agreed.

I almost expanded on that theme, then realized I had no heart for it, having left my good cheer behind at the school.

We rode around to the stables and dismounted. The lads there went about their business with the horses as usual, but apparently they knew something of the happenings of last night. Elizabeth endured their staring curiosity in silence. It would have been unseemly for her to answer their unasked questions.

"It's probably all over the place by now," I said as we trudged toward the house.

She nodded. "Today is Saturday. I shall have to decide what to wear to church."

I gulped at the implications. The whole village would see her tomorrow. Her bruising would not nearly have faded by then.

"And if anyone asks, I shall answer them truthfully," she added, looking serene.

Jericho was on the watch for us. He opened the side door and saw to our cloaks and my bag of books.

"What's happened today?" I asked.

"It's been perfectly calm. Your mother kept to her room until the early afternoon, when she came down to eat. Mrs. Hardinbrook sat with her and the doctor looked in several times. They're all up there in her sitting room now, having tea and playing cards."

"What about Father?" That morning I had asked Jericho to especially keep his eyes and ears open on my behalf. I had also told him what Father had said in regard to his being sold. At least one of us had been spared from suffering the tortures of an unknown future for the day.

"He had a very long talk with her—" He broke off, for Father emerged from his library and strode toward us. He looked quite grim but his greeting was warm. Jericho, sensing that he was redundant, vanished.

By now I couldn't contain myself. "Father, tell me—"

"Yes, Jonathan, I did speak with her." He looked very tired and my spirits fell, for I knew what he was going to say. "She would not be moved, laddie."

"Oh, Father." I felt a knot tightening at my throat as surely as if I'd been standing on a scaffold with a hangman. "Please, I don't want to. Can't you try again?"

"She was like a stone. She won't be moved on this." he said, his voice as thick as my own. "You are to go to England and Cambridge."

Elizabeth groaned and put an arm around me.

"Then God have mercy on my soul," I said mournfully, and found it impossible to hold back the tears wanting to spill out.

CHAPTER
FOUR

LONDON, AUGUST, 1773

"Ho, sir! Would yer likes ter get married?"

The nearly toothless young man who accosted me as I descended from the coach was sodden with gin.

"I've a pretty wife for yer, sir! Sweet 'n' willing."

That's not how I would have described the woman lurking just behind him. Over-used and apathetic came to mind. She was also drunk.

"A good 'ousekeeper and seamstress. She knows a' there is ter know 'bout threadin' a needle, haw-haw!" He jabbed an elbow into my side.

It was an even chance that if his ribald joviality didn't knock me over his breath would. I pushed him off and checked to make sure my money was still in place. It was, thank goodness, so I bulled past him, seeking the sanctuary of the inn.

"A pretty wife, sir. A good wife ter carries a' the family name!" he cried after me.

Now that was an idea. Bringing home such a wench for a daughter-in-law would certainly set Mother on her ear, or even flying head-first over a cliff.

I smiled at that pleasing picture. Suitable reparation for all that I'd been put through.

My thoughts were as sour as the sea smell clinging to my clothes. Instead of the clear air washed by miles of ocean waves, they stank of filthy bodies, damp wood and, disgustingly, rat droppings. Such was what I'd discovered upon opening a trunk in search of new linen. I'd grimly shook out the cleanest-looking shirt and neckcloth and donned them. Bad as they were, the stuff was still better than what I'd been wearing. I was to meet my English cousin at this inn today and futilely hoped to give a good impression of myself.

"A pretty wife for yer!" said the pander to the next man off the coach, who cursed and shoved him out of the way much as one would an annoying dog.

The door of The Three Brewers beckoned. I ducked through, bumping into another man before me. The entrance hall was dark compared to the outside, and he'd paused to let his dazzled eyes adjust. We begged one another's pardon, and I pretended not to notice as he surreptitiously touched a pocket where he must have his own money secreted. Perhaps I was not as well dressed as I thought, that or pickpockets had so great an income in London that they could afford such clothes that would allow them to pass for gentlemen.

The porter intruded at this point, giving a cheerful welcome and ringing his bell for a waiter to come see to us. We were shown into the strangers' room with others from the coach and there made our needs known. I was famished and settled that part of my business promptly, even before taking a chair. Used to dealing with an endless number of similar starving guests, the man wasted no time in seeing to everyone's comfort. This inn had a favorable reputation, and I was thankful and pleased that it was living up to the praise.

A noisy family with an infant shrieking in its nurse's arms rolled in. They disdained the strangers' room and were shown to some more private place away from the other guests. Well and good, for my brain was feverish from the journey and lack of food, and I might have been tempted into slaughtering an innocent had they remained.

Only when a hot plate of fatty, boiled beef was placed before me along with a deep cup of wine did my disposition improve. I hurriedly handed over a shilling and fell upon my meal with ravenous abandon. When the plate was clean, I followed it up with pigeon pie and an excellent boiled pudding. Nearly replete, the dessert of apples and walnuts filled the last empty corners. It was the first fresh food I'd had since we'd run out of eggs on the ship. If I ever gnawed salt beef and weevil-infested bread again it would be too soon.

Well, perhaps not. Given the chance to turn 'round and sail straight back to Long Island today, I'd have taken it. I was dreadfully homesick and likely to remain so. Rapelji had said to regard this as an adventure.

If adventures meant bad food, coarse company, weeks of staring at miles of bottomless cold gray water, bumpy coach rides and encounters with a gin-soaked pander and his trollop, then he was welcome to mine. To be fair, London promised many interests and excitements, and the victuals of The Three Brewers were filling, but not as good as Mrs. Nooth's table at home.

I cracked two walnuts against each other and wished for a speedy return. Regardless of Mother's presence, it was at least familiar. I smashed the shells into smaller shards and picked out the meat.

Mother. Other men regarded the word with warmth and sentiment; all it inspired in me was anger and frustration.

Father's reasoning had not moved her to change her mind, neither had my tears—not that I wept in her sight. To do so would have only invited her contempt. Instead, I arranged for a private interview, hoping that a direct plea might work, but it was an absolute failure before I ever opened my mouth to speak. The naked disgust on her face as she looked upon me shriveled my liver down to nothing. I had no experience dealing with the mad, nor did I wish to acquire any. My only desire was to leave the room and never see her again. Since my effort at persuasion had died stillborn, I had to supply another reason to justify my visit. Red-faced and with the sweat tickling under my arms I blathered out a stuttering apology to her and concluded with a little speech of gratitude for her kindness toward me.

I did not state what I was apologizing for; I would not give a name to an evil that only existed in her sick mind. Thankfully, she did not refer to the events of the previous evening. Had she done so I'd have fled. I *did* feel like a complete fool, for this was uncomfortably like an admission of guilt.

If one wishes to count childish fibs, then it was not the first time I'd ever lied, but it was the first time I had ever lied at length and so convincingly. The further I went, the worse I felt. Even as the words bubbled up into elaborate constructions of remorse, I vowed to *never* place myself in such a position again. The experience left me feeling foully humiliated and in no doubt that if I hadn't utterly tarnished my honor this day, then I'd very definitely thrown a shadow upon it.

It was an impossible situation, as Elizabeth maintained, but what else could be done? The woman was mad, but she was our mother and until we came of age, we were unhappily subject to her whims. The other problem, as Father had pointed out, was the money. For a good education I needed the sum that she'd set aside for me—which would be denied if I insisted on Harvard. Very well, then I'd go to Cambridge. If groveling to this demented creature for a few minutes would curry her favor, then I would grovel, and did so. Thoroughly.

It worked. A creaking, rattling ghost of a smile drifted across her face, smacking of arrogant triumph. I'd been forgiven. My future was assured. It was time for her evening tea. I had permission to be excused.

After that bitter degradation, I was less ready to so harshly judge Beldon and Mrs. Hardinbrook for their toad-eating.

My shameful scene with Mother concluded, I went to see Father. It took me a while to work up the courage, but I finally introduced an idea that had been stirring uneasily in my brain: the possibility of having her declared incapable. I had feared he would be angry with me, but came to realize that he'd already thought it over for himself.

"How do we prove it, laddie?" he asked. When I faltered over my answer, he continued. "It would be different if she wandered about raving at the top of her voice all the time, but you've seen how she is. She's been in a temper over that incident, but you need more than that to take to court. In public her behavior has always been above reproach."

"But we've plenty of witnesses here to the contrary."

"To what would be dismissed as an unpleasant altercation within a family. No court would judge in our favor with—"

"But surely as her husband, you are able to do *something*." I could not quite keep a whine from invading my tone. Damnation. I was better than that, but desperate.

Father's face darkened, and with an effort, he swallowed back his annoyance. "Jonathan, there are some things that I will not do, even for your sake. One of those is compromising my honor. To go down the path you are suggesting would do just that."

My gaze dropped; my skin seemed aflame. For the second time I stammered an apology, only now I meant what was said.

He accepted it instantly. "I do understand exactly how you feel, I've been there many times. Life is not fair, but that doesn't mean we can't make the best of what fate—or your mother—drops on us."

Cold comfort, I thought.

The morning after those talks marked the official opening of Elizabeth's quiet campaign against Mother. We rose early and left early for the church. She'd managed to keep out of Mother's sight since the fight for fear that Mother might stop her from showing herself in public once she saw the extent of the damage done. Elizabeth's dress had been carefully chosen for its color, which brutally accented her fully developed bruises. She made no effort to hide them. Being a favorite among the women of our village, she was surrounded by a group of the concerned and the curious almost as soon as she stepped from the carriage. While I sent the driver back to the house for the rest of the family, Elizabeth made excellent use of her time.

I still disapproved, but since she was telling the plain truth, I had no difficulty supporting her. When the carriage rolled up again to discharge Mother, Mrs. Hardinbrook, Beldon, and Father, the atmosphere of avid curiosity mixed with revulsion was nearly as thick as a morning fog. Distracted by her guests, Mother did not notice it. A few late-comers who hadn't yet heard the tale came over to greet her and meet her friends, but as soon as they detached themselves, others took them aside for a confidential whisper. Mother had been oblivious to the subtle change in the people around her, Father was not. But what he guessed or knew, he kept to himself and stood next to his wife in our pew.

Somehow we got through the service and returned home, me to brood on my disappointment, Elizabeth to her first feeling of triumph. She was all but glowing with satisfaction when I found her in the library. This dampened somewhat when she looked up and successfully read my face. Not wishing to intrude upon her, I'd kept my news, or lack of it, to myself throughout the morning.

"She wouldn't listen, would she?" she asked, all sympathy.

I threw myself onto a chair. "I don't think she knows how. I talked with Father, but it's hopeless. He can't do anything."

"You're not angry with him?"

"No, of course not. If he could help, he would. I'm going to have to leave."

"I wish I could come with you, then."

"So do I, but you know what Mother would make of that."

"Something evil," she said. "What will you *do* at Cambridge?"

"Be miserable, I'm sure."

"It will be a long, long time. When you come back, you'll be all grown up. We won't know you."

"You think I'll change so much?"

"Perhaps not, little brother. I'm being selfish, though."

"Indeed?"

"Whatever shall I do with myself while you are gone?"

"You'll miss me?" I gently mocked.

"Certainly I'll miss you," she said.

"Nothing selfish about that."

"I'm selfish because all I can think of is my own troubles, of spending day after day facing that horrible woman and her toadies without you here to comfort me. I should really be worrying about you being off by yourself."

"Oh."

"Don't think badly of me, Jonathan."

"I don't. Believe me, I do not. I've just never thought of how things might be for you while I'm gone."

"Then thank you for thinking of it now. But it mightn't last forever, you know. You saw how it went at church today. She and that precious pair plan to go calling tomorrow, but I believe many of the people they'll visit to be unavailable. Oh, dear, what's wrong?" Her forehead wrinkled at my expression.

"I just don't feel this action is worthy of you."

She started to either object or defend, then caught herself. Her face grew hard. "Indeed, it is not, but she hurt me terribly and I want to hurt her back. It may not be very Christian, but it does make me feel better."

"I know, I just don't want you to become so accustomed to it that it consumes you. Otherwise when I return, I shall not recognize you, either."

The feeling behind the words got through to her. "You believe I might become like her?"

"Not at all, but I should not like to see you influenced by her into becoming someone you are not."

"God forbid," she murmured, staring at the floor. "Mirrors can be awful things, can't they? But they do give you the truth when you bother to look in them."

"I don't mean to hurt you …"

"No. I understand what you mean."

"What will you do?"

"Whether my actions demean me or not, I will see them through. If Mother leaves, well and good, if not, then perhaps I may adopt Father's example and leave the house myself. I have many friends I can visit, but give me some time, little brother, and trust in my own sense of honor."

There was a word to make me wince.

Hopes of a reprieve from Cambridge dashed, there was little else to do but follow Father's advice. I played the puppet in Mother's presence, and it paid handsomely. The allowance Father was able to arrange for me was more than generous. Perhaps she was trying to buy my affection. Perhaps she just didn't care. Only later did I realize that her purpose was for me to make an impressive show to others. She gave many tedious lectures instructing me on how to behave myself once I was in England. I'd had lessons a few years before, but for a while feared that she'd hire another dancing master to refresh my memory about correct posturing in polite company.

The next month saw me through a round of farewell parties with our friends, fittings for new clothes, and careful decisions over what to take along. As Elizabeth had predicted, Mother's reception into our circle had turned decidedly cool, but there were some occasions that required the presence of our whole family, so the woman got her share of social engagements. These were enough to satisfy her, but Elizabeth was sure that once I was off to England a dramatic drop in invitations would take place. She promised to write me in full detail. Perhaps her first letters would be in the very next ship to arrive in port after my own.

Something to look forward to, even if the news was over two months old.

As the hubbub of The Three Brewers played around me, I used my penknife to work out more pieces from another broken walnut. Across the room an argument was going on between two drunken workmen that looked to develop into a full-blown battle. Their accents were so thick I couldn't make sense of what they were shouting, though the swearing was clear enough. A group of ladies huddled together and stopped up their ears, except for one who fell to praying. She started with a little scream when one of her friends accidentally brushed her ear with an upraised elbow.

My teeth crunched against a bit of overlooked shell. I spat it out and continued munching more cautiously.

One of the men took a wide swing at the other and missed, generating a lot of amusement in the crowd. Bets were made, but called off when the landlord and a couple of younger men intervened and escorted the drunks outside. I had half a mind to follow, to see if the fight would continue, but was too full of food to be bothered.

I loutishly spat another shard of walnut, pleased with the knowledge that what went unnoticed here would have sorely offended Mother.

Across the room the ladies had unstopped their ears and put their heads together for a good talk. One of the younger ones smiled at me. Resuming my manners, I nodded back, lazily wondering who and what she was. By her dress, manner, and the company around her I decided that she was not a whore, or else I might have done more than nod. I hadn't forgotten the promise to myself about taking the earliest opportunity to lose my virginity.

The pander and his woman came to mind again, only to be dismissed with disgust. I wasn't that desperate or drunk.

The young lady turned her attention back to her friends. My face grew warm as I deduced by their manner that they were talking about me. From the smothered smiles and bright looks thrown my way I concluded that their opinions were highly favorable. I smiled back. Perhaps an opportunity was about to present itself.

Or perhaps not. The fight between the workmen had developed into what sounded like a proper war. Though I hadn't followed the two combatants outside, others had, and in a few scant moments sides were taken and blows were struck. Members of the inn's staff abruptly disappeared, though two of the maids clogged the room's one window trying to keep up with the course of the battle.

"Jem's got that 'un!"

"Arr, he's bitin' orf 'is ear! Get 'im, Jem!"

Then both girls squeaked and jumped back. A young tough with a bleeding ear sprawled half in and out of the opening. Before his admirers could rush to his aid, he raised up, threw us a foolish grin of pure glee, and bobbed from sight. The girls returned to the window to cheer him on.

The more refined ladies of the neighboring table had produced screams of alarm, and crowded toward the door for the purpose of escape. They were hampered by others in the hall without, who were apparently trying to get out for a better view of the fight. The smiling girl was among them.

So much for that opportunity, however slim it had been. I stood, brushed stray crumbs from my clothes, and made for the window. Offering my apologies to the maids, I pushed past them and stepped through it into the courtyard to see what all the commotion was about.

A wild-eyed man who had lost his shirt, but retained his neckcloth, rushed past me waving a bucket and howling. The man he seemed to be pursuing was making an equal amount of noise but in a slightly different key. A dozen other men were having a sort of wrestling match with one another in the middle of the yard. On the edge of their muddy sprawl of arms and legs, I spotted the porter swinging a cudgel and bellowing in triumph each time he connected successfully with someone's head. He'd worked out a simple routine of knocking a man senseless, then moving on so the waiters could pull the body from the fray. They had the start of a fine stack of them, though it wasn't much of a discouragement to newcomers eager to join the riot.

"What's it all about?" I asked a young gentleman next to me, who was content to be a witness rather than a participant. He wore dusty riding clothes and an eager expression on his long face.

"God knows, but isn't it grand? Five shillings that that big fellow with the scar will be the last to drop."

"Done," I said, and we shook on it. I kept my eye on the porter and was not disappointed. Before long, he worked his way 'round to the fellow in question and gave him a solid thump behind the ear. The result fell short of my expectations, for he only went down on one knee, shook his head, and was up and swinging as though nothing had happened. The waiters wisely passed him by.

"Bad for you," said the gentleman.

"There's time yet."

My faith in the porter's arm was given a second test. As he made another circle of the gradually diminishing fighters, he was able to use his cudgel on the man again. This time more force was applied and the fellow was knocked to both knees. He got up more slowly, but he did get up.

"What's his skull made of?" I asked. "Stone?"

"Cracked him a good one, though. He's drawn blood, see?"

That was a good sign. Stones don't bleed. I called encouragement to the porter for another try, but he was distracted when the man with the bucket blundered into him. Both fell over into the general melee and were momentarily lost. The porter emerged first, roaring with outrage. When he swung his cudgel back to deal with the newcomer, it caught the scarred man in the belly by mistake and he suddenly dropped from sight.

"Third time's the charm," I said. We waited, anxious for different reasons, but the man remained down. The waiters darted forward and dragged him out. Three more men waded in to help the porter and amid groans, curses, and with the breaking of a few more skulls, order was gradually restored to the courtyard.

The gentleman shook his head and paid up. "What a show. Pity it was so short." He was about my age, with a high forehead, cleft chin, and a broad, childish mouth, the corners of which were turned down as he settled his debt. His was not the frown of an unhappy loser, merely concentration for the count. He had very wide-awake blue eyes that added to the somewhat foolish but generally good-natured cast of his overall expression.

"Pity indeed," I agreed. "Since there's second no chance for you to win this back may I buy you something to ease the sting of your loss?"

He cheered up instantly. "That's very generous of you, my friend. Yes, you may. It's too damned hot out here, don't you think?"

We retired to the common room, but found it quite clear of waiters, maids, and guests.

"Probably still cleaning up the mess," he said, then bellowed for assistance. A pot-boy cautiously appeared, and I promptly sent him off to fetch us beer.

"Unless you'd prefer something else?" I asked.

He threw himself into a chair, putting his feet on the table. "No, no. Beer's what's wanted on a day like this. I've been on the road all morning and have a great thirst."

"Traveling much farther?"

"Only to this roach trap. I'm supposed to meet some damned cousin of mine and take him home."

"Really?"

"Damned nuisance it is, but—" A new thought visibly invaded his brain. "Oh, dear, suppose he's out there among the wounded?" He launched from the chair toward the window and leaned out, shouting questions to the men in the yard. I sat back to watch the show. He excused himself to me and went over the sill to investigate something, but returned just as the beer arrived.

"Did you find your cousin?" I asked.

"Thought I had, but the man was too old."

"What does he look like?"

"Oh, about this tall, forty if he was a day, and bald as—"

"I mean, what does your *cousin* look like?"

"Oh … him. Damned if I know. He's fresh off the boat from one of the colonies, so I should spot him quick enough. Probably gets himself up with feathers and paint like a red Indian. I saw an engraving once of a frontiersman, dreadful taste. He was in a canvas suit covered head-to-toe with white fringe, trousers going all the way to his ankles, bare feet, and topped it all with a beard like a prophet. Can you imagine?"

"Sounds dreadful. What's he over here for? New clothes?"

"Come to get an education. We're going to be at Cambridge together, but since he's supposed to be reading law and I'm doing medicine, we'll likely be spared one another's company for the most part."

"What? You've never met the chap and you don't like him?"

"I daresay I won't if he has Fonteyn blood in him. Not that I'm too very much against my own family, but some of the folk out of Grandfather Fonteyn's side of things would be better off in Bedlam, if you know what I mean."

"Bedlam?"

"That great asylum where they put the mad people. Damn, but that was good beer. Here, boy! Bring us another! That is, if you care to have another one, sir."

"Yes, certainly. You intrigue me, sir. About this cousin of yours... would he be about my age, do you think?"

He squinted at me carefully. "I'd say so." His mobile face suddenly went slack, then his eyes sharpened with alarm. "Oh, good *God*." He nearly fell from his chair getting his feet down from the table.

"I'm not that awful, am I?" I asked, after he'd sorted himself.

His jaw flapped as he tried to put words to a situation that required none. As he floundered, the beer was set before us.

"Would you care for anything to eat, Cousin?"

"A pox on you, sir, for misleading me," he finally cried.

"And my apologies, sir, for being unable to resist the temptation to do so."

"Well-a-day, I've never heard of such a thing!"

"Perhaps it is my Fonteyn blood showing through. Jonathan Barrett, at your service, good cousin." I stood and bowed to him.

"A *fine* introduction this is, to be sure." He stood and gave a hasty bow in turn. Then we bestowed upon each other a second appraisal.

"Well?" I said.

"Well, what?"

"Do we become friends or act like our less genial relations?"

He blinked.

I grinned.

"Oh, pox on it!" He extended his hand and smiled broadly. "Oliver Marling, at your service."

"Oliver 'Fonteyn' Marling?" We shared the same middle name, I knew.

He made a face. "For God's sake, call me Oliver. I absolutely *detest* my middle name!"

Not that I'd had any misgivings about the man after the first few moments of speaking with him, but now I hailed him as a true kinsman in heart as well as by blood. We enjoyed more than a few beers that afternoon, ate like starving pigs that evening, drank an amazing amount of spirits, and talked and talked and *talked*. By the time we'd passed out and had been lugged upstairs to our room by the staff, we were the best of friends.

THE MORNING SUNLIGHT was mercifully subdued through the tiny window, but its brightness was still enough to dangerously heat my brain to the bursting point. My eyes felt as though someone had poured gravel into each socket. I groaned, but refrained from touching my head for fear that it might pop from my neck and go rolling around the floor. The noise alone would have killed me.

All I could see of Cousin Oliver were his riding boots, which were on the pillow next to mine. For all the movement on that side of the bed he might have been a corpse. A blessing for him if he were dead, for then he'd be spared the abominable pain of recovery. Our drinking bout was such as would have left Dionysus himself flat on his face for a week.

Around and below us came the sounds of the inn, which had apparently awakened some time ago. With no consideration whatsoever for our possibly mortal condition, business was proceeding as usual.

When I'd reached the point where walking around in agony would be no different from lying around in agony, I made an attempt to get out of bed. The thing was rather high, so the drop was an awful shock. The thud I made upon landing must have been heard throughout the rest of the house. It certainly echoed through my fragile head with alarming consequences. How fortunate for me that I was now within grasping distance of the chamber pot. I seized and dragged it toward me just in time.

The next few minutes were really horrible, but when the last coughing convulsion played itself out, I felt slightly improved. I wanted to crawl back to bed again, but hadn't the strength for it. Shoving the pot away, I flopped on my back on the bare floor and prayed for God to have mercy on one of his more foolish sheep.

Some idiot pounded on our door as though to break it down. Without pausing for an invitation, one of the waiters entered and looked things over.

"Thought I'd 'eard you stirrin', sir. Would yer be wantin' ter breaks yer fast now?"

I was wanting to break his neck for shouting so loudly, but couldn't move. All I could do was give him a glassy stare from where I lay at his feet and think ill thoughts.

"Well, p'haps not. Tell yer what, I'll 'ave some tea 'n' a bit of bread sent up. Twill do 'til you find yer legs, haw-haw." Booming with his own cleverness, he left, slamming the door so hard I thought the bones in my skull would split open from the sound.

There was a bowl and a pitcher on a table across the room. The idea occurred to me that splashing water on the back of my neck might be of restorative value. I managed to get to my knees and crawled over. The pitcher was empty. It seemed pointless to exert effort to return to bed, so I gave up and sat with my back to the wall, waiting for the man to reappear with the promised tea.

He must have been distracted by other duties. The whole long dizzy morning seemed to pass before he pounded on the door again and came in with his tray.

"Yer lucky, sir. Cook just had some fresh made, 'ot 'n' strong." He put the tray on another table, poured out a cup, and brought it over. I held it tenderly with trembling fingers and sipped. "That'll set yer right as rain. Now what 'bout this 'un?" He indicated Oliver, who had not yet moved.

"Leave him," I whispered.

"Shouldn't leave 'is arm draggin' on the floor like that. 'E'll lose all feelin' in it." He helpfully pulled Oliver's arm up, but it only dropped down again. A second attempt got the same results, so he lightly flipped Oliver over on his back. Bidding us both a good morning, he left, thundering down the hall and stairs like a plow horse with eight legs.

I drained the cup, waited a few minutes, and decided the stuff would stay down after all. Pushing against the wall, I stood, staggered to the table, and poured another, but drank it more slowly. Bit by bit, my brain began to cool and a few of the more alarming symptoms subsided. The chance that I would ultimately recover seemed more likely now.

On his back, with his mouth sagging wide, Oliver began to snore. There was an almost soothing note to it, though it gradually increased in loudness. To take my mind from my own miseries, I waited, interested to learn just how loud he could get. When one is in the throes of a terrible recuperation, the oddest details are welcome distractions from the pain.

My interest soon waned as the very blood under my hair began to throb in time to his rumblings. It was a wonder he did not wake himself from the noise. He snorted and snarled, gave out a gasp as though he'd inhaled an insect, and suddenly a prodigious sneeze exploded from his slack lips. It was enough to stir the cobwebs in the far corners. This did succeed in waking him, poor man. He stared at the ceiling with the same kind of glazed stupefaction as I had earlier.

Still whispering, out of respect to his heightened senses, I said, "It's just under the bed on this side."

He didn't take my meaning at first, but gradually his face turned a predictable green, and with the color came comprehension. He floundered onto his stomach, clawed for the chamber pot, and made his own contribution to it.

"Oh, God," he moaned pitifully afterward, quite unable to move. With a cautious toe, I shoved the pot and its offensive contents back under the bed. Oliver put his hands over his ears and moaned again as it scraped over the bare wood of the floor.

I was merciful and said nothing, and poured him half a cup of tea. His hands were unsteady. Still lying on his stomach, partly off the bed, he drank it, and I caught the cup before he could drop it.

"Well-a-day," he murmured, his head hanging down and his mouth muffled by the bedding. "We must have had a magnificent time last night."

"Indeed we did. We may never survive another. Was it you or that other chap who poured wine on the fiddler?"

"What other chap?"

"The little round fellow who lost his wig in the fire."

"He didn't lose it, you threw it there."

I took a moment to recollect the incident. "Oh, yes. The fool was bothering the serving maid and I thought he needed a lesson."

"Good thing for you he wasn't the sort to demand satisfaction or you'd have had to be up at dawn."

So terrible was the idea of getting up that early with such a pain in my head that it hardly bore thinking about. "Was it you or him?"

"What?"

"That poured the wine on the—"

"Oh. Him. Definitely him. Fellow had too much to drink, y'know. Disgraceful. What did you think you were doing defending that wench's honor, anyway?"

"I just can't abide a man forcing his attentions on a woman."

"Didn't know they raised knight-errants in the colonies. Have to be cafrill ... I mean, careful. The next man might force the issue, then you'd have to kill him and marry the girl."

"Why should I have to marry the girl?"

He paused in thought. "Damned if I know. What time is it? What *day* is it? Is there any more tea?"

There was and I gave it to him. Neither of us were ready for even the simplest of food, so we left the bread alone. When we each became more certain of our slow improvement, I slowly opened the shutters to bring in some fresher air. The chamber pot was rapidly becoming a nuisance.

Oliver managed to leave the bed and join me at the table. He surveyed himself, peered closely at my face, and shook his head.

"This won't do. Can't go home looking like this. Mother would burst a blood vessel if she knew about this drunken debauch and we'd never hear the end of it."

In our rambling talk last night, he'd made frequent mention of his mother. His descriptions bore a remarkable similarity to my own parent. "Won't she be just as angry if we're late?"

"Oh, I can say your ship was held up or something. We needn't worry about that. A day's rest will do us a world of good, but I don't fancy spending it cooped up here. What we want is a bit of activity to sweat the wine out of us."

He lapsed into a silence so lengthy that I wondered if he wanted me to take on the responsibility of finding a solution. Being an utter stranger to London, not to mention the rest of the country, the odds against my being of any help in the matter seemed very high.

"Got it!" he said, animation returning to his vacuous face. "We'll go over to Tony Warburton's. You'll want to meet him, so it may as well be now."

"Won't we be an intrusion?"

"Hardly. Tony's used to my turning up at odd times. He's part of our circle, you know, and since you're with me, that means you're in, too. He's studying medicine as well, but I'll see to it that he doesn't bore you with it."

Oliver assured me his friend would not only welcome our visit, but insist that we stay the night. With this in mind I gladly settled things with the landlord and saw to it my baggage was brought down. It took a surprising number of servants for this task, and several more turned up to receive their vails for services rendered during my overnight stay, including many that I'd never seen before. Perhaps they'd been on duty when I had not been in a condition to remember them later. It sufficed that some of the shillings I'd won from Oliver magically vanished in much less time than it had taken to win them.

In the courtyard, Oliver stood ready by his horse, a big bay mare with long, solid legs and clear, bright eyes. I couldn't help but express my admiration for the animal and in turn received a list of famous names in her pedigree. None of them meant anything to me, but they sounded impressive, nonetheless.

He had hired an open pony cart for our conveyance, meaning to lead the mare rather than ride her. The cart's inward-facing benches would allow us to enjoy conversation, yet there was enough space to stow my luggage. Another advantage was that the cart was narrow enough to navigate London's crowded streets with reasonable efficiency.

I say reasonable, because once we left the inn and were well on our way, the noise and crowds of the city were nearly overwhelming to my country-bred senses. Everywhere I looked were people of all shapes, classes and colors, each of them busy as ants with as many occupations as could ever be imagined, plus a few beyond imagining. My long-ago visit to Philadelphia had not prepared me for such numbers or variety. Even the busy colonial city of New York, which I had glimpsed on my way to the ship that carried me here, was a bumpkin's muddy backwater village compared to this.

The air hummed with a thousand different voices, each calling their wares or services, begging or just shouting for no other purpose than to make noise. Soldiers and sailors, chimney sweeps and their boys, panders and prostitutes, well-dressed ladies and their maids, men of fashion and threadbare clerics all jostled, laughed, argued, screeched, or sang with no regard for anyone but themselves and their business. I forgot my aching head and fairly gaped at the show.

"Is it always like this?" I asked Oliver, raising my voice as well so he could hear me, though he was hardly an arm's length away.

"Oh, no," he bellowed back. "Sometimes it's *much* worse!"

I thought he was having a joke on me, but he'd taken the question quite seriously and expanded on his answer. "This is a normal working day in the city, y'know. You should be here on a holiday or when there's a hanging or two at Tyburn, then things really liven up!"

Oliver drew my attention to various places of interest whenever possible. The buildings loomed so high in spots that it was apparent that the sun even at its summer zenith was an infrequent visitor to the streets between. In one patch of open area, though, he was able to point out the masts of a ship standing improbably among the buildings and trees.

"That's Tower Hill, of course, and the ship itself is on perfectly dry land."

"What good is that, then?"

"Oh, it's done no end of good for the navy. If some unwary soul has the bad luck to stop for a look at it he has to pay dearly for his curiosity."

"What? You mean they offer a tour of the place?"

"For a very costly price."

"Is the fee so great?"

"Great enough for most. The fellow offering to show them around is part of a press gang. More than one hapless lad fresh in from the country has been trapped that way and may never set foot on land again. Foreigners are fairly safe, and so are gentlemen, and since you're both in one, you've nothing to fear from them. Still, I can't help but pity the poor men who wander into that pretty snare." He gave a sincere shudder and by some leap of thought I got the idea that he may have had some personal experience in the matter.

We jolted and wove our way through the many streets for over an hour, though the distance we traveled could not have been more than a couple of miles. The views and distractions were many, and Oliver was pleased with my reactions to them, enjoying his role of playing the guide as much as I was playing the sightseer.

Presently, Oliver gave the cart man more specific directions and we stopped before a tall and broad house of fine white stone with black paint trimming the proportionately broad windows. Because Oliver had mentioned the tax upon windows, I could see that the owner of this place was in such a financial position as to be untroubled by the added expense. This looked to be a highly favorable exchange for the mean little room I'd had at the inn.

We left the cart, mounted the front steps, and Oliver gave the bell a vigorous pull. A servant soon opened the door and welcomed us inside. He was well acquainted with Oliver and, after sending a footman off to inform the master of the house about his guests, showed us to a parlor and inquired how best to provide for our immediate comfort.

"Barley water, if you please," said Oliver, after a brief consultation with me. "And some biscuits if you have 'em and some ass's milk if it's fresh."

The butler appeared to be somewhat puzzled. "Nothing else, sir?"

"Crispin, if you'd drunk all that we had last night and woke up with all the agonies of perdition we had this morning..."

Abrupt understanding dawned upon Crispin's face, and he vanished to see to things, including the cart waiting outside. He soon returned with another fellow carrying a large tray and made us feel at home, explaining that his master would be delayed from joining us immediately. Apparently we've arrived a bit earlier than Mr. Tony Warburton was accustomed to rising, so he had to dress. In the meantime, the barley water, though not as good as beer, quenched our thirst, and the biscuits settled the rumblings in our stomachs.

"I took the liberty," said Crispin as he poured the milk from a silver pitcher, "of adding eggs and honey to this. Mr. Warburton swears by its restorative powers."

"Lord, is he studying to be a physician or an apothecary? Never mind answering that. If old Tony has frequent occasion to turn to this for relief, then he's going to be a drunkard. Oh, it's all right, Jonathan, no need to look shocked. Tony knows it's all in jest. He's really a frightfully keen student, but like the rest of us, enjoys having a good time when he can."

The mixture in the ass's milk was more than palatable and after seeing to Crispin's vail and to the footmen for fetching my luggage in we were left on our own.

Our room was decorated well and in good taste, though a bit stuffy. I suggested opening a window, but Oliver pointed out that the close air within was preferable to the noisome odors without. Sensing my restlessness, he tossed me a copy of the *Gentleman's Magazine*. Father subscribed to it himself, but the issues we received were necessarily out of date by at least two months owing to the long ocean crossing. This one was only a month old and I welcomed the somewhat fresher news.

I flipped idly through the pages, taking note of an article about a comet that on my voyage had caused much excitement and interest back in the middle of June. It was fascinating to me that the same object I'd seen on the other side of the ocean, was—that same night—also seen in England. How high had it been? How fast had it been going to have hurled itself over such a vast distance?

Owing to clouds, the writer was unable to add to what I had been able to see trailing across the southern sky from shipboard. My chief memory was not so much of the comet, but the superstitious reaction the sailors had had to it. During the time that it was visible, there had been much muttering, praying, and wearing of charms against any evil it might bring. Though our captain was a man of very solid sense, he let them have their way in this, but saw to it that they were kept busy lest they brood upon their fears and get up to mischief.

I moved on to another article describing the bloody war raging between the Turks and Russians. There was an annex page that folded out into a very excellent map of Greece, and from it I was able to pick out some of the famous cities that had been mentioned in my study of the language with Rapelji. The many details delighted me, and I hoped that my father would share it with him when his issue arrived. I was about to comment to Oliver about it when the young master of the house chose that moment to make his entrance.

He was a bit haggard in his appearance, a match to our own, no doubt, and despite the amount of time he'd had to ready himself, he was clad informally in a sweeping mustard-colored dressing gown, plain cotton stockings and bright red slippers. An elaborate turban covered much of his head, though it was very askew, showing the light, shaven scalp beneath. His eyes were a bit sunken and his flesh pale, but his manner was hearty as he came forward to greet us. Oliver introduced us and we made our bows to one another. Tony Warburton just managed to catch the turban in time to prevent it from dropping off at our feet.

"I hope this is no imposition," said Oliver. "That is, us turning up on the doorstep like peddlers?"

"My dear fellow, I am delighted you've come," Warburton said, righting the turban and himself. He fell wearily into a chair. "The truth is something's happened and if I don't tell someone, I'm certain to burst."

Oliver threw me an amused glance to assure me his friend's somewhat theatrical attitude was normal. "What has happened? You're looking a bit done in."

"Really? I feel wonderful."

"Not some calamity, I hope?"

"Hardly that. It's truly the best thing that's ever happened to me in my entire life."

My cousin now gave me a quick wink, which Tony missed, for he was staring wistfully at the ceiling. "If it is good news, then by all means, please share it."

"The greatest news possible for any man." He tugged absently at his indifferently knotted neckcloth. "Oliver, my best friend, the best of all my friends, I'm in love!"

Oliver clasped his hands around one knee, pursed his lips, and leaned forward with polite interest. "What? Again?"

CHAPTER
FIVE

TONY WAS QUITE OBLIVIOUS to his friend's skepticism.

"This is well and truly real love," he continued. "This is what I've awaited my whole life. Until last night all my existence has been a wasteland, a wilderness of nothing, a desert...."

He went on like that for quite some time until Oliver managed to get in another question.

"Who is this girl?"

"She's not a girl; she's a fairy princess come from *A Midsummer Night's* what-you-call-it. No, she's more than that; she is a goddess. She makes all other women look like ... like ..."

"Mortals, I suppose. What's her name, Tony?"

"Nora. Isn't it beautiful? It's like some rare flower on a moonlit hillside. Oh, wait 'til you meet her and you'll see what I mean. My words fall utterly short of the reality."

Oliver doggedly went on. "Nora who?"

"Jones. Miss Nora Jones."

The name was still unfamiliar to Oliver. "She sounds wonderful. Where does she trade?"

Tony snapped his head 'round, full of outrage. "Good God, man! She's a respectable *lady*. How dare you?"

Oliver made an about-face of his own toward true contrition. "I do beg your pardon, I'm sure. I had no idea. My most humble apologies, to you, to her and to her family. Who are they, anyway?"

Tony settled back and after a moment's consideration, accepted the apology. "The Jones family, I suppose."

"From Wales, are they?"

"France, actually."

"France? How can someone named Jones be from France?"

"Obviously they're not, you great fool—she's just *come* from France! Been living abroad for her health and only recently returned to London."

"How did you meet her?"

"Robert—that's Robert Smollett"— he said as an aside to me— "had a musical evening on last night and she was one of the guests. She was there with his sister and Miss Glad and Miss Bolyn and all that crowd. She stood out like a rose in a field of weeds. She's the most beautiful, the brightest, the most graceful creature I ever had the fortune to clap eyes upon."

"She must be something if she can eclipse Charlotte Bolyn," said Oliver. "But we shall have to see her for ourselves to make sure your praises haven't been overly influenced by the strength of your feelings."

Tony smiled with patronizing confidence. "Of course, of course. Seeing is believing with you. But I can promise that you will not be disappointed. The Bolyns are giving a party of their own tonight and I've been invited, which means you can both come with me. It's in honor of some foreign composer who's gotten to be favorite in the more fashionable circles, but if we're lucky, we won't have to waste any time on him. Think you can come?"

"Given the chance to prepare. My cousin may need a bit of help. His clothes have been crammed into a sea chest for the last couple of months and—"

"Oh, that's nothing. I'll have Crispin look over the lot and dust everything off for you."

"Dust was hardly my concern, Mr. Warburton, considering that I was on board a ship the whole time," I put in.

Tony waved away my reservations. "Just leave it all to Crispin. You're in the hands of an expert. He never lets me out the door unless I look respectable. I only got away with this costume because he was busy with you two. You must both forgive me, I was up very late last night."

We protested that we were not in the least offended, then he lapsed into more praise about Nora Jones.

"I'm going to marry her, Oliver. I mean it. I'm quite serious this time, so stop laughing. Those other girls were a fool's whim, a passing fancy. This is the real and true thing. I know. I even dreamed about her last night. Thought she was right there in my room, so I shall have to marry her to save her reputation. For God's sake, don't you dare repeat that to anyone. The gossips in this town would turn a beautiful dream into a ditch of night soil given half a chance."

"And just how beautiful was this dream?" asked Oliver, unable to suppress a grin.

Tony's pale skin reddened. "None of your damned business, sir! I wish I'd never mentioned it. What are you here for, anyway, besides to distract me from joyful thoughts of my one true love?"

Oliver told him about our own party last night and the need to recover away from his mother's sharp and disapproving eye.

"Can't blame you for that," said Tony. "It's just as well my parents and the rest of the family are away at Bath taking the waters. Lord have mercy, I can hardly wait to take my examines this year. As soon as I set up a practice, I'm getting my own place. I might even be able to take Crispin along, if I can persuade him. He's a terribly superior sort, y'know. Might think it beneath himself to leave this household for another, even if it is mine. Servants!" he concluded with a shake of his head.

Oliver commiserated; I said nothing. Jericho could easily have come with me, but was convinced that if he left, his place in the house might be filled by another servant more suitable to my mother than myself, despite Father's promise to the contrary.

Jericho and I had discussed the subject seriously and thoroughly and had concluded that he would be happier left at home. Though I respected his wishes, I could not be accused of being content myself with the outcome. Now that I was off the ship and in surroundings similar in many ways to that home, I missed his company.

It was for the best, though, for I realized he would look after Elizabeth in my absence and had left him a sufficient amount of money to post letters to me at regular intervals. I had charged him to send reports of all the other news that my sister might be unaware of or ignore from lack of interest. He knew how to read and write for I had taught him, having followed Rapelji's example that a lesson is more thoroughly learned when one must teach it to another. However, Jericho and I had long ago decided never to speak of it, for many people thought it dangerous to own educated slaves, and his busy life might be unpleasantly complicated by their disapproval. Father was in on the secret, though, and, of course, Elizabeth.

I wondered and hoped that they were all right and enjoying good health. That one hope and many, many nebulous worries about them returned sharply to mind, along with a familiar ache to my heart. "Why such a long face, cousin?" Oliver asked.

"I feel like 'a stranger in a strange land,'" I replied mournfully.

"Eh?"

"He means he's a long way from home," explained Tony. "What we need is something to occupy the time until this evening. I was going to go someplace today, but I'm damned if I can remember where. Crispin!"

His shout brought the butler and a quick question got a quick response.

"You are to visit Bedlam today, sir," he said.

"Bedlam? Are you sure?"

"Your ticket for entry is on the hall table, sir."

Oliver was all interest. "Really? That would be a treat."

Tony was dubious. "You think so?"

"Oh, yes. You know how fascinated I am in such things." He turned to me. "You used to be able to get in whenever you pleased, but the governors of the hospital shut that down. It's a shame too, because they were bringing in a good six hundred a year from the admissions. Now one has to have special permission and a signed pass. Not everyone can get it, you know. This is a wonderful bit of luck."

"For you, perhaps," said Tony. "I don't feel I'm up to it, even if it is for the furtherance of my education. Why don't you go in my place, then tell me all about it later? I don't share your passion for studying lunatics."

"Surely you won't want to miss this opportunity?"

"Surely I do. I have other ways to entertain myself; I'm sure of it."

"This is hardly for base entertainment, Tony. I'll be going there to learn something."

His friend burst into laughter. "Oh, the things I could say to that."

Oliver scowled. "What things? What?"

"Nothing and everything. You're better than a thousand tonics, my dear fellow. You two go on to Bedlam and get all the education you want, but please, leave me to rest up here. After the excitement of meeting sweet, lovely Nora, I still feel quite drained and need to recover. I want to be at my best tonight."

Oliver's scowl instantly vanished and he gave up trying to fathom the cause of his friend's amusement. "If you're certain."

"Yes. I shall do nothing more strenuous today than compose some sonnet, an inadequate tribute to her beauty."

That ultimately decided things for Oliver. He pulled out a great gold watch. "Very well. We've plenty of time, perhaps we can even take in Vauxhall, too."

Tony held up a cautioning finger. "But I thought you wanted to remain sober?"

"Damn. Yes, you're right. We'd better stay away from there 'til later."

"Come back at six and I'll have my barber scrape your chins off."

We took our leave of Tony Warburton, redeemed our hats and walking sticks from a footman, then sent him off to secure a couple of sedan chairs for us.

"I think it's worked out for the best for him not to come," Oliver remarked as we waited outside. "When he's in this kind of a humor, he's likely to try out lines of his poem on us."

"He's such a bad poet?"

"Don't ask me to judge that. One and all, my friends assure me that I can't tell the difference between Shakespeare and popular doggerel."

"Then what's the problem?"

"It just occurred to me what bad idea it is to enter Bedlam with a lovesick fool who's sure to disrupt things by lapsing into verses about his wife-to-be whenever the fancy takes him. We might never get him out again."

The chairs arrived, and I listened closely while Oliver haggled over the price with the men. The only way to cease being a stranger in this land was to learn how things were run and the minutiae of local customs. Since I would be living here for at least four years, it was to my best advantage to keep my eyes and ears open at all times.

This resolve, I was to find out, was somewhat restricted once I got into my sedan chair. Though it had two large windows on either side, the view was much more limited than the one I'd enjoyed on the pony cart. Owing to my natural height, my head nearly brushed the roof and frequently did so as the bearers bounced along their way. We passed by other chairs with more top room, something necessary to the ladies within who wished to preserve the state of their hair. I noticed that the leather ceiling of my own bore oily evidence that more than one woman had been here before, leaving behind a dark stain mingled with white flecks where the lard and rice flour had rubbed off.

"Have a care, sir!" one of the bearers warned when I leaned too far out a window to catch a glimpse of the myriad sights we passed. My enthusiasm was an endangerment to their balance. Having no wish to crash face first into the filthy cobbles, I forced myself to keep still and resolved to engage some other means of travel for the return trip. Anything, up to and including being pushed along in a barrow, would be considered. Confined like this and cut off from conversation with Oliver, the hundreds of questions popping into my head with each new sight had to go unanswered. There being so many, I regretfully knew I'd never remember them all later, for surely they would be replaced by others.

At least I was spared the grime of the streets and shaded from the sun, but despite these advantages, the ride was long and wearisome. If not for the guiding presence of my cousin I should also have been quite lost, for I had no idea where we were or where we had come from. Though the bearers might have little trouble navigating to and fro through the crowds boiling around us, I would not have been able to find my way back to Warburton's unaided.

Though our destination was a hospital for lunatics, it turned out to be a pleasant and restful sight; I'd expected something much smaller and uglier than the building before us. Vast and long, three stories high, with tall towers marking the corner turning of each wing and the tallest of all in the center, Bedlam, once known as the hospital of Bethlehem, looked as fair as any edifice I had so far seen in this great city. We stood at the beginning of a wide lane leading directly to the central entrance from the street. On either side, a simple white fence enclosed sections of the front grounds, protecting the perfectly spaced trees within. If one grew tired of observing the inmates, this wholesome patch of greenery would serve to soothe the eye.

There were few people about, though the quiet air carried an odd note to it that I did not immediately identify. As we drew closer to the entry, it increased and became more varied until I finally identified it as the drone of human voices. Drone would serve for want of a better word, for it frequently broke off into high laughter or outright screaming. The hair on my head began to rise and for the first time I questioned my cousin's wisdom in bringing me with him.

Unaware of my misgivings, he presented his ticket to the proper authority and after a delay that only increased my unease, we were assigned a guide to take us around. Though Oliver was a medical student, I was not, but no question against my being here was ever raised. Oliver said the right things and asked intelligent questions, while I nodded and imitated his manner so as to not arouse suspicion. In truth, I need not have gone to such trouble. On the one hand, no one was too curious about us, on the other, after five minutes, I would not at all have minded being expelled.

Our guide led us into the men's wing only, the women's side being barred to us. Some of the more lucid inmates were allowed to take their exercise in the halls, all of them closely watched by their keepers. Only because they were somewhat better dressed than their charges, and armed with clubs and keys, was I able to tell them one from another.

Though assured by our guide that the straw in the cells was frequently changed, the stench of filthy bodies, night soil, and rotten food pervaded every breath in the place. My cousin and I found some relief by holding handkerchiefs to our noses, which amused the guide and the other keepers. They maintained that they were quite used to it, and we should soon be, too. I prayed that we should not stay so long as to verify the truth of their statement.

Some of the more interesting cases were pointed out to us, and Oliver took time to study each with an absorption that surprised me. Flighty as he seemed most of the time, here he was a genuine student, apparently serious in his pursuit of knowledge when the fit was upon him. It was contagious, for his comments to me quickened my own curiosity and sparked a lengthy conversation on the causes of madness.

"You and I both know that it can be passed along in the blood," he said. "There are whole families running loose that should be chained up in the basement. But some of these cases just seem to come out of nowhere as if the wretch had been struck by lightning. That fellow back there in the straw cap preaching so fervently to the wall is an excellent example. You missed hearing about him, but his keeper said that his was such an occurrence. He was once a curate and while doing his rounds one day, he just fell right over. They thought it was apoplexy or too much sun or the flying gout, but he fully recovered the next day, except for his wits, which were all gone. Now he thinks he's a bishop and spends all his time in theological argument with invisible colleagues. To add to the singularity of his circumstances, his arguments are quite sane and sound. I listened to him and he makes more sense than others I've heard of a Sunday."

The poor man was certainly in a minority, for all those around him either stared at nothing with frightened or blank faces or raved in their cells, rattling their chains and howling in a most pitiful way. If any one became violent, others might follow, so the keepers had to watch them constantly. I'm sorry to say that when drawn to one of the barred windows set in the stout door of a cell, the creature within began screeching in a most alarming way at the sight of me. I fell back at once, but that alone did not calm him and he continued until a keeper opened the door and threw a bucket of water on him. This inspired much merriment in those others who were able to appreciate it. The screams turned to sputtering, died away, and his door was again locked.

"That's the only bath 'e's like to get in a twelvemonth," the grinning keeper confided to me. "Lord knows 'e needs it." Considering his own utter lack of cleanliness, I thought he had no reason to judge another, especially one unable to care for himself. With my handkerchief firmly in place I caught up with Oliver, who was talking to a lad whose sullen expression reminded me of young Nathan Finch back home.

"I don't belong 'ere," he insisted. " 'm not like them others. I never 'urt no one nor meself, so they got no call to put me 'ere."

"Is this true?" Oliver asked our guide.

"'Tis true enough the way 'e tells it. He never 'armed 'imself or others, but they put 'im 'ere anyways."

"Why? If he's not mad—"

"Oh, 'e's mad enough, sir, for they found 'im 'sponsible for slittin' open the bellies of a dozen cattle. Said 'e could 'ear the calves 'nside callin' ter get out 'n' 'e were just 'elpin' 'em along lest they smother. They'd a lynched 'im at Tyburn for 'is mischief, but 'e were judged to be too lunatical for it to do 'im any good, so he were brung 'ere. Leastwise 'e won't get no more chance to cut up no more cattle." Laughing heartily at this observation, the guide patted the lad on the head, and moved on. Looking back, I saw the boy make a murderous face at us, followed by an obscene gesture. Harmless or not, I was glad to see that he was solidly chained to a thick staple set in the floor.

The hideous stenches, the noise, the pervading sadness, anguish and rage assaulting us from every direction were exhausting. After two hours, even Oliver's earnest quest for knowledge began to flag and he inquired if I was prepared to leave. Out of consideration for his feelings, I tried not to appear too eager, but indicated that a change of scene would not be unwelcome.

He consulted with the guide, who quickly led us to the entrance where we settled with him and were invited to return at our earliest convenience. Again, he laughed at this, giving the impression that he was not expressing hospitality, but something more sinister. We were well down the lane before finally slowing to a more dignified pace.

"What did you think of it?" asked Oliver.

"While I can appreciate that seeing the sights within was a rare opportunity, I can't honestly say that they were entirely enjoyable."

"I'll be the first to agree with you on that point, but it was certainly of excellent value to a student of the medical arts. I hope I can remember everything for Tony later."

"If not, then please consult me. I'm sure I shan't forget a single detail for the rest of my life. I hope that man of his does as promised with my clothes, the stink of the place clings to me still. I shall want to change them, but what I'd most like is a decent bath."

"Well, if you think you need one," he said, but with some doubt in his tone. "I'm sure something can be arranged before the party tonight. There's the Turkish baths at Covent Garden, but we haven't the time or deep enough pockets, I should think."

"How much could it cost for a bit of soap and water?"

"Very little, but it's the extras like supper and the price of the whore you sleep with that add up, and that can go as high as six guineas."

I abruptly forgot all about Bedlam. "Really?"

Oliver misinterpreted my reaction. "Yes, it's disgusting, isn't it? Even if you forgo the bath and meal, the tarts there will still demand their guineas. And they're not much better looking than the ladies that trade at Vauxhall, who are considerably more reasonable in their prices, I might add."

My head began to reel with excited speculation. "Where is this place?"

He waved a hand. "Oh, you can find it easily enough. But another time, perhaps. We'll have to get back to Tony's before that barber he promised disappears."

It was just not fair. I'd spent a horrid afternoon in Bedlam when I could have been wallowing in a scented bathing pool like a turbaned potentate with any number of beauteous water nymphs seeing to my every desire. Though Oliver and I had much in common, it seemed that our ideas on practical education were quite different. I wanted to ask him more about his experiences at Covent Garden and Vauxhall, but we'd reached the end of the lane and had to consider our mode of transport.

After expressing my preference of a cart over a sedan chair, we managed to find one going in the desired direction. This one had outward facing seats and was crowded with other passengers, two of whom were ladies of the respectable sort. Their inhibiting presence kept me from obtaining more details from Oliver, so I had to content myself with conversation on less exciting topics than the tarts of London.

Our trip seemed shorter, whether by speed of the horse, or the amusing nature of my cousin's comments as we traveled. The streets were just as busy as ever as people hurried to finish their errands before nightfall. Oliver said that the city could be a deadly trap to the unwary or the unarmed, and if the footpads were bold enough during the day, they were positively bloodthirsty at night. Since we would be going over by carriage, with footmen running before and behind with torches, we would probably be safe enough.

"Can you defend yourself?" he asked.

"Oh, yes." With an easy twist, I opened my walking stick to reveal part of the Spanish steel blade within. Oliver whistled with admiration. "It was a present from Father," I added. "He'd ordered it nearly a year ago, intending it for my last birthday, but delivery was delayed. As it was, it made a fine parting gift for my trip here."

"Or anywhere," he added, his eyes lighting up with a touch of envy. "I shall have to take you along to the fencing gallery we have at Cambridge so you can show us your skill."

"I should look forward to that." It had been ages since my last match at home, and I wanted the practice.

"Tell me, before you left, did you have any opportunity at all to put it to use?"

"Use? What? Against the rebels? They're miles from where we are."

"No-no-no! I meant against all those bloodthirsty red Indians!"

"Eh?"

He explained his eagerness to hear whatever exploits I might have had fighting savages, being under the misapprehension that the colonies were comprised of besieged forts under constant threat from roaming hoards of feathered fiends. My lengthy explanation about the complete lack of hostile natives on Long Island disappointed him, but served to fill the time until we reached Tony Warburton's front steps. Though ostensibly a guest in the house and therefore not subject to paying for lodging and board, I might have spent much less money had I remained at The Three Brewers. The many vails were adding up, and my supply of pennies dwindled before I came to an understanding with the butler that all things could be settled at the end of my visit. This promise, rather than putting the servants off, caused them to be more attentive than before, so my request for a bath was greeted as an easily met challenge rather than an impassable obstacle.

Because Mrs. Warburton was a great believer in maintaining a clean body (hence the family holiday at Bath), facilities were at hand, even if they weren't exactly ready. Two stout boys carried her bathing tub to my room and then lugged bucket after bucket up the stairs to fill it, while another man lighted a fire to warm the room. Though it was August, the weather was cool today, and they weren't going to risk my catching a chill while under their care. Their concern might also have been that if I died from that chill I should be unable to pay them for their trouble. Even so, the water they brought was barely lukewarm.

Ah, but it was water, and I sank gratefully into the cramped tub for a much-desired soak. With a fat bar of soap and a flesh brush I was a happy man. Oliver and Tony came in for a short visit to view "the antics of this rustic colonial" as they joked to me. In turn, I shocked them by briefly recounting the many times on the crossing voyage that I had voluntarily stripped and had myself doused with seawater from the deck pump.

"Well-a-day, man, 'tis a wonder you're not dead," Oliver exclaimed with hollow-eyed horror.

"On the contrary, I found it to be refreshing and greatly improving to the appetite." I left off telling them about the awful food.

"He *is* still alive," Tony pointed out.

My cousin conceded that I was, indeed, still alive, by the grace of God and no thanks to my foolish habits.

"You made mention of Turkish bathing, Oliver. How is it so different from this that it is better for the health?" I asked.

"For one thing you're not slopping about in a drafty room, but working up a proper sweat wrapped in a hot blanket."

This didn't sound much like the marble-lined pool surrounded by the graceful seraglio I'd envisioned. He apparently didn't hear my invitation to continue his description, suddenly recalling a task he'd left undone in his room. Tony chuckled at his departure.

"Oliver is a bit bashful when it comes to talking about his winching," he said. "It seems he'd rather do it than waste time in discussion, which is quite sensible, after all. Perhaps later I can persuade him to take you 'round to meet some of our fair English roses after the party."

Well-a-day, I thought, a deep shiver coursing through me at the prospect. I applied the soap to the brush, and the brush to my flesh with happy diligence.

As the boys carried the buckets of dirty water back downstairs, I worked to get my hair combed and dried before the fire. Mother had insisted on fitting me out with a wig, which I suffered to accept in order to keep the peace. However, the one she chose was a monstrous horse-shoe toupet nearly a foot high with a sweep of Cadogan puffs hanging from the nape. No doubt another man would look quite handsome in it, but my first glimpse was enough to convince me that my own appearance would be extremely grotesque. I would sooner sport a chamber pot in public than to be seen wearing that thing. Brightly oblivious to my pained expression at the buffoon in my mirror, Mother pronounced that it would be perfect for any and all social functions I should be fortunate enough to attend and gave me lengthy instructions for its proper care. This upcoming musical evening would have met with her rare approval.

But she was thousands of leagues away and unable to command my obedience; I blithely cast the wig aside. This was no light decision for me, though.

During today's travels, I had ample opportunity to observe that no matter how mean their station in life, every Englishman I'd clapped eyes on that day (except for only the worst of the wretches in Bedlam) wore a wig. Foreigners like myself who chose to eschew the custom were either laughed at for their lack of fashion sense or admired for their eccentricity. Since I had a full head of thick black hair, I would take a bit of sinful pride in what God had given me and wear it as it was, tied back with a black ribbon. In this I was almost copying Benjamin Franklin, at least in general principle.

He'd made himself quite popular in polite society by choosing to dress simply and make an affectation out of his lack of affectation. He'd made a sober, but good-humored contrast to all the court peacocks, and had enjoyed no lack of female companionship. Though I utterly disagreed with his politics and those of his fanatical friends, I could admire his cleverness.

Tony Warburton's barber came and went, leaving my face expertly scraped and powdered dry. He grumbled unhappily over my attitude about the wig, which he had expected to dress. If all gentlemen made such a calamitous decision to go without, he would lose more than half his income. Before sending him on, I compensated him with a generous vail, having made it a practice to always be on good terms with any man who plays around my throat with a razor.

Crispin lived up to his reputation; all my clothes had been cleaned, aired, and laid out as though new. After careful thought, I picked my somber Sunday clothes, but offset the severe black with an elaborately knotted neckcloth and highly polished shoes with the new silver buckles. One of the younger footmen had been detailed as my temporary valet, and I was pleased with his attention to detail, though I said little lest he develop an exaggerated idea about the size of his vail when I left.

"Heavens!" exclaimed Tony when he and Oliver came to collect me. "They'll think you're some kind of Quaker who came by mistake."

"That or a serious student of the law," I returned with dignity.

Oliver agreed with me. "I think he's made a wise choice. Everyone will expect him to be either an uncivilized savage or an insurrectionist lout. Dressed this way he looks neither, and they may trouble themselves to stop and make his acquaintance first out of sheer curiosity at the lack of spectacle."

"Thank you, Cousin. I think."

"Don't mention it," he said cheerfully, and led the way downstairs.

WITH FOOTMEN RUNNING before and behind our coach, their torches making a welcome light in the darkness, we suffered no interference from criminal interlopers on our coach ride to the Bolyn house. It was an enormous pile, and though it probably presented a pleasant face to the world, I hardly noticed for all the people. There seemed to be hundreds milling about, reminding me of the crowds I'd seen in the streets earlier, but infinitely better dressed, with less purpose and more posturing. Oliver wanted to stop and talk whenever he saw a familiar face, but Tony kept us moving, for he was anxious to see his Miss Jones again and introduce her.

We did pause long enough to pay our respects to our host and hostess, and Oliver's prediction that my garb would inspire a favorable impression proved true, at least with them. I was asked many questions about the colonies, which I rather inadequately answered, hampered as I was by having lived in only one small part of them. Most of the interesting news had happened elsewhere, though I was able to provide some information regarding events in Philadelphia. For that I could thank Dr. Theophilous Beldon, who had quite exhausted the novelty of the subject in his efforts to cultivate my friendship before my departure.

He would have loved it here, for I saw many dandies of his type roaming the house and grounds, bowing and toad-eating to their betters to their heart's content. Several in particular stood out so much from the rest that I had to stop and gape. Elizabeth often accused me of being a peacock, but then she'd never seen these beauties.

Their wigs were so white as to blind an observer and so tall as to brush the door lintels. Instead of shoes, they appeared to be wearing slippers; a silver circle served in place of a buckle. They were painted and powdered and so richly dressed that for a moment I thought some members of the French court had wandered in by mistake.

I had certainly given thought to augmenting my own wardrobe while in London, but if this was an example of fashion, I would sooner go naked and said as much to Oliver.

"Oh, those are members of the Macaroni Club," he informed me.

"A theatrical troupe, are they?"

"No, scions of wealthy houses. They've done their grand tour of Europe and brought the name back from Italy."

"Name?"

"Macaroni."

What Italian I had learned did not include that particular word, so I asked for a definition.

"It's a kind of dish made of flour and eggs. They boil it."

"Then what?"

"Then they eat it."

I tried to work out how boiled flour and eggs could be made edible and gave up with a shudder.

"Everything these days is done *a la macaroni,* you know. You could do worse than follow their example." He looked upon them with wistful envy.

"Truly," I said, as though agreeing with him while thinking, *if worse existed.* "If you admire them so much, why don't you?"

"Mother won't let me," he rumbled, and for a few seconds a singularly nasty expression occupied his normally good-natured face. I'd seen it briefly last night when we'd talked about ourselves and our families while getting so terrifically drunk. It worked across the lean muscles of his cheeks and brow like a thunderstorm. Even without any knowledge of our family ties, I would have recognized the Fonteyn blood in him at that moment. He seemed aware that he was revealing something better left hidden and glanced away as though seeking any kind of a distraction to help him mask the thoughts within.

"Awful, isn't it?" I said aloud, without meaning to.

Though surprised, he instantly understood my meaning and looked hard at me, his eyes oddly clear and sharp with sudden weariness, as though waiting for an expected blow to fall now that I'd gotten his attention. None did.

The odd silence between us lengthened. "I just know it really is awful," I murmured, trying to fill it, but unable to think of anything better to say.

Some of the tightness of his posture, which I hadn't noticed until he shifted restlessly on his feet, eased. The anger and hatred against his mother that had battered against me like the backwash of a wave began to gradually recede.

"Yes," he said, the word emerging from him slowly, as though he were afraid to let it go. He sucked in his lower lip like a sulky child.

There was more that could have been voiced, months and years of it, perhaps. But nothing more came from him. Vacuous good humor reasserted itself on his face, first as a struggle, then as a genuine feeling. He dropped a hand on my near shoulder with a reminder that we should not lose sight of Tony, then carefully steered me through the crowd of Macaronis like a pilot taking a ship through dangerous waters.

Despite the people pressed close around, each talking louder than his neighbor to be heard, I discerned the clear tones of a harpsichord nearby. This was supposed to be a musical evening. Being unable to play myself, I had cultivated an appreciation for the art and expressed the hope that I might be allowed the time to enjoy the artist at hand.

"You'll have buckets of time, I'm sure," said Oliver. "The fellow here is frightfully good, but new here and his name escapes me. Knowing Bolyn's ambitions, he's probably German."

"What's his ambition to do with his taste for music?"

"It's well known that the king prefers German music, and Bolyn must be hoping that an evening like this will somehow get him royal attention."

"To what end?"

"Who knows? He's probably angling for at least a knighthood; they usually are. I never saw much point to playing such games. There was one fellow I knew whose father was knighted and the only advantage he noticed was for the tradesmen, who doubled all their bills."

We moved out of range of the music, through some wide doors, and into a graceful garden surrounding the house. Lanterns hung from flower-festooned poles, taking the place of the sun, which had departed on our drive over. Here we caught up with Tony, who had grown fretful.

"She's supposed to be here," he told us. "Mrs. Bolyn assured me that she acknowledged her invitation." Nervously, he tugged at his neckcloth. The afternoon's rest had restored his color and now it all seemed gathered in two dense spots high on his cheeks.

Love must be a frightening thing indeed to put a man into such a state, I thought, and wondered if I would turn into a similar wreck if the conclusion of this evening lived up to my expectations. I was in pursuit of physical gratification, though, and aware that other young men achieved it without exhibiting Tony's alarming symptoms. Perhaps if I were careful, I would not fall in love with my hired mistress, and thus be spared such agonies. I was more than willing to take the chance.

The estate had a marvelous garden with thick grass and a hedge maze lighted by paper lanterns. Somewhere within musicians played. A table with cold meats and other things was set up near the entry along with many chairs and benches. Though Tony claimed to have no appetite and moved restlessly on, Oliver and I did, and tarried to take full advantage of the offerings. We each promised the other not to overindulge in the matter of wine and with that understanding made up for it by our consumption of food. In between bites, he would point out this person or that to me, always with some amusing note about them, which helped to fix their names in my memory.

"Over there is Brinsley Bolyn—that's Charlotte's brother, you know. She's the raving beauty this year, but no one's been allowed to propose to her yet. They say their father is holding out for someone wealthy enough to do his family some good."

"Are they descended from Anne Boleyn? Or rather from her family?"

"No, but they like to think it and have put the story about so long and so often that people are beginning to believe them. I'd put as much stock in that claim as I would the footman who takes on his master's name and title and insists on being called 'my lord' by other servants."

"Are there any real titles here?"

"I'm certain of it. Bolyn's spent enough on this to try to impress them. They wouldn't dare not be here." Oliver nodded in the direction of a slight fellow conversing with a fat man. "There's Lord Harvey, for one. His title outlived the family fortune and he's looking around for an heiress to help him recover their lost dignity. Of course he hasn't a chance with Charlotte. Her dear papa guards her too well. I wonder why he's talking with old Ruben Smollett? That's Robert's father. Robert's part of our group, y'know. Unfortunately for Lord Harvey, Smollett's oldest daughter only just turned twelve. I doubt if his creditors will wait until she's old enough to be married off."

Tony rushed up just then, his eyes alight and hands twitching. "Wipe the grease from your faces and look lively, you two. She's here!"

"I should never have guessed," said Oliver. He obediently dabbed the corners of his mouth and passed his plate to a convenient footman. I reluctantly left my own tasty burden on a table where someone's lap dog jumped up to finish it for me. "Lead us to this paragon of beauty, my friend."

Oliver meant only to mock Tony's enthusiasm, but once we'd turned a corner formed of hedges we could see that his praises had been well placed.

"By God, Tony!" he gasped.

"Just as I said. The peerless Miss Nora Jones is truly a goddess. What say you, Mr. Barrett?"

Words altogether deserted me. The young woman conversing with her friends on the path before us was beyond them, anyway. She had dark eyes, a pleasing nose, a mouth perhaps too wide for convention, and a chin too sharp, but the totality of their merging was such as to strike even the blind speechless. I felt as though I'd taken a step and found the stairway mysteriously shortened, leaving me jolted from head to toe and ready to fall over.

"Just as I said!" Tony repeated gleefully.

Indeed, *yes,* I thought, and my heart began pounding so loud in my ears I could scarce hear anything else.

CHAPTER
SIX

"I'll introduce you to her in a minute," Tony promised.

"Why not now?" my cousin demanded.

"Because you look like a dying fish. When you're able to properly breathe again, I'll invite you over. In the meantime, I must have a word with her."

He excused himself and joined the group of women. They received him kindly and with some giggling as he solemnly bowed to each. He reserved his lowest and most courtly bow for Miss Jones, who accepted it with no more than a nod and a polite smile. Evidently she was still unaware of his true feelings for her, though they were painfully obvious to anybody who happened to be glancing their way.

"His parents may not approve of this," Oliver remarked.

"Of what?"

"Him wanting to marry her. Old Warburton is a dreadfully practical man with a horror of penniless girls with no name. Unless she has money, property, family, or all three, they'll have to elope."

"So you're taking Tony seriously?"

"I think so this time. I've chided him on his susceptibility to beauty and for falling in love with a new girl every other week, but there's something different about this one."

That was an understatement. She was no less than astonishing. I couldn't pry my eyes from her. I also felt a familiar stirring that made looking away imperative lest something embarrassing develop within the snug confines of my black velvet breeches. But I continued to stare at the unearthly beauty not a dozen feet away, shifted and dithered uncomfortably, and had a passing thought about being caught oncleft sticks.

Then she looked right at me.

Oh, those *eyes*....

I gulped—unsuccessfully, for my mouth was dry—and my heart gave a lurching thump that everyone must have heard. She certainly seemed to, for she smiled, looked me up and down, and smiled again. By then I was certain the world had paused in its spin only to start over faster than before to make up for the time lost. In contrast to the one she'd bestowed upon Warburton, this smile was warm with interest. I had to turn and see if anyone was behind me, hardly able to believe that I was the focus of her attention.

She tilted her head to say something to Warburton, who instantly broke away and came back to us.

"Would you like to meet her now?" he asked.

Would the incoming tide like to meet the land? That's how I surged forward.

Warburton made introductions that included the other ladies, but hers was the only name that I heard, hers the only face that I saw.

She inquired about my health, and I mumbled and muttered something back. With my blood running all hot and cold through my loins, I was too distracted to make intelligible speech. It was wonderful, but agonizing, for I truly wanted to make a good impression upon her, yet found myself unable to think of anything to say or do except act like a stunned sheep.

Hardly a minute had passed and she was drifting off with Warburton. No doubt he would find some secluded spot in the garden, make his proposal, and that would be the end of any chance I might have to improve my own acquaintance with her. The color suddenly drained out of my world.

"Something wrong?" asked Oliver. "Good heavens. Perhaps you'd better sit down. You're ill."

"I'm fine," I lied.

"You are not and nearly being a doctor, I should know. Come over here and I'll find you some brandy."

He led me to a bench and made me sit. Helpless, I watched Warburton and Miss Jones disappear in the crowd. I had had my chance and now it was lost. When Oliver returned with the promised spirits, I heartily wished the glass to be loaded with hemlock. I obediently drank without tasting a drop, and either owing to the heavy meal or the force of my mangled emotions, it had absolutely no restorative effect.

"What has happened?" Oliver demanded, his face puckered with concern. "Oh, don't tell me. I can see it now. Good heavens and well-a-day, but this is turning into an interesting evening. Just promise me you won't get into a duel with Tony and murder each other over her."

"What?"

"That's how these things usually end up, and Tony's been my friend for years and years, and I've gotten fond of you even if you are half Fonteyn and I'd rather not have you running each other through…"

I held up a hand. "Peace, Oliver. I'm not the sort of fellow to come between a man and his potential bride."

"That's a relief to hear. I mean to say, I wouldn't have known which of you to second."

For his sake and the sake of his jest, I smiled, but it faded the moment someone else claimed his attention and took him away. I remained on the bench thinking of everything and nothing and hoping to catch a glimpse of Miss Nora Jones again. A few of the young ladies that had been in her company descended upon me and tried to open a conversation, but I doubt that my replies to their remarks made much sense. When they drifted on it occurred to me that I was being a fool about the whole business. Yes, I had met an extremely beautiful girl, but it was an idiot's dream to think that I'd fallen in love with her at first sight.

Now *that* was a terrifying word: love. The very fact that it had so swiftly cropped up in my mind had an immediate sobering influence. It was utterly impossible, I concluded. Impossible because I knew nothing about love, about this kind of love, anyway. I did love my sister and father, my home and the people there, even my horse, but what did any of that have to do with what I was feeling now? Nothing. Perhaps some of the food I'd eaten had gone bad and the symptoms had manifested themselves at the same time I'd clapped eyes on Miss Jones.

Life would be so much simpler were that true.

"Mr. Barrett?"

I gave a start. "Yes?"

A middle-aged woman with a pleasant smile and kindly eyes looked down at me. "I'm Mrs. Poole, Miss Jones's aunt."

A knot formed in my throat. I tried to gulp it down so my voice wouldn't crack. "Yes? I mean, I am very pleased to meet you." Belatedly, I found my feet and made a bow to her.

"As am I," she said. "Would you mind very much coming with me? My niece—"

I didn't hear the rest. It was blotted out by a strange roaring in my ears. I did not think it had anything to do with the digestion of my dinner. She led the way into the garden and I followed. We turned corner after corner until I thought we should run out of space to walk. We did not seem to be very far from the house, though. The hedge maze must have been of a very clever and intricate design. Then my knees went jellylike as we turned one last corner and came upon Miss Jones standing in the faint nimbus of light from one of the lanterns scattered throughout the place. Her eyes brightened and she extended her hand to me once more.

"Good evening again, Mr. Barrett," she said in her angel's voice.

I stammered out something polite, but before I could follow it up with anything better, a dark thought intruded upon me. "Where is Tony, that is, Mr. Warburton?"

"Gone back to visit with his other friends, I expect."

"I thought that he ... that he was going to—" I broke off, belatedly realizing Warburton's intentions toward her were none of my concern. I found breathing to be a bit of a struggle.

"Yes," she said serenely. "He did propose to me, but I turned him down."

My eyes must have popped just then.

"We had a nice talk and got everything sorted out," she continued. "I am happy to say that once Mr. Warburton realized that I have no wish to marry, he pledged himself to remain my very good friend, instead."

Now what did she mean by that? I decided I didn't care. "Perhaps we may also become friends, Miss Jones." My words were light, but difficult to bring forth. Not knowing quite what to say or do, I babbled on. "I should like that very much."

"Of course, Mr. Barrett. That's why I asked my aunt to bring you here. I wanted to get to know you better, too. I hope you do not think ill of me for doing so."

"Not at all."

"Good. I do tire of all the rules that society has invented to prevent men and women from holding intelligent converse with one another. Sometimes it is tediously impossible. If it weren't for my dear aunt ..."

At this second mention of Mrs. Poole I glanced around, thinking that she might take this opportunity to put in a word, but she was nowhere in sight. Leaving us alone didn't seem quite proper, or at least it would not be so back home. Here in England, though, the customs might be different.

"She's a little way up the path," said Miss Jones, correctly discerning my thoughts.

"Indeed?" I was feeling hot and cold again. All over.

Her mouth twisted into a wry smile. "Oh, dear, this is perhaps new to you, isn't it?"

"I ... uh ... that is ..."

Now she took my hand and came so close that all I could see were her wonderful eyes. They were darker than a hundred midnights, but somehow caught the wan light and threw it back like sparks from a diamond. I found myself blinking against them.

"It's all right, Mr. Barrett," she whispered soothingly.

And so it was. A great calmness and comfort overtook me as she spoke; a cheering peace seemed to fill me in the soft silence that followed. My worries and self-doubts over this new situation vanished as though they'd never been, and I came to realize that my inexperience, rather than trying her patience, was entirely charming to her.

Not quite knowing how we got there, I found myself sitting on a bench in the shadows chatting with her as though we'd known each other for years. She had me tell her all about myself. It didn't take long; I hadn't done very much yet with my life and thought any lengthy reminiscences of it might bore her. I need not have worried, for she seemed to find everything of interest. It was highly flattering and most encouraging to my own esteem, but eventually I ran out of subject matter. I burned to know more about her and thought that if I could put the right combination of words together I would learn everything.

While I paused to think, she took advantage of it to shift the subject slightly.

"You really are so very beautiful," she told me, her fingers brushing my cheek.

"Shouldn't I be the one to say that to you?" I asked. Without, I was surprisingly calm, but within I wanted to leap up and turn handsprings.

"If you wish."

"Perhaps you hear it too often."

"Often enough," she admitted. "And there are other subjects one may talk about with equal enthusiasm."

"If you asked me to name one, I don't think I could possibly meet the challenge."

"I judge that you underestimate yourself, Mr. Barrett. What about love? Have you ever loved a woman?"

Some of my earlier awkwardness returned.

"Oh, it's all right to talk with me about such things. Other girls might not be so minded, but I have always had a great curiosity. With some men, one may tell right away, but with others..." She shrugged. "So tell me, have you...?"

"I have never loved a woman," I admitted. "I have never been in love... at least not until I saw you."

She was pleased, which pleased me, but I had hoped for a warmer response. No doubt other men had confided similar sentiments to her and repetition had dulled the meaning for her. I wanted to be different from them, but did not know what to say or how to say it.

As it turned out, I said nothing, for we were suddenly pressing close and kissing. While growing up, I had seen others so engaged and had concluded that observation had little to do with active participation. My surmise proved to be more than correct. Until this moment I had had no real inkling of the incredible pleasure such a simple act could produce between a man and a woman. No wonder so many people took any given opportunity to indulge themselves. This was far more addictive than drink, at least for me.

My first efforts were less polished than enthusiastic, but she had me slow down to a pace more suitable for savoring and each minute that passed taught me something new. I was a very willing student.

She pulled away first, but not very far. "You've never before loved a woman?"

"No."

"Would you like to?"

I was not so far gone as to be confused by what she meant. "More than anything in my life."

"And I should very much like to be that woman. Will you trust me to arrange things?"

"Arrange?"

She drew back a little more. "I think it's best if we are both very prudent about this."

I understood and immediately agreed, but wasn't prepared to give up her company just yet. Neither was she and we pursued our initial explorations until I was faint for want of air. Nora—for she had become Nora to me by now—did not seem to need any, but allowed me time to recover.

She knew that I was there with Oliver and Warburton and my disappearance for the evening would raise questions requiring an answer.

"Tell them that you met one of the servant girls and came to an arrangement with her," she suggested. "It's a common enough practice, so you need not provide more details than that. I shall excuse myself to the Bolyns and leave. You'll find my carriage waiting at the west gate of the grounds."

"I'll be there," I promised.

She had me go first. The maze wasn't too difficult; I found my way out after a few false paths and was nearly knocked over by the light and noise upon emerging. The contrast between the activity by the house and the intense interlude in the garden made me wonder if I'd dreamed the whole thing. But a few moments later Nora glided out, graced me with a subtle and fleeting smile, and moved on. My heart began to hammer in a way that no mere dream could inspire.

I grew nearly feverish searching the crowd for some sign of my cousin. My patience was nearly at an end when I spied Tony Warburton standing off by himself holding a half-full tankard by its rim. Distracted as I was, I noticed that he looked a bit disturbed, like a man trying to remember something important.

"Hallo, Barrett," he said, coming out of it as I approached. "Oliver told me you weren't feeling well."

"I'm better. Fully recovered, in fact." Almost word for word, I passed on the excuse Nora had provided for me. In the back of my mind, I thought that I really should feel some sort of remorse for what I was intending to do with the love of this man's life, but there was not a single twinge against my conscience. Nora had made her choice and who was I to argue with a lady?

"Yes, well, I wish you a vigorous time, then. Which one is she? Oh, never mind."

In spite of myself I couldn't just run off. He looked damnably white around the eyes. "Are *you* all right?"

"Yes, I think so. Little dizzy, but that'll be the drink, I expect." He raised the tankard and drained off a good portion of it. "Go off and enjoy yourself with your English rose. We'll see you in the morning? You know my street? Good, good, but not too early, mind you. Enjoy yourself."

Walking away, I glanced back, troubled. He had returned to his preoccupied state. It was so different from the excitement that he'd shown earlier. As a jilted suitor, surely he should have been morose or angry, anything but this calm puzzlement. I wondered what in the world Nora had said to him.

Nora.

Concerns for Warburton mercilessly cast aside, I asked directions and made my way to the west gate.

◆ ◆ ◆

OLIVER HAD WONDERED about Nora's finances. If one could judge anything by the well-appointed coach and matched horses drawing it, then she had no worldly worries at all. The only reason that I had the mind to notice it was the dismal fact that Mrs. Poole was unexpectedly with us. I had completely forgotten about her and got a bad shock when I entered the coach to find her sitting next to Nora. Both of them were amused, but not in a derisive manner.

"How nice to see you again, Mr. Barrett," she said. "I'm so glad that you and Nora have become friends."

"Er…yes," I responded idiotically. I dropped into the seat opposite them, confusion and doubt invading my mind and cooling my initial ardor. Was Nora setting things up to play some kind of cruel trick on me? It did not seem likely. What might she have told her aunt about us? I could hardly assume that Mrs. Poole knew of our plans for the rest of the evening. It wasn't the sort of thing one confided to one's chaperone.

"How do you like England?" she asked with bland and benevolent interest.

Nora gave me a slight nod, a sign that I should answer. Perhaps her aunt was totally ignorant; that, or she knew all and had no objections, which struck me as odd.

"It's very different from home in ways that I had never imagined," I said truthfully.

The coach lurched forward. The noise of the wheels made quiet talk impossible so Mrs. Poole found it necessary to raise her voice to continue her conversation with me. Nora contributed little herself, content to simply watch me with her bright eyes. This, of course, made it difficult for me to hold up my end, as my thoughts were constantly wandering back to her. By the time the coach rocked to a final stop, my mind was in a particularly unsettled state.

A footman opened the door and assisted the ladies out. He was a young, handsome fellow with a cool demeanor, a trait he shared with the driver and the other footmen. All were in matched livery and carried themselves with quiet pride. For the first time since the practice was forced upon me, my offered vail was politely refused.

At a word from Nora, I followed her up the steps to the wide doors of her house. Within, all was clean and orderly and in careful good taste. I glimpsed a dozen paintings and sculptures decorating the front hall, booty from her tour of the continent, perhaps. I had no time to ask, for Mrs. Poole took my hand.

"The party has quite worn me out. You'll please excuse me, Mr. Barrett, if I retire now?"

I did so with mild surprise, but the lady favored me with another sweet smile and went upstairs accompanied by a maid. All the footmen magically disappeared. Nora and I were happily alone.

"I'm sorry about the interruption," she said. "I could hardly leave my aunt behind at the Bolyns'."

"It's all right, but I confess I am puzzled by her attitude. All of this puzzles me."

"What, that a lady like myself should bring a man home as I've done with you?"

"Well, yes."

"And yet if a man brings home a lady, no one thinks much on it."

She certainly had a point there.

"Now, if a lady is so inclined, should she not be allowed the same freedom as a man?"

"I suppose..." I glanced toward the wide stairs where Mrs. Poole had taken herself.

Nora took my hand in two of hers. "Put your mind at rest, dear Jonathan. My aunt and I have a perfect understanding of one another on such matters, as do my servants. My only demand of you is your discretion. May I rely on it?"

I could hardly blurt my answer to that one out fast enough.

"Very well, then. Now... would you like to see my bedroom?"

Strangely, it was on the ground floor, but by the time we reached it I was out of breath, as though we'd run up several flights of stairs. The air seemed very scarce once more. My chest was tight and my knees trembled with an intriguing mixture of fear, anticipation and lust. Nora was aware of this and enjoyed her effect on me, but in a sympathetic manner. She gave my hand a reassuring squeeze before pushing open her door.

She drew me into a room decorated for delight. Candles were everywhere, burning away with a supreme lack of thrift to turn night into day for us. Each added its small warmth to what was being produced by the fireplace, comfortably dispelling any chill that might have lingered from our drive over.

The walls were papered halfway up with Oriental-looking flowers on a dark pink background. The ample bed was draped with embroidered tapestries to match, and the sheets—when I got close enough to touch them—were of ivory-colored silk and scented with rose. A special recess in one wall opposite the bed held a lovely and striking portrait of Nora, wearing antique clothes.

"It is very like you," I said. "What was the purpose of the costume?"

"A whim of the artist. He was very talented, but eccentric."

"Did he love you?"

"How did you guess?"

"Anyone seeing this work would know."

Her lips curled in a smile that any man might die for, and I found my arms going around her, drawing her tightly to me. We resumed the kisses begun an age ago in the maze.

"Slowly, Jonathan, slowly," she cautioned. "This is a special time for you. Don't let it go by so fast that you'll not remember what was done."

I laughed at that impossibility. With her help and encouragement— for I won't deny that I was nervous and shy—we began the lengthy and fascinating necessity of removing one another's clothes. As things progressed, I discovered a hundred places other than her mouth where a kiss might be joyfully applied. As for my first sight of a naked woman, I admitted some surprise at the silky fluff between her legs. I'd been misled by the lines in the Song of Solomon where the bride's own charms were compared to jewels. The reality Nora possessed was hardly a disappointment, though, and certainly worthy of careful exploration.

"Heavens," she said in turn when the last of my things dropped away. "I have chosen an eager stallion. Gently now, we'll find a place to stable him in good time."

This did not take long, fortunately, for I was almost to the point where I had to have release or go mad from the waiting. But Nora had grown warm enough under my hands and mouth to be in a similar state of near-bliss. She gave a soft, happy cry as I went in and held the small of my back so hard as to nearly break it as we traveled from near-bliss to its totality in a few swift moments.

When I finally caught my breath, when the sweat on my temples cooled and dried, when my heart stopped thundering between my ears, when my eyes rolled down to their proper place and I could see Nora beneath me, her head thrown back on the pillows, I knew that I was helplessly and hopelessly and forever in love with her.

Unable and unwilling to stop, I began kissing her again.

✦ ✦ ✦

"YOU ARE SO VERY BEAUTIFUL," she said, repeating her earlier judgment. She teased my hair with gentle fingers.

I pulled them down to my lips and nibbled at them. It seemed the thing to do.

"And vigorous, too. Midnight's just gone by; are you not yet tired?"

"Never," I mumbled. "I shall always be ready and waiting for you."

Something like a shadow flowed over her face, but vanished before it could take hold. "Of course you will, but wouldn't you like something to strengthen you first?"

Since she'd awakened the idea, I realized I'd worked up a tremendous appetite in the last few hours of activity. Disengaging from my grasp, she slid from the bed and crossed to a table holding several covered plates.

"Some cold meats and cheese?" she asked. "Some wine?"

Trailing after her, I wouldn't have cared if it were stale water and weevil-infested ship's biscuits. She saw to it that everything was within easy reach and watched while I ate.

"You must have something for yourself," I said. She shook her head. "No, thank you."

As the food took the edge off the worst of my hunger and the wine made its way to my head, a dark thought began to curl unpleasantly through my mind.

"You've done this often before," I pronounced.

"What do you mean?"

"The servants being so well rehearsed, your aunt's cooperation, this all ready and waiting...." I gestured at the table.

"Yes. That is true, Jonathan."

"Who were they?"

"It doesn't matter, does it? You're the one here now. I only rarely ask anyone to come home with me as I've done with you."

"And who will be here the next time?"

"Please listen and understand, Jonathan." Her mouth hardened slightly and her eyes snapped. "Listen."

I felt myself instantly sinking into their darkness.

"Please listen to me...."

And I did. And I *tried* to understand.

She loved me, but she loved others, too, and would continue to seek them out. That was her nature and she wasn't going to change for my sake or for anyone else's. However, she could not abide jealousy in any form, and told me that I should not give in to it. Above all, I should never be jealous of her other lovers; otherwise I would never see her again. I knew she meant it and, nearly choking, I swore to do as she asked. The impossibility of her request knotted my throat with tears. How could I *not* resent those unnamed interlopers?

But she talked to me, sweetly, soothingly.

Her voice filled my whole world.

Her voice *became* my world.

Then, like the sun breaking through a black cloud, it became entirely possible.

The best and easiest task I could ever take upon myself was to please her. And what she wanted of me was certainly within my abilities. I would love her and willingly share her and enjoy the privilege and honor of it with others. We would be like courtiers of old, gladly waiting upon the pleasure of our lady.

I had listened. I now understood.

My head and heart were at peace.

I finished my meal, content to simply look at her and marvel at the perfection of her face and figure. Nora was not as quiescently minded, though, and came around the table to sit on my lap. Since neither of us had bothered to dress, I found this to be very inspiring and began to express my feelings to her in a such a way as to leave no doubt over how I intended to conclude things.

I started to rise up to carry her back to bed, but she told me to remain in the chair. With a quick shift, she straddled my lap. I gulped, a little shocked at this new presentation of her boldness. I would never look at horseback riding in the same way again.

The chair creaked under our combined weight and exertions, but even if the damned thing had collapsed, we wouldn't have noticed or paused. She wrapped her legs around my waist and its back and pressed close upon me. Her lips dipped down along the column of my neck, her teeth and tongue dragging against my now very sensitive skin. With a sigh, she fastened her mouth on the very pulse point of my throat and began sucking there.

At first it felt no different from the other kisses she'd given that I'd received with such joy, but it continued much longer and with no sign that she planned to stop. Not that I wanted her to; it was utterly wonderful. And the wonder of it only increased when she opened her mouth wide and her teeth dug deep and hard into my skin, finally breaking it. A full-blown cry of ecstasy burst from me then, along with the climax that overtook us both.

My loins were spent soon enough, but instead of the all-too-brief moment of glory I'd known before, the sensation there continued to increase. It spread to flow throughout whole of my body and went on and on and on, building upon itself like a great storm cloud seeking to touch the moon. Each breath I took was a long gasp of gratification; each exhalation a pleading sigh for more.

My brain was afire; my body shuddered as though from fever as she held to my throat and drank the blood flowing from the wound she'd made. The triumphant couplings we'd shared before were *nothing* compared to this. I moaned and writhed and could have wept from the ecstasy that blazed like lightning over and throughout my flesh. One of my hands snaked up, the fingers pressing upon the back of her head, a silent invitation to dig deeper, to take more, to take as much as she liked, to empty me completely.

But she had more control of herself than I. An hour might have passed for us locked together like this or a week. I was too overwhelmed to know or care until she began a gradual and slow drawing away from me; something I sensed at once and tried to hinder. She licked and kissed me in a most tender way, but remained firm, and eventually and most reluctantly I came back to myself again.

I don't remember getting there, but we'd returned to her bed, for it was only then that I really woke up, soaked to the bones with a vast and heavy weariness. She'd donned a dressing gown and was kneeling on the floor to put her face at a level with mine. She'd put out many of the candles, and those that remained seemed to have a strange effect on her eyes. The whites were gone, darkened... flushed with crimson through and through.

"How do you feel?" she asked, her brows drawn together with light worry.

"Cold," I croaked.

She tucked the coverlet around me and crossed to the fireplace to add more wood. Despite my listlessness, I noticed that the firelight shone right through the thin fabric of her gown, revealing every graceful line of her figure. In my head, I wanted to take action about it, but my body inarguably insisted upon rest.

"Better?" She leaned over me, stroking my forehead with one finger.

"Tired." And dizzy. Warburton had been dizzy....

"Have some of this." She held a cup of wine to my lips, but I could only manage a small swallow. "It will pass. I fear I've asked too much of you tonight."

Warburton...white around the eyes...and dizzy.

"What did you say?"

I dredged more air into my lungs. "Warburton. You did this to him earlier." I touched my neck where she had kissed...*bitten*...?

"It's all right, Jonathan. Please trust me. Everything will be all right."

"What have you done?" Limited as my experience had been before this night, not once had I ever heard of women biting and taking blood from their men. My once-solid feeling of well-being was slipping away like a ragged dream.

"Exactly what you know I have done," she calmly replied. "There's no need to be alarmed."

"What do you mean? Of course I should be alarmed."

"You're not hurt, are you? Does it hurt now? Did it hurt then?"

No...I thought. Far from it.

"Only the idea of it is strange to you but, my darling, let me assure you that it is entirely natural and necessary to me."

"Necessary?"

"For how I live, how I'm best able to love."

"But the way we did it earlier..."

"Was the way of most men and women, yes. Mine was a divergence that gives me the greatest form of pleasure, not just for myself, but for my lover. Did you not find it so? You didn't want me to stop."

"I must have been mad. Damnation, Nora, you were *drinking my blood!*"

Her features dissolved from concern to amused chagrin. "Yes, I was. But be honest, was it so terrible?"

That took all the wind out of me.

Wry amusement surpassed her chagrin. "Oh, my dear, if you could only see your face."

"But...well, I mean...well, it's damnably *strange*."

"Only because it's new to you."

"This isn't, well, harmful, is it?" I asked.

"Hardly. You may wobble a bit tomorrow, but sleep and good food will restore you."

"You're sure?"

She kissed my fingers. "Yes, my darling. I would never, ever harm you. If it were within my power I would protect you from all the world's evils."

I settled back, overtaken by another bout of dizziness and the oddity of dealing with her ... preferences. It was hardly without struggle, but I found myself curiously able to accept them. The sincerity of feeling behind her last words was so sharp that it was almost painful to hear, but at the same time a thrill went through me. I'd hardly dared to hope that she would love me as I was loving her.

She was absolutely right about her needs not being so terrible, quite the contrary, in fact. And if she'd started kissing me again in the same spot and in the same way I would not have stopped her. The mere thought of her lips light touch on my throat revived me greatly in mind and in spirit. My body, sad to say, was not yet sufficiently recovered for me to put forth the invitation just now, but soon.

Gingerly, I explored the place on my throat with my fingers. It felt slightly bruised, nothing more, and the only evidence of her bite were two small, raised blemishes.

"They're not very noticeable," she said. "Your neckcloth will cover everything."

"Have you a mirror?"

"Not handy, and I don't like to trouble the servants this late."

"Good God, what time is it?"

"Close on to three, I should think. Time to sleep. My people will see that you get home in the morning."

"Not too early," I said, echoing Warburton's instruction. Instead of resentment toward him, I now felt an almost brotherly compassion and camaraderie. "Poor Tony. He's so terribly in love with you."

"Yes." She rose and lay down next to me, but on top of the coverlet. "Perhaps too much in love."

"Don't you love him?"

"Not in the way he wants. He wants marriage and children, and that is not my path."

"Why not?"

"It's too long a story and I don't wish to tell it."

"But I know nothing about you." The whites of her eyes were not so flushed now. The darker pupils were slowly emerging from their scarlet background.

"You know enough, I think." She stroked the hair away from my brow and kissed me. "You'll learn more in the nights ahead."

The dreamlike comfort that had begun to envelop my thoughts abruptly whipped away once more. "No I won't. I'm going up to Cambridge tomorrow, God help me. I'll never see you again!"

"Yes, you will. Do you think I'd let anyone as dear to me as you get away?"

"You mean you'd come with me?"

"Not with you, but I can take a house in Cambridge as easily as in London. The place is a dull and windy fen, but if you're there ..."

Her mouth closed over mine, warm and soft and tasting of salt.

Not salt. Tasting of blood. My own blood.

But I didn't care. She could do what she liked as long as I had a place in her heart. She wholly filled mine.

We talked and planned for a little while, but I was exhausted and soon fell asleep in her arms.

I AWOKE SLOWLY, lazily, my eyelids reluctant to lift and start the day. I had no idea of the time. The room's one window, though large, was heavily curtained. I was alone in the big bed. Nora must have risen earlier and gone down to breakfast.

Rolling on my side, I noticed a fold of paper on the table by the bed. Written on it was the simple message, "Ring when you are awake." Next to the paper was a silver bell. I did as instructed and presently a large and terribly dignified butler appeared and asked how he could be of service to me.

"Where is Miss Jones?"

"Gone for the day, sir, but she left a message for you." I sat up with interest. "Yes?"

"She will try to meet with you again tonight, but if she is unable, she will certainly see you in Cambridge within the week."

My disappointment fell on my heart like a great stone. I'd hoped for more. A lengthy love letter would have been nice. A week? That was an eternity. "Where has she gone?"

"She did not confide that information to me, sir."

"What about Mrs. Poole? Would she know?"

"Mrs. Poole left early to go visiting, sir. I do not think she will be able to help you, either."

"Damn."

"Would you care for a bath and shave, sir?"

"Really?" Considering all the trouble Warburton's servants had been to yesterday, this was an unexpected boon. I accepted the offered luxury and while things were being prepared for me in another room, sat at the table and composed a note to Nora.

Like my first kisses, it was chiefly more enthusiastic than polished, but sincere. Some parts of it were doubtless overdone, but love can forgive anything, including bad writing. When I came to a point where I could either go on for several more pages or stop, I chose to stop. It struck me that the whole thing was highly indiscreet, and Nora had specifically asked for my discretion. Virtuously, I recopied it, but changed the salutation to read "My Dearest Darling," rather than "My Dearest Nora." I signed it with a simple "J" and threw the first draft into the fire. That was as discreet as I cared to be for the moment.

Her servants saw to my every comfort and made sure I was groomed, fed, and dressed in clothes that had been magically aired and brushed anew. I was—as Nora predicted—a little wobbly, but that was hardly comparable to the twinges in a number of my muscles and joints unaccustomed to certain horizontal activities. I also found it necessary to tread carefully in order to spare myself from another kind of unexpected discomfort, for there was a decided tenderness between my legs due to last night's many goings-on. Perhaps a few days of rest would not be so bad for me, after all.

A coach was engaged to take me to Warburton's. It was early afternoon by now, but I had no great concern about my tardy return—not until Nora's coach stopped at the front steps and Oliver burst out the door.

"My God! Where on earth have you been?"

"I told Warburton—"

"Yes, yes, and so you went off for the night. Well-a-day, man, you could have at least given him a hint on where you'd be so I could find you."

"Is there some trouble?"

"Only that we're supposed to be on our way to Fonteyn House to meet Mother by now."

Oh dear. With that pronouncement of doom hanging in the air like a curse, he hustled me inside.

Warburton greeted me with a grin and a wink and I had the decency to blush to his face. Courtiers to Nora we might be, but I wasn't yet ready to talk about it with him now. If ever.

"You're white as a ghost, but seem well enough," he said. "Poor Oliver thought you'd fallen in with a press gang or worse."

I regarded his own pale skin with new eyes. "Yes. I do beg everyone's pardon. It was wrong of me to go off so suddenly. I didn't think that I would be so long."

"One never does," he purred. "Come in and sit and tell us all about her."

"Absolutely not!" Oliver howled from the stairs he was taking two at a time. "As soon as they bring down your baggage, we are leaving."

Warburton shrugged expressively. "Another day, then. She must have been extraordinary, though, eh?"

I had to remember that he was still under the impression I'd been with some servant girl. "She was, indeed. That is the only word that could possibly describe her."

His eyed widened with inner laughter. "Heavens, you've fallen in love, and after but one night. Do you plan to see her again?"

"Yes, I'm sure I will. At least I hope so."

"Then you'll have to lay in a supply of eel-skins. No offense against your lady, but you don't want to pick up a case of the clap or pox while you're with her. They'll also keep you from fathering a brat, y'know."

"Uh..."

"No arguments. There's not a doctor in the land who won't agree with me. Oliver would tell you the same, only I'm sure he's too shy, but once you're up at Cambridge, ask him straight out, and he'll tell you where you can get some. Or me, if you can wait that long. I won't be leaving for another week or so."

He was different from the preoccupied man I'd left last night, and very different from the high-spirited suitor I'd first met: genial and interested in things outside of himself. I again wondered what Nora had said to him. I knew just how persuasive she could be but this taxed all understanding.

Oliver returned, followed by several footmen wrestling with my trunk and other things. He had asked the coach that brought me to wait and now supervised its loading. Finished, he rushed back and wrung Warburton's hand.

"Sorry to have to hare off, but you know how Mother is."

"It's all right, my dear fellow. I'll see you at the same rooms later this month?"

"Certainly! Come on, Jonathan. I'm not Joshua, I can't make the sun stand still, though God knows it would be damned convenient to do so right now." He seized my arm and pulled me out. I waved once at

Warburton, who grinned again, then tumbled down the steps and into the coach. Oliver's fine horse was tethered behind, its saddle and tack littering the coach's floor and tripping me as I charged inside. By a lucky twist, I managed to correctly land my backside on a seat.

Oliver collapsed opposite me with a weary sigh. "Damn good fortune you picked this instead of a chair or wagon. When we're clear of the town traffic, we should make good time."

Once more I apologized to him.

"You needn't worry about my feelings, it's Mother who may take things badly. Some of her friends were at that party last night and it could get back to her that we were out having a good time instead of hurrying home to introduce you to her. She has to have things her way or it's the devil to pay otherwise."

That sounded uncomfortably familiar. Ah, well, if his mother and mine were so alike, I would only have to endure her for a short while. Cambridge had suddenly become highly appealing to me, and if I was anxious to get there and take up my studies, then she could hardly object to such an attitude. All I need do was keep silent on the source of its inspiration.

"Has Warburton spoken much about Miss Jones?" I asked.

"Eh? No, I don't think so. He got a bit drunk last night, but that's all I can recall. I suppose his proposal was a failure, but usually when a girl turns him down he sulks in bed for a week. He seemed in good spirits today."

"Why do you think it was a failure?"

"Had he succeeded, he would have told us."

"You seem rather incurious."

"It's hardly my business." His expression changed from indifference to interest. "Oh-oh, are you thinking of—"

"Of what?"

"If the beauteous Miss Jones has turned him down, it would smooth the path for you, wouldn't it, dear Coz? Only I'm not sure what Tony would make of that. He has the devil's own temper at times."

"The jealous sort, is he?"

Oliver shrugged.

That could be another reason why Nora refused his offer. "Jealous or not, it is the lady who should have the last word on whom she chooses to spend her time with."

"Yes, I've always thought that way myself. So much the better if she chooses to spend it with you."

I lost my power of speech for a few moments.

"Don't look so surprised, I saw you following the girl's aunt into the maze. From the look on your face I knew it wasn't to have a quiet talk with *her*. You needn't worry; I'm not one to tell tales. I've found that it's healthier to stay well removed from any romantic intrigues that are of no direct concern to me. All I ask is that if you have a question, come on out with it. This hedging around for information is bad for my liver."

So. Dear Cousin Oliver wasn't as simple as he pretended. Perhaps it was the Fonteyn blood. I chuckled. "All right. You've my word on it. I'll even drop the subject. It's bad manners to talk about a man when he's not present, anyway."

"Heavens," he said, returning to his normal careless manner. "Then what *shall* we talk about?"

"There's one thing that comes to mind. It's what Warburton was saying to me in the hall before we left."

"What's that?"

"He said you'd help."

"If I can. Help about what?"

"I'm not exactly sure. Could you please tell me…What's an eel-skin?"

CHAPTER
SEVEN

MY INITIAL MEETING with the family's reigning grand matriarch, Elizabeth Therese Fonteyn Marling, left me with the kind of lingering impression that months afterward could still raise a shiver between my shoulders. She had lived up—or perhaps down—to my worst expectations and more. She and my mother were eerily alike, physically and mentally, though my aunt was of a more thought-filled and colder nature, which, considering Mother, was really saying something in her favor. After that, it was about all I *could* say in her favor.

Her husband had died years ago—Oliver had only a faint memory of him—and since then she was the uncontested head of both the Fonteyn and Marling clans. She held her place over all the others, including the men, by the force of her personality and the wealth she'd inherited from her father. As my father had done, her husband had signed an agreement forswearing all rights to her money before he was granted permission to marry her. Whether it had been a match based on love or property I was never to find out.

Fonteyn house was nearly as great in size as the Bolyn place, but with much larger grounds and so many more trees pressing close on its flanks that one could mistake the lands for primeval forest. Our coach passed through very wide iron gates with spikes topping the bars, and though it was still light, I fancied a decided gloom settling upon us. That, I thought, came from Oliver, who by turns either babbled about nonsensical things or dropped into profound silence. He seemed distinctly uncomfortable, but when I asked him what was amiss, he would only shrug.

"She's a bit of a lion," he said, meaning his mother. "Just agree with everything she says and you should be able to escape with only a few claw marks rather than a full mauling."

After dealing with my own mad matriarch, I thought myself braced and ready for what lay ahead.

The coach rolled up to the front and huge doors opened from within. As we got out, a handful of young footmen rushed from the darkness of the house to see to the unloading of my baggage. They hurried as though their lives depended on it.

Oliver stayed one of them and murmured to him. The lad nodded several times, put down his burden, and hared off into the house.

"He's announcing our arrival to Mother," Oliver explained. "She's usually in her drawing room this time of day, but it's best to be sure."

"Perhaps I should change first." Except for some boots I'd pulled on for the journey in case we had to do any walking, I was still in the somber clothes I'd worn to the party. Thanks to the attentions of Nora's servants they were still presentable, but I thought perhaps a different coat would be more suitable to the occasion.

"No, no, you're fine. In fact I think she'll approve of your apparent sobriety. She detests anything smacking of the frivolous."

Before I could offer further objections Oliver took my elbow and guided me into the ancestral stronghold. I needed his help, for it only then struck me just how much wealth it had taken to build such a pile. There is a great difference in knowing the family to be rich and seeing the evidence of the fact. Grandfather Fonteyn had done very well for himself, it seemed, when he began buying land out from under his neighbors and using the revenues from the acreage to purchase more. Of course, it had taken him decades to build up his fortune and an exceptionally prudent fist to hold onto it, but by and large the family—that is, the Fonteyns and Marlings—lived well.

Though not in anywise a castle—it was much too modern—Fonteyn House exuded an oppressive atmosphere reminiscent of the Medieval dungeons described in Rapelji's beloved history books. Though this structure boasted as many windows as Warburton's, these were shrouded with thick curtains, blocking all light and warmth from entry. The halls on either hand stretched into a chill gloom so thick I could not see their far end. The main staircase also led up into darkness.

"This way," he said, indicating the left-hand wing. Our boot heels sounded loud as we trod over the black and white marble floor. For a moment I had an absurd impression of being a chess piece on an impossibly large board, perhaps a knight about to be sacrificed to the opponent's queen.

Oliver paused before a set of doors. Closed fast, they looked to be sturdy enough to fend off a real siege. "In here. You're on your own, I'm afraid."

"You're not coming in?"

"I'll be behind you, but will have to be silent for the most part. She'll dismiss me early on, so you'll be alone and unsupported."

At this point I actually wavered.

He saw it. "I'm really sorry, Coz, but she has her ways. It's all to a purpose. She wants to see you sweat. She's a fiend toward those she wants under her thumb, and this is how she begins the bullying."

"Oh, indeed?" Father had taught me how to deal with bullies of all types.

Oliver saw that as well. "For God's sake, don't take it as a challenge. There's nothing she likes better, and she knows far more than both of us together how to put down what she sees as defiance. Trust me, your interview will be much shorter and less scathing if you play the obedient and humble sheep."

I could see he was absolutely serious. In light of the things he'd already told me and what I'd gleaned from Father before my departure, it seemed sensible to take his advice. "All right. I'll tread carefully."

He looked relieved. "Excellent. We'll have some good brandy afterward. Lots. You'll want it."

He knocked twice on one of the doors, then opened it like a well-trained footman, standing out of sight of whoever lurked inside.

With a dry mouth, I straightened my spine and went in. The room was long, with a low ceiling and but one window. Candles burned in all the corners, but were hard-pressed to push back the gloom. A fireplace was at its mid-point, dormant now. Above it hung a full-length portrait of old Grandfather Fonteyn himself, painted during his prime to judge by his apparent youth and antique clothing. A strangely unremarkable face. Either the artist was an inferior talent, or he'd been most careful not to reveal the truth about his subject. He'd painted a likeness, but nothing of the soul as some were able to do. He had done something with the eyes, though, for they seemed to look right at me from their height.

I refused to let a bit of paint and canvas perturb me. The old man was dead and gone, and I had his living descendent to worry about.

Next to the fireplace between two large candelabra ... a throne.

Or so it seemed to me. I gathered the impression of a large and richly carved chair and velvet cushions. Its proportions were such that they might dwarf an ordinary occupant, but the women seated there seemed to fill the whole of its space and beyond. She was of a normal height to match my mother, but possessed a quality in her bearing that made her seem much taller than me.

As I crossed the length of her drawing room, there came to me the creeping sensation that I'd not left home after all, for she looked uncannily like Mother, right down to an identical ivory scratching stick clutched in one hand. Dear God. I barely heard Oliver trailing ghost-like behind me.

Elizabeth Marling raked me over with her hard little eyes, her thin mouth growing thinner as it pulled back into an easy sneer. The surrounding lines in the heavily painted skin had been incised there by many years of repetition. I could expect no mercy or understanding from this woman, nor even the pretense of familial affection.

Oliver, using a quiet, flat voice that seemed to not be his own, made introductions, formal as a lord chamberlain.

My aunt snorted at me. "Marie said that you were a devil and you've the looks for it, boy, but if you've any ideas of devilry while you're under my watch you can put 'em out of your head this instant."

Such were her first words of welcome to her only nephew, delivered before I'd completed my bow to her. "Yes, Aunt Therese," I mumbled meekly.

"You will address me as 'Aunt Fonteyn,'" she snapped.

"Yes, Aunt Fonteyn," I immediately responded.

"It's a good name and better than you deserve. If you didn't have a half share of my father's blood I wouldn't waste my time on you, but for his sake and the sake of my dear sister Marie, I'll do what I can to civilize you."

"Yes, ma'am. Thank you, ma'am." Civilize? What did she think I'd do, use the soup tureen for a chamber pot in the middle of supper with the local curate?

Tempting thought.

"Something amusing you, Jonathan Fonteyn?"

"No, ma'am." I managed to hide the inevitable wince my middle name inspired.

"How is my sister?"

"Well, ma'am, when I left her."

"Have you letters? She would send letters with you."

"Yes, ma'am." I had a thick packet of them folded in oil cloth in one pocket, hastily retrieved from my boxes on the ride over. I held them out.

"There." She pointed the scratching stick to a small table to my right.

I placed them on top as though they were a fragile treasure. Mother had strictly charged me with their care and delivery. She gave me to understand that should the ship sink I was to save them before saving myself. They'd spent the entire crossing in the small chest where I kept my more treasured valuables. In all that time I wondered what was in them, but honor prevented me from breaking any of their wax seals and reading the contents. Intuition told me I wouldn't have liked what was there, anyway.

"You, boy," she said, addressing Oliver as though he were a servant of the lowest order. He seemed to be staring hard at some invisible object just off her left ear. "Get out of here. Have Meg bring tea. Mind that she has it hot this time if she knows what's good for her."

He fled.

She turned her gaze back upon me, and I strove to find whatever it was that Oliver had seen. There was nothing, of course, but it was better than trying to face down her basilisk glare.

"Naught to say for yourself, boy?" she demanded.

"I deemed it best to wait upon your pleasure, Aunt Fonteyn."

"Ha! Talk like your father, do you? He could make a pretty speech twenty-odd years ago. Does he still have that sly and easy tongue?"

"He enjoys a good, intelligent conversation, ma'am," I said, trying to be neutral.

That stayed her a moment. Perhaps she was considering whether or not I was making an impertinence about our own exchange. My voice and expression were all innocence, though. Mother might have pounced upon it, but Aunt Fonteyn let it pass. Probably waiting for a more vulnerable opening. The checkered black and white marble pattern served as a floor here, too, a continuance of the likeness to a chess game. Though we were on a level to each other, this queen seemed to loom over me, ready to strike me from the board.

"What about that sister of yours? How is Elizabeth Antoinette?"

Elizabeth, God bless her, hated her middle name as much as I did mine. I was glad she wasn't present for she might not have been able to hold on to a bland face. "She was well when I last saw her."

"She look much like your mother?"

"Many have remarked on the resemblance, ma'am, and say that they are very alike."

"In looks only, I'm sure," she sniffed, as though it were a crime rather than a blessing not to share the same temperament. "The Barrett blood, no doubt. Anyone to marry her, yet?"

"No, ma'am. Not before I left."

"She's past twenty, isn't she?"

"Nineteen, ma'am."

"She'll be a spinster for life if she doesn't hurry along, but I suppose there's nothing suitable on that miserable island of yours."

She made my beautiful home sound like a barren rock barely able to stand clear of a high tide. What *had* Mother been writing to her?

"And you? Any prospects?"

Nora's sweet face flashed across my mind's eye. I would not defile that private delight by mentioning her existence to this creature. "No, ma'am."

"And just as well. You're to have none, y'hear? Not without my approval."

"Yes, ma'am."

"We'll see how you settle in. If you behave yourself we just *might* be able to find some wench who'll put up with you, providing she's got decent money and a name."

"Yes, ma'am."

"Until then you'll keep your attention on your studies. There are no wastrels in this family, y'hear?"

"Yes, ma'am."

"Going to practice law, eh? Then I hope to God you do better at it than your father."

I'd expected a taunt like that and did not react. For the next two hours and thirty-two minutes I stood statue-like before her doing my level best not to react to anything she said.

She lashed me with close questioning about my life and future and meted out summary judgments, all severe, of my answers. I recall the passage of the time very well because of the presence of a clock on the mantel. It was clearly ticking, but I grew certain that the mechanism of the minute hand was defective, for the damned thing hardly seemed to move. I could have sworn days had passed rather than hours before she finally, *finally* dismissed me.

I nearly reeled out the door, exhausted, yet horribly stirred up inside, and sweating like a blacksmith. It was a nasty, familiar feeling; one I'd thought I'd left behind with Mother. Here it seemed doubled, for it was doubly undeserved. Mother was all bitterness and reprisal for imagined slights; Aunt Fonteyn had no such delusions. She enjoyed inflicting pain for its own sake. She was worse than Mother, for Mother's graceless treatment of people might possibly be excused by her unstable mind; Aunt Fonteyn had no such defense for her behavior. Mother could not help herself, but my aunt was very much in control of her conduct.

Oliver met me in the hall with a full-to-the-brim cup of the promised brandy. I was in such haste to drink, the first gulp left me choking.

"Steady, now, Cousin. Give it a chance to work," he cautioned.

His sympathetic concern made me smile in spite of my red-faced anger. "You've done this before, have you?"

"Far too often."

"How do you bear it?" I asked, meaning to make it light, but it did not come out that way.

In response to my tone, his eyes flashed at the solidly shut door to his mother's lair. "By knowing that if God has *any* mercy, I'll live to dance on her grave," he whispered with a raw vehemence that made me blink. He seemed to realize that he had perhaps shown too much honesty and made an effort to cover with a careless gesture at my cup. "Come, finish that off and I'll show you around the old ruin, introduce you to some of the ancestors we've got framed on the walls. They're a dull and dusty lot, but quiet company. Your duty's done until supper."

I groaned slightly at the thought of actually sharing a meal with my aunt.

"It won't be too bad," he said with a kindly assurance that reminded me achingly of Elizabeth. "Just agree with everything she says and afterward we can get properly drunk. We'll leave for Cambridge at first light. My word of honor on it."

❖ ❖ ❖

WITH MUCH RELIEF, we did indeed depart, and well before dawn. Though still sickly from too much wine and another dose of Aunt Fonteyn, it was preferable to recover in a lurching coach than under that woman's roof. I don't remember much of this last part of my long journey from Long Island, just hanging out the coach window to be sick a few times, moping for Nora, and gaping with unhappy shock at the dreary monotony of the countryside as we got closer to our goal.

The thoughts of Nora were the best and worst part of the ride. I had no word from her, of course, but hoped for some. Several times I entertained the happy fantasy that she was well ahead of us and already waiting for my arrival or perhaps she might even catch up with us in her own coach as if in some popular ballad.

I was in love, a state that does not lend itself to logical thought. Eventually I stopped looking out the window and filled the time by speculating how long it would really take her to catch up to me.

Too long, I concluded, shifting restlessly in my seat while Oliver sensibly snored away the hours.

We arrived in Cambridge the next day, choosing to spend the night at an inn to give ourselves and the horses a rest rather than pushing on into exhaustion. Had we known how black the sheets were we'd have made other, cleaner sleeping arrangements, such as the stables. Certainly they would have had fewer fleas than the ones we endured.

Nora had expressed a low opinion of the place that was to be my home for the next few years. True, there was little enough in the countryside around Cambridge to draw my interest, but the many buildings comprising the university were no less than magnificent. Oliver was very familiar with the area and I was glad to have him as guide, else I would have soon lost myself amongst the various colleges. He knew his business and with a surprising lack of confusion led me through the intricacies of where to go, which tutor to see, and finding a place to live.

The last was the easiest, for I was to share rooms in a house with Oliver and Tony Warburton, taking over one previously occupied by a friend who had passed his examines at the last term and left. With hope pulsing through my brain, I immediately wrote a loving note to Nora to inform her of my new address and posted it off to London. Cambridge wasn't very large, but I wanted to take no chance on our missing one another.

One day succeeded the next, and I was kept extremely busy, for there were a thousand new things to learn before the start of the term. Between them, Oliver and Warburton had a number of friends who drifted in and out of the rooms to talk, share a drink, or even take a nap. Not surprisingly, many of them were also studying medicine, though there were a few reading law like myself. A sharp contrast to the placid pace I'd known on Long Island, I readily embraced the variety of this hectic new life fully and strove to enjoy every stimulating moment.

But Nora was always in my head, and though fully occupied, my hours were frequently far too long. I worried, fretted, and kept a lookout for her all the time that I was awake and dreamed about her when I was not.

Each time I saw a coach and four—and there weren't that many in Cambridge—my heart leaped toward my mouth, only to drop heavily back into place from disappointment when it turned out not to be hers.

One drizzling evening almost a week later Oliver and I were returning from a dinner with some other scholars. A coach waited on the street outside our house. I recognized it instantly, swiftly discounted the recognition, for I'd grown used to having my expectations dashed, then threw aside my doubts once I saw the driver's livery. I rushed forward, leaving Oliver flat-footed in the thin mist calling an annoyed question after me.

The coachman knew me—fortunate, since I had forgotten his face— and had a folded bit of paper ready to hand over as I approached. It was an invitation. I gave it only a quick glance, enough to pick out the words I wanted most to see, before hauling myself into the coach, too impatient to wait for the footman's assistance.

Oliver trotted up, his mouth wide and eyes popping. I waved the paper at him. "She's here!" I cried from the window as we pulled away. He did not find it necessary to ask who and waved back with his walking stick to wish me luck. Just before I withdrew inside, I caught a glimpse of a man emerging from our house. Tony Warburton. He paused to stare for a moment, then turned to Oliver, obviously with a question to ask. It looked like my poor cousin would be caught in the middle of things after all.

Heartlessly, I left him to it. Any guilt I might have felt in taking the place Warburton desired for himself simply did not exist. I was going to see Nora and that's all that mattered.

She lived surprisingly close, and I speculated that she'd arranged it so on purpose, for surely she could have afforded something more fashionable elsewhere. Not that the house we stopped at was a hovel. It proved comfortable enough once I was ushered inside, but it was decidedly smaller than her London residence, and bore signs that the unpacking was still in progress.

"Why, Mr. Barrett! How nice to see you again!" Mrs. Poole rustled down a steep stairway. "You're looking very well. Does the academic life suit you?"

Though I wanted to see Nora more than anyone or anything else, I was moved to patience by the sincere goodness of the woman's manner. "I believe so, ma'am, but I have not yet begun my studies."

"I am sure that you will do well once you start. Nora tells me that you have a fine mind."

In the short time we'd spent together, Nora and I had hardly concerned ourselves with intellectual pursuits. I searched Mrs. Poole's face for the least hint of a false note or derisive humor and found none. She was about the same age as my mother and aunt, but there was a universe of difference between their temperaments. She guided me to a room just off the entry and saw that I was comfortable. A fire blazed against the damp, and hot tea, cakes and brandy were at hand. Candles burned in every sconce and in the many holders scattered throughout the room as if for a party. I could not help but be reminded of that first night. My heart began to pound.

Mrs. Poole excused herself with a fond smile. She was hardly out of the room before Nora swept in.

My memory had played tricks with me in her absence. The face and form I'd carried in my head differed slightly from the reality. I'd made her taller and set her eyes closer together, forgotten the fine texture of her skin, the graceful shape of her arms. Seeing her now was like meeting her anew all over again and feeling that perfect, most enchanting shock as time stopped for me. My heart strained against the pause as though it alone could start everything up once more. It needed help, though, and that could come only from Nora.

Her eyes alight, she rushed toward me. All the clocks in the world resumed ticking even as the blood began to swiftly pulse within my whirling brain.

The next few minutes were a blur of light, of joy, of holding her fast while trying to whisper out my love in broken words. Broken, for I was constantly interrupted as she pressed her mouth upon mine. I finally gave up talking altogether for a while, which really was the best course of action to take, considering.

"I was afraid you'd forgotten me," I said, finally breaking off to breathe.

"Never. It took more time than I'd expected to ready everything for the journey."

"Can you stay?"

"For as long as I like." She smoothed my hair back with her fingers. "That shall be for a very long time, I think."

My heart soared.

Further talk could wait. We were too hungry for one another and climbed the stairs to go straight to her room. As before, Mrs. Poole and the servants were nowhere to be seen.

The bed was different, but the silk sheets and feather pillows were there, along with her portrait and dozens of candles. I helped her from her clothes, my hands clumsy as I tried to recall how I'd done it before. Nora chuckled at my puzzlement, but encouraged me as well. My turn to laugh came when she tried to undo the buttons of my breeches. I had grown decidedly inspired while undressing her, and they'd become rather a tight fit. She was having trouble finding enough slack to accomplish her task.

"There!" she crowed finally. "Isn't that much better?"

My back to the bed, I teetered unsteadily on one leg as she worked to pull my breeches down. "Indeed, but I think that things might be improved if we..." Giving in to a second's loss of balance, I toppled onto the mattress, dragging her down on top of me, laughing. The bedclothes and pillows billowed around us like clouds.

My heart was flying.

Thus began my *real* education at Cambridge.

Nora taught me much about love, ever interested in helping me explore and develop my own blooming skills. While others might revile her experience, I reveled in it. She filled my life, my thoughts, the food I ate, and the very air I breathed. The whole world seemed to sing from her presence.

Not without interruption, though.

Once the term started I had to face the necessity of more mundane learning. But for her gentle urging to begin the work, then finish what I'd started, I might have abandoned the university completely to spend all my time with her.

My activities were—to my mind—unevenly divided between study, socializing with my friends, and Nora. I wanted to be with her constantly, but yielded to her sweet insistence that she had to have some hours apart for herself and her own friends. Soon we settled into a pattern that suited us both. I visited her several evenings a week as my studies permitted. Unless I had to get up early the next day, I would stay quite late, and occasionally the whole night. Her only irritating custom was to always wake first and leave me to sleep in. Irritating to me, for I would have liked to have the opportunity to love her once more before departing. I chided her on it, for at the very least she could stay for breakfast.

"I am not at my best in the morning, Jonathan," she replied. "So do not ask me to remain with you."

"The afternoons, then," I said.

"No." She was firm, but kind about it. "Your days are your own as are mine. This has always been my way. I love you dearly, but please do not ask me to change myself. That is the one thing I will not do for you."

Put in that context, I could hardly refuse her, though it troubled me at the time.

Not for long. After a time it did not seem important.

Of her other friends I saw little and we did not socialize. If I arrived too early, I either waited in the street or Mrs. Poole would chat with me until whatever visitor there departed. Many of them were fellow students, Tony Warburton being in their number. They were young, of course, invariably handsome, fit and usually moneyed. None ever stayed very long, hardly more than five minutes, as if they had only called to pay their respects before going on to some other errand. They gave scant attention to me or even to one another, which struck me as odd. Whenever we met elsewhere her name never came up in conversation.

Oddly, I had no jealousy for them and though they were aware of me, sensed none directed at myself. Tony Warburton seemed to be the exception to this, though much of what I thought I observed had to come from my own imaginings. Now and then I'd feel a sharp pinch of guilt in my vitals, and doubtless the feeling would spill over onto my face in his presence. In turn, I was prone to interpret any odd look or comment from him as part of the resentment he should have for my taking the special place in Nora's heart he'd ardently hoped to achieve for himself. As the weeks passed I wondered whether I should talk to him about her, but when I raised the subject with Nora, she resolutely discouraged it, telling me not to worry.

Warburton's manner toward me was otherwise as open and friendly as when we were introduced, but some points of his personality had altered enough so that even Oliver had to comment.

"He's not as preoccupied over women these days, have you noticed? Used to fall in love at regular intervals, y'know."

"Perhaps he has been studying hard," I said.

"Drinking, you mean."

That I had not noticed. "We all drink, Oliver."

"Yes, but he's been doing more than the rest of us, and that's quite a lot."

"He never seems the worse for it."

"Tony holds it well enough, but I know him better than you. I think his mind is yet fixed on Miss Jones. He didn't make much of a row when she refused him, which he's never failed to do before. He doesn't like to be disappointed when he's set his heart on something he wants."

"Perhaps because he's still friends with her," I murmured.

"I've known that to hurt more than help. Sometimes it's best to make a clean break or else one or the other party ends up pining away for things that cannot be."

"If he loved her I could agree with you, but he's said and done nothing to indicate that."

"Not while you're around, anyway."

"He's spoken to you?"

"Not exactly, but he puts on a damnably grim face when he knows you're going over for a visit. He sulks awhile, then gets drunk."

"He hides it well."

"Doesn't he just? You don't notice because he's always passed out by the time you get back. He's always all right in the morning—except for a bad head."

We all suffered from that malady at frequent intervals. "Should I do anything about him, you think?"

"Don't know, old lad. Just thought I'd mention it, is all."

This is a warning, I thought.

After that Oliver refrained from further talk on the subject. More than once he'd stated that what went on between me and Nora and Nora and his friend was none of his business and seemed content to let it remain so. I respected this and did not attempt to draw him farther out, but now that I'd been made aware of them, I did note the small changes in Warburton, and thought about them frequently afterward. Again, when I spoke of him to Nora, she told me not to be troubled.

THE SOCIAL DRAWBACKS of an institution like Cambridge became apparent from the start, as I realized with dismay that the majority of my activities precluded the presence of women. There were dinners and parties of all kinds, but for tutors and students only. Not once but many times Nora and I discussed the utter unfairness of such ridiculous social partition.

Yes, we did find time to talk. One can occupy oneself with love-making for only so long before requiring a respite. During these intervals I discovered Nora's mind was more than equal to her beauty. We found much common ground between us regarding people and politics, history and literature. Nora was very well read and, though barred from the many volumes in the university library, she somehow managed to gain access to them in pursuit of her own literary amusements. I assumed that one of her other friends assisted her in this.

"If it weren't for books I would become quite mad," she confessed while paging through a rare volume I'd gleaned from a bookseller and presented as a gift for her library. She had a passion for history and a particular interest in biographies. This one was about the lives of various European monarchs.

"You are the sanest person I've ever met," I said. We were in her parlour downstairs. She'd made it a very pretty place with new flowered paper enriching the walls and the kind of furnishings to comfort a weary body. A large fire in the grate warmed the whole room. "Why ever should you go mad?"

"Why should any of us?" she countered, which was hardly an answer. Perhaps I was expected to supply one.

I sank onto a wide settee, an idle thought passing through my head about what an excellent support it would be for love-making. All in good time. "My father thinks it's in the blood."

"He's probably correct," she said absently. She knew all about Mother's side of the family by now.

"Are you worried you might be risking yourself?" I asked this in light of her sensual preferences. "You know ... you *could* be courting the possibility of madness whenever you drink from me."

She looked up from her book, surprised until she saw my smile. "Oh, my dear, hardly that. I agree with your father's opinion regarding one's natural inheritances, such as hair or eye color. In regard to myself, if I did not have such friends as these" — she gestured at her shelves of books— "my life would be unbearably tedious. You have no idea how heavy an empty hour can be even when surrounded by people. I do. I once endured years of them, years of grinding ignorance and boredom muddled together with contempt and jealousy for that which I could not understand." There was no pain in her tone, though, only gloomy regret.

"How old were you?" It could not have been so very long ago.

Her smile returned. "I was not old, Jonathan. I was young; very, very young."

I'd never asked her age, but by even the most generous estimate, she could not have been more than four and twenty, if that much. "I see. And now you are very, very old."

"Yes," she said lightly. "I'm positively ancient."

I fell in with her humor. "But you magically preserve yourself by drinking my blood."

"Of course."

An idea lanced through my skull, a rather obvious one. Why had it never occurred to me before? "And that of others like Tony Warburton?"

Her gaze turned guarded against any suggestion of jealousy from me. There was none, only curiosity. "Yes. I have to, you see. There's not enough in you alone to sustain me."

"You speak as though you live upon it," I said seriously.

"Well...I do."

There followed a lengthy silence from me as I sought to comprehend her meaning. "You're not joking, are you?"

She stood by the fire, my book in hand, watching me carefully. "No."

"You must be." My voice had gone up a little. A small breath of unease curled against my spine like a draft.

"Believe what you will."

She was *not* joking. "How can you? I mean, *how* is it possible?"

Nora shrugged. "It's how it is with me. Accept it."

"Surely you must know. Were you born like this? Did your mother nurse you on milk...or blood?"

She made no reply.

My unease was roughly swept aside by something else, something more solid than the air but just as invisible. Darker. Colder. It edged beneath my skin, oozed along my muscles, squeezed my lungs, chilled my racing heart.

Her secret, like a curtain hanging between us that I had previously— perhaps wittingly—ignored, was torn away by that invasion. I caught my first glimpse of what lay beyond. The full understanding I thought I wanted burst upon my brain.

"Jonathan?"

"It's true?"

"That I live on blood. Yes." Her tone was steady, her demeanor...still watchful.

"Is *that* why there are so many handsome, hearty young men around you, why they come calling so often, why you require their silence...."

"Yes."

"And I am one of them. You—your *favorite*." *Oh, dear God....*

She fixed her gaze hard on me. "Jonathan, calm yourself."

My mind swooped like a bird struck by an unexpected rush of wind. I found myself struggling to right myself, but felt trapped, pressed down, held in place by the power of her eyes.

"*Calm* yourself." Her voice was firm and clear and more forceful than normal. It streamed through my ears, my thoughts, my body, rising to drown me from within. I abruptly gave up fighting. It was the only thing to do. Anything else was foolish. Nothing else was important. Not my new knowledge. Not my new terror. Not even myself.

She was seated next to me. When had she moved?

"Listen and hear me out, Jonathan."

Her melodious tone soothed, reassured, filled me with peace. I could not find tongue to speak. Could only nod.

"I do what I must to live and maintain myself," she said. "The others come by and for a moment or two I gift them with a unique pleasure, and they gift me with life. The ones who can afford it provide a small donation of money. I have none of my own, no family, no fortune, no other means to live."

"They give you money?" My voice was normal once more, but at the same time it sounded as though someone else were using it. The sudden tranquility she'd impressed upon me was in danger of splintering like thin ice on a deep pool. I was walking where I did not wish to go.

"When I ask, when I'm in need. A little from each, so they are not beggared, the same as with their blood. If that makes me a whore, then so be it."

I stirred, writhing inside. "No ...."

"I've *no* other way!" She collected herself and stared hard until I felt at ease again. "But ... you understand that now. You completely understand. Don't you?"

"I ... yes."

"And it's all right. It doesn't bother you in the least. I'm still the woman you love."

Her gaze wavered, and I felt my mind clearing a bit, the darkness on my heart lifting. I did seem remarkably serene, considering.

"There's one very important difference, Jonathan. You are not merely my favorite. You are the man *I* love. I may receive some pleasure from them and give it, but you are the *only* man I take to my bed. You're the only man I want there. Believe that, if you believe nothing else."

And I did. Wholly. My heart grew so full I thought it would burst. I wanted to touch her, but she still held me fast with a mere look, watching for some minutes. Only gradually did the apprehension leave her expression and tension depart from her posture. Only then was I able to move. I lifted one hand, fingers touching her face very lightly. With some surprise I realized there were tears glistening on her cheek.

"Oh, Nora. Please don't cry. There's no reason."

"There are a thousand. But it's all right now. I'll stop." She found a handkerchief and used it. "I just don't want to lose you. Or hurt you. Ever. But sometimes I can't help it because of my nature. It forces me to—"

"It doesn't matter. Truly it doesn't." I meant it with all my soul. "I'll show you ...." I eased her arms around my body. She gave no resistance as I pulled her close. Turning slightly arranged us so her lips almost brushed my neck.

"Jonathan ...."

I cast free of my neckcloth and presented my bare throat to her, leaving no ambiguity as to what I desired to give. I loved her. Trusted her. *Wanted* her.

"But here ...? We can go upstairs."

Now it was my turn to fix her with a look. "Yes, we can. But I want you to do with me as you do with them. Right here, exactly the same."

"Why?"

"So I won't have to wonder what it's like."

Her eyes went wide. I'd surprised her.

"Then after, if you choose, take me to your bed."

The room was very silent as I waited for her response. I heard only the fire cracking and—it could have been fancy only—the very beating of my heart.

Her arms suddenly found strength and pulled me close. I gasped when she bit down, and it was from pure joy.

PACKETS OF LETTERS from home eventually arrived, months out of date but eagerly welcomed. I always read the last one first to be certain that all was well before putting them in proper order.

Elizabeth's were the longest, with page after page covered with news and the kind of observations she knew would amuse me. She lightly recounted the most mundane events of home, making them interesting; her writing was so clear that I could almost hear her voice in my ear again. I missed her dreadfully.

Father's letters were shorter, but full of affection and pride, which in turn gave me pride in myself as well as a certain humility that I should have the high regard of such a man. He'd left many friends behind in England and encouraged me to seek them out to give them his greetings. In this task I was more than a little remiss, for some had died, others lived too far away, and by now I had friends of my own to occupy the days. I did manage to look up one or two old fellows who remembered him, but having little else in common with them, the visits were awkward. As quickly as common courtesy allowed, I would excuse myself to return to my own haunts, duty done.

Jericho had the least to say, curtailed by his own lack of free time and anything to write. This was a comfort, for it meant that the household was still running smoothly. He did state that Elizabeth's silent feud against Mother had eased somewhat. My canny sister made her point with the more alert members of the congregation that Sunday, but the less sensitive had ignored her bruises or simply disbelieved how she'd gotten them. This small group became part of Mother's new circle of friends. Though Elizabeth held them in contempt, they did divert much of Mother's attention from her.

Mother did not write at all. This was a relief, for it released me from the duty of writing back, and God knows I had nothing to say to the woman. I suppose it was the same for her.

Other notes were enclosed, from friends, from Rapelji, and surprisingly, from Dr. Beldon. He was cordial and warm and floridly polite to the point of fawning. His letters I regarded with distaste, but felt obligated to answer. My replies were brief, and by their brevity, hopefully discouraging to further correspondence. It never worked. I would have felt ashamed, for he was an interesting and intelligent man, but those qualities were undermined by his toad-eating ways, else I might have welcomed his friendship.

My letters home were about my life at Cambridge and the direction of my studies. I wrote of my new friends and of Cousin Oliver, but left out quite a lot on the rest of the family. Doubtless Mother would be reading them and my honest opinions of her dearest relatives would have turned her apoplectic. These views I confided to a private journal I kept that she would never see. Of Nora, at least in my letters home, I said nothing.

The last months of that year fairly galloped past. Though I did well enough in my studies, they did not hold my interest. Compared to Rapelji's style of tutoring what I worked on now seemed childishly easy.

His most valuable lesson to me had been the cultivation of a good memory; this, combined with his frequent drilling of Latin and Greek, stood me through the most difficult of my reading. While other lads often despaired of pounding anything into their heads, I seemed to soak it up like a cleaning rag. This pleased me, for it left more time to devote to Nora. As the days grew shorter with the approach of winter, so did my nights with her lengthen and grow richer.

"This is my birthday," she said one evening in November in the same tone of voice one uses to comment on the weather.

We were comfortable in her drawing room, idly pushing around a deck of cards. Coal snapped in the fireplace; I was warm and pleased to sit back and digest the excellent supper I'd recently shared with Mrs. Poole, who had long departed for bed. Nora had been at the table but had not eaten, as was her custom, and was quiet for the most part. Perhaps this announcement explained her preoccupation. Why had there been no marking of the event?

I expressed my congratulations and regret that I had no present to offer. "I wish you had told me."

"I hardly ever tell anyone. People make such a fuss over it, and there's little enough that I want."

"There must be something."

"Yes, or else I wouldn't have mentioned it. It's not anything one may buy from a shop. It's something only you are able to give me."

This sounded most promising. "What, then?"

She wore a curious look as though appraising me as she had at the Bolyns' party. There was a change in her manner, though. This time her usual cheerful confidence seemed dampened. The quiet affecting her this evening was surely connected with her birthday. Some people take no joy from them, and I was surprised that Nora might be one of that number.

I took her hand and leaned close. "What is it you want?"

A shadow, not really visible on her face, but as a subtle shifting throughout her whole body, came and went.

"Nora?"

"Do you trust me?" she abruptly asked.

"Yes, of course I do."

"Are you afraid of me?"

"Nora, really! What an absurd question."

"Is it, I wonder."

"Tell me what's troubling you."

The shadow vanished and she offered me a smile in its place. She caressed my neck with her fingertips, a familiar gesture by now and one that never failed to excite me. "Nothing, darling Jonathan."

I was inclined to be doubtful. "Are you sure?"

She gave no direct answer. "Come upstairs."

Well... I'd never yet refused *that* invitation, and notwithstanding her odd mood, I was not going to begin tonight.

As always with this pursuit, we fed upon one another's enthusiasm, seeking and gaining arousal with each touch and kiss until both of us were ultimately seized with that furious eagerness unique to love-making. We gave in to it, gladly surrendering our thoughts, our bodies to its heat. Nora laughed as she rode me, until she dropped forward and suddenly smothered the sound against my throat. I felt the light, sharp prick of her teeth, then I could have laughed, cried or shouted as though from fever when she finally pierced the skin and began to tap the life welling from it.

She'd timed herself to match my own readiness. Somehow, she always seemed to know.

A speculation drifted through my mind that this present coupling could not possibly surpass the previous one.

But once more Nora proved me wrong.

Before my body had quite exhausted itself, she hooked a leg around one of mine and rolled until I was on top. This was a change, for usually she would hold to my throat for a much longer period. Drops of blood from the tiny piercings in my neck splashed on her breasts. She brushed at them, then licked her fingertips clean. I pressed harder into her, anticipating a furtherance of our pleasure when she resumed taking her fill from this fresh position.

"My turn," she whispered, rocking under me, matching my rhythm. Her hand came up and one of her long nails suddenly gouged into the white flesh of her own throat until she bled. She gasped a brief plea to me, telling me what to do, but it was unnecessary. I closed my lips over the wound and for the first time drank the life from *her* body....

Red fire.

So it felt as it coursed into my mouth, gusted into my belly, and thundered to each shuddering limb. It seared my bones, ate outward through the flesh, scorched my skin until Nora and I must both be consumed by the blaze. The totality of pleasure I'd known only seconds ago now seemed like a candle's flame against the sun. It was too much to bear, far too much—yet I would not stop.

Nora cried out—again and again, as if in pain, but holding fast to me as I had to her that first night, urging me to take more, to take everything from her. I drew deep, abruptly aware that the strength I'd freely given moments ago was flowing back. Sweet and bitter, hot and cold, pleasure and pain, life and death, all tumbled madly together like autumn leaves caught in a spinning windstorm.

Nora cried out—arching, convulsing, this climax far more intense than any we'd ever before shared. It touched off an identical response from me; we were finally and truly *one* body, not two. Never before had we lost ourselves like this within each other.

Delirious, we spiraled into the measureless depths of a crimson vortex, into everything and nothing, ultimately whirling down, down, down to finally collapse, sated, in a wonderful, bottomless silence that had no name.

I DRIFTED AWAKE, sprawled comfortably on my back, light-headed, for a moment not recalling where I was, but strangely unconcerned.

Candles burned in every corner of the room. Rather wasteful, that. One, or at the most two, were enough. They seemed very bright to my sleep-puffed eyes, flaring to the point of hurtful dazzle whenever I blinked. I was often like this of a morning after a night of drink, but this time was spared the unsettled stomach and twice-thickened tongue tasting of....

What was that? A taint of iron and salt in my mouth. What had...? Oh.

I remembered. With a little shock.

At the time, caught up in the frenzy, it had been the right thing to do, but now I was faintly scandalized by the drives of my own lust. Thinking over the experience with a cooler mind, it seemed... perverse.

Which was a very illogical judgment considering that Nora had been drinking my blood for months without protest from me. To the contrary, I adored the act, at times positively craved it.

Certainly Nora had wholly desired for me to partake from her. There was no doubt in my heart that I had well-pleased her in the extreme. That was good, very good indeed, but I wasn't sure if I could repeat this night. The idea wanted some getting used to, but after that... I thought I could manage.

Not *too* soon again, though; it was exhausting. If we did that *every* time we made love... by God, I'd be an old man in a week.

Nora lay next to me, one arm on my chest, her fingers spread wide as though her last deed had been to caress the hair there. I covered her hand with my own and slothfully considered whether or not it was worth the effort to rise and put out the candles. Some of them had begun to gutter, and their flickering, uneven light was a mild annoyance to the contented, thoroughly satisfied state of my mind and body.

There was a clock on the table across the room. It was well past two. Nora and I had slept for hours. I was strangely wakeful. And hungry. The table, except for the clock, was bare. That was sufficient to decide me. I'd take care of the candles on my way down to the kitchen.

Turning gently so as to disturb Nora as little as possible, I noticed her eyes were slightly open.

I smiled into them. "You are truly astonishing," I said softly, bending to kiss her.

She did not respond. Her eyes remained open and unblinking. "Nora?"

I gently shook her. Her body was inert under my hands.

She's asleep, she's only asleep. I shook her until her head lolled from side to side. Her eyes did not change, were as blank as sooty glass.

No...

I reached across for the silver bell by the bedside and rang it, roaring for help. Eternities crawled by before the bedroom door opened and a sleepy Mrs. Poole looked in. She correctly read from my agonized face that something was wrong and hurried to Nora's side of the bed. She put a hand to her niece's brow. I was in agony.

"Ah," she said, smiling. "Nothing to worry about, young man."

"Nothing to—"

She cut me off and pointed to the mark on Nora's throat, then to my own. "Taken from each other, haven't you?"

"I—"

"That's all it is. It only puts her into a heavy sleep until she recovers."

The woman must have been blind or mad. "She's not *breathing*, Mrs. Poole!"

"No, she's not, but I tell you there's nothing to worry about. It's like catalepsy. It'll wear off in a few hours and she'll wake none the worse. Bless your soul, but she should have warned you this would happen."

I could not bring myself to believe her. Nora was so utterly, damnably *still.*

Mrs. Poole patted my shoulder in a kindly way. I suddenly realized I was naked with only the sheets to cover me; Nora was equally exposed. However, Mrs. Poole was unperturbed, her concern centered solely upon my agitation. "There now, I can see you'll only listen to *her* word on it. Wait here and I'll fix things right up." She toddled away, her slippers scraping and scuffling as she went along the hall and down the stairs.

Nora remained as she was, eyes open and blind, lips parted, heart—I pressed an ear to her breast—as silent as stone. I backed hastily from her, from my fear. Had I killed her? She often said she was careful not take too much for me, lest I weaken and fall ill, but what if, in my inexperience, I'd gone too far?

I clawed haphazardly for my clothes, pulling them on against the chill that had invaded me. I was nearly dressed when Mrs. Poole returned, carrying a cup of what I first took to be red wine.

"This will do it for certain," she promised, throwing another smile my way. She hovered over Nora, dipped a small spoon in the cup and wet the girl's lips. "Just a few drops of the life-magic..."

"What is that?" I found myself asking.

"Beef blood," she replied. "We had a very fresh joint today and this is what drained off. Cook was saving it for something else, but—"

"Beef blood?" I echoed.

"Nora prefers—well, you and those other fine young gentlemen know what she prefers to have—but this does just as well." She let another few drops ease between Nora's parted lips. My own heart nearly stopped when those lips suddenly moved against one another. Her tongue appeared and retreated, tasting. "That's my girl. Come awake so Jonathan knows you're all right."

Nora's dead eyes closed slowly, then opened to look at me. "Jonathan?" she drowsily murmured.

Now it passed that I was the one unable to move.

"There, there," said Mrs. Poole. "Drink this down first, my girl." She lifted Nora's head and held the cup until Nora took it herself. She drained it completely, giving a little shiver—of pleasure, that was clear—when it was gone.

"What is the time?" Nora whispered.

"Late, but you've hours to go yet. Really, Nora, you've been very naughty not to have spoken to him beforetime. I would suggest an apology. You've frightened him terribly." As though to counteract the gentle rebuke, Mrs. Poole pulled the bedclothes up, almost tucking Nora in like a child.

Nora looked at me. The whites of her eyes were flame red. Evidently the beef blood, like my own, brought about that same strange effect. "Jonathan?"

I shook my head. And shivered. Not with pleasure.

She glanced at Mrs. Poole, who frowned. "It's your own fault, girl. Sort it out. I'm off to my bed, if you two don't mind. Try not to shout or you'll alarm the neighbors." Mrs. Poole took the cup and bade me goodnight, shutting the bedroom door softly on her way out.

"You were..." But I could not finish.

She sat up against the pillows. "I know," she said pensively. "I should have explained to you before we started. It's...difficult for me to find the right words sometimes, especially with you. Other times it seems best to say nothing at all."

"Best for yourself?"

"Yes," she said candidly, after a moment's thought. "And now you're afraid of me again."

I could hardly deny that truth. "Perhaps you will simply 'talk' me out of it as you have before."

"Or perhaps you will do that for yourself."

I started to speak and ask her meaning and found it unnecessary. All I had to do was think of my father and remember his struggle to explain his estrangement from Mother. "'I could see myself turning into her own little dancing puppet,' he'd said."

Her look sharpened. "Who said?"

"Father, talking about his wife." The room was deathly silent. I held my breath, half-expecting a response, but she made no reply. "You don't want me to be a puppet, do you?"

"No," she finally murmured. "I never did."

After all, her life was filled with puppets: handsome young men who gave her blood to live on and gifted her with money to live with, each one happy with his lot, each one under her careful control. This night I had truly become the sole exception to her pattern. In asking myself why, I knew the answer as well as I knew every curve of her flesh. Whatever fear I'd felt melted as though it had never been.

"I'm very glad to know that," I said, my voice growing thick.

She must have seen the proof of that on my face. "You are. You really are..."

I moved back to the bed, climbing in beside her, drawing her close, holding her, for she seemed in need of it. "No more persuasions, Nora. No more secrets. They only hurt *you*, don't you see?"

"But sometimes the truth is impossible to speak."

"It need not be. You've a very clever girl. You can always find a way. Just trust *me* to accept. Even the impossible. Have I not done so just now?"

"More than I ever hoped for. I feared—"

"Oh, we're all done with that. Forget it. Forget fear."

"If I could."

"Ah—none of that! Or I shall be very cross," I whispered fiercely, with a mock anger that eventually made her smile. Her body relaxed against mine, as though she had indeed shed a burden. "Haven't you heard? 'Perfect love casteth out fear.' Now you don't want to go arguing with St. John do you? I thought not."

"I don't think this was *quite* the situation he had in mind."

"Love is love, and there's little enough of it in the world. Let us cherish what we have and trust in its strength, not fear our weaknesses."

"Yes. We will do that...."

✦ ✦ ✦

AND EVENTUALLY no more words were necessary.

My blood quickened, growing hot, insistent, and pulsing hard against the little wounds on my neck. In other places, too. The fever I'd shared with her earlier returned, flooding me head to toe with a need more overwhelming than any before it.

It mirrored her own need. So ... we obliged one another.

CHAPTER

EIGHT

CAMBRIDGE, JANUARY, 1776

Celebrating the New Year with Oliver and several of our friends had once again been a merry but depleting experience. It took a few days of rest before I was in a condition to notice my surroundings again and so discover the packet of mail from home one of the more sober servants had left on my study desk. Breaking the seal, I found that it disappointingly contained but one letter, the singularity enough to cause me alarm before I even read it. After reading, I was in no better state, and once the whole import of the news it contained sunk in I was utterly horrified.

I had to see Nora.

It was fully dark out, and raining, but she'd be receiving visitors despite the weather. I threw on some protection against it and bolted from the house.

The streets were slick with water and mud. Some of the houses had lighted their outside lamps, but these were little better than distant will-o'-the-wisps against the murk. It hardly mattered. I could find my way to Nora's blindfolded.

Mrs. Poole let me in, smiled, and said, "I'm sure she'll be out in just a few minutes."

Yes. True. A few minutes with each of them. That's all it took to get what she needed. I couldn't begrudge her that, but this time the waiting was thorny. The letter rustled in my coat pocket as if reminding me of the calamity contained in its lines.

"Shall I take your things?"

Thus Mrs. Poole gently reminded me of my manners. I gave over my hat and slipped free of my cloak, dropping my stick in a tall, oriental-style jar holding similar items left behind by previous visitors. "Where are the servants?"

"Some are in bed, others are busy in the kitchen. I don't mind, Jonathan. Heavens, but it is a wet night out. If you'll excuse me I'll see that this is hung by the fire. That is, if you are staying awhile?"

"I don't—I mean—yes. I think so. Yes."

"Is there something wrong?"

My world was coming to an end, that's all. "I need to talk to Nora."

She chose not to press farther and left. Too nervous to sit, I paced up and down the hall, my boot heels thumping on the painted wood floor. I wanted Nora to hear and hurry herself. Unsuccessfully, despite the fact it meant nothing more to her than nourishment, I tried not to think about what she was doing beyond the closed door of her drawing room.

They were certainly quiet, but then it wasn't really a noise-making activity: perhaps a gasp or sigh, the slip of cloth on skin, a soft murmur of thanks from one to the other, and, if she was in need, the click of a few coins passing from one hand to the other. Except for paying over any money, my own experience was too ready to supply details, though in fact I heard exactly nothing. The walls were solid and the door very thick and snugly fitted within its frame. Even a moderate amount of sound would not have escaped.

I paced and turned to keep warm. It had been a bad idea to relinquish the cloak to Mrs. Poole. I glared at the door. Damnation, how long did she need? It wasn't as if she had to take her clothes off, and all the man had to do was loosen his neckcloth for her to ...

The door swung open. I belatedly thought that it might be better to step into a side room and give them the privacy to say goodbye, but it was too late now. And not overly important. To the departing young man I would doubtless be just another one of Nora's many courtiers stopping to "pay my respects."

Damnation. The man with Nora was Tony Warburton, still wearing his hat and cloak. They saw me at the same time. Nora's face, always beautiful whatever her mood, lightened with that special joy only I seemed to give her. Warburton's darkened briefly and didn't quite recover. He used to be better at hiding it and often as not hardly bothered anymore.

Nora noticed, but let it pass and greeted me cordially. "What brings you here at this hour?" Her eyes were flushed scarlet from this, her latest feeding. Like many other things about her that had at first upset me, I was now so used to it as to overlook it entirely.

"I must talk to you. It's extremely important."

She could tell by my manner that I was greatly distressed. "Of course. Tony, if you don't mind?"

Warburton seemed not to have heard her. He remained in one spot, looking hard at me. His neckcloth was back in place, but not as neatly as he was accustomed to wearing it. There was no mirror in the drawing room for him to do the job properly. There were few mirrors in the house at all, I knew. He was pale, not so much from blood loss as from high emotion.

"Tony?"

"Yes. I do mind," he said at last. His voice was too charged to raise above a whisper, but with all the pent-up choler behind it was more effective than a bellow.

Nora's ruby eyes flashed on him, but he glared at me. My own immediate troubles dimmed. That which had lain unspoken between us for so long was starting to surface.

But I had no heart for such a confrontation. "Never mind," I said. "I'll go. I apologize for my intrusion."

Nora curtailed my effort to avoid a problem with a sharp lift of her chin. "Nonsense. You're here now and—"

"Of course you'll see him," said Warburton. "You'll always see *him*. No matter what it does to others."

"Tony...." she began.

"No more. I bear no more of this." His voice had dropped even lower with suppressed rage. I barely heard. Nora, standing next to him, had no such difficulty. She came around to stand directly before him.

"Tony, listen to me. Listen to me very carefully."

The air in my lungs settled there as though it had gone solid and could not be pushed out. I knew the tone in her voice, felt the power of it singing through my own brain, though it was not directed at me. I also knew what it was costing her.

But Warburton seemed too incensed to succumb to it. "No more. You want too much of me. Do you know what it's been like for me these years having to be content with your crumbs while he—"

"Tony...."

"No!"

Nora dropped back a step, clearly surprised. This instantly transmuted into anger, but Warburton was too engulfed by his own to care.

"Always taking, taking, taking. First our blood, then our money. Did you know that that's how she makes her wage, Barrett? How she's able to afford her houses, servants, and all the rest? She collects a little from each of us every time she does it. Only a little, mind you, so it's not even missed. Gifts, she calls 'em. Well, no matter the name she chooses to put on the payment, a whore's still a whore whether she spreads her legs for it or not."

I started forward to knock him flat, but Nora was ahead of me. Her open hand lashed out faster than my eye could follow. Warburton grunted and staggered from what must have been a fearsome blow. The whites of his eyes flashed briefly before he shook it off. I made toward him, but Nora imperiously and inarguably signed for me to hold back.

"Mr. Warburton, I see no reason for you to remain any longer or to ever return once you've left," she said evenly.

Warburton blinked a few times as her words penetrated. His long face crumbled in on itself as he comprehended what he'd done. "Nora, forgive me. I didn't mean ... it's just that I ...."

"Get out of here." She glided past him to open the front door herself. Spatters of rain and a wave of cold air tore through the hall.

For a long time he made no move. I hoped Nora would ask me to force him out, though it would certainly end in a challenge and a duel. There was no reason to think that it might end otherwise, anyway. Nora coming between us had only postponed the formalities. I wanted to break his neck.

He finally stirred, started to speak, then aborted because of the venomous look she had for him. He winced as if from another blow and turned from her, eventually striding away and into the pouring darkness of the street. Only when he was lost from sight in the misery of the rain did Nora close the door.

"I'm sorry," I said.

"Was his jealousy your fault?" she demanded. She was visibly trembling.

"This was ill-timed. I should have waited elsewhere, or first sent a note."

"You know you're welcome here anytime. So do they." She waved a hand to indicate her other courtiers. "So did he. I'm the one to apologize to you, Jonathan. I should have seen this coming. Prevented it."

"How? By talking to him?"

"In my way."

"I thought you'd already done so."

"I have. It just never seemed to work as well with him. I don't know why, perhaps it's his drinking." She shook off her speculations and came to me, her hands outstretched. "I'll try again, but later, when we've both cooled down."

"But, Nora...."

"'A wholesome tongue is a tree of life, but perverseness is a breach in the spirit,'" she said, quoting from Proverbs. "There is something wrong in Tony's spirit."

"He mortally insulted you!"

"He told the truth and you know it. Granted, by the manner in which he told it, he meant to hurt me."

"For which I'll repay him handsomely when the chance comes."

Then she went still and distant and I felt the wash of her anger flow over me like an icy wave. "This is not your concern, but mine, Jonathan."

I was suddenly unable look at her or say what I'd been about to say. My outraged objections died away, unspoken, not out of fear of offending her, but from the tardy admission to myself that she was right.

"Please, leave it to me."

Had she ordered or demanded I just might have ignored it, but she gave this as a request, and that steadied me down. Much as I wanted to play the knight-errant and avenge the insults thrown at her, it was for her to resolve things her own way. Interfere, and I would be no better than Warburton.

"Very well," I conceded.

Her face softened. I'd said nothing specific, but it was as good as a promise to her. She knew I would keep it. "Thank you." The strain that had unhappily pushed between us vanished. "Come in by the fire. Would you like some tea?"

I declined, but let her guide me into the drawing room to the settee by the fireplace. "What will you do about him?"

"Whatever I can, if I can. I think it was a mistake for me to have continued with him after I'd met you."

Cousin Oliver had also expressed a similar opinion. Often.

Nora's face suddenly twisted. With a shock, I realized she was crying. She was not a woman to easily give in to tears and disliked doing so. I quickly stood and gathered her in my arms, giving her the comfort of soaking my shoulder.

"I'm sorry," she mumbled.

"It's all right to cry when you're hurt."

"It's just... oh, God, but I *hate* losing a friend."

Whatever his faults, Warburton did have looks and no small portion of charm. Beyond the necessities of nourishment, she had enjoyed his company and counted upon him as a friend as I had. No more, alas.

The storm gradually passed and she pulled herself in to once more resume her usual air of self-possession. I started to offer her a handkerchief, but she'd brought her own out. It was spotted with a small amount of blood. Warburton's. I looked away as she dabbed at her eyes and blew her nose.

"Please don't tell me there are others to take his place. I'm not like that, Jonathan. I can't just engage any young man for what I do. It's not a matter of having to take whoever comes my way because they're handy. If it were for the blood alone it would be different. But there's more to it for me than mere feeding. I have to at least like the man to touch him I that way, and I do like Tony. Or I did."

"You need their love as well," I whispered.

"Yes. And more. It's so easy for men to love me, but for them to accept what I am .... Even after I've talked to them, influenced them ... it's not always there. Those are the ones I have to let go, and it's never easy."

"Like Oliver?"

That startled her. "You knew?"

"I suspected. He's never said anything, of course, only acted a bit reserved about you."

She nodded. "He's a very sweet young man, and I dearly enjoyed listening to his prattle, but it became obvious that he was uncomfortable about my needs. I made him forget all that happened, though some ghost of that memory may still remain. He is reserved, he just doesn't know why."

"I can see that such power of influence that you have is a great help in avoiding unwanted complications."

"A help or a bad habit. I'm glad there are no such things between us anymore."

"Mmm." We sat close together on her settee and stared into the fire. Concerns over Warburton faded as I remembered what had brought me here. My heart began to ache.

Though she could not see my expression, she was quick to sense the change in my mood. "What is it, Jonathan?"

"I have some bad news." God, was that *all* I could say about it?

But she heard the pain in my voice and turned around to face me.

I fumbled out the letter with some idea that she could read it for herself, but changed my mind. A summation was enough. More than enough. "My family. They want me to come home."

Now she did take the paper from me and read it through. She said nothing.

Words were inadequate.

"It's Father's writing, but I know it *must* be my mother's idea. Only she would be fool enough to tear me out of here before my studies were complete. It's so utterly witless! How could she do this to me?"

"Are you unhappy only about your studies?"

"Of course not! I hope you don't think—"

"No, Jonathan," she said gravely. "I know you better than that."

"They don't know about us, you see. So I don't understand why."

"From what you've told me of your father he would be most reluctant to have you break off your education here ... unless they really need you as he says."

"Our home is hardly in the thick of things. As far as anyone's concerned all the turmoil is in Boston, Philadelphia, and Virginia. We're miles and miles from those places, surrounded by British troops and other Tories, why should they need me?"

"It might be a case of want, rather than need," she gently pointed out. "I think that your father is afraid."

A bitter retort to gainsay that almost burst from me, but died when I saw her sad look. I took back the letter and read it again. The truth, as seen from this view, seemed to jump out and strike me right in the heart. I hadn't wanted to see it before; to do so would mean ...

"But I can't leave you, Nora," I said, tears creeping into my own voice now. "I couldn't bear it."

"Hush," was all she said. She pulled me close, until my head rested on her breast, and wrapped her arms around me, comforting and warm. Part of me wanted to weep, but I did not. What would be the use?

I ALL BUT CRAWLED BACK to my room some hours later, dejected and hopeless and with no idea of how to avoid my duty to my father. I'd cautiously asked Nora if she would be willing to come to Long Island with me, but she was unable to give an answer. That had hurt, for I'd wanted her to immediately say yes. She was honest, though. She really did not know what to tell me.

"There is so much to think about," she said. "Give me the time to think it."

Pressing her for a decision would be importune. All I could do was accept and await. At least she'd not given a flat-out refusal.

The last person I wanted to see was Tony Warburton, but there he was lolling in his chair in the sitting room we all shared, apparently waiting for me. Two empty wine bottles stood on the table next to him and he was in the process of draining away a third as I walked in. Nora's intervention had only postponed the inevitable. Somehow, I would have to resolve things with him in a way that would not result in a duel.

"Barrett," he said. He looked embarrassed and shy and his gaze did not quite meet mine. All his anger was gone.

I hadn't known what to expect: a challenge, censure, insults—anything but remorse. My own anger magically evaporated. I was sorry for him, but did not feel up to more talk, especially since he was drunk. I made to go past to my own room, but he lurched from his chair to head me off.

"Please... Barrett, please hear me out. I just wanted to apologize." His words were slurred, but sincere. A drunkard's sincerity, I thought. Oh, well, forgiveness was easy enough to find in my present mood. I had other things on my mind now.

"It's all right. I shouldn't worry about it anymore if I were you."

His slack jaw waggled a bit. "Oh, I say, you are such a decent man. I'm...I've been so wretched since... I said a lot that I don't mean, and I'm truly sorry."

"Yes, well, don't worry about it."

"But I—"

"Get some sleep, Warburton."

"No, I need... I *must* apologize to Nora as well. I was too horrible to her. I won't ask her to forgive me, but I will apologize. I only want to do that and then I shan't bother her again. On my honor." He spread his hand over his heart.

"Tomorrow, then."

"Tonight! It must be tonight."

"No, you're much too... tired." I nearly said "drunk."

"Tonight," he obstinately insisted and pushed away from me. He found his cloak and dragged it over his shoulders. "You must come. She won't see me unless you're there."

I thought of trying again to persuade him to sleep, but knew it wouldn't work. He'd had just enough to be unreasonable and need watching, but not so much as to be incapable. He would go, with or without me, and in his condition he'd probably fall and drown in a gutter. Perhaps the cold air would help clear his head and I could talk him out of it for the moment. I hoped Nora would understand if I could not.

The weather hadn't improved; we were soaked when we reached her house. Warburton had forgotten his stick, so I'd lent him mine to steady his steps. He leaned on it now and complained about what a thoughtless oaf he was. I shivered and silently agreed with him as we tottered over the last few yards.

"At least knock first," I admonished, but he opened the door himself and walked right in.

"*Shh,*" he said, finger to his lips. "Don't want to wake anyone. Only Nora, but she'll be awake. Keeps late hours, y'know. Very, very late hours." He broke off into a sodden grin.

"What is this?" Nora emerged from the drawing room where I'd left her. "Jonathan, what is going on?"

I felt supremely foolish standing there holding Warburton up. "He wanted to apologize. I couldn't stop him and thought it better to come along."

Her exasperation never quite developed. She saw Warburton's condition and how things stood. Or wobbled. "Very well."

Oblivious to us, Warburton broke away from me to plow into the drawing room, muttering about the brandy there.

"One more drink and he'll have to be carried home," I said. "I'm sorry, Nora."

She dismissed my contrition with a smile and a shake of her head. "Go take care of him. I'll see if there's any hot tea or coffee left in the kitchen."

As expected, Warburton was pouring brandy for himself. He looked up as I came in. "Where's the beauteous Miss Jones?"

"She'll be back."

"No. I want her here. She must be here." His sentimental repentance was rapidly vanishing, threatening to turn into belligerence.

I sighed. The tea would have to wait. "I'll fetch her."

He brightened. "You're a true friend, Barrett."

A patient one, I thought, turning away. Calling for Nora at the door, I only just caught her murmured acknowledgment from down the hall. Behind me, I heard two quick steps, but there was no time to look back to see what he was doing.

Something went *crack*. The room was engulfed in a dull white sheet and my legs collapsed from under me. I didn't see so much as feel the floor coming up.

When the white leached away I became acutely aware of a hideous knot of agony on the back of my head and my inability to move. I could breathe and suffer pain. That was all.

And see. Yes. That was Tony Warburton standing over me. Holding my stick. His movements were in control and quite steady. His face was no longer slack from drink.

His face...

Dear God.

"A true *friend*, Barrett," he whispered.

I tried to speak. Nothing happened. Too much pain was in the way.

Holding the cane in both hands, he gave it a twist. I'd shown him and others the trick of it during practice at the fencing gallery. The handle came free and out slid a yard of Spanish steel, sharp as a razor.

No...

I must have made some sound; he raised one booted foot above my belly and shoved down hard with all his weight. Air vomited from my lungs. No breath, no movement, no way to warn Nora—Who was just coming in the door, but he was ready for that and whipped around in time with the blade level and his arm went straight and all she could do was give a little wondering gasp as the steel vanished into her breast.

She seemed to hang frozen in the air, held up by the thin blade alone. Her quivering hands hovered around it as though seeking a way to take hold and pull it out. Her eyes flashed first shock, pain, and more pain as she realized his betrayal. They flickered down at me, fearful. I was able to open my hand toward her. Nothing more.

Blood appeared on the ivory satin of her bodice. Over her heart.

Warburton made a soft exhalation, like a laugh.

Nora swayed to one side and fell heavily against the wall, flinging her arms out for balance. Warburton, still holding the sword-stick, followed her movement as though they were dancers.

Within my mind, I howled.

Without, silence.

Silence... until Nora slipped to the floor with a whisper of fabric and her lips forming a sound halfway between a sob and a moan. Her wide skirts floated around her like flower petals. She stared at him the whole time, eyes brimming with anguish and anger and sorrow and loathing;

stared until her eyes became fixed and empty and all motion and feeling drained away to nothing, leaving nothing.

Only then did Warburton draw the blade from her body. He swept it clear with savage efficiency. Drops of her blood spattered the flowered wallpaper like tiny rose buds.

He turned. Looked from her to me. He loomed tall as a giant and swung the sword so that the point lightly tapped, tapped, tapped just below my chin. He smiled at me. Cheerful, bright, interested in everything, and utterly normal—the same smile I'd seen the day I first met him. The smile of a sane man who is not sane.

He reached down to tear open my neckcloth, the easier to draw the sword across, from ear to ear. Better to remove the impediment than to cut through it. It flashed through my mind that things might look as though I'd killed Nora and then myself. He couldn't know about my letter from home, but that would inspire an explanation for this slaughter.

He placed the sword's edge against my throat. I felt its hot pressure. Part of me would welcome what was to come for I would be with Nora, another part raged against it, denied it, fought it—

And could do nothing, *nothing*, to stop him. He batted my feeble hands away with no effort.

Useless. Useless.

If heaven were not my destination, then hell could offer no worse than the absolute helplessness I felt in these last seconds.

The blade pressed upon my naked skin. It was stained with her blood. He made that soft laughing sound again. All I could manage was a groan as his arm flexed to drive—

Something seized his wrist like a striking snake. The sword jerked up and away from my throat.

Astonishment froze Warburton for an instant. He stared, all incredulous, before reason returned and told him that what he saw simply could not be possible. She had to be—must be—dead. The blood was yet there on her dress...God in heaven, I could *smell* it. No one could survive such an awful wound....*No one human*, I wailed.

Almost as though my very thought had leaped into his head, Warburton flinched and backed from her, but she held fast to his arm, using his impetus to regain her feet. He tried to shake off her grip. Failed. Desperately clouted her head with his free hand. She didn't seem to feel it. Their natural difference in size and strength should have worked in his favor but it was as though none existed, and he was suddenly aware of it.

There was a dull snap, Warburton cried out, and the sword-stick dropped from his nerveless fingers. Gasping, I was just able to crawl toward it, take it up.

But Nora did not need my help.

Her eyes burned with something beyond fury. She was still beautiful, but the hellfire blazing in those eyes had transformed her from goddess to Gorgon; to look upon her now was to see your own death...or something worse.

And Warburton looked.

His jaw sagged as though for a scream. No sound came forth. I glimpsed in his face only a reflection of the horror he saw and that was enough. No shriek or howl or cry flung up from the depths of hell could have possibly expressed it.

Silence, dark and heavy and alive and hungry. Silence, like an eternity of midnights condensed into a single moment, ready to burst forth and engulf the universe forever. Silence, except for my own pained breath and the hard laboring of my heart.

No one moved. Warburton was like a man of stone, frozen in place by terror like a sparrow before a serpent: aware of what was to come, but unable to fly from it. Only his face changed, the sane insanity evaporated, exposing the pitiful, raw despair beneath.

Then Nora whispered, "No," and released him, soul and body. There was a thump and thud as he toppled to the floor.

She stood over him, hands loose at her sides. He cowered away until stopped by a wall, then curled his legs up to his chest, arms wrapping tightly around his head. He choked convulsively once, twice, then began to weep like a heartbroken child, long keenings of pure despair.

I wanted to weep as well, but for another reason. Dragging myself up, I stumbled toward her.

IT WAS AN HOUR before I stopped trembling. The churning in my guts never quite settled, and the back of my head put forth lances of pain whenever I moved too fast. Nora wrapped a piece of ice from the buttery in a cloth for me to hold over the spot. She said the skin was broken, but would not need to be stitched together.

Her manner was as smooth and cool as the ice. Her gaze roved everywhere, never quite meeting mine. She'd withdrawn from me without leaving the room. When I put my hand out to her, she would only touch it briefly and then find some other task to distract her away. At first I thought it had to do with me, until I perceived that her mind was turned inward, and what ran through it was not pleasant.

The sad drone of Warburton's crying had finally ceased and after a bout of prosaic sniffing and snuffling, he'd fallen asleep. We left him on the floor where he'd dropped and kept our distance as though he carried some kind of pestilence.

"Shall I take him home?" I asked.

"What?" She stirred sluggishly, having lingered over the lighting of a candle. Dozens of them burned throughout the room except for a dim patch around Warburton.

"It will cause less notice if I'm the one to take him home."

"What will you tell Oliver?"

"I'll think of something."

"Lies, Jonathan?"

"Better than the truth. More discreet."

I'd meant this to bring her comfort. Her lips thinned as she chose a more ironic interpretation.

"Everything will be all right," I told her, hoping she would believe it. She shook her head once, then looked past me toward Warburton. "He tried to murder us, Jonathan. I can forgive him for myself, but not for what he nearly did to you. I was the indirect cause of that."

"He was mad, it's past now."

"He *is* mad ... and will probably remain so."

"What do you—"

"I've seen it before. I may have stopped myself in time, but who's to say how it will be for him when he wakes up?"

"Stopped yourself?"

"From totally destroying his mind."

There was no need to press for further explanation; what I'd seen had given me more understanding than I wanted. I shifted, made uncomfortable by the memory.

Nora opened a cupboard and produced yet more candles and lighted them all.

"What darkness are you trying to dispel?" I asked.

"None but that which lies within me. These little flames help drive away the shadows ... for a time."

"Nora—"

"I live in the shadows and make shadows of my own in the minds of others. Shadows and illusions of life and love that fill my nights—until something like this happens and shows them up for what they are." Her hand brushed over the front of her ruined dress. Certainly the sword had pierced her heart, yet she'd recovered and lived. What manner of creature was she? Goddess or demon?

Though I but dimly perceived her meaning, her words and how she said them frightened me. Instinct told me she was working up to something, but I didn't know what, and in my ignorance I was unable to gainsay her.

"At least you're not a shadow, Jonathan. I can thank God for that comfort, whatever may come."

This sounded ominous. "What do you mean?"

Now she sat by me and looked at me fully. "I mean that I love you as I've loved very few others."

My eyes filled. "I love you, too. I would sooner cut my heart out than leave you."

"I know," she said with a twisted smile. "But others need you, and I am needed here." She glanced at Warburton. "To correct my mistakes, if that's possible."

"What are you—" But I suddenly knew what she was talking about, and she gave me no chance to alter her decision. It was now my turn to learn of betrayal and in the learning, to forget it.

To forget many things.

"Please forgive me," she whispered.

And I did.

Without struggle, I slipped into the sweet darkness of her eyes.

IT HAD TAKEN NO SMALL AMOUNT of time and trouble to arrange my passage home. I had to find the right sort of ship and a trusty captain with a long history of successful crossings, then wait for his arrival in port. Then there was the packing. I'd acquired many more books and clothes since coming to England and they all had to be put into boxes and trunks, carefully wrapped in oilcloth against the sea damp.

My instructors had an understanding of my situation and obligingly made concessions about my studies. I crammed several months of learning into one, and happily passed with honors in late March. My university training was yet incomplete, but perhaps I could finish things out at Harvard later. This year's course was over, at least.

Fresh April loomed, bringing more rain, but I was not looking forward to the voyage taking me away from it, though the shipping company had assured me the winter storms of the Atlantic were over. *What about the spring ones?* I wondered glumly.

Ah, well, there was no turning back at this point. I'd have to pray that Providence would be kind and brave it out with the rest of the passengers. My things were packed, I was ready and waiting at the port, and in two months, God willing, I would see Sag Harbor low on the western horizon and soon after that my welcoming family.

My companions for the trip looked to be an interesting lot: some clergymen and their wives, a bright-looking fellow who said he was an engineer, an artist and, inevitably, some army officers. The growing rebellion in the colonies demanded more and more men for His Majesty's service. In the next few weeks we would doubtless grow quite sick of one another, but things were all right for now.

As he had been the first to greet me, my good cousin Oliver was now the last to bid farewell. We were waiting for the ship's launch to come for me and the others in a tavern by the docks. We'd secured seats by the only window to be the first to know of its arrival. We drank ale to pass the time. I didn't care for mine much. Ale was for celebrations, not for partings.

"I stopped by the Warburtons' on the way over," Oliver said, his expression falling as it always did about the subject of his friend.

"How is he?"

"About the same."

It was a great mystery, what had happened all those months back, to Tony Warburton. Oliver had initially noticed something was wrong, but had mistaken it for drunkenness. Everyone was well-used to seeing Warburton drunk. This time, he simply hadn't sobered up. His clothes were sopping wet from the weather and—Oliver discovered—his right wrist had been badly broken. He could not tell anyone how he had come by his injury, nor did he seem much concerned about it.

He still smiled and joked, but more often than not what he said was incomprehensible to others, as if he'd been carrying on a wholly different conversation in his head. He made people uneasy, but was unaware of it. He hardly turned up for his studies, and then had no concentration for them. Sooner or later he'd wander from the lecture hall. His friends covered for him until his tutor had enough and called him in for a reckoning. After that interview, his parents were quickly sent for and Warburton was taken back home to London.

Like Oliver, I'd also stopped in at the Warburton home see him and say good-bye. I was received with absentminded cordiality. He favored me with his old smile, but for some reason imparted a horrific feeling in me. I tried talking to him; he paid scant attention. The only time he showed any animation was when his eye fell upon my sword-stick. His face clouded and he began rubbing his crooked wrist where the ill-healed bones still ached. He shook his head from side to side and the watchful footman whose job was to keep track of his young master stepped forward and suggested that I should leave.

"It's awful, isn't it?" I said. It was a bleak gray day out. A perfect match to our mood.

Oliver agreed. "I plan to look in on him, though. Now and then he has a lucid moment, the trick is to get them to last. Wish I knew the cause of it. The doctors they've taken him to say anything from the falling sickness to the flying gout, which means they haven't any good idea. And the treatments! Everything from laudanum to bathing in earth." He looked both grim and sad. Warburton had been his best friend.

"That's probably the launch to take me out to the ship," I remarked, pointing.

"Not long now." He turned from the view and craned his neck toward the crowds strolling up and down the quay.

"Looking for someone?"

He shrugged. "I just thought that ... well, that your Miss Jones might have come by to ... you know, see you off."

No, she wouldn't be coming. It was daylight and Nora never ... never ... something. I'd gone blank on whatever it was. Annoying, but probably of no importance.

"She's been very busy lately," I told him. "Poor Warburton's condition deeply affected her, y'know." Soon after Warburton had left for London, Nora had also moved back. "His mother told me that she often comes to visit him. Seems to do him good, though it doesn't last for long."

Nora's sudden departure from Cambridge had puzzled Oliver. "You and she you didn't have a quarrel or anything, did you? I mean, when you got that letter to go back ..."

"What an absurd idea." But he did not appear convinced. "Let me assure you that we parted the best of friends. She's a lovely girl, truly lovely. It's been a delight to have had her friendship, but all good things must come to an end."

"You're pretty cool about it, I must say. I thought you were madly in love with her."

My turn to shrug. "I loved her, of course. I shall certainly miss her, but there are other girls to meet in this wide world." I winced, feeling a sudden lurch of illness in my belly.

"Something wrong?"

"Nothing, really. Just a headache." I absently rubbed the back of my head and the small ridge of scar hidden by the hair. Acquired on some drunken debauch earlier in the year when I must have stumbled and fallen, it occasionally troubled me. "You'll look after her for me as well, won't you?"

"If you wish. Won't you be writing her yourself, though?"

"I . . . don't think so. Clean break, y'see. But I'd feel better if you could let me know how she's doing. It strikes me that though she has many friends, she's rather alone in the world. I mean, she does have that aunt of hers, but you know how it is."

"Yes," he said faintly. Oliver didn't much approve of Nora, but he was a decent man and would do as I asked. I looked at him anew and realized how much both of us had grown in the nearly three years of my stay. In many ways he'd become the brother I'd never had. The weight of the world fell upon my spirit as I again faced the awful possibility that I might never see him again.

The launch glided up, and ropes were thrown to hold it to the dock; the oars were secured. A smart-looking ship's officer jumped out and marched purposefully toward our tavern. It was time.

"God," I said, choking on the sudden clot of tears stuck in my throat.

Oliver turned from the window and smiled at me, but the corners of his mouth kept tugging downward with his own sorrow. He made no comment. We each knew how the other felt. That made things better and worse at once.

"Well, I'm damned sorry to see you go," he said, his own throat obviously constricted and making the words come out unevenly. "You're the only relative I've got who's worth a groat and I'm not ashamed to say it."

"But not in front of the rest of the family," I reminded him.

"God forbid," he added sincerely, and the old and bitter joke made us both laugh one more time.

Ignoring the stinging water that blurred our vision, we went out to meet the officer.

CHAPTER
NINE

LONG ISLAND, SEPTEMBER, 1776

"They was my hosses 'n' wagon, Mr. Barrett, 'n' still mine but for that bit of paper. I figger 'twill take another bit of paper to get 'em back 'n' want you to do it for me."

Thus spoke our neighbor, Mr. Finch, seated in Father's library. Our guest and future client was angry, but holding it in well enough; I would have been in an incoherent rage over the theft. Father only nodded in neutral agreement.

Finch's problem had become a familiar story on the Island as the commissaries of the occupying army diligently worked to fill their own pockets as well as the bellies of the imported soldiers they were to supply.

"What sort of paper?" asked Father, looking grave.

"It were a receipt for the produce I were sellin' to 'em. I had my Roddy read it, but they left out how much I were to be paid 'n' said it would be filled in later." He placed the document before Father.

"And you signed it?" He tapped a finger against a mark at the bottom of the sheet.

Finch's weather-reddened face darkened. "They give me no choice! Them bloody soldiers was standin' all 'round us with their rifles 'n' bayonets fixed to skewer us 'n' grinnin' like devils. I had to sign it or they'd a' done God knows what 'n' more besides. Damned Hessians they was, 'cept for the officer 'n' 'is sergeant. Couldn't make out a word of their talk, but the way they was lookin' at my young daughters was enough to freeze your blood solid."

Another too-common evil. We'd all heard of the outrages committed by the soldiers on helpless womenfolk, and when their men tried to defend them they were often as not murdered. The army sent from England made little distinction between the rebels and the king's loyal subjects, not that a war was any excuse for their mistreatment of the common people.

In addition to wholesale theft and the occasional riot, many of the military had taken to using unprotected women as their own private harem whenever they pleased, whether the ladies were willing or not. There had been courts-martial held, but the attitudes of the officers more closely resembled amusement rather than intolerance for the brute actions of their men. Thinking of how I would feel should Elizabeth face such a threat, I could well understand why Finch had readily cooperated.

"So I made my mark," he continued. "Then one of 'em hops up and makes to drive away 'n' when I asks the officer what he thinks he's doin', he says the receipt included *what* the goods come in as part of the sale. 'The king needs hosses,' he says as cool as you please. I was a-goin' to argue the point with 'im, but those men was licking their lips 'n' my girls was startin' to cry, so it seemed best to leave 'n' try another way. The poor things only come along to help me 'n' in return git shamed 'n' have to see their da shamed as well. Roddy felt awful about it, but he read the paper over 'n' couldn't find a way around it. Said that the way it were written could be taken as havin' mor'n one meaning."

Fairly well off compared with other farmers, Finch still could not afford to lose a good pair of work animals and a wagon. Still less, though, could he afford harm to his family.

"Anyways, if you c'n see yer way through to gettin' my property back, you'll not find me ungrateful, Mr. Barrett," he concluded.

Father's desk was stacked with similar complaints. He was himself a victim of the rapacious commissaries and their clerks. With a signed receipt from a farmer selling his goods, they could fill in whatever amount they pleased on the sale. It was usually a more than fair sum of money, but none of it ever reached the farmer, for that went into the pockets of the commissaries. Any complaint could be legally ignored, for the victim had signed, hadn't he? He was only trying to squeeze additional money from the Crown, the cheat. Any who refused to sell their surplus could have the entire crop confiscated. That, too, had happened.

"Will we be able to help him, Father?" I asked after Finch had left.

His answer was a weary grimace. "We'll do what we can, laddie. There's some forgery at the bottom of this case, else they wouldn't have been able to take the horses and wagon. That might make a difference. At the very least we can raise a bit of noise over it. Because of the way these things work, one can't help but expect to see the corruption sweeping in, but this business is getting completely out of hand. I'll write to DeQuincey. He's busy playing pot-boy to General Howe, but perhaps he'll take a moment to remember his neighbors."

Nicholas DeQuincey was one of the most ardent supporters of the king's cause and had been among the Loyalist troops waiting to greet General Howe's army when it landed on Staten Island two months ago. Apparently he was so loyal he was willing to turn a blind eye to the resulting depredations of Howe's army. That Father was planning to ask for help from such a man was a clear indication to me that he'd pretty much given up hope of using the civil courts to settle matters. Now it would fall to calling on friendships and favors to achieve justice.

I ran my thumb over a pile of papers outlining various complaints against the occupying army. There was little hope in me that anything would come of them, even with DeQuincey's intervention.

"It's not fair," I muttered.

He looked up from the letter he was composing. "No, by God, it isn't. It's bad now and will only get worse. If that Howe had played the wolf instead of the tortoise he'd have captured Washington before he and his rabble ever had the chance to leave this island. At least then we would have seen the beginning of the end to this tragic nonsense. I don't know how far Washington will retreat, but there's enough country north of here for him to drag the fight out for months."

Months. Good lord.

Father finished his letter and addressed it. While he worked, I was busy turning Finch's complaint into language suitable for a court presentation. The day after I'd arrived home, Father had taken me on as his much junior partner. It was not official so far as the court was concerned, for I still needed to pass my examines, but I was glad of the honor and the chance to use what I'd learned in Cambridge. We hoped that after the rebellion was over and things got back to normal again I could finish my schooling at Harvard.

But he treated me as a respected colleague and commissioned the making of a fine desk to match his own. They were pushed together front-to-front for convenience, though it often led to confusion. Much of our labor overlapped; we were still working out how to avoid making a muddle of all the paper.

Of this new project, a second copy of Father's letter needed to be made by me, though that was really a clerk's job. We had no clerks; the two lads that had been with us had long-since departed to their families or to join up with Loyalist troops. I possessed no inclination to follow the latter example. Father hadn't encouraged me in one way or another on that decision, but I shared his opinion that the fighting was better left to the soldiers who knew how. He needed my help more than they and more than one incident had occurred to justify my remaining close to home.

Back in January, while I'd been making arrangements to return, Father had had the bad luck to be in Hempstead when a rebel troop led by the fanatical Colonel Heard had ridden in to force known and suspected Loyalists to sign an oath of obedience to the Continental and Provincial congresses. Father signed rather than submit to arrest, but found little reason to be bound by his agreement.

"A forced promise is no promise," he told me. "They'll make no new friends to their cause with such methods and only turn the undecided against them."

Had Father been undecided before, this insult had clarified things for him.

For a time. Now our British saviors seemed to be doing their best to alienate those that had shown them the greatest support. Father's vast patience showed signs of erosion as each new case came in. We'd seen five people that morning. That officer, his sergeant, and the troop of Hessians had been very busy. Doubtless they were also benefiting from their "legal" thefts.

When I'd finished my draft, Father paused in his own work to look it over.

"Is it all right?" I asked after a moment.

He gave a pleased nod. "Wait 'til we get you in court. If you do as well there as you do on this..."

If we ever had another court. The exacting work of civil law was yet another aspect of life interrupted by the rebellion. At this rate I would be serving an unnaturally long time at this apprenticeship.

Someone knocked on the door. At our combined invitation it silently opened and Jericho announced that the midday meal was ready. Heavens, where had the morning gone? Father shed his wig, we put away our writing tools and marched out in Jericho's wake to assume our accustomed places at the dining table.

The library was in a corner room of the house and, with both sets of windows open, subject to a pleasing cross breeze that made it comfortable in the hot months. The dining room was not so advantageously located and had but one window. It was flung wide in a futile hope of freshening the close air within, but the wind wasn't in the right direction to provide much relief. We sat and stewed in the heat, picked lightly at our food, and imbibed a goodly share of barley water drink.

Little had changed in the years I was absent and this ritual the least of all. Mother would hold forth on the most tedious topics, or complain about whatever had offended her in the few hours since breakfast, usually quite a lot. She was well-supported by Mrs. Hardinbrook and, to a lesser extent, by Dr. Beldon. Both had become fixtures in the household, though Beldon could be said to be a contributing member by reason of his doctoring skills. He'd proved to be an able enough physician, but was still liable to fits of toad-eating. Elizabeth was formally polite to him, Father tolerated him, and I avoided him, which was sometimes difficult because the man was always trying to court my friendship.

Today Mother was full of rancor against yet another rise in prices.

"...four times what they charged last year for the same thing. If we didn't have our own gardens we should starve to death this winter. As it is, Mrs. Nooth will have to work day and night to build up our stores once the crops really start to ripen. It's a disgrace, Samuel, and absolute disgrace."

"Indeed it is, Marie," Father said, taking a larger than normal draft. He had wine as well as barley water.

"Of course, *if* we have anything left to harvest," she added. This was a not too subtle reference to the crop sold to the first commissary to come through the area. Under circumstances very similar to Finch's, Father had had to sign a blank receipt for a load of grain. The grain was collected, but we were still waiting to be paid for it.

Father spared a glance for me and raised one eyebrow. I smoothed out the scowl that was preventing me from properly chewing my food.

"I got a letter from Hester Holland today," Elizabeth said to me. She wanted to change the subject. "She'd heard that all the DeQuincey boys were serving under General Howe."

"Then God keep them safe and see them through to a swift victory," Mother responded. She didn't like Miss Holland, but the DeQuincey clan held her wholehearted approval. Mother was not beyond doing some toad-eating of her own, and the DeQuinceys were a large and influential family. They had money as well and a match between one of its scions and Elizabeth was something to encourage.

"Amen," said Mrs. Hardinbrook, but it was rather faint. She also had hopes for arranging an advantageous marriage, but in three years she had yet to successfully interest Elizabeth in her brother or her brother in Elizabeth. It was very frustrating for her, but amusing to watch, in a way.

Beldon was entirely aware of her efforts and now and then would occasionally commiserate with me on the subject. He had polite and honorable admiration for my sister, but that was as far as it went, he assured me, perhaps hoping to gain some praise for his nobility of spirit. I'd met others of his temper at Cambridge, men with a decidedly indifferent attitude toward women. Soon after my homecoming I'd made clear to him that I was not of that number, a fact he graciously accepted, though the toad-eating continued as before.

"Hester wrote that some of the soldiers being quartered in the old church are very handsome," Elizabeth said. Unlike Hester, she wasn't the sort to idly gossip about such things and I wondered why she'd bothered to mention it, until I noticed that she'd directed the remark in Mrs. Hardinbrook's direction. The lady had once taken pains to be present when a company of commissary men had marched by our gate to their camp, wearing her best dress and most winning smile, waving her handkerchief to the thieves. Elizabeth thought—not without reason—that she was a great fool.

I now perceived this innocuous statement to be an acid comment on Mrs. Hardinbrook's immodest behavior. It might also be taken as an indirect reminder of Beldon's preferences and the futility of altering them with a marriage. Mrs. Hardinbrook had an outstandingly thick skin, but a twitch of her brows betrayed that she had felt the blow. Beldon's lips curled briefly—with humor, I was relieved to note, not offense.

Mother, innocent of this byplay, took it as something to pounce upon. "She would, I'm sure. Elizabeth, you really must try to cultivate a better class of friend than that Holland girl. If she's keeping company with soldiers then she's no better than a common tavern slut."

Mrs. Hardinbrook smirked, entirely missing the implication that she could be included in Mother's judgment.

Elizabeth's face flushed and her mouth thinned into nonexistence. For a few awful seconds she looked astonishingly like Mother during one of her rages. Father's eye fell upon her, though, and he solemnly winked. Her anger subsided at this reminder not to take anything that

Mother said seriously. They had had plenty of opportunity to practice such silent communication and once again it had spared us all from a lengthy row.

Beldon had noticed—for he was always alert to what was going on around him—and visibly relaxed. Whenever Mother became unduly upset it always fell to him to calm her down. His bottle of laudanum had proved to be very handy in the past, but as a good doctor he was reluctant to rely on it for every ill happening in the house. I'd seen more than one opium eater ruining himself at Cambridge, so on that point he and I were in accord.

"I saw Mr. Finch's eldest earlier," he said. "While waiting for his father he acquainted me with the family's misfortunes."

"Hmm," grunted Father discouragingly, unwilling to speak of business at the table.

"Mostly just to pass the time, I fear. A decent young man, but dull." Beldon had clearly caught the hint and made his tone of voice lazy and bored, as though it were hardly worth the effort to speak. "He mentioned some other things as well. Tedious stuff," he added. "Most tedious."

He'd struck just the right balance between getting his message across yet not arousing anyone's curiosity. Mother and Mrs. Hardinbrook duly ignored him, having no interest in farmers' gossip.

Father looked up at this. Beldon met his gaze briefly, then contemplated the wallpaper beyond. I could almost hear Father say "damnation" to himself. He grunted again and nodded at Beldon, then at me. This meant we were to both come to the library after the meal.

Silence reigned after that. The heat was too much for even Mother to maintain a dialogue of her many grievances for long. She turned down a thick slab of hot pie and excused herself. She usually had a nap in her room at this time of day unless there was entertaining to be done. Nothing was planned for tonight, and no one hindered her exit.

Mrs. Hardinbrook was a woman with an appetite that no amount of summer heat could ruin. She had her pie with an ample slice of cheese on the side, and an extra glass of wine. Groaning under that load she would certainly follow Mother's example and snore away the rest of the afternoon. One by one, the rest of us excused ourselves and left.

Elizabeth had been the first out and waited for us in the library. She'd also caught Father's signal and was interested to hear Beldon's news. Such informal gatherings had been called before; Beldon questioned her presence only once. He ventured that the gentle nature of her sex justified her exclusion from "business" but the tart reply she gave to his suggestion swiftly altered his view of her.

Father settled him in his chair, Elizabeth and I took over the settee, and Beldon perched on a windowsill to take advantage of the breeze. Something of a dandy, he sported his wig at all times and in all weathers no matter how uncomfortable it must have been for him. He flicked a handkerchief from his sleeve and mopped at the shining beads drenching his forehead.

"Tell me what you heard," Father instructed without preamble.

Beldon did so. "This is rumor, mind you, but young Roddy trusted the source."

"What source?"

"Some sergeant working with the commissaries. He was at The Oak and boasting about his successful collections to one and all. Roddy and Nathan Finch were keeping quiet in a corner and heard him talk about how the commissaries were not going to content themselves with waiting for the farmers to come to them. He did not exactly mention what they were planning, but it seems obvious that they will start visiting individual households next and making more direct collections."

Father snorted. "Wholesale thievery is what it will be."

Beldon smiled unpleasantly. "They've dug themselves in well enough. They're familiar with the country and people by now and will be sharp to see anything suspicious."

Elizabeth had kept up on events. "You mean if anyone is hiding livestock or grain from them?"

"Exactly, Miss Barrett. They'll rake over this island like a nor'easter and take what they please—all in the king's name, of course, and the devil for the people they take from, begging your pardon."

"How is it that you know how they work?"

He paused, held in place by Elizabeth's penetrating look. Nothing less than the truth would suffice for her and he must have known it. "From '57 to '59, I served under General James Wolfe during the campaign against the French," he said matter-of-factly.

We glanced at one another, brows raised and questions blooming at this revelation. *This* was news.

"You served in the army?" asked Father after a moment.

"Yes," he said shortly. "Wasn't much older than your son here at the time."

He'd not intended to surprise us, otherwise the toady in him might have provided a greater flourish for such a piece of information. For the first time I began to wonder if just possibly the toad-eating might be a pretense. When a man is thought to be a harmless buffoon, other men discount him as a threat and drop their guard. I'd seen such in others while at school, and they were never called out to duel. Interesting, were it true.

"Why have you never mentioned this before?" asked Father, when he'd recovered from giving Beldon a wondering reappraisal. Elizabeth and I had unabashedly mimicked him.

Beldon's mouth curled inward as though he regretted imparting his history. "It happened a long time ago, sir. It is not one of my happier memories and I beg that none of you mention it to my sister. Deborah, as you may have noticed, enjoys talking and I fear she may try everyone's patience with the subject."

It abruptly occurred to me that Mrs. Hardinbrook knew nothing about this chapter of Beldon's life, else she would have long ago spoken of it in the hope of making him more attractive to Elizabeth. Recounting the exploits of a war hero would have been irresistible to her—unless Beldon had not been particularly heroic....

I pushed that unworthy and dishonorable speculation aside. Some of Father's friends had also been involved in that great conflict and were equally reticent about their experiences. Whatever reason Beldon had for keeping quiet would be respected.

Similar thoughts may have rushed through Father's mind, for he said, "You have our word that we shall say nothing to your sister or anyone else, Doctor." A quick look to each of us guaranteed our nodding agreement to this promise. "Now tell us what we should expect from these soldiers."

"More of the same, I shouldn't wonder," said Beldon. "No one would suffer overmuch from their collections if they were honest enough to pay good coin for what they take, but we've seen proof that that is unlikely to happen. My suggestion is we send word to the citizenry hereabouts to start preparing new and very secret spots to conceal their excess. Have a portion set aside to be taken away, some portion placed in their usual storage places and hide all the rest, which should be the greater part of a household's supply. Each house should have several such stores just in case one is discovered or even betrayed."

"Deception against the king's soldiers?" Father mocked.

"Defense against the jackals professing to serve those soldiers," Beldon countered, referring to the commissaries. "They serve only themselves and will continue to do so. I've seen their like before and no amount of feeding will sate *their* appetite for money. General Howe can chase Washington and his rabble from one colony to another until winter comes to freeze the lot of them to perdition, but these fellows have no such distractions. They will continue their plunders in the king's name until nothing remains."

No one of us could doubt that. In his many letters to me, Father had often mentioned what a prize Long Island would be should the thing come to a full-blown rebellion. In July we heard talk that Washington was planning to send men through the counties to drive all the cattle and sheep they found into the eastern end of the island and shoot the herds to keep them out of British hands. Not surprisingly, this was met with strong opposition, and from his own men. They were not terribly anxious to confront the Loyalist owners of the stock. It seemed that earlier efforts to disarm these citizens had failed. They'd made it clear to the rebels that they were entirely prepared to defend themselves and their property from Congressional thieves.

Washington fumed, the New York convention stalled, and in the meantime General Howe's brother, Vice-Admiral Richard, Lord Howe, arrived with his hundred-fifty ships crammed full with hungry soldiers. Washington's attention became happily engaged elsewhere. Later, General Howe made his landing at Gravesend Bay and saved the king's loyal subjects from the threat of ravaging rebels.

Unfortunately, he had scant interest in saving them from his own men.

"We'll have to have a meeting," I said. "Perhaps at the church after services. It's the best way for everyone to hear it all."

"Aye, including the soldiers, I think," said Father, reminding me of the new additions to our congregation. Some of us still hadn't determined whether the men were there to worship God or to make sure sedition was not being preached. "This is the stuff that charges of treason are made of. They'll think we're conspiring with those rascals over in Suffolk County rather than looking out for our own."

Instantly, I jumped to an alternative. "Then we'll call upon only those we trust and inform them directly."

Father's eyes glinted. "Which means there's nothing in writing that may be held against us. I think you've a talent for this, laddie."

I couldn't help but grin. Having grown used to the physical and mental stimulus of Cambridge, I was sorely missing a challenge; this business promised to be rare entertainment. It might also prove to be much more interesting than those old university amusements, which chiefly consisted of getting drunk whenever the chance presented itself. "I can start at first light tomorrow."

"But not alone. Dr. Beldon, do you not go on mercy calls?"

"You know I do, sir," he said, wiping his brow once more, then pausing as he pondered the reason for Father's query.

"I think you should go with Jonathan on his errands."

I started to ask why Beldon's company was necessary and bit it off as comprehension dawned. A doctor had an infinite number of reasons to be riding from house to house. Beldon's profession would provide us with excellent cover should we be questioned by suspicious folk, whether they be rebels or soldiers in the king's army.

"Very good, sir," said Beldon wryly, understanding and approving.

"And what shall I do?" Elizabeth gently demanded. She clearly wanted to go with us, but the unsettled state of things abrogated her unspoken wish. She, too, had heard of the outrages and was not so foolish to think herself immune to such insults.

"With Jonathan gone I shall need you to help me with the work here," said Father. "You write faster and more clearly than he does, anyway." I took no umbrage at Father's opinion of my penmanship, for it was true.

Elizabeth's archness vanished. She enjoyed helping Father and had done so in the past. Mother disapproved, of course—for it was not lady-like to play the clerk—but not so much as to forbid it.

"Between us I want to plan out how to conceal the surplus to last through the winter. I'm keeping in mind that we may have more than our own to feed. Your mother"—here he paused as though trying to overcome an indigestible bite from his last meal— "has written to those cousins of hers offering them asylum until the rebellion is past. They have yet to reply, but we will have to be prepared. We'll need a second buttery, someplace to store the smoked meats..."

"Flour, sugar, spirits, yes." Elizabeth's face lightened. "I shall talk with Mrs. Nooth and Jericho about all of it. We'll have more hidden treasure than Captain Kidd."

"If I might recommend one more suggestion," said Beldon. "That is, I'm sure dear Deborah would be mightily interested in offering her assistance to you, but she is, after all, a rather busy lady."

This was met with another awkward moment of silence, then Elizabeth nodded. "Yes, Dr. Beldon. I believe it would be better not to disturb her or Mother with such mundane chores as these will doubtless prove to be."

Beldon looked relieved. And so he was able to politely pass on his lack of confidence that his sister could ever hold her tongue in the wrong company.

✦ ✦ ✦

"He's not such a bad fellow, is he?" Elizabeth said as we strolled slowly around the outside of the house in the somewhat cooler air of the early evening.

"Beldon? I suppose not. I think he'd be better off without her, though." There was no need to mention the lady's name.

"Wouldn't we all?"

A few steps to the side of us, Jericho stifled something that might be interpreted as a cough. Or a laugh. It was quite a display from a man who took so much pride in a lofty household station that often demanded great reticence. However, he was away from the house and treading the same grounds we'd tumbled over as rowdy children; he could allow himself to be himself to some extent. We could not go back to those days, but the memory was with us and comforting company.

"I think that staying here has been a beneficial experience for him," she said.

"In what way?"

"He's allowed the chance to be with a less demanding company of people, for one thing."

"He was hardly in isolation in Philadelphia."

"Yes, but his social life was certainly limited, if Mother and that woman are anything to judge by. Like attracts like, y'know."

I had no trouble imagining Beldon surrounded by a large group made up of the sort of people Mother would approve of, and freely shuddered.

"Since you've returned I've looked at him as though through your eyes and noticed that he's not the toad-eater he was at first."

"I've noticed no change."

"That's because you avoid him."

True.

"When he's away from her he can be quite nice."

"Good God, you're not thinking of—"

Elizabeth laughed. "Hardly. I'm just saying that he has a gentle nature and more than a spoonful of wit, but marriage to him is the last thing on my mind. His as well, I will confidently add."

"More's the pity for Mrs. Hardinbrook, then. She does so want to be your sister-in-law."

Elizabeth shuddered in turn. "What about you, little brother? Did you not meet anyone in your wide travels? You mentioned going to parties with Cousin Oliver. Surely there were young ladies there . . . ."

"Indeed there were, and the lot of them as interested in the Fonteyn money as Mrs. Hardinbrook."

Except for one. Heavens, I hadn't thought of Nora in months. Perhaps if I'd asked her, but no; she'd said she never wanted to marry. She really couldn't because...because...well, for some reason. I absently probed for the scar on the back of my head. It was mostly gone by now. Harder to find.

"Something wrong, Mr. Jonathan?" Jericho inquired.

"Touch of headache. Must be the day's heat catching me up." I dismissed it and turned my mind to other things. "Remember the Captain's Kettle?" I asked, using our childhood name for it. We'd spent hours there, playing treasure hunt.

"Where you nearly broke your neck? Of course I do," Elizabeth replied.

"I was thinking that it would be an excellent place to hide our cattle. It's away from the usual roads and has shelter and fodder a-plenty."

Elizabeth murmured her approval and added the idea to the growing list of things to be done that she kept in her head.

"I'll ride by there tomorrow and look it over to be sure."

"Do you wish me to come along, Mr. Jonathan?"

Jericho knew all about my errands. How he knew was a mystery. "I suppose you could, if you want to. But won't you be busy here?"

"Jericho is offering to play the chaperon for you," Elizabeth explained.

I chuckled and shook my head. "I've nothing to worry about. The good doctor and I understand one another."

"A pity his sister doesn't. The year you left she got so tiresome about him that I spent two months with the DeQuincey girls just to get away from her."

And from Mother. Elizabeth had given me every detail in her letters. Unable to stand the constant judgmental scolding any longer, she'd arranged an invitation to visit her friends, packed some trunks, and departed with her maid. Mother had been livid about it, for Elizabeth hadn't shared her plans with anyone except Father, who pretended a detached interest in the matter as if it were unworthy of his notice. Eventually Mother seemed to adopt the same attitude (with Mrs. Hardinbrook aping her, of course) and things settled down again. So Jericho assured me when he wrote. When Elizabeth finally returned, she found Mother's disinterest in her to be a welcome improvement over their previous relationship.

But even with such respites, three years of tension and temper had

had a wearing effect on my sister. She was older and certainly wiser, but much of her natural lightness of spirit had vanished. There was a watchful weariness in her expression that was forgotten only when she was away from home or with me. The rest of the time she wore it or assumed a bland mask as hard as armor. It was a trait she'd picked up, unconsciously I thought, from our long-suffering servants.

Some of them had left after they'd decided Mother's "brief stay" was becoming permanent. We'd lost two cooks, several maids, and five stable lads to her ire. All had been replaced as needed, and we still had the slaves, but when Mother was around, none of them had an easy time of it. Mrs. Nooth had remained, thank God, or the whole household might have fallen apart.

"I think," said Elizabeth, pausing in her stroll, "that this would be a good place for the second buttery."

"But this *is* the buttery," I pointed out.

"Yes, and what better place to hide it? Don't you see? We'll have some of the lads dig the present one that much deeper, make a false wall only we know about."

"Like a priest's hole?"

"But much larger."

"We can do the same thing for our other stores as well."

"Be sure to suggest it to those you talk to tomorrow. And please do be very careful, Jonathan."

I was thinking of making a jest at Beldon's expense, but the somber look on Elizabeth's face stopped me. Should the commissaries, should anyone either on the rebels' side or simply up to mischief find out what was being planned, everything we had could be confiscated. With no notice whatsoever Father and I, Beldon too, could be arrested for treason and even hanged. By our own countrymen. The only worse punishment could have come from the rebels. Had they been in charge of the Island, I doubt that things would be much different except they would not have left us out of their battles. Their rabble's maxim that anyone not for them was against them had caused much grief and suffering. More than one man had been tarred and feathered by mindless mobs and died horribly from it.

"I shall be very careful," I promised her. "Anyway, this won't last long. Just for the season, I'm sure. Beldon thinks that once Washington's great Continental Army gets a taste of real winter, they'll scurry back to their hearths like rabbits to a burrow. Then General Howe can round up the so-called Congress and put an end to the matter."

"I hope so. Do you think they'll be hanged?"

"Only if they're caught. They were foolish enough to sign that treasonous declaration two months ago. What presumptuous gall they had to imagine they represented *everyone*...." I'd read a copy of the ridiculous document along with Father and like him had raged against the inflammatory language of the charges against the king. (Though under our present circumstances I thought that the point about the military being independent of and superior to the civil power was well made. Now, issues that should have been decided in courts were being contested in battle.) We both concluded the absurd paper should be consigned to the flames and its writers and signers to the gallows.

But... that was General Howe's problem, not mine, I reminded myself. I had other matters to worry about.

✦ ✦ ✦

WELL BEFORE DAWN Jericho woke me out of a lethargic dream state as he came in with my morning tray. A vivid picture of Nora Jones had been before my mind's eye, but faded rapidly as I tried to hold on to it. Then it was completely gone and I gave up in mild frustration to the inevitable. Everyone's mind is full of doors that open only during sleep, and mine were the sort to slam solidly shut at the slightest hint of waking.

The dreams troubled me, for their content—whenever I had the rare instance of recalling one—was disturbing. Now and then my drowsy mind would throw out a bit of memory that made no sense, yet during the dream itself I had no difficulty in understanding. The most familiar one concerned Nora. We were at the Bolyns' party again; I danced with her in the maze, kissed her, made love with her. Pleasant enough, and true enough, in the way of a dream, but both of us were splashed from head to toe with blood. It was warm and just turning sticky, the heavy smell of it clogging the air. I could almost taste it. Neither of us and no one else ever seemed to notice, though.

The other dream memory was more mundane, but for an unknown reason much more frightening. It was really nothing: only Tony Warburton smiling down at me from some high place. The first time I remembered having it I'd awakened in a cold, slimy sweat, lighted every candle in the room, and shivered under the coverlet like a child. This reaction eventually passed, but I was never quite comfortable with that one.

"It will be very hot today," said Jericho as he went to the wardrobe to choose clothes for me.

I sipped tea, holding the cup in both hands. "It was hot yesterday."

"More so today. Eat what you can now. You won't want to later."

He was always right about such things. I worked my way through the food he'd brought, slowly adjusting my thinking away from senseless dreams to the tasks awaiting me this day. Even with Beldon's company, I planned to enjoy myself.

"Do you wish a shave?" Jericho asked.

I brushed a finger along one stubbled cheek. He'd shaved me yesterday and had we been following our usual routine, I wouldn't need another until tomorrow. Should I have a clean chin while calling on our neighbors, or not? Not, I decided, and said as much to Jericho. Most of the farmers and other men shaved but once a week for their churchgoing and thought it good enough. I didn't want to put them off by playing the dandy. That was Beldon's province.

"Is Dr. Beldon awake yet?" I mumbled around some biscuit.

"Oh, yes. Sheba just got his tray for him."

No need to comment how inappropriate it was for a young girl to be taking up Beldon's breakfast rather than one of the house lads. Not that Beldon made himself offensive in any way with anyone of either sex. The girl was safe enough with him, as was any lad in the house, for he was really a decent sort.

Except for the toad-eating, I reflexively reminded myself. Upon consideration, I found it odd that Mother was capable of throwing herself into a foaming rage at an erroneous assumption of impropriety between myself and Elizabeth and yet could entirely ignore the doctor's preferences. I'd once mentioned it to Father, who opined that Mother simply did not know or, if she did, contemptuously disbelieved the possibility. Whether her ignorance was willful or not, Beldon was aware of it, and like many other facets of life, it seemed to amuse him.

Jericho laid out my old claret-colored coat. I had put on some muscle since I'd last worn it and the seams had been opened to enlarge it, the work carefully covered by braid trim. While nowhere near being threadbare, it was less than new and thus the correct item to wear while making informal calls upon our neighbors during their working day. Next to it he unfolded a fresh linen shirt, breeches, and my second-best riding boots. When I expressed a partiality for a straw hat to wear against the sun, he pursed his lips, shook his head, and brought forth the correct head covering for the coat.

"No wig?" I queried lightly.

He started to reach for a box, but I hastily called him off.

Since Beldon had no valet to help him he came down to the library ten minutes ahead of me. Father, in his dressing gown and silk nightcap, was with him and once more going over the names of the people we were to see. Beldon thought it was too short a list, but Father pointed out that it was better to see a few at a time rather than rushing about in noticeable haste.

"You're a doctor making your usual calls on your patients and Jonathan is along to visit with their families."

And to act as guide. Beldon knew most of our neighbors by now, if only from seeing them every Sunday at church, but he was less sure of where they lived unless they were regular patients. Rapelji, for example, was not in that number. His housekeepers, Rachel and Sarah, were adept at keeping him in excellent health with their herb lore. Many of the local farmers were content to see the sisters for their illnesses as well, sparing themselves from paying a doctor's fee.

I noted that Father's mistress, Mrs. Montagu, was not among those named, though her home was along the route we would take. Perhaps he would see to informing her himself later. I hoped so. With all our late troubles, I felt that he was in need of some pleasant, relaxing company.

Father let us out the side door facing the stables and wished us good luck. Our mounts were ready, the doctor on a hack he'd purchased some time ago, and a similar working horse for myself. Rolly would have been a better ride, but could draw unwelcome attention. I had no desire to lose him on the high road to some avaricious officer with a sheaf of blank receipts in his pocket.

Beldon spent a moment fussing with his box of medicines, making sure it was secure, then swung up. The horses may have sensed a long day was ahead and made no effort to use up their strength with unnecessary prancing or high spirits. We paced sedately down toward the front gate.

"It's good to finally be off," said Beldon. "I hardly slept last night, thinking of this."

I made a noncommittal noise I'd learned from Father. It was useful for expressing almost any sentiment, the interpretation of it being left to the listener.

"You do realize that I shall be making real calls, don't you?"

I said that I did.

"One of the Coldrup daughters has her migraines, and the youngest at the McCuin's broke his arm. ..."

He chattered on, a man interested in his work. He reminded me of

Oliver in that regard and because of it I was better able to tolerate his company. He was, as Elizabeth said, "not such a bad fellow." I distracted myself from the normal tedium of the ride with speculation about his history. Except for a store of anecdotes which his sister imparted in boundless detail about their life in Philadelphia, and the little snippet he'd dropped the previous afternoon, I realized that none of us knew very much about him, not really. It seemed a shame. Perhaps—if once one could get past the toad-eating—he could become a friend.

We turned east into the waxing force of the rising sun. As Jericho had prophesied, it was going to be very hot. I squinted against the searing light and tilted my hat down. I couldn't see where I was going too well, but the horse knew his business and kept to the road.

We passed Mrs. Montagu's gate on the right and a mile farther down I indicated for Beldon to leave the road. The Captain's Kettle was in this area. Our property line crossed over at this point. The boundary had been a bone of contention between Mrs. Montagu and Father soon after her husband had died fourteen years ago. Two sets of surveyors had come up with very different interpretations of where the correct line lay and the matter had ended up in court. Father had argued his case and would have won it had Matilda Montagu remained at home during the proceedings. Upon meeting her, he became abruptly sympathetic to her claim and dropped the litigation. With his sympathy and her gratitude as a beginning, they proceeded to form a lasting, satisfying, and highly discreet friendship.

I led the way now, weaving my horse between the trees. I hadn't been up here since that April ride so long ago, but the landmarks were unchanged. Within, I had the unnerving feeling that I would once more see Father and Mrs. Montagu walking hand in hand in the distance. That was foolish, of course, but the feeling lingered and strengthened as we drew closer to the kettle.

Birds squawked and squabbled overhead. Insects hummed and dodged them. The air was thick with their noise, yet seemed muted, flattened by the growing heat. There didn't seem to be much activity where we were.

"I don't think we're alone," said Beldon, barely moving his lips, speaking just loud enough for me to hear him over the movement of the horses.

One can usually sense when someone is watching; I just hadn't recognized the feeling. "Where?"

"Ahead of us. On either side. I think we should go back."

I wholly agreed with him and the two of us turned in unison without another word. It could be children at play or a pair of lovers on a tryst, but it could also be any number of less innocent threats. Better to return after the prickling on the backs of our necks went away.

We did not get that chance, though. Before we'd gone fifty yards a hard-looking man in uniform stepped out from a dense thicket of bushes, aimed his rifle at us, and in a rough and accented voice ordered us to halt.

I knew the uniform. Everyone on the Island did. He was a Hessian.

CHAPTER
TEN

A SECOND MAN joined him and barked out another order at us.

"Down!" the first one translated.

Beldon and I exchanged looks. Heroism was the last thing on our minds. Not that we had anything to be heroic about. Once we'd identified ourselves we'd be able to leave.

I hoped.

We cautiously dismounted and kept hold of the reins. We studied the soldiers and were studied in turn. They saw by our clothes that we were gentlemen, but there were plenty of so-called gentlemen opposing the king these days. The men were flushed and their sweat-stained uniforms showed evidence that they'd been hiking through the woods for some time, perhaps even all night. It was certain to me that they had some purpose to the exercise, perhaps an ominous one for myself and Beldon. Beldon's horse, supremely unconcerned with the situation, dropped his head and began tearing at the grass.

The second man barked a question, but before the first could translate it, I hesitantly answered.

"This is Dr. Theophilous Beldon and I am Jonathan Barrett," I said in rather slow German. "This is my land. Why are you here?"

Though I'd only previously used it in my academics, my German was apparently intelligible. It surprised them, and to my tremendous relief the grip on their rifles slackened. The second man came to attention and identified himself as Detricht Schmidt and gave his rank, but I did not know that particular word. He could have been anything from a simple soldier to a colonel, though his manner and the lack of trimmings on his uniform made the latter very unlikely. Their officers were very fond of show. I repeated my last question and finally got an answer.

"They're looking for a band of rebels," I explained to Beldon. "At least that's what I think he said. Something about stolen horses."

Beldon nodded, also impressed by my linguistic gifts. "Where is his commander?"

"*Close by,*" said Schmidt, after I'd asked.

"Here," repeated the other man agreeably, waving an arm at the surrounding woods. His accent was heavy, but probably no worse than mine must have sounded to his ears.

"We want to go," I said to him in slow English.

Both of them shrugged. I tried to say the same thing in German, but garbled it up. However, Schmidt understood enough of my meaning. "*You must stay,*" I was told.

"Here halt," his friend emphasized, making a sitting gesture with his palm toward the ground. Both were nodding and smiling, though, so perhaps they'd decided we were not with the rebels.

"They must want their commander to look us over first," I said.

Beldon was amiable. "Then let's all be pleasant about it, since it can't be helped." He smiled in return and pulled a snuffbox from his pocket, offering a pinch of its contents to our captors. They accepted with many friendly thanks and another piece of our initial tension broke away.

Schmidt excused himself after a moment and disappeared into the trees. The other young man gave his name as Hausmann and complimented my German. "Schmidt soon back," he promised.

"*Is your commander English?*"

"*Jawohl, Herr* Barrett."

"Where are the rebels?"

He shrugged, but it caused him to recall that they might be nearby and he checked the surrounding open area uneasily. "Trees—go," he suggested, wanting to get into their cover. "*Schnell, bitte.*"

Beldon and I led our horses in, grateful for the shade, though it cut us off from the wind. Hausmann kept his distance so as to have room to bring his rifle to bear if we made it necessary. He'd relaxed somewhat, but it was clear that he was ready to deal with any threat until ordered to stand down by his commander.

"How many men are here?" I asked, repeating a question from Beldon.

Hausmann puzzled out my meaning right away, but would only smile and shake his head.

"Not a good idea to give away the strength of your troop," Beldon, the former soldier, explained.

And I thought he'd only been trying to make conversation. I had better luck asking Hausmann where he was from and if he had any family. For that I got the name of his village and a number of relatives and their history in that district. Much of it was too rapid for me to follow, but I made encouraging noises whenever he slowed down.

"Your family?" he asked politely. "Your land all?" He indicated the area.

"Our land," I said.

He looked both envious and admiring. "Land is good. Here land I want."

"Here?"

He waved to show he meant some other land than what we stood upon. "Farm. Woman. *Das Kleinkind.* "

"What?" asked Beldon.

"He wants to have a family."

"What about the one he left in Europe?"

"I think they're all dead. He said the wars killed them."

Before he could express any sympathy, the three of us turned at the sound of several men approaching. Schmidt had returned. With him were two more Hessians and two men wearing the uniform of the king's army. "Lieutenant James Nash," said the one with the most braid, making a succinct introduction.

I recognized the name. He was behind the theft of Finch's wagon and horses. He seemed a bit old to be a lieutenant, in his late forties, I guessed. Perhaps he'd been unable to advance further for lack of funding, patronage, talent or opportunity. This new war was probably his last chance to change his luck and acquire some security for his old age. Too bad for Finch.

I introduced myself and Beldon to him and informed him as politely as possible that he was trespassing. I did not employ that particular word, but he knew what I meant.

"My apologies, sir, but we're on the king's business and cannot make distinctions between public and private lands. Those damned rebels don't and we have to follow where they run."

"I believe your men mentioned they were horse thieves."

"Aye, they are," he added with some warmth. "Tried to take a wagon too, but we foiled that."

I refrained from looking at Beldon and kept a very straight face.

"What a shame. That they took your horses, I mean."

"We'll find 'em," he assured me. "If you know the area, you can help us."

I smiled graciously and hoped that it looked sincere. "I should be delighted to lend you any assistance, Lieutenant. That is, if I may take your invitation to mean that we are no longer in detention?"

"You never were, but my men do have to be careful. Some of the louts are armed and not afraid to shoot. I think they're headed for Suffolk County with their booty."

Or to Finch's farm.

"You've gone over this acreage thoroughly, then?"

"Not quite. Know of any hiding places?"

"These woods," I said truthfully, but vaguely. "But horses would slow them down. If they're in a hurry, then they'll be likely to swing back toward the road or find more open countryside."

"*Herr Oberleutnant!*" Another Hessian rushed away from us, shouting.

"He's spotted them," said the sergeant. He snapped out orders to the men and they spread into the trees. Nash was content to let them do the sweaty work and followed more slowly. He wanted us to come with him.

"I have my rounds to make," Beldon protested, hoping to end the business.

"Won't be long. Best if we all stay together. You don't care to catch a stray bullet if things go badly, do you?"

Beldon did not, and we resigned ourselves to Nash's company. He led the way, his stocky, paunchy body moving easily and making his own path. We did the best we could leading the horses. Despite the shade, the heat was worse now. I was damp from face to shanks and a bramble scratch between my sleeve and riding glove began to sting from the sweat. Nuisance. It was all one foolish, bloody nuisance.

Nash's men had entirely vanished, but I could hear them crashing along. They were heading in the direction of the Captain's Kettle. If the rebels were local—and I was certain they were—then the kettle would be the first sanctuary they'd think to use.

"*Down here! Down here!*" one of the Hessians called in the distance. It could only mean that they'd found it. Nash speeded up a little.

Damnation. Not only had the rebels trespassed our land and possibly thrown unwelcome suspicion upon Father, but they'd promptly given away our own best secret. We'd have to think up some other place to hide our stock this year.

Since they knew about the kettle, I suspected the thieves had to be the Finch boys, Roddy and Nathan. I mentioned this in a whisper to Beldon, who reluctantly concurred.

"I hope they have the sense to run," he muttered, his mouth tight and the corners turned down. If caught with the horses they would be hanged. Rebel or no, it was not a fate I could wish upon anybody.

"Mind yourself," I muttered back. If Nash heard him...

Someone fired a shot.

Beldon dropped and I instinctively imitated him. The horrid crash was well ahead of us, though, and isolated. A rifle, I thought. The noise was different than that from a pistol. No other shots sounded. Nash urged us to hurry and plunged forward, which struck me as a ridiculously foolish course of action. No soldier, I. Neither of us were armed. I felt terribly vulnerable.

Hausmann appeared and relayed information to Nash, who understood him.

"Nothing to worry about," he told us with faint contempt. "Fellow tripped on a root. Accidental discharge." Apparently he overlooked the fact he'd been quick enough to take cover, too.

"Thank God for that," Beldon breathed out. He produced his handkerchief and scraped futilely at his streaming forehead. I sighed as well, but my heart wasn't yet ready to retire from the place where it had lodged halfway up my throat. As though reading my thought, Beldon grinned at me. I found myself returning it. That seemed to help.

Nash caught up with some of his men now and questioned them. They were pointing and gesturing. From this I deduced that they'd discovered the kettle and were trying to explain its geography to him. My horse swung his ears forward and neighed. Ahead of us and down, another horse answered. The trees were very thick here. If you weren't careful you could fall right into it. Beldon tied his animal up and walked over to investigate with the others. I did the same and hoped Nash wouldn't ask me anything awkward.

"Did you know about this?" he demanded, pointing to a break in the trees. From here it was easy to see the drop-off.

"Of course I did," I said blandly.

"Just the place for a horse thief to hide, so why didn't you tell me about it?"

"I'm hardly familiar with how a horse thief thinks, Lieutenant. It never occurred to me to mention it." True enough. "Had your man not given the alarm, I would have taken you here." Blatant falsehood, but hopefully God would forgive me that one.

Nash may have had further comment on the subject, but seemed more concerned with retrieving his...king's property. "Well, things have worked out. We got the horses back."

"Won't the thieves be close by, though?"

"That shot seems to have frightened them away. We're safe enough. Come on."

Beldon looked dubious despite Nash's confidence. "As simple civilians, may we be excused from this exercise? I have no desire to inflict any more damage to my clothes than they've already suffered."

Nash again gave him the half-amused, half-contemptuous look that professional soldiers reserve for the rest of the world and went off after his men.

"You think they're still around?" I asked.

"I do not know. One thing I am sure about is that I should be very reluctant to enter a place like this." He stepped closer to the edge of the kettle and nodded at the woods on the opposite side of the depression. "With all his men down there, any rebels up here would have no trouble pinning them and picking them off as they pleased."

"Shouldn't we warn them?"

"There's probably nothing in it. They're chasing farm lads, not soldiers. I think—"

But I didn't hear the rest of Beldon's opinion. Across the kettle, I caught a glimpse of a pimply face suddenly obscured by a cloud of thick smoke. Roddy Finch, I thought. Of course. He'd be the one to...

Something struck my chest with enormous and sudden force. I was shocked. The only thing I could think of was that for some insane reason Beldon had picked up a large stone and smashed it against me with all his strength. The breath rushed out and I staggered back from the blow.

Not Beldon. His hands were empty. He wasn't even looking at me; his head turned, strangely slow, his gaze meeting mine for an instant.

His normally tranquil expression sluggishly altered to alarm. I saw my name form on his lips, flowing out little by little, one syllable at a time.

My heels caught on something as I staggered back. My legs wouldn't respond. My arms thrashed wildly at empty air.

Beldon thrust his hands forward, but was too slow to catch me. I completely lost my balance and dropped. My back struck the earth solidly, driving a last pocket of breath from my lungs.

It dazed me. I'd thumped my skull in the fall. My slack tongue blocked my throat. I tried to shake my head to one side to dislodge it. I could not move.

Stunned. Only stunned, that's all. It would pass. Like the time I'd fallen into the kettle.

Patches of bright sky leached through the leaves high overhead. Beldon came into view above me. He was bellowing. I couldn't understand the words, only that they were too loud. I winced and tried to tell him to lower his voice, that I was all right.

A gurgling, wheezing sound. From *me*. From my chest. A vast, invisible weight had settled upon it.

Beldon's face was twisted into an awful mixture of rage and grief and terror and helplessness. What was wrong? What had happened?

The weight on me was crushing. My God, I couldn't *breathe*.

He put his arms under my shoulders and lifted me a little. He was trying to help me get air. But nothing happened. I clawed at my throat. At my chest. He pushed my hands off, but they'd already found the problem. They came away smeared with blood. Far too much blood.

No....

I choked, tried to speak. The stuff flooded up my throat like hot vomit and spilled from my nose and mouth. I was drowning in it. Drowning in my own blood.

Beldon was talking to me. Yelling, perhaps. Weeping? Why...? What—?

Good God, *no*. It can't be.

My body thrashed, out of control as my lungs vainly tried to work. The terrible pressure on my chest spread, crushing me into the earth like a giant's boot heel. I had to fight it or be smashed into a pulp like a worm.

Beldon, damn him, was trying to hold me still. He didn't understand.

Air. Please, God. Just a little air...

I breathed blood instead. Choked. Sputtered it out again. Beldon was covered with it. Like that dream of Nora...

The memory whipped from my mind. I struggled to clear my clogged throat.

Elizabeth. Father....

Just a little air. Just a little that I might see them once more. God, I was on *fire* from within. What burned me?

Fight it.

My efforts produced only a bubbling, gagging noise. I was already panicked; to hear and know that dreadful, disgusting sound was coming from me....

Fight it!

The blazing pain abruptly ebbed. The weight on me eased.

Fight...

Eyelids heavy now. Couldn't blink. Couldn't focus on anything. The light and leaves above blurred and merged and danced together, receding.

...it...

A shuddering convulsion shook my body from head to toe. I was aware of the movement, but not really feeling it. Beldon cried my name in a hopeless wail.

But I was unable to answer as a soft stillness settled upon me. I lingered just at the threshold of waking and sleep. He was shaking me, trying to rouse me. It should have worked, but all that was me was in retreat. It was like rolling over against cold morning air and pulling the blanket down more snugly to seize another few minutes of blissful, warm rest.

Beldon stopped the shaking. I pushed the sleep off briefly, wondering what troubled him. He was yet within view, but his head was bowed as for prayer.

The pain was all gone now. No air yet, but I didn't seem to need it. That awful weight was also absent. Good. Good.

Nothing left to do now but give in to the sleep. Which I did, slipping away into the silence and sweet darkness.

I WOKE UP SMOOTHLY, with none of the usual attendant grogginess. The room was blacker than ink. Must have been well past moon set. That, or Jericho had closed the shutters of my window and drawn the curtains. I should have been baking from the day's lingering summer heat, but was not. Neither warm nor cold, the only feeling intruding on my general awareness was that my bed was uncomfortably hard.

Damnation. I must have passed out drunk on the floor. It wouldn't be the first time.

But...I hadn't really gotten drunk since leaving Cambridge. I was home. Surely Jericho would have taken care of me.

The back of my head rolled from side to side on the wooden planks, each irregularity of the bone against an unyielding surface made apparent by my movement. Damn the man. Even if my drunkenness offended him, he could have at least spared a pillow for me.

My shoulders pressed down heavily as well. And my backside. And my heels. I'd grow numb and stiff if I stayed like this.

He'd thought to give me a blanket, but had drawn it completely up over my head. I was having trouble pulling it from my face .... I could *not* pull it away from my face. When I tried to move my arms, my elbows thumped into—

What? The sides of a *box*? Where in God's name was I?

My eyes had been open through this. Or so I thought. It was difficult to tell, everything being so black. They were definitely open now. In the cramped space I inched one hand up and felt to be sure. Cheek. Lashes. Lids. Outer corner. *Blink.*

Nothing. I saw nothing.

It was the damned blanket. I tugged and came to realize it was wrapped around me and somehow tied over the top of my head like a—

No. That was ridiculous.

Almighty God, but it was quiet. I could only hear my own stirrings in what I now accepted as a small, enclosed space—the rustle of cloth, the scrape of shoe heels on wood, even the soft creak of my joints—but absolutely nothing else.

But there *had* to be some sound. It was always there, even when one did not listen, there were hundreds of things to be heard. Wind. Bird song. The whisper of leaf and grass blade. One's own pulse, for God's sake, thumping against the eardrum.

Silence. Perfect. Unremitting.

Even my heart?

No. It was there—had to be; I was just too alarmed now to hear it.

I pushed against the blanket or whatever it was that covered me and encountered the lid of the box I was in. Oliver and some of his cronies were having a game with me. Waiting until I was drunk, they'd put me in here for a bad joke. A positively foul joke. Oliver wasn't the sort to be cruel, though, so ....

But I was *not* in Cambridge. My mind was seeking any answer but the truth. I already knew it, or thought I did, but to face it—no, impossible. Quite impossible.

Perhaps Oliver was drunk, insensible in another room, that had to be it.

My shoulders strained and muscles popped as I pushed on the lid.

The bastards had nailed it down. The thing wouldn't budge. I'd be damned before I gave them the satisfaction of hearing me call for help. Oliver had had no part in this. It was too spiteful.

Warburton, perhaps.

Warburton, white around the eyes and looking drunk. But he hadn't been drunk.

Warburton, curled up on the floor, weeping.

Nora, looking down at him.

Nora, looking at me.

Nora, talking to me. Telling me all the things that I must forget.

I shook away that memory as if it were rain streaming in my face. Just as persistently, it continued to flood down.

Rain. Yes, that was right.

It had been raining. Cold. Icy. Tony Warburton striding away into the night. And when I saw him again he was drunk and repentant. But he hadn't really been drunk. He'd tricked me to going over to Nora's and when she'd walked in, he'd ...

No. That was only in a bad dream.

To the devil with them. I could not bear the silence and darkness any longer. My voice roared out—

And went no farther than the confines of the box. The flat sound of it thrown back on itself told me as much.

Beldon had also called for help. He and I had been ... I'd just seen the Finch boy raise his rifle. But he couldn't have—that simply could not have happened to me. I couldn't believe, didn't dare believe. To do so meant that I was ... had been ... they wouldn't have done this to me.

I was *alive*. The living aren't trapped in the ground like this; God would surely spare the worst of sinners that horror. I could still think, move, speak, even smell. The odor of musty cloth and new wood and damp earth were making me sick.

Earth. In the *ground*. *Trapped in the ground*.

I heaved against the lid, calling for help. I did this many times, keeping the unthinkable at bay a little longer.

Useless. My arms dropped to my chest, drained, shaking with weakness.

Now I knew without doubt, without any deceiving fancies, *exactly* where I was, and no yell, no scream, no plea, no sobbing prayer would free me from this.

My *grave*.

For maybe a count of five I lay frozen, then:

No. *No. Nonononononono.*

I bellowed, I shrieked, panic seizing me wholly as I clawed at the lid tearing my hands on the unyielding wood. I had to *get out*—

And, for a fraction of a moment, I ceased to *be* at all, turned into a mindless screaming *thing.* Then my cries faded and died, along with the pain of life, and I seemed to be floating, falling, but slowly. I fancied the earth bearing indifferently down on me, trying to hold me into itself, yet I pushed and pressed my way past it, like, and yet unlike, a swimmer. Instead of cleaving soil, it was as if it flowed *through* me.

My thrashing body suddenly hurtled free of its prison and heavy as stone, rolled down a slight grading. Arms and kicking legs ripped at the shroud, almost free—

I was...on the ground. Not in it. Open ground. Trees. Their leaves whispering to one another. What a sweet song for my starved ears. I could still smell earth, but it wasn't as cloying, diluted by other scents carried on the wind. Clover, grass, and a skunk, by God. I never thought I'd welcome *that* pungency.

Able to use my arms again, I finally tore away the cloth shroud binding me.

Shroud. I sat up and forced myself to look.

My shroud. Yellow with age, for it had been stored in the attic since my birth, as was the custom. We all had one, Father, Elizabeth, Mother, all the servants, all our friends. Death was always around us, from a summer fever to a bad fall from a horse. One prepared for death as soon as one was born. One had to accept it, for there was no other alternative.

Nora, my mind whispered uneasily. I shook my head violently.

Take stock. Where...?

I was...in a graveyard. The one I passed each Sunday going in to hear the sermon.

But I could *not* be.

I pushed the impossibility away. It kept returning like a nagging fly.

I pushed away the burgeoning fear. It held back for the moment.

An unbidden image came to me of standing at the edge of the drop off, of noting without alarm the puff of smoke across the way, of not knowing what it meant, of falling, of pain, of blood....

Without any thought behind the action, I began unbuttoning my waistcoat. My fingers moved on their own, and it was with mild surprise that I looked down to see my clothes parted and my chest bared. The wound that some hidden part of my mind expected to find was there, right over my heart, but closed up and nearly-healed. The surrounding skin was bruised and red, but not from inflammation. There was no pain. Not any more.

Nora.

I grew very cold. Not from the soft air flowing past me, but from the stark memory of her slumping down, run through with my sword-stick. It had caught her in the heart. The blood covered her dress. Warburton had laughed and turned upon me. My dream, my nightmare, had been true. Nora had died and returned...and had made me forget.

Made me forget everything.

Our love. *How* we had loved. All of it plucked from my mind like ripping pages from a book.

Not completely, it seemed. Those lost pages were fluttering back into place again. Each memory with a sweetness offset by a last, bitter betrayal.

Had she been cruel or kind? From the bits and pieces returning, I knew that she *had* truly loved me and would have done anything to protect me from harm. But she also had herself to protect, and so I'd been made to forget not only all that made her different from others, but my deepest feelings for her, made to wall away half of my very soul. The enormity of her gentle perfidy numbed my battered mind. I drew my arms around my legs and rocked back and forth, overcome by the misery.

My eyes stared without seeing at the bright night sky, at the humps and angled shapes of the gravestones surrounding me, at the church's great gray shadow creeping over the ground. As a child, I would have taken on any dare but this one, to spend a single moment in this place after dark. Was I now become some lost spirit rejected by both heaven and hell? Was I condemned to be trapped here? Was this my punishment for falling in love?

Such questions as these hammered at the barrier of desolation I'd built up. Eventually their absurdity broke through, allowing a vestige of reason to slip in.

Such sinister imaginings were suitable for a ghost story, or the overdone drama of a stage play, but not for me. I wasn't a spirit or the recipient of divine vengeance, though I had no doubt now that I had died. My heart was silent. My lungs only worked when I consciously used them. How strange it was not to breathe.

Nora had been the same. I could almost laugh to remember how alarmed I'd been when I'd noticed that. It had been on the night when we'd first exchanged blood. She must have blocked my mind from re-marking on it before.

I was... I was like Nora now. By giving my blood to her and taking hers into myself, she'd passed on—what? Her immunity to death?

Why hadn't she told me what to expect?

Perhaps she hadn't known herself, I logically answered. There was much she'd never told me. Far too much, apparently.

Then I did laugh. I laughed until I wept. Couldn't stop. Didn't want to stop., Giving myself up to a malignant self-pity blacker than the confines of my vacant grave, I moaned and howled and cried, my voice striking off the side of the church to cast itself to the open air. I did not recognize it. I did not even recognize myself, for I'd been turned into a most miserable wretch by the overwhelming despair of losing her.

◆ ◆ ◆

THE STORM PASSED.

Eventually.

My temper was not such as to leave me in the depths for very long. Sooner or later we must all emerge and deal with mundane practicalities.

I wiped at my nose and swollen eyes with the lower edge of my shirt. They'd dressed me in my best Sunday clothes. I'd even been given a proper shave. Poor Jericho would have had to do it. I swayed where I sat, nearly plunging into the darkness again by simply thinking of how he must have felt.

Later. I would worry about it later.

Levering stiffly to my feet, I kicked away the shroud and brushed at the earth clinging to my breeches.

What next?

Go home, of course.

It seemed a good idea. Then it soured. They thought me dead. I'd terrify them. What would they think? How could I possibly explain myself? How could I explain Nora?

How—I was looking at the undisturbed mound of my grave—in God's name had I escaped *that*? The flat marks where the spades had tamped the dirt down were still there, blurred a little where I'd rolled off. There were footprints all around as well, men's and women's. I had no difficulty imagining the mourners standing by it, listening to the service being read and weeping through the words. They were the real ghosts of this place, the living, with their grief twining about the low stones like sea mist. The dead were at peace; it was the ones they left behind who suffered.

Where did that leave me, who was neither alive nor dead?

Later.

My bones felt leaden; I was worn out by sheer emotion yet questions continued to pop into my head. I ignored them and trudged out of the churchyard. One foot before the other for a time, then I could rest. A little sleep in my own bed and I'd sort it all out for the others in the morning.

God, what would I *tell* them?

Later. Later. Later.

Forsaking all thought, I walked and let my senses drift. The road dust kicked up by my steps, the night insects at song, wind rustling the trees, these were most welcome distractions. Normal. Undemanding.

"'Oo's there?!'"

The intrusion of a human voice jerked me back to myself.

"Speak up! I've a rifle on ye." Despite the man's bold declaration, there was a decided quaver in his tone.

"Is that you, Mr. Nutting?" I called back. Something like relief flooded me as I recognized Mervin Nutting, the sexton. He was sheltered beneath the thick shadow of a tree, but I had no trouble spotting him. The puzzlement was that he could not see me standing not fifteen yards away in the middle of the road.

"'Oo are ye?" he demanded, squinting right at me, then moving blindly on. He held a pistol, not a rifle, and his hand shook. "Stand forth!"

"I'm right—" Oh, dear. Perhaps this was not such a good idea after all: confronting the man who had most likely dug my grave and filled it in again. My mouth snapped shut.

"Come on! Show yerself!"

I backed away a step. Quietly. Took another. My shoe crunched against a stone. Nutting swung in my direction with his pistol. He looked terrified, but determined. His clothing—what he wore of it—suggested that he'd recently been roused from bed. His house was close to the church; he must have heard my ravings and come to investigate. No wonder he was so fearful.

"Come on!"

Not this time, I thought, moving more carefully. Better to leave him with a mystery and to speculate at The Oak about hauntings than to reveal the truth and frighten him to death.

"Vat is it, Herr Nutting?" A second man came up behind him, shrugging on a Hessian uniform coat while trying to keep hold of his lantern. He must have been quartered at Nutting's house.

"Thieves or worse," was the reply. "Hold it high, man, so we can see." He joggled the Hessian's arm.

"*Vorsicht! Das Feuer!*" the soldier yelped, worried about dropping it.

The lantern may have helped them, but I perceived no real difference for myself. It was like a candle against full daylight. My eyes were used to the dark by now, but surely my vision should not be as clear as this.

Emboldened by having company, Nutting advanced them onto the road. I saw every detail of their faces, even the colors in their clothes; in turn, they were limited to the radius of their feeble lamplight. I kept backing away, but was unable to judge the right distance to avoid its most outside reach.

"*There!*" the Hessian cried. He pointed straight at me.

Whether Nutting understood German or not was debatable, but he got the general idea and brought his pistol to bear. He shouted an order. Or started to. I didn't wait for him to finish and pelted down the road faster than I'd ever run before. The pistol roared behind me and I nearly fell flinching from it, terrified of being hit.

Thank God Nutting was better at disposing of ale than shooting straight, and his companion was thankfully unwilling to proceed without more arms. I gained distance. Far behind, but still visible to me, they shouted for me to return. A most foolish request.

Well, that had woken me right up. I slowed to a walk, albeit a quick one. I was not breathing hard. Good God in heaven, I wasn't breathing at all.

I groaned at that reminder.

What was to become of me?

All the questions returned, full force, and I had no answers. Time would take care of most of them, no doubt, but the encounter with Nutting made me realize what awaited when I got home. Not that I'd be facing another pistol, but my return from the dead would certainly inspire the most dreadful fear at first. Was I ready to do that to them? Would it not be better to …

I didn't care. I needed them. They … they'd just have to hear me out. That was all there was too it.

The last mile home is always the longest, and I was growing very tired. My eyes hurt. I'd ask Beldon to look at them and hopefully prescribe some drops to soothe things. Heavens, but it would be good to see even Beldon the toad-eater again. How dreadful he had looked that last time. He had so desperately tried to help me, the poor fellow.

The sun would be up soon. My eyes were beginning to burn like coals from the growing brightness. This sensitivity worried me. Common sense suggested that it would be better to avoid true daylight when it came, at least until I got used to it.

Nora. She NEVER *came out during the day.*

She'd slept—slept the day through however long the seasons made it. It had been her one unbreakable rule. We'd almost had an argument about it once. We'd gone to a party that had lasted all night. I wanted to watch the sunrise with her and she'd flatly refused, insisting on going home once she'd realized the time. I'd been stung by this, offended that she couldn't give up an hour of sleep for me, but she'd talked to me in that way of hers until it ceased to matter.

I'd forgotten that until now. She'd made me lose so much. Every memory that returned possessed both comfort and pain and no small measure of unease. I'd accepted—or had been made to accept—her differences from other people as eccentricities, but if a serious purpose lay behind each, then it was to my interest to imitate her.

I needed shelter from the sun, then, and very soon. Even now I had to shade my eyes against the glare stealing above the horizon. It was much worse than during my morning ride with Beldon yesterday.

Had that only been yesterday? Or today? Had I been truly alive just this morning? How long had I been in the—

Later, I said firmly.

The house was too far away to reach in time; I'd have to settle for the most distant of our outbuildings, an old unused barn. It had once been the property's main barn and close by had stood the original house. That had burned down decades earlier and the remaining stone foundation and chimney had become a childhood playground. We'd been forbidden to go into the barn, but had explored it anyway. Children either have no concept of mortality, or honestly believe they will live forever. We'd come to no harm, though I later shuddered at the risks we blithely took then. The place had been filled with discards and old lumber, rats and snakes.

The doors were gone, but I'd expected that. Dodging a growth of ivy that had taken over the walls, I walked in, cautious of where I put my feet. The trash I remembered had long ago been hauled away and probably burned. Just as well. The stone floor was still in good condition, though clumps of grass and weeds grew in cracks near the entry as far as the sun reached in. They would serve as a guide for me to judge where the deepest shade might be found. It was noticeably darker inside despite the gaps in the high roof. Birds and other small animals had found refuge here. Hopefully, I would be safe as well until my eyes adjusted.

Outside the light grew unbearably bright. Perhaps I was being unrealistically optimistic about being able to shortly leave. I fled to the most protected part of the place, a horse stall in a far corner. The brick walls were high, what must have been a dark and cheerless spot for the former occupant, now offered a unique comfort to me.

"But I want to go home," I whispered, peering over the wall. I had to shield my eyes with my arm. The light was utterly blinding.

My limbs stiffened. No pain, but they were horribly difficult to move. So much had happened; the fatigue was catching me up. Rest. After a little rest I might feel better.

I was reluctant to sit. The floor was filthy with dust and other small rubbish I preferred not to think about, but there was no choice. My legs folded on their own. My knees struck with a jarring double crack that deprived me of balance. I pitched over and landed on my side. My thoughts were as stiff and sluggish as my bones. I felt no fear. I'd had a surfeit of it in the last few hours and could produce no more.

Dragged down by the natural pull of gravity, I rolled flat on my back. My eyes slammed shut on their own. The world may have spun on about its business, but I was no longer a part of it.

✦ ✦ ✦

HARDLY AN INSTANT LATER my eyes opened again.

I lay as I'd fallen, but this awakening was far superior to the last one. My mind smoothly picked up its previous thread of thought as though I'd only blinked rather than dropped unconscious to the floor. I felt alert and aware and ready to deal with whatever the dawn brought. Fluidity returned to my limbs; the wooden hardness of my joints vanished. I easily stood to take note of my surroundings.

Changes had taken place. Important ones.

Though the strength of the outside light was about the same as before, it now fell from a different direction. The west.

By God, I'd slept the whole day away if I could believe that it was now sunset. It was yet painfully bright, but gradually dimming to a more comfortable level with each minute. Soon it would be fully dark—at least for other people. For me, well, at least I should be able to avoid accidentally running into anyone out for a late walk on my way—

Home. I desperately wanted to be *home*.

Supper would be over by now. They'd probably be in the drawing room: Mother and her guests to play cards, Father to read, Elizabeth at her spinet. Perhaps not. The house was in mourning, after all. My heart ached for them and for myself. I would hurry. Once there I would somehow find the right words.

Futilely, I brushed at my clothes. As if how I looked would matter to Father and Elizabeth when they saw me. I couldn't wait to see their faces, all of them; once over the shock it would be better than Christmas. I'd ask Mrs. Nooth about food first thing, because I felt quite starved for…heavens, I was too hungry to know what I wanted to eat, though doubtless anything left from the last meal would suit just fine.

Swiftly, I marched from the barn and down the overgrown path leading to the road. The lack of food had me somewhat tired in body, but strangely sharp in mind. The strength of last night's terrors and doubts and worries had faded. I even found myself smiling about the encounter with Mr. Nutting. He'd only gotten a bad fright, though; I'd make it up to him at The Oak later, the Hessian, too, if he liked ale. I'd be the talk of the county, the Lazarus of Long Island.

My confidence faltered. How would the membership of the church receive this particular resurrection? Even the better educated might be reduced to a superstitious dread. The common folk I hardly dared consider. Would I be viewed as a heavenly miracle or an infernal mockery?

Later, I reminded myself once more and kept going.

Had they caught Roddy Finch yet? I'd been so occupied with my own immediate sorrows that I'd had no thought to spare for the man who had…killed me. No thought to spare and, until now, no anger. Murderers were hanged and rightly so, though in this case there was sufficient mitigation to prevent it. You can't hang a man for murder if the victim turns up to call things off, but the pimply-faced bastard would pay for this if I had to flog him myself. I was very definitely prepared to do it as my anger was not just for me but for the awful grief he'd caused my poor family.

On the other hand, he might probably hang anyway, for the horses he'd stolen back from the Crown.

My mind started to spin a bit at the complications. I'd have to talk with Father, sort it all out with him. Later.

Less than half a mile from my gate, I became conscious of a wagon rattling up the road behind. I saw it long before the driver could see me and debated whether or not to take cover until it passed. Sooner or later the news would spread of my return so I supposed it would make no difference to wait for him. Besides, he might be obliging enough to give me a ride. My feet were beginning to drag as my empty belly snarled to life. I consoled myself that soon Mrs. Nooth would put it to rest with her excellent cooking.

The driver was a stranger, though obviously a farmer or worked for one. I waited until certain the lighted lamps hanging from his wagon had picked me up from the general darkness, then gave him a friendly hail. He was startled, for the times were unsettled and a man out after sundown was subject to justifiable suspicion.

"Who be ye?" he demanded, pulling on the reins. There was a long rifle propped next to him on the bench, and he seemed ready to reach for it.

"I'm Mr. Barrett, at your service, sir. I live near here."

"Good e'en to ye," he replied cautiously, looking me over. "Have a spot of trouble?"

I fought down the urge to laugh. "Yes, quite a lot of it. I suffered a fall and am trying to get home." Close enough to the truth.

"Musta been a prodigious fall, young sir," he said agreeably. "I can give ye a ride if ye c'n tell me if 'm on the right road to Glenbriar."

"That you are, sir. And less than a mile from my own gate."

He took the hint. "Good, commun up, then." He made room for me on the seat and I readily joined him. "Name's Hulton. 'M on my way to sell goods to the soldiers." He got the horses moving again. "Sun go down, but thought I'd push through."

"You're welcome to spend the night at my home. Or, if you stay on this road you'll pass The Oak. They'll put you up there right enough. I'd be careful about dealing with the commissaries, though."

"They not payin' good coin?"

"Even worse." I explained in detail about the blank receipts and the theft of Finch's property. Hulton took it all in with a stone face, then shook his head.

"'F that be how things stand, then I may as well go home ag'in as go on. Least 'f the rebels steal from me I c'n get the soldiers to hang 'em, but who'll hang the soldiers?"

"The rebels, if they win," I said.

His eye sharpened. "You one of 'em?"

"Good God, no. My family are all loyal to His Majesty, God bless him."

"Amen," he said, amused by my wholehearted sincerity. "Still, can't 'ford to lose m' goods to anyone, be they soldiers or rebels. This'll take a bit of figgerin'. Can't figger like this. Need grease for the wheels to turn, y'see." He reached under the bench and pulled out a jug. Though one hand was busy with the reins, he expertly removed the cork and treated himself to a hearty swallow without dropping anything. "Care for a bit? Best applejack on the Island. Make it m'self."

I balanced my thirst against the ill effects drink would have on my empty stomach. The latter growled threateningly against the restraints of good sense. "Perhaps just a sip...."

The stuff felt both warm and cold going down. I expected it to be unsettling and wasn't disappointed. I also expected it to go straight to my head; instead, it just seemed to roil in my guts like too many fish crammed into a small bucket.

Hulton grinned, taking my expression as a compliment to his skill as a distiller.

I hiccupped. Rather badly. The applejack wanted to come back up again. Hand over my mouth, I apologized and explained that I hadn't eaten all day.

"Shoulda said somethin'," Hulton gently scolded and produced a basket from under our seat. "Go through that. My missus cooked me a chicken to eat on the way. Take what ye please."

I unwrapped the greasy cloth covering. The applejack rumbling inside was most certainly affecting my senses. The chicken, which might otherwise have set me to ripping at it like a starved mongrel, smelled repulsive. There was a fat loaf of bread squashed in next to it. I tore off a piece and bit into that instead. It was crusty, tender, and obviously still fresh, but tasted wrong. I forced it down my throat. It immediately went to war with the drink.

Hulton took another swig from his jug and offered it to me again. This time I politely refused. As I worked to chew through another piece of bread, he asked for more details about the commissaries. I offered them, but the flow of talk was interrupted by my frequent swallowing in order to keep the food down. Hulton noticed.

"Not settin' with ye?"

I shook my head.

"Then don't eat it."

What a practical suggestion. I'd been cramming the bread in because

I thought I needed it, not because it was good. Hulton wrapped the basket up and put it away. "Not sick, are ye?"

I wished he hadn't mentioned that. The aftertaste of the applejack in my mouth was absolutely vile. As for the bread, I concluded that Mrs. Hulton must have been a perfectly awful baker. "Perhaps I've been without food too long," I said aloud.

"Aye. Go without 'n' 'tis best to start up ag'in easy. Maybe soup."

Soup. Ugh. I nodded to keep my lips sealed tight. Hulton thankfully did not produce any. I gulped and pressed a hand hard against my belly. It was beginning to cramp.

"Gate here. This be your place?"

Thank God. "Yes. Thank you, Mr. Hulton. You've been very kind."

"'M well paid 'f you saved me from losin' m' stuff. Thank'e for the offer to stay, but I'll be on to The Oak. I want to hear all the talk 'n' figger that's the place for it. Mebe summun else thought all this through ahead a' me so I won't have to a'gin. God speed to ye, Mr. Barrett."

When the wagon fully stopped, I dropped down. The hard landing stirred my guts up to new rebellion. Pausing only long enough for a final wave of farewell, I stalked straight to the gate, but at the last moment veered to one side. The cramp was worse, doubling me right over. Arms clutching my middle, I retched up the bread and applejack onto the grass. There wasn't much, but I kept spitting and coughing as though my body wanted to rid itself of even their memory. Finally done, I weakly straightened and staggered over to rest against a tree.

I was *still* hungry.

But not for bread or soup or fowl or anything else that came to mind. Not milk or fruit or cheese or wine or ....

She always and only drank *blood*.

How was I to ... acquire it?

The despair I thought I'd left behind in the graveyard seized me once more, mixed with sheer terror of what must come if I wanted to live. I sank to the ground, unable to move.

Sweet God, Nora, what have you done to me?

CHAPTER
ELEVEN

LIFE-MAGIC, Mrs. Poole had called it as she let a few drops of beef blood slip between Nora's lips.

I could conclude from that example there was thankfully no need to seduce or assault any innocent lady for my own nourishment. After all the time spent with Nora, I knew better. The taking of blood from another human had an entirely different significance for her than just to keep her body fed. I wasn't remotely ready to consider the complications of that aspect of my changed nature yet. Like a thousand other things, it would have to wait until later.

With a sigh of either resignation or acceptance, I got to my feet and opened the gates just enough to slip through. The weariness I'd noted before was much more pronounced. Manifested first in my bones, it had spread to the muscles and outward to drag at my very skin. I could lie down and rest, but knew that wouldn't help. Every moment streaming past stole away a little more strength. The time would eventually come when none remained. I trudged along the drive, shoulders slumping and head down to watch where my steps fell.

But my mind was wide awake and in need of distraction from the body. Unable to supply any answers about my immediate future, I fell to speculation over my past. Without a doubt I had become like Nora, but what—and I used the word in the most literal sense—was Nora? What had I become?

Most definitely not a ghost, I wryly concluded, not unless ghosts got hungry. I also had doubts that they expended much worry on whether road dust would permanently ruin the polish of their best shoes. (Yes, it was a foolish bit of diversion, but in my unsettled state of mind I needed it.) Anyway, I'd never really believed in ghosts since I was a child. Even then, such lapses of reason had been limited to foggy nights when the normal atmosphere thickened by sea mist lent itself to imaginings of supernatural creatures.

A demon, then? Since I believed in God, I knew there was also a devil. Had some fiend from hell taken possession of my mind and body, sending me forth from the grave to trouble the world? That did not seem too very likely, either. Besides, I'd had no difficulty calling upon God for help earlier when I'd panicked while trapped in...

How had I escaped that damned *box*?

For every other change within me I had some memory of Nora to serve as a pattern to follow, but this was a most singular exception. My recollection of what had happened was most confused. The moment had been muddled by a solid and sour-tasting fear that was yet powerful enough to raise a groan and set me shuddering as if from fever...

If I continued to give in to the fear I'd never learn anything.

By force of will I straightened my shoulders and made myself stop trembling. Decisively, I shoved the fear away; an unwieldy thing, but controllable if I put my mind to it. Tempting as it was to sink to my haunches and wail like an infant, I would not surrender to it this time. There was too much to think about.

One last shake of the head to clear out the remnants, a deep breath, and I was in command of myself again and not a slave to outside forces or inner alarms. Measured against the rest of the wide world it wasn't much, just a small victory, but it was mine, and I held it close and tight.

That was better. I resumed my walk toward the house.

Now I would have to try to assume a detachment from the experience. A doctor must do much the same thing in order to allow him to proceed with the more unpleasant aspects of his art when they became necessary. If Beldon could do it, then I would, too.

In my mind's eye, I placed myself back in the ground once more. Without fear to obscure things, I was able to form a clear picture of that awful time—if one may make a picture from absolute darkness. Between the onset of panic and my sudden roll off the heaped earth, I found it. There had been a blank instant when I felt as though I were falling.

No...that wasn't quite it. Close. It was more like floating in water; except that didn't really describe it, either. A bit of both, perhaps? The result was that I had ceased to be trapped in my coffin and somehow came to rest on the ground some six feet above it.

The line from Revelation about the sea giving up its dead recalled itself to me, and I toyed with the thought that that great and terrible prophecy had come to pass in some way. Only toyed, mind you. To assume that I alone had been singled out in such a manner struck me as being the height of folly-filled arrogance.

My recollections of other passages of the Bible and how they related to my situation were not very encouraging. There were some very firm laws against the drinking of blood, at least in the Old Testament, and some mention made of it in the New. Well, I could let myself starve in an effort to deny the necessities of my changed nature, or I could yield to its demands and, like many another poor sinner, ask God to forgive me and hope for the best.

Moral questions at rest for the moment, I returned to my original puzzle of how I'd escaped the grave. Reason dictated that answers lay in some other direction than divine intervention, most likely within myself.

If Nora had been able to survive a sword thrust into her heart, what other seeming miracles might she have been capable of carrying out? In this light, my physical rising from the grave could be...

I paused in my tracks, feeling a hot burst of excitement within. Would I be able to repeat that escape?

I did not know.

And I was too apprehensive to even consider an attempt to try. Also, too hungry.

Intuition and appetite, having taken temporary precedence over reason, told me that I had no time to spare for experimentation, fascinating as it might prove to be.

Get moving and keep moving.

It was a great relief to me when the high white walls of my home loomed into sight amid the trees. It was a great hardship not to rush straight up and start hammering on the front door. Before undergoing any happy reunion, I would most definitely have to feed myself first. I couldn't possibly face the many questions and tide of emotions to come in my present state. Nor did I wish to suddenly acquaint them with the peculiar dietary needs my change required. One shock at a time.

How I was to satisfy those needs gradually became apparent as I walked around to the back of the grounds. The two points on my upper jaw where my canine teeth emerged were feeling decidedly odd. Exploring the area with my tongue and finally my fingers, I learned that these teeth were longer than before and starting to jut outward at a slight angle from the rest. Nothing strange there; I'd seen Nora in the same condition often enough. Experiencing it for myself induced a mixture of anticipation and dread, not unlike losing one's virginity. I couldn't help but compare it to that first night with Nora, for though I was certain of having an extraordinary time, I had misgivings about botching things.

But whatever might lie ahead, this involuntary alteration of my teeth was—in its unique way—indisputably pleasurable.

I skirted the house and minor outbuildings and headed for the stables. Chores done and their own stomachs filled, the lads had long since retired to their quarters above. Some were well asleep, others still settling in for the night. I felt both wonderment and charm that I could hear them, for like my eyes, my ears had likewise undergone a tremendous improvement over their original condition.

One bedtime conversation persisted; the two speakers were also the youngest, the only ones with enough energy left at the end of a long day to put off their slumbers a little longer. Their talk was filled with speculation on how long the rebellion could last and whether or not they'd have a chance to join up with Howe's men before it ended. They certainly stretched my patience before exhausting the subject to begin drifting off to their dreams of soldiering.

My belly ached painfully over the delay, but the pauses between comments began to lengthen, and finally went unbroken. I gave them another quarter hour, then eased through the door for a cautious look around.

The first members of the household to greet me were our dogs. We had an even half-dozen hunting hounds that slept where they pleased. Two of them favored the stables year round, probably because of the vermin there. The smallest was a very talented rat catcher. He now bounced to his feet and joyfully rushed me. His brother roused and followed and the two of them knocked me right over and halfway out the door again. I was buried under wet tongues, stub-clawed feet, and small whines of eager welcome. They totally ignored my hushed pleas for silence. I gave up and let them have their way. Though terribly distracted by hunger, this was a homecoming to cherish. They, with their own heightened senses, could discover no evil fault within me. I found that most reassuring. Perhaps the rest of the family would follow their example.

The dogs eventually calmed down to go sniffing about the yard, and

I reentered the stable on tiptoes, listening for signs of disturbance from the lads above. Nothing but the occasional snore. Good.

The first stall I came to was Rolly's. God, but it was good to see him again. He seemed to think the same as I moved inside and patted him down. He bobbed his head and exhaled a warm blast of breath into my face. I ran a hand along the sleek line of his neck, taking in his scent as well, then stopped. Through the great curved wall of his chest I could hear the very beating of his heart.

Oh, but that was a tantalizing sound. And the smell. More than the ordinary, comforting fetor of stable and horses was here for me. One scent alone caught my full attention, drew me toward it, quelled any feeble protests. Dark and heavy and irresistible, it leached right through his skin and crashed against my spinning brain with the force of a nor'easter. I made hushing, soothing noises to Rolly, telling him to be quiet, then sank to my knees. And he did remain quiet, even as I felt out one of the big surface veins in his foreleg. He didn't once flinch as I brought my lips to the best spot, then used my teeth to cut through his thick flesh.

It welled up fast and though I swallowed as quickly as possible, some overflowed and dribbled past my chin. I ignored it.

The warmth of Rolly's living blood washed into me, spreading from my empty belly to saturate all my limbs. It was though I were drinking summer sunlight. My flagging strength returned in full, increased, doubled, tripled.

As the aroma was more enticing than any solid food I'd ever had, the taste was a thousand times better—not at all what I'd expected. During our exchanges, Nora's blood had certainly possessed a unique and erotic quality that enabled me to drink it without the least revulsion, but for all the sensual pleasure imparted, it still tasted like blood. That which I now consumed was wholly different, as was its effect on me. Instead of being engulfed in a blaze of red fire whose heat invariably took me to a supreme climax, I was inundated with the kind of sweet contentment that a starving man must feel when, after years of privation, he at last eats his fill.

I don't know how much I drank; it must have been quite a lot, perhaps as much as a tall beer flagon, perhaps more, but some inner signal told me when no more was needed. A little blood continued to seep from the wounds I'd made, but I pressed them with my hand until they clotted over. This was very messy, of course, but I'd take care of that soon enough.

Sitting back in the clean straw of the stall, I considered what I'd just done and decided that this sort of feeding was something I could not only put up with, but actively enjoy. I also considered what it might be like should the time come for me to take some lady to bed. The intuition I'd given free rein to tonight told me that that experience promised to be no less than incredible. As wonderful as it had been to be on the receiving end of Nora's kisses, how much better might it be to be the one giving the kiss—in this, my changed state?

Well-a-day, as my good cousin Oliver would have said. Perhaps I would eventually find out.

Quitting the stable, I started for the well, but changed my mind. Drawing water would be too noisy, and I didn't want to rouse anyone until I was presentable again. There was a clear sweet stream not a hundred yards from the house, better to use it, instead. As though spoiling for a footrace, I trotted lightly toward it, my previous exhaustion completely forgotten.

I startled two rabbits and a bush full of dozing birds along the way. The birds squawked and fell into guarded silence, but the rabbits dodged swiftly away into cover. I followed them for the sheer joy of movement. Had it been open ground, I thought I'd have had a chance of catching them, too. I'd never been so fresh and alive before; had Nora also felt this? She'd been so serene and sedate; I wanted to turn Catherine wheels, to leap, to fly to the moon.

I had to settle for kneeling by the stream and cupping up water to wash away the stains of drying blood. Though comfortable enough splashed against my face and neck, it was extremely cold on my hands as I dipped in, biting cruelly as though it were mid-winter. They'd gone blue and were starting to shrivel before I'd finished. On the walk back I had to rub hard to revive feeling in my fingers. Very odd, it seemed, but having suffered an excess of odd experience in so brief a time, the matter was hardly worth notice.

There were too many other things to consider, the most important being how best to approach my family. Having seen me unquestionably dead and the corpse buried, I had no illusion that their first reaction would be utter terror. There was no way around that one. Hopefully, the joy to follow—once I'd explained things—would more than compensate their initial distress.

I would have to begin with Father and rely on his courage and wisdom to help me deal with the others. But inert as my heart had become, I could feel it shrink at the idea of approaching him. The simple fact was that I was highly embarrassed about the whole business, for it would involve a lengthy confession on my intimacy with Nora, something I had only dared to confide to my private journal.

Heavens, I hoped that no one had found it and was lightly turning over those pages. Such thoughts as I'd recorded there were for my eyes alone....

Later? I questioned.

Later, an inner voice wearily confirmed.

As for any difficulties I might encounter with my family... in every possible way I had taken on Nora's abilities, so I had no doubt that if it came to it I could enforce my will upon them. I could ease their fears, even alter their very thoughts, if necessary.

But this was an abhorrence to me, for it meant that I might momentarily be forced to adopt my mother's hated precept of "doing it for their own good."

If it must be, then so be it. I needed them.

Surely they would forgive me even as I'd forgiven Nora. If that happened, well and good, but if not, then I'd learn to live with it somehow. I would gladly ease any fear, but that's as far as it would go.

They would *not* be my dancing puppets.

Approaching the side door closest to the stables, I slowed and pondered a new problem: how to get inside my own home. With the times being so terribly uncertain, Father had had heavy bolts fixed to all the doors and ground-floor windows. Despite the warmth of the season these were always firmly locked at night. The heat was no real hardship, since everyone slept on the next floor or in the attic and those windows had no need to be secured. Standing back, I saw that all the ones on this face of the upper story were wide open, even the one to my room. Convenient, but only if I were a bird and able to fly in.

Or float?

I started to dismiss that one, but reconsidered as the idea had a lunatic attractiveness to it. If I could induce myself to that very odd state I'd achieved to escape my grave, even learn to control it...

No. I shook my head. That was far too fanciful. Frightening, too. I was absolutely not going to explore that possibility. Besides, there had to be an easier way in. I had only to find it. A ladder would be just the thing. I seemed to recall there being one lying on its side against the house somewhere in the back, or perhaps in the stable....

Going around to the rear of the house, I spied the cellar doors and gave them a hopeful try. Bolted. The hinges on the right half were rather free, though. There was enough play between the metal and the wood for me to force my fingers in and give an experimental tug.

For the second time that night I found myself bowled over on my backside. The right half flew up with a sharp crack as the hinge nails slipped from the wood. I'd gotten the balance all wrong or miscalculated my own strength. The door slammed down into place and would have made the devil's own row if I hadn't caught it at the last second. My hand was bruised, but nothing worse. Righting myself and cursing with quiet intensity at the pain, I lifted it just enough to get inside.

The place was dank and dark, the latter coming as a surprise to me. I'd grown so used to being able to see impossibly well at night that I was momentarily nonplussed. Without a candle, I was doomed to blundering my way around any number of hazards like an ordinary man. Not having the means to make a light, I backed up and loosened the bolt on the doors and pushed on the half with the broken hinges. It slid to one side with an unhappy scrape that had me wincing at the noise, but the opening provided more than sufficient light. Now I'd be able to make my way up to the kitchen without stumbling over anything and breaking my neck.

As it was the custom to keep the fire banked and ready for the next day's cooking, the kitchen was very warm. I fled through it, for despite my lack of regular breathing, the lingering food smells still managed to penetrate my nose and set my stomach writhing. I briefly thought about returning for a candle, but decided it was unnecessary. From here I could easily find the way to my room.

I took my shoes off before going upstairs and was careful to avoid the spots in the floor that creaked. The silence filling the place seemed to be a listening one. I hated playing the fugitive, but nothing else would have been right. I wasn't sure what would be, though, having consigned that problem to the nebulous and now fast-approaching future. Doubtless something would work itself out. After all my exertions my clothes were, as Mrs. Nooth might have said, "in a state." Confronting my family while so disheveled was not at all desirable, but that had become less important than changing for the sake of my own comfort. Once out of them and free of their attendant reminders of the grave, I'd feel much better and more of a mind to think.

An easy push on the door and I was standing in the familiar security of my own room.

The first impression I got was that it had been given a better than average cleaning by Jericho. The table I used for study was no longer stacked with its clutter of papers and open books. The former were gone and the latter all firmly closed and lined up in their case. This angered me. I hadn't finished with those yet and he knew it....

But he also knew I'd never return to them again. I had died. Oh, my poor friend.

Other details impressed themselves upon me. On a table by the bed someone had placed a burning candle in a small holder within a wide bowl of water. I hadn't seen this sort of thing since Elizabeth and I had been very young children and wanted a light to chase away the night terrors.

The bed itself had been turned down as if waiting for my return. Laid out at its foot was the elaborate dressing gown Elizabeth had made me; on the floor were my slippers.

I recoiled from this otherwise innocuous sight. It was perfectly innocent, until you remembered that the missing occupant was dead and supposedly gone forever. Had they turned my room into some kind of horrid shrine to my memory? It was repellent, but then I might not have felt differently had I come in to find the place stripped of belongings and bare of all evidence of my existence.

It would change. Before the night was out, everything would be changed back. Perhaps not the same as before, but better than this ghastly, grief-filled present.

First things first. I had to get these things off.

Hastily, I stripped from my coat, peeled away shirt and breeches, and scraped free of stockings and underclothes. The air gently flowing in from the window was agreeable to my naked skin. I stretched to let it touch every part of me and combed back my tangled hair with my fingers. Marveling, I saw that the scar on my chest marking where the ball had shattered flesh was much fainter and smaller than before.

My Sunday clothes I left in a pile on the floor, though I did remove the silver buckles from the shoes, intending to place in their usual case in the wardrobe.

The wardrobe, unfortunately, unexpectedly, unhappily, and unreasonably, was quite, quite empty.

I stared at it like a brainless buffoon, jaw hanging and eyes popping for a ludicrous amount of time until white-hot outrage flooded through me. Couldn't they have waited just a little while before disbursing my things among themselves and the servants? I could understand the basic need to put me into the ground the same day I'd died, for the weather was far too hot for delays, but it wouldn't have hurt to let a decent interval pass by before performing this other ritual of death.

Slamming the door, careless of the noise, I grabbed up the dressing gown and pulled it on, my movements made stiff by anger. I tried the top drawer of the chest at the foot of the bed. Empty. Not even a dusting of lint remained in the corners. Disgusted, I slammed it shut as well. I had nothing else to wear other than the dressing gown or my grave clothes, and I'd be damned before I put them on again. Fuming, I returned to the wardrobe and checked its drawers. I didn't really think I'd find anything, but then I wasn't thinking at all at this point, being too furious for it.

Empty, empty, *empty*. The little treasures left over from boyhood, too worthless for a sensible man to keep, too priceless to throw away, were gone.

Even my private journal, my diary, keeper of all my thoughts...gone.

This was the last straw. How *dare* they?

The door to my room slowly opened. Elizabeth stood there, a shawl draped over her night dress, gripping a candle in one unsteady hand. She managed to look both uncertain and alarmed.

I was yet too insensate to be rational. All thought, all consideration of what had happened had been driven from my mind. With what I felt was justified exasperation, I turned on her. "Damnation, Elizabeth, where are my things?"

My sister had paused to look in upon me, doubtless drawn by the noise I'd been making. It was a normal sight to see her there. In the past had she not come in countless other times for a late conversation before retiring?

In the past. The past before I had *died*.

She froze, stock still, held in place by the unimaginable, paralyzed by the inconceivable. Her great eyes were stricken and hollow. No sound came from her open mouth. She didn't seem to be breathing at all, and despite the warm glow of her small light, her skin went dreadfully ashen.

I froze as well, first with surprise at her expression, then with shock at my own unbounded stupidity as I belatedly realized that I was surely God's greatest fool.

Contrite, I reached out to her. "I'm sorry. I—"

She dropped back a step, her lips parting for a scream that she was too frightened to release. Never had I seen such a look of blank terror on anyone's face, much less that of my own sister. Remorse welled within me, choking my voice.

"Please don't be afraid. I'm not a ghost. Oh, please, Elizabeth."

She dropped her candle. The tiny flame went out in the fall; the stick struck the floor with a thud. Melted wax sprayed over the painted wood.

She backed away one more step, making a soft *oh* as she did so.

"For God's sake, Elizabeth, don't leave me. I need you."

"No," she finally whispered, her voice high and blurred with tears. Oh, the impossibilities were legion. I'd had the time to confront them one by one, get used to them, accept them; poor Elizabeth was having to do it all at once.

"It's all right. I *am* real. I—"

"What do you want?" Her words were so thin that I barely heard them. She seemed just on the point of tearing away and running.

My heart was breaking for her, for myself. I could feel it cracking right in two. "I want to come home."

"It can't be."

It must—or I should be forever lost. I needed my family, my home, they were all I had, without them I was truly dead. I could not go on without them. The impossible *had* to become possible.

My hand still out, I moved slowly toward her, close enough to touch, but careful not to do so. "It's all right. I am here. I am real. There's no need to fear, I would never, ever hurt you. *Please....*"

Perhaps the agony of feeling rather than the inadequate words broke through, but something inside her seemed to waken. I could see the change gradually come to her face. Her eyes now traveled to my trembling hand, and with painful caution, her own rose to take it. Our fingers gently touched. I remained still, waiting for her thoughts to catch up with her senses.

"Jonathan?"

"I'm right here. I'm not a dream." I encompassed her tentative fingers lightly, fearing she might pull away, but unable to stop. She did not draw back, though, and after a long moment her own grasp strengthened. Hardly aware of the movement, I sank to my knees, awed and humbled by this raw proof of her courage and love. As if in mirror to my own, crystal-bright tears streamed down her cheeks.

"Oh, little brother...," she began, but could not finish. Instead, she opened her arms and drew me close, and we clung to each other and wept as though we were children again, finding common comfort in the sharing.

When the worst of the storm had passed, she pulled a limp handkerchief from the pocket of her gown and swiped at her eyes and nose. "I've none for you," she said apologetically.

I smiled a little, that she should worry over such a trifle. "Never mind."

We looked at one another and I felt awkward and abashed to have been the cause of any distress to her. Elizabeth seemed to vacillate between joy and terror. Both of us realized it at the same time and that this was not the place to settle our many questions.

"Come," she whispered. I found my feet and followed her. My legs were shaking with relief and trepidation.

She'd left the door to her room down the hall open, but shut it as soon as we were inside. Within was evidence of the restlessness that had kept her up at such a late hour. The rumpled bedclothes were turned back and several candles burned themselves away to dispel the darkness of the night and of the soul. Her Bible and prayer book were open on her table along with a bottle of Father's good brandy. While she rummaged in a drawer for fresh handkerchiefs, I poured a sizable drink for her.

"You need it," I said.

"By God, I know I do," she agreed, exchanging a square foot of soft white linen for the glass. I blew my nose as she drained away the brandy. Much stronger than the wine she was accustomed to, the stuff had its usual immediate effect on her, for she dropped right into her chair as her legs gave out.

I stared as if seeing her for the first time. In truth, I was seeing her with new eyes. How must Lazarus have looked upon his own sisters after his return from the dead? The comparison now struck me as being downright blasphemous, but I had no other examples to draw from in my memory. Did he see how vulnerable they were? Did he feel as aged and wearied by his experience? Or perhaps they were better sustained by the strength of their faith than I. At least none of them had been so alone in their ordeal.

The listening silence of the house washed against me, so profound that I could hear Elizabeth's heart beat. Once part of the background, now it seemed to fill the room with its swift drumming. I knelt again and took her hand, pressing the inside of her slender wrist to my ear. This was music, the greatest music I'd ever heard. And the music was but one of a thousand, thousand other precious, fleeting things that I might never have appreciated or even known, but for Nora's ... gift.

Elizabeth spread her fingers to caress my hair. "Oh, Jonathan, how is this possible?"

"I have no easy answer for you."

A smile fled over her face. The color was returning. "I don't think I could expect one."

"Is everyone all right? Is Father all right?"

Her expression fell. "What happened absolutely shattered him."

"Good God, I must go to him—" I started for the door.

"He's not home," she said. "He went out late this afternoon. He went to Mrs. Montagu. I made him go," she added, as if she had to apologize for his absence. "She couldn't possibly come here and he needed to see her and she him. They needed each other."

Poor Mrs. Montagu. She loved me, too. "That's all right, I understand, but soon I must see him."

"Of course. We'll have to go over right away."

"Yes. It'll be better for him if you're there. But please, tell me where my clothes are."

I must have sounded very forlorn. She suddenly slapped a hand over her mouth to stifle laughter that threatened to go to tears again. She leaned forward and held me, her head resting on my shoulder. I wanted to let her stay, but there was so much to do yet. She may have sensed it and pulled away to blow her nose. It had grown rather red. I loved it. I loved her.

She made a vague gesture to indicate my room. "That was Mother's doing. After the ... services she ordered Jericho to pack everything up. I think Dr. Beldon got some of your better shirts. Oh, God, oh, God." She struggled against another sweep of emotion, shaking from the effort.

"I'll sort it out with Beldon," I said quickly. "Is he all right, too? He looked so awful when ... when ..."

She broke off her work with the handkerchief to stare at me as we both realized the time for explanations was upon us. Everyone, even Father, would have to wait. "You must tell me," she whispered. "Tell me everything."

I rocked back on my bare heels and stood, pacing the room once or twice to put my thoughts in order. She watched my smallest move, her eyes wide as if she were afraid to look away or even blink, lest I disappear. Her hands clutched the arms of her chair like talons. Tonight her world had lurched and tumbled and yet she was prepared to face the next fearful blow. Very brave, but not the best state of mind for listening.

Elizabeth's cat lay on her bed, a tawny tom of considerable size and phlegmatic temperament. I picked him up and stroked him into a rumbling purr, delighting in the sensation of his warmth and softness. As with so much else, that which had been commonplace was now a wonderment to me. I took him over to Elizabeth and put him in her lap. He adapted to the change with indifference and continued his low murmur of contentment. She responded to it and began petting him. Her posture relaxed somewhat, though her eyes never left me.

Where to begin? In the churchyard? In my coffin? The ride with Beldon? Or much further back, with Nora? That was a tale I thought I'd never share with anyone. Ah, well, Elizabeth wasn't the sort to blush easily; I wasn't as certain about myself.

I tried to keep my story short and simple, and as neither could remotely describe it, tangled on some things. Elizabeth didn't help when she interjected questions, but my own embarrassment was the worst hindrance.

Elizabeth impatiently interrupted. "Jonathan, please stop trying to protect my sensibilities and just tell me what you mean. Was she your mistress or not?"

And I'd hoped not to shock *her*. I gave up and spoke plainly, making it easier for a time, until I got to the part concerning the mutual blood-drinking. Bereft of the rousing feeling leading up to it, the act lost all erotic attraction and sounded absolutely disgusting. Elizabeth's color faded again, but she did refrain from interruption on this. She could see how extraordinarily difficult it was for me to talk about it.

She had another glass of brandy, taking half during the fight with Warburton and finishing it when I came to my waking up in the coffin. Then I did try to spare her by passing over it quickly enough, but she fastened upon that which had left me so thoroughly puzzled.

"How did you escape?" she demanded.

"I'm not sure I know what to tell you," I answered with equal parts of truth and apprehension.

"Is it so terrible?"

"One could say that. One could also say that it is entirely absurd as well."

She pressed me, but my explanation, when it came, was met with gentle skepticism.

"I don't blame you," I said. "It's not something I can believe, and I've been through it."

For several minutes she was quite unable to speak. When she did, she had all the questions I'd posed for myself and was just as dissatisfied with my inadequate answers.

"Can you just *accept* it?" I asked, my heart sinking as Nora's must have done on other, similar occasions with me.

"If we lived in a time when intelligent and reasonable people still believed in witchcraft this would be so much easier to take," she replied.

"Can you?" It was almost a prayer.

"It's not a matter of 'can' but of have to, little brother. Here you are and here you stand. But, by God, if this night ends and I wake to find I've dreamed it all, I shall never, never forgive you."

I began to smile, but smothered it. The feeling behind the mocking threat was too tender for crude levity. She'd finally reached her limit and this was her way of letting me know. I went to her and took her hands in both of mine. They were very cold.

"This is not a dream. I have come back and I will not leave again."

"God willing," she added quietly.

"God willing," I echoed.

She bowed her head over our clasped hands, whether for prayer or out of sheer weariness, I could not tell. Then she looked up. "Jonathan ... do you have to drink blood as she did?"

"I'm afraid I do."

"Will you do the same things she did?"

My God, she was wondering if I'd be seducing dozens of young women in order to feed myself. An interesting idea, but not an example I intended to follow. "No, I will not do that. There's no need." I explained about my business with Rolly. "It didn't hurt him and I was much revived," I added, hoping that the knowledge might make her feel better.

"Oh," was all she could say.

"Probably best if you don't think about it," I quickly suggested.

"It sounds so awful, though."

"It's not, really. Not to me."

"What will you tell everyone?"

I was surprised. "The same as I've told you."

"*All* of it?"

Oh, dear. Sharing the truth with Elizabeth and Father was one thing, but spelling out the details of my intimacies with Nora to every yokel in the county was quite another. And as for popular reaction to what I required for sustenance ... "Yes, well, perhaps not."

Elizabeth took notice of my distress. "Never mind. We'll talk to Father and decide what to do later."

Later. My favorite word, it seemed. I was growing impatient with it.

"We must find you clothing," she continued. "I'll get your shirts from Dr. Beldon's room—"

"Will you now? And what do you plan to tell him?"

"Nothing. He's not at home tonight."

"Then where the devil is he? You shouldn't be here alone."

"I'm hardly alone with all the servants—"

"Where is he?"

"Hunting." She said this with a meaning that passed right over me.

"I don't understand."

"Right after the…services for you, he left with the soldiers to go looking for the men who shot you."

I backed away until I bumped into her bed, then abruptly sat. While I'd been stumbling about, wholly occupied with my own problems, the world had spun on regardless. My life thread had been cut, knotted together, and worked back into weave again, but no one other than Elizabeth knew about it. "You must tell me everything that's happened since I…"

Might as well say it.

"…since I died."

"Oh, Jonathan."

"I know of no other way to put it, so let the words be plain and honest. It's only the truth, after all. Now tell me. I must know all that's happened."

It was Elizabeth's turn to gather her wits and decide where to start. She was usually so self-possessed that her present discomfort was painful to watch.

"Did Beldon see who shot me?" I asked, hoping it would prompt her to speech.

It did. "No. He heard the shot and saw the smoke, then turned in time to see you fall. Do you not know who it was?"

"Roddy Finch."

She stopped petting her cat and went white. "Then it's true. Beldon said he thought the Finches were behind the horse theft, but I just couldn't believe that they would have—"

"Well, one of them did," I stated with no small portion of bitterness. The Finches had been schoolmates, friends, part of the Island itself as it related to our lives. The treachery was monstrous.

"But for Roddy Finch to do such a thing?" She looked ill and I could sympathize with her up to a point, but no farther.

"For *anyone* to do such a thing," I reminded her. "If they catch him, he'll be hanged."

"But you're alive," she protested.

"He was stealing horses at the time, you know. They'll get him and those with him for that, if nothing else."

She groaned. "I don't want to think about it."

"Neither do I." There was no need; it was out of my hands and someone else's concern. "What happened afterward? What about the soldiers?"

"They brought you back. Both of you. Beldon was in a horrible state and weeping so hard he couldn't see and had to be led by one of the soldiers. I was working with Father in the library and we saw them from the window, bringing the horses in from the fields like some ghastly parade. Father rushed past me and out to the yard. God, I can still hear the cry he gave when he saw you. I shan't ever forget it."

I went to her and put an arm around her wilted shoulders, giving what comfort I could. "You needn't go on about that part. I couldn't bear to hear it, anyway. Let's get ready and go to him. We'll have to walk. If we stir up the stable lads now I'll be here all night talking to them."

"I don't mind. The air will clear my head."

With much tiptoeing, whispered directions, and the occasional mis-step in the dark, we found some clothes for me, then went to our rooms to dress. As promised, Elizabeth raided Beldon's room for a clean shirt and stockings and I borrowed the rest from Father. It felt odd, pulling on an old pair of his breeches, but we were of a size now, and I didn't think he'd mind. My other boots and shoes had vanished, requiring that I use the one pair that remained, the ones I'd been buried in. I duly replaced the silver buckles.

Elizabeth was very informally garbed in a dress she favored for riding. It was hardly a step up from what some of the servants wore, but she found it comfortable and needed no help getting into it. Out of habit, custom and regard that she'd be calling upon Mrs. Montagu, she covered her loose hair with a bonnet and drew on a decent pair of gloves.

We slipped out the side door, shutting it firmly, but were unable to reset the bolt. It would only be for a few hours, though. Cutting around to the front, we set off down the drive to the road at a good pace, though I felt like running again. However badly our reunion had begun, Elizabeth and I were together at last and one large portion of my enormous burden was lifted. Soon Father would understand everything as well and with their help ...

My mind took a sudden turn down a path I'd studiously avoided until now. "Elizabeth ... how did Mother take it?"

She looked at me sharply. "I was wondering if you would ever get 'round to her."

"Is she all right?"

"She wouldn't dare not be."

"What do you mean?"

"You know how she is, all that she does is determined by how she wants others to think of her. I don't believe the woman has a feeling bone in her body."

I pressed for details and got them. My mother had been shocked, of course, but while others around her were giving in to their grief, she busied herself getting the funeral organized.

"'Someone has to see to it,' she said, and the way she said it implied that we were all weak fools. My God, even Mrs. Hardinbrook had tears to shed for you, but not Mother."

I shouldn't have really been surprised. I was also deeply hurt. "She's a sick woman, Elizabeth."

"I'm sorry, I shouldn't be telling you this."

I waved it off. "In a little while it won't matter."

We reached the road soon enough. Elizabeth tripped on some old wheel ruts, and I had her hang on to my arm for guidance.

"You must have eyes like a cat," she muttered.

"Or even better. I am not without some advantages."

And I would have enlarged on the subject but for an interruption that for an insane moment hurtled me right back to that hot morning by the kettle. I actually felt the sun's heat on my face and the air lying heavy in my lungs. Without any thought behind the gesture, my hand fell protectively upon my chest as a Hessian soldier emerged from behind a tree with his rifle ready and ordered us to stop. A second, then a third joined him and jogged toward us, their pale faces grinning like fiends in the moonlight.

CHAPTER
TWELVE

ELIZABETH GAVE NO OUTWARD SIGN of alarm, but her grasp on my arm tightened.

The soldiers closed on us, and one of them shouted something.

In my halting German I asked them what they wanted. An ugly brute on our left sniggered as he looked at Elizabeth, but his companions thankfully did not seem of a mind to pursue his idea. I repeated my question. It finally got through to them that I was speaking in their language. As with the other Hessians, it had a favorable effect; unfortunately, the answer I got was far too rapid and complicated for me to follow. They were very skittish.

The same man shouted again and got a reply from someone coming up behind us. I saw him before the others did.

"Another bloody Hessian," I told Elizabeth. "I hope this one speaks English."

"What are they all doing here?"

"I got the impression they want to ask us the same question. Mind yourself against that villain on the end. He's not polite."

She made a brief nod and murmur of agreement.

The newcomer was the sergeant in charge of those who had stopped us and at first glance seemed a sensible, solid type. He gave me a brief greeting in English that was far more tolerable than my German, then conferred with his men. I gathered from their talk that a number of others were scouting up and down this part of the road.

"What are you looking for?" I asked, when he was free to place his full attention upon me.

"Perhaps for you, young sir," he said. "There are rebels here all around. Why are you and this female out so late?"

With all the haughtiness I'd learned at Cambridge, I drew myself up and made formal introductions. I was careful not to be too condescending, but made certain that he knew he'd gotten off on the wrong foot. His men's vulgar reactions to my sister would have more than justified my calling him out if he'd been a gentleman, or caning him since he was not, but circumstances required that I be flexible in the matter of honor for now.

The sergeant, who gave his name as Lauder, was not impressed. "Have you any papers, sir?"

"Papers?"

"Some papers to say you're who you are."

"My brother's word is proof enough in these parts, Sergeant Lauder," said Elizabeth. "If you need more than that, then you are welcome to follow us and our father will be more than happy to provide it."

"Your father will have to come to see you, miss. My orders say to bring in anyone out after curfew."

"This is utterly ridiculous," I said. "What curfew?"

"The curfew that has been ordered," he answered, as though no further explanation were required.

"I have never heard of such a—"

He raised a hand. "You will come along now."

"Who is your commanding officer?"

"Lieutenant Nash. He will see you in the morning."

"Nash? But he's—"

"But I know him," Elizabeth said at the same time.

I stopped to look at her.

"He came to the funeral," she said under her breath.

"Awfully decent of him," I muttered in return, thinking low thoughts about Nash's judgment that the rebels had left the area of the kettle. If he hadn't been so damned optimistic...

"That is good, then," concluded Lauder, ignoring this aside. "He will be most pleased to welcome you."

I wrenched myself back to the present. "An army camp is no place for a respectable lady, Sergeant. I insist that you allow me to return my sister to our home—"

"I have my orders."

"You have no right—"

"I have my orders," he repeated, tenaciously patient. The man had turned woodenly polite, but was implacable.

Damnation. The glum look on Elizabeth's face indicated an exact concordance of thought between us on the situation.

"I'm sure Nash will sort this mess out for us once we talk to him," she said.

I sighed and nodded. I expected that he would be cooperative enough—once he got over the shock.

Elizabeth maintained her grip on me, but kept her head high. The sergeant's now-respectful attitude toward her had been noticed by his men and their discipline was such that no more coarse remarks or signals were to be heard from them. Now that the initial excitement of a successful capture had passed, they were looking more sleepy than lustful, thank God.

"What's brought you out at this hour?" I asked the sergeant. "Even the rebels you're chasing must retire sometime."

"A farmer came in to tell us of a young man who had some misfortune on the road. Lieutenant Nash sent us to find him."

So Farmer Hulton had been gossiping in the tavern. "He turned all of you out just for that?"

"It was a most strange thing to hear."

"And what was so strange?"

"The young man told the farmer his name was Barrett. Yesterday the only young Mr. Barrett in the area was shot down dead by rebels. You are here and say that you are Mr. Barrett." Now he broke his wooden facade down enough to bestow upon me a look of amused suspicion.

"Oh my God," said Elizabeth.

"Sorry, miss," added the sergeant, misinterpreting her reaction.

"There's been a terrible mistake," she told him.

He invited her to go on, but his continued amusement was plain.

"Don't you see? That was my *cousin* who was killed."

"Pardon, miss?"

Elizabeth brought us all to a halt, Lauder regarding her with polite interest, me with dawning dread. What in heaven's name was she up to?

"My poor cousin, whose name was also Barrett, was the one killed yesterday," she said.

"I am sorry, miss."

"It was my brother here that the farmer met on the road."

"I see, miss."

"So there's no need to detain us."

Lauder shrugged minimally. "You must still come along." He moved on and his men herded us forward.

I squeezed Elizabeth's hand. It had been a good try.

She wasn't ready to give up yet. "Sergeant Lauder, I fully appreciate that you must perform your duty, but you are interfering with the king's business."

"In truth? It must be very late business."

"My brother and I were taking a very important message to our father from Colonel DeQuincey, who is on General Howe's staff."

"What message?"

"We are not at liberty to say."

"May I see this message?"

"It was not committed to paper, Sergeant. Surely you know how dangerous it could be if—"

Lauder held up a restraining hand. "It is not for me to say, only to follow my orders."

After that there seemed to be no further purpose to argument. Elizabeth subsided for the moment into a state of smoldering indignation that no word of commiseration from me would dispel. It gave her a goodly energy, though, for she set a smart pace for the rest of us in our march toward Glenbriar and The Oak, where Nash and his men were quartered. Not half an hour more passed before the road made a last gentle curve and I saw the familiar sign.

It was an old building, one of the first large structures on the Island with upper and lower stories and a vast cellar below, famous for the choice and quality of drinks kept there. The windows on the ground floor were open and some lamps and a candle or two were burning, but no one was presently in the common room.

Lauder left us standing outside while he entered, in search of additional orders, no doubt. Elizabeth crossed her arms and jerked her chin up to indicate her displeasure. Even the brute who had not been particularly polite kept his distance from her.

The sergeant returned shortly and issued a brief command to his men.

"What is it? What's going on?" Elizabeth demanded.

"You will be placed in the cellar until morning," he said.

"The what?"

"The cellar of the inn."

I started to object, but Elizabeth was well ahead of me.

"Absolutely not! We're loyal subjects of the king and will not submit to such insulting treatment. Where is Lieutenant Nash?"

"Those are my orders, miss—"

"To the devil with your orders, sir!"

"'It must be so, miss. I have summoned the landlord to—"

"Lieutenant Nash!" she bellowed up at the windows above us. She was quite loud enough to wake everyone in the surrounding houses much less those hapless souls trying to sleep at The Oak. Lauder attempted to suggest that she exercise control and quietly go along to the cellar, but found himself drowned out by her continuous shouting. Then he indicated for his soldiers to restrain her and carry her off.

The first man who reached out to her got a punch in the eye from me. He dropped like a stone. The others, seeing me as the greater threat now, closed in. I lost sight of Elizabeth in the confusion of arms and legs and fists that followed.

Having my kind of upbringing, I'd no experience at street brawling, but natural instinct and anger made up for it. I had a vague impression of hitting one in the stomach, connecting with another's chin, and kicking a third in a place where no gentleman would have presumed to strike. In what seemed like an instant, the lot of them, including Sergeant Lauder, were prostrate in the dust and moaning. Coming back to myself, I regarded the scene with no small astonishment as I could not make out how I'd been able to do it.

Elizabeth, from her vantage in the doorway of the tavern, stared at me with wide-eyed wonder. "My God, Jonathan."

"Get inside," I snapped.

She ducked through the door with me at her heels and as one, we shot the bolt into place.

"My God," she repeated. "Four to one and all of them soldiers. What else did they teach you at Cambridge?"

"Ha," was all I could reply, being still too surprised myself for coherent speech.

She thought to go to a window to fasten it shut, lest the sergeant and his men gain entry that way, but found it unnecessary. "They're not getting up," she reported.

Surely I hadn't hit them that hard. I joined her looking out on the yard and found it to be true. Though there was some movement in the ranks of the wounded, none of them were attempting to stand just yet.

"We'll have to talk to Nash soon or there will be the devil to pay for this," she said.

I almost objected to this sudden degrading of her language when it occurred to me that she was greatly enjoying herself and our circumstances. "Very well," I said, though the encounter to come with Nash was not something I looked forward to with any eagerness.

The row had been more than sufficient to stir the heaviest sleeper and the narrow stairs leading to the upper rooms were becoming crowded with the curious in various states of dress and undress. The company, all men, upon seeing that a lady was present, either finished putting on the clothes they had, or quickly retired to acquire more for modesty's sake. Elizabeth had the presence of mind and the courtesy to turn around and allow them the privacy to retreat.

Stumping downstairs against the flow came Lieutenant Nash. He'd managed to throw on the necessaries, but lacked a coat or even waistcoat, and his feet, though in shoes, were without stockings.

"What the devil's going on here?" he demanded sleepily. He pointed an accusing finger at me. "You! What's happening here?"

I was standing in deep shadow at this point, thankful for it, and reluctant to come forth.

"I'll handle this," Elizabeth said, and moved into the light. "Lieutenant Nash?"

His aggressive manner commendably altered. "Good heavens, is that you, Miss Barrett?"

"Yes, and I must beg you for your help."

Nonplussed, but attempting to be gallant, he reached the bottom of the stairs and gave a dignified bow. "No need to beg, Miss Barrett, I am entirely at your service."

"Thank you, sir. Your Sergeant Lauder and his men wrongfully arrested us and were going to lock us in the cellar for the night. I only ask that you call him off long enough to hear me out."

"Arrested *you*, Miss Barrett? Upon what charge?"

"He was not very clear on that point, sir. He is, however, very devoted to his duty and I fear he will continue with his arrest unless he receives instructions to desist."

Nash opened and shut his mouth a few times, but decided to take action on her behalf. He unbolted the door and spent some time outside surveying his men. As Lauder was not yet in a condition to offer detailed explanations the business was concluded more quickly than one might otherwise expect. Through the window, more citizens, prompted by curiosity to forget about the curfew, had gathered to investigate. Some other soldiers had also emerged, and Nash ordered them to disperse the crowd before coming in again.

The landlord of The Oak now appeared and was demanding to know the cause of the uproar. Nash looked expectantly at Elizabeth.

"Would you please show us to a more private room, Mr. Farr?" she asked sweetly.

His instincts as host helped him to maintain some composure and he gestured toward a door at the back. Elizabeth swept up a candle and glided ahead, but turned just enough to make sure that Nash followed her. She was such an uncommon sight with her regal bearing, humble clothes and mysterious manner that he'd forgotten all about me. In their wake, I passed the landlord.

"Would you please bring along some brandy, Mr. Farr? The lieutenant is going to need it."

Farr rocked back on his heels. "My God!" He whispered, going deathly white.

I made hushing motions with my hands. "It's all right. There's been a dreadful mistake, is all."

"But I 'eard as they *buried* you...."

I shook my head, assuming an air of exasperation. "Very obviously they did not, Mr. Farr. Now, please get that drink and have one for yourself as well." I left him goggling and shut the door in his face.

Elizabeth had placed her candle on a table and was facing me as I walked in. The flame settled and the shadows stopped dancing. Nash now turned around, his expression one of expectation. It sagged into open-mouthed shock as he recognized me.

Elizabeth closely echoed my words to the landlord. "It's all right. There's nothing to fear."

Nash appeared not to heed her. He fell away until his back was pressed to a wall. I could hear his heart thundering so hard that it seemed likely to burst from his chest. His eyes, with the whites showing in abundance, tore from me to Elizabeth and returned.

"Sweet Jesu," he whispered, as though in agony from a mortal wound.

And then the fatigue swept over me as I realized this was yet another in what promised to be an exhausting series of difficult confrontations. I could go all through it, as I had with Elizabeth, or ... I might try an alternative. It might serve to at least abrogate his fear.

I stepped closer and looked at him straight. "Nash, you must listen to me..."

In this, I was repeating as nearly as I could the tone and manner that Nora had used often enough on me. I was not at all sure that it would

have the same soothing effect on this terrified man until I realized that
I'd already had some small practice at it with Rolly. It had worked then,
it would work now.

I focused upon his eyes and spoke softly, as one might to lull a child
toward sleep. Elizabeth's close presence, the room around us, the voices
of the men outside, all retreated from my mind. I was aware of myself
and Nash and nothing else.

His breathing slowed, as well as the laboring of his heart.

"You must listen to me...."

His eyes ceased to be so large, then clouded over.

"There's no need to be afraid," I droned on. My head began to ache
from the effort.

His whole face and posture went slack.

"Do you understand?"

"Yes...." he whispered back.

That was all I wanted to hear. I stepped away from him. My head
cleared and piece by piece the rest of the world returned to its proper
place in the universe.

Elizabeth stood rooted to her allotted portion. Even as I'd taken the
fear out of Nash, she seemed to have embraced it once more herself.
"Jonathan, what have you done?"

"It's just a way of calming him. Nothing to worry about."

"Did... she do this to you?"

"Yes."

"I'm not sure I like it."

I shrugged. What mattered was that it had been successful. Nash
wasn't fainting with fear or screaming the house down. He was, in fact,
looking quite normal under the circumstances. His eyes had cleared and
he regarded me with no little puzzlement.

"Mr. Barrett?"

"Please sit down, Lieutenant." I indicated to Elizabeth that she
should take a place at the table. She did so and we joined her. I was
feeling lightheaded from all the activity. When Mr. Farr came in with
a generous tray, I welcomed the interruption as a chance to order my
thoughts.

Farr was very nervous and clumsy for he could not look away from
me. I smiled reassuringly and told him to be of good cheer, that everything would soon be explained. He left the room in haste, shutting the
door with more force than necessary. Beyond it, I'd glimpsed a dozen
faces eaten up by curiosity trying to peer inside.

"An explanation, Mr. Barrett?" prompted Nash, sounding very normal.

Elizabeth had recovered somewhat from her apprehension, and both her brow and lips were puckered as she waited to hear what I was going to tell him. I suddenly wished someone else, someone quicker and more knowledgeable about such matters, was with us to do it in my stead. But Nora was very much elsewhere. It was up to me, but I wasn't sure I was up to it.

Absurd, I suddenly thought. For the next hour or more I might be delayed here trying to explain the inexplicable to this man and was it really any of his business? It was not. There were more important things for me to do while the night lasted than revealing my whole life to this stranger.

I reached for Elizabeth's hand to give her a reassuring squeeze, then once more fixed my gaze upon Lieutenant Nash.

It was easier this time.

✦ ✦ ✦

PICKING UP THE BRANDY BOTTLE, I poured some into a cup, then tilted it toward Elizabeth questioningly. She shook her head. I had sore need of its bracing effect myself, but knew better than to try. The once appealing smell drifting in the air around us now made my stomach churn. I passed the cup to Nash, who seemed willing enough to drain it.

Elizabeth looked more than a little dubious over what I had just done to him. She still did not approve, but saw that necessity outweighed any moral objections. Nash was different from the landlord in that he'd witnessed my death and burial, but under my influence he'd been able to accept an unlikely but more convenient story about my return from the dead. The truth, being so implausible, simply would not do this time. Besides, I knew that if a lie is repeated often enough it will become truth and the best person to begin the repetition was Nash.

"I hope everything is clear, Lieutenant," I said, sitting back. My head pained me quite a lot now.

He sounded absolutely normal. "Yes, Mr. Barrett."

"Now I suggest that you take yourself out there and offer some assurances to your men about this situation. Then I would very much appreciate it if you could arrange for a safe escort for my sister and myself."

"It will be a pleasure, Mr. Barrett," he said with a courteous and sincere smile. So saying, he rose, bowed to each of us, and went into the common room. The rumbling conversation there ceased upon his appearance, then started up as he was bombarded with eager questions.

Pale faces once more peered in at us, eyes wide, wearing the same foolish expressions usually found on sheep.

I smiled and waved back at them until the door shut, then crossed my
arms on the table and lowered my head into them with a weary sigh.

"I hope it works," said Elizabeth.

"It will have to. I'm too tired to think up anything else."

"You didn't anyway," she pointed out. "I did."

Very, very true. I'd taken her improbable story about a cousin bearing
the same name and influenced Nash into believing *that* was the man
who had been killed. It was hardly perfect, but would do, at least for
those few in the army who were concerned with what had happened.
Our immediate family and circle of friends would have to hear the facts,
or something close to them, but that could wait until later.

"Are you up to the journey back?" she asked.

"Yes, of course I am." I straightened and put some starch into my
spine. "I was just resting my eyes."

"It was ... most strange to watch you do that."

"What did it look like?"

"Like two men talking, but there was something more going on beneath the talk. As though you both understood one another but everyone else would miss the meaning."

"You didn't, though."

"No. I knew, but that poor man ...."

"Is now going to do his best to help us," I told her gently.

"Well and good, but please don't mind if I choose to worry."

"What is there to worry about?"

She dropped her gaze, but only for an instant. "I last felt this way
when you went off to England. I was afraid you'd change so much that
none of us would know you anymore. As it was, you did change, but
were still the same. I don't know if that has any sense."

"It does."

"You were all grown up, of course, more polished, but still yourself.
Now this night I've seen and heard things that would drive anyone to
madness. I know that you are here, but some part of me cannot trust it.
Are you my brother come back from the grave or have I gone mad after
all and just don't know it yet?"

"You're the sanest person in the world, Elizabeth. Don't ever doubt
yourself."

"It's just ... I'm frightened. And I'm not used to being frightened. The
worst part is that I've been frightened of *you.*"

Oh, but it hurt to hear her say that, though it was no great surprise. First shock, then joy, and shock again once she'd had time to think things over. All the unnatural aspects of my return were probably battering her like hailstones. That's how I was feeling.

"You wonder if I'm a miracle or a monstrosity?"

Her gaze dropped once more.

"I've no answer to that. It could be both, for all I know. There have been tremendous changes within me. I'm able to do things that I can scarce comprehend, but I am yet the same brother you had before. Though I could dispel your fears as I did with Nash..."

She gave a small start, raising her head sharply.

"...I will do *no* such thing. Not to you and not to Father. Never. That would be unspeakably vile. It's also a great risk."

"In what way?"

"The risk is to me—of losing you both by being absolutely truthful about this...change. I'm trusting you to accept me, whatever and however I am now. If you cannot, then I am lost. I will not force my will upon either of you; I swear that on my sacred honor."

The taut lines altering her expression eased as bit by bit she shed her fear. "And what about others?" She indicated the door. Nash's authoritative voice came through it as he repeated my own words to the men there.

"It's rather out of my hands now. If they wish to be afraid, they will be, so I suppose I can't help that. As for myself, I wish with all my heart that someone could take away *my* fears."

"Oh, Jonathan."

"As for the rest..." I shrugged.

The rest included Jericho, Mrs. Nooth, all the servants, Mrs. Hardinbrook, Beldon, Mother. So many...so many...so many...

"I only want to see Father," I whispered, dropping my head down on my arms again.

Elizabeth's hand rested lightly on my shoulder a moment, then she rose and opened the door. "Lieutenant Nash? My brother would like to leave as quickly as possible, please."

✦ ✦ ✦

WHETHER BECAUSE OF MY INFLUENCE or his desire to oblige my sister, Nash swiftly completed arrangements for our escort. We privately informed him of our destination and the need for discretion. Though Father's friendship with Mrs. Montagu was close to common knowledge in the area, they were each so well respected in their circles that everyone was content to overlook it. Nash agreed, as he had been in the world long enough to understand and do likewise.

He also extended himself and placed two horses at our disposal. He stated his willingness to conduct the escort himself and took one, I the other, and Elizabeth was boosted up to ride behind me. Astride. It could hardly have been a ladylike display for her, but she held tightly onto my waist and made no complaint.

Nash had a man march before us with a lantern, which seemed foolish to me since I could see so well and might have led the way. I held my peace on the subject, though. Any display of my new abilities would needlessly stir them up.

The stars provided me with more than sufficient illumination and now that I had a moment of leisure to consider them, I felt a fresh awakening of awe at their beauty. They were like tiny suns, but unlike the sun itself, could be looked at directly. There also seemed to be many more than I was accustomed to seeing. Thousands on top of thousands of them crowded the sky like clouds of glowing dust motes. The light they shed upon the land was quite even and diffuse so that there was a singular lack of deep shadows in the surrounding countryside. Only beneath the thickest clusters of trees did I spy anything approaching real gloom.

Nash spoke up: "Miss Barrett?"

"Yes?"

"On the road you told my sergeant that you were on the king's business in regard to a message."

"What? Oh. Yes. Our father is a friend of Colonel DeQuincey, who was the one sending it. I fear that I cannot divulge the contents to you, for we are both under oath."

Nash was disappointed, but willing to persist. "I do find it odd that such duties must require a lady to be out so late."

"You are not alone in that opinion, Lieutenant," she said agreeably.

"Also that none of my men reported any messengers upon the road."

Then she took a chance, stepping out on the framework of lies she had formed and that I had placed in his mind. "My brother was the messenger. He is well acquainted with the geography hereabouts, so it is not surprising that he was able to avoid any encounters."

He turned his attention upon me. "You must have prodigious knowledge, indeed, sir. One can scarce throw a stone into the woods without it striking one of my men."

"True enough," I said. "I did not have an easy time keeping out of their way."

"But if you were on the king's business, then surely you would have had no need to avoid them."

"Being delayed was what I wished to avoid, Lieutenant Nash," I said stiffly. "My limited knowledge of German combined with the misfortune of falling from and losing my horse and papers all served to turn me into a most suspicious character in the eyes of Sergeant Lauder. After hearing Hulton's story, I can see why you sent your men out, but I keenly regret the loss of time." He started to reply, but I continued. "However, your speedy assistance in correcting the matter will not go unmarked or unrewarded."

He clearly understood my meaning and managed a slight bow from his saddle. "Your servant, Mr. Barrett." He was an officer in the king's army, which made him a nominal gentleman, but the pay was meager enough to keep him open to compromise on some points. With the prospect of a bribe coming in the near future we could count on him to contain his curiosity for the moment—longer, should it become necessary for me to influence him again.

The night was getting on and despite—or perhaps because of—all the excitements, Elizabeth was growing sleepy. Her head rested against my shoulder, matching the rhythm of our plodding horse. But for my change, I should have been in the same state. Though I'd experienced a certain mental lethargy after dealing with Nash and was suffering a great heaviness of spirit from the consequences of my change, I was yet energetic in body. Perversely, I found it to be annoying. I should have felt sleepy as well. I missed it. Our country custom of rising and retiring with the sun was, I thought, ingrained in my very bones. No more. That whole part of my life was now completely reversed. The nights that lay ahead did not bear thinking about, for they looked to be rather lonely. I could not expect anyone else to reverse themselves just to keep me company. Noticing that her hands were coming loose, I roused Elizabeth. She jerked awake with a gasp.

"Just a little farther," I promised her. "We've already passed the turning to our gate."

She murmured an inarticulate acknowledgment and endeavored to stretch a little. "I hope Mrs. Montagu has some tea. I should very much like a cup or two."

"I'm sure she will, but I suggest you go first and make the request before they see me. There's bound to be an uproar once I walk through the door."

Now she did come alert. "Heavens, yes. How are we going to do this? If I burst in on them in the dead of night with this news they'll think I'm as mad as Mother. And if you come in with me it could be worse."

"Actually, I did have the idea that you should precede me. Of course you don't want to burst in. Just knock on the door and take Father off for a quiet chat to get him prepared. Tell him whatever you need to about Nora and—"

"Jonathan, my dear little brother, there is no way in the world that I could possibly provide him adequate preparation for this."

"I'm under no illusions on that point, but I hope you will try."

"I shall, but no matter what I say, he's going to have a terrible shock when he sees you."

Alas, yes.

The man walking ahead with the lantern had paused, waiting for the rest of our parade to catch him up. Nash leaned down to confer with him, then straightened to squint ineffectually into what for him was true darkness.

"What's the matter?" I asked. I'd also looked around and saw nothing unusual.

"Lauder's other men aren't at their stations," he rumbled.

Several reasons for that came to mind: they'd fallen asleep or were detained out of sight while attending to bodily needs or they'd some-how lost their way from the road. I did not give voice to them, for they sounded foolish enough as thoughts.

"Stay here a moment while we scout ahead," he told us and kicked his horse forward. The half dozen Hessians that marched at our heels followed on his barked order. I reined my animal to keep it in place and watched them go.

"This does not bode well," she whispered into my ear.

We waited, listening for…well, anything. I was ready to kick my mount for a fast race home at the first hint of trouble, but all was silent, only the ordinary sounds of the night came to us.

One man finally trotted back and beckoned us to follow him.

Nash and the rest were gathered about the narrow course that broke off from the main road to lead to Mrs. Montagu's house. The men were watchful, but not nervous.

"Where are the others?" I demanded.

"Hereabouts," Nash replied with false conviction. Considering the fiasco yesterday that had cost me a normal life, I was annoyed at once again seeing evidence of Nash's incompetence.

I stood in my stirrups for another look. Nothing but trees, fields, and empty, dusty road before and behind. Not quite empty. There was something lying across the ruts a little ahead, close enough to notice, but too far to identify. A fallen branch, perhaps.

"They must be very good at woodcraft," I commented. "I perceive no sign of them at all."

"It's a thick night," he said. "No moon. None of us can see much."

The damned idiot. Men gone missing and him overlooking the danger of it. We could be surrounded by rebels and he'd prefer to get shot than admit something was wrong. "I think we should go on to our destination, Lieutenant."

"Certainly."

"*Herr Oberleutnant!*" The man with the lantern had pushed ahead and stumbled over whatever it was on the road. His strident tone brought us all to attention. Nash moved toward him. I trailed along, having the idea of there being safety in numbers. Elizabeth tightened her hold around my waist.

They were all bending over it and the alteration of their manner was such as to make me stop short. I signed to Elizabeth that I was getting down and swung a leg over the horse's neck and slipped off. She dropped next to me.

I pushed into the middle of them and recoiled at once. At our feet lay the body of a young Hessian. His head was thrown back so his mouth was wide open as though for a scream. In contrast, his eyes were calm and quite dull. Limbs flung every which way, his chest was cracked open like an eggshell. The intensity of the bloodsmell struck my senses like a harsh slap. The stuff covered him and had soaked into the earth.

"Oh, my God," whispered Elizabeth.

My first instinct was to turn and drag her away from the awful sight, which I did. She made no protest. Her feet tangled one against the other; I lifted her up by the elbows until we were well distanced and set her down with a jolt. She swayed against me, gasping for air.

"My God, it was just how *you* looked," she said, freely trembling.

Her words cut right through me, gouged into my vitals, and tore out again leaving behind chaos and a kind of blank agony.

Too much had happened. The rest and retreat I so desperately needed now forced themselves upon me. For a few minutes I simply could not think. It's a truly terrible thing to go through, when nothing—absolutely *nothing*—fills the mind. You don't really forget anything, not names or facts or memories, you just can't get to them. I was a sudden simpleton, unable to move or speak, unaware of time or events. I was a closed box, sealed fast shut, nothing would go in or out. Like a coffin.

Elizabeth's voice finally made a crack in its hard surface. She shook my shoulders, insistently calling my name.

"I'm all right," I replied to whatever question she'd asked.

"Are you?"

I breathed in a great draft of fresh night air and managed to recover a little of what passed for my wits. A glance at her worried face helped most to sort things. It was damned selfish to give in to such weakness when she needed me. I decided my legs would hold me after all. "Not really, but it will have to do. What of yourself?"

She was unwell, but not the kind to faint, and told me as much.

"Stay here," I said. An unnecessary request. She wasn't about to budge. I was compelled to return for another view of the calamity. Awful as it was, I could not allow myself to be bullied by my fears. It would be bad, but better than giving myself over to foul imaginings.

It was bad enough, but worsened when I recognized him.

The dead man was Hausmann, the young fellow who had wanted land, a family, a new life. His life taken, his dreams dead, the children to come never born, he was so horrible and yet so pathetic. The two balanced each other to promote equal amounts of revulsion and pity. Was *this* what had happened to me? Was that the sight that had made my father cry out so?

Yes and yes.

Then unexpectedly, came the rage. It washed over me like a scarlet tide, fiery hot, frighteningly strong.

Who had done this?

Nash had dismounted and was regarding his man with a sad, hard face. During his life he had probably seen much of death, but he did not appear to be overly callous. He looked at me and something flinched in his face. I ignored it.

"Nash, I want to get the bastard who did this."

"We will, Mr. Barrett," he said, sounding nettled, perhaps, that I was presuming too much upon his goodwill.

To the devil with it. "Nash, listen to me ...."

He flinched again, his eyelids fluttering as if against a strong wind.

"Tonight we are going to hunt down whoever did this and take him. Do you understand?"

He struggled for breath. Not all of the men could follow my words, but they read my intent well enough. Those closest to us fell back.

"Do you understand?"

He was unable to speak and only just managed to nod. He'd gone very white and, when I released him, staggered a little. One of his men muttered and made a surreptitious gesture with his hand. I'd seen something similar while visiting one of the Dutch towns on the west end of the Island. It had been explained to me as being a sign to ward off the evil eye. I ignored that, too. Let them think what they liked as long as they obeyed Nash's orders—and Nash obeyed mine.

I gave instructions, then grabbed up my horse's forgotten reins and stalked back to Elizabeth. "Nash has picked out two trustworthy men. They're to escort you safely to Father—"

"What?"

"I'm going to stay and help him settle things."

"You're what?" She had heard me, but wasn't ready to accept it.

"I have to do this."

"You have to see Father."

"Later."

"Jonathan—"

"No. *Listen* to me. The bastard that killed me may have killed that poor soul as well. I can't let another hour pass without doing something about it."

She looked over at the men standing by the corpse. "But Father—"

"Will understand."

"Are you so sure?"

I was and I wasn't and could form no answer for her, only frame another question. "Do *you* understand?"

Again she looked past me, then right at me. Her hand touched my chest where the rifle ball had shattered every aspect of our lives, then fell away. "I'm afraid I do."

Relief, elation, love. "Thank you, sister."

"Thank me later, when I'm in a better mind to take it."

I lifted her up onto the saddle and gave her the reins. "If I'm not back before dawn don't worry. It only means that I had to find shelter for the day. Whatever happens, you'll be able to meet me at the old barn tomorrow after sunset. I'd come to the house, but...."

She leaned down and her fingers dug into my shoulder. Her voice shook. "As long as you *do* come back, because I couldn't possibly bear to lose you twice."

CHAPTER
THIRTEEN

NASH AND I MADE A THOROUGH INSPECTION of the area and drew a few conclusions. Hausmann had been shot at fairly close range and died where
he'd fallen. His rifle, bayonet, powder horn, and other gear were gone,
along with whatever coin he might have possessed. Nash took the strip-
ping of the body in stride and even seemed to approve.

"It'll make it that much easier to identify the rascals and hang 'em,"
he said.

There'd been at least two, perhaps more. The footprints were too
muddled for us to make much sense of them. Our own tracks added to
the confusion, but I was able to find where the rebels had crossed the
road to head over the fields.

"They may be trying to get back to Suffolk County," I grumbled.
"They'll find no lack of help there. The whole place stinks of sedition."

"Oh, yes, the `Sons of Liberty.'" He added, "More like the sons of
bitches. But if they're going to Suffolk, I should think it would be faster
to stay on the road."

"Not if they know the land. The road curves farther along and would
take them too much out of their way."

"We can't hope to follow them at night, not through all that with only
a lantern." He motioned at the fields.

"Then have your man put out the light so our eyes can get used to
the dark."

"Mr. Barrett, this is most impractical!"

225

"Or leave it by that poor boy's body. At least then no one will fall over him."

He had no objections to that suggestion. Someone had placed Hausmann in order, straightening his limbs and covering his face with a handkerchief. With the lantern sitting incongruously in the dust close by his head, he looked more macabre than when we'd first found him. My anger welled up again, for him, for me, for the grief that had happened in my wake and that which was to come.

Nash sent one man back to Glenbriar on my horse to fetch more troops. He might have been content to wait for their arrival, but I was very conscious that the night was swiftly passing.

"If we tarry here the rebels will either bury themselves in Suffolk or have found a boat to take them across the Sound. We must set out now and let the others catch us up as they can."

"Their orders are to look for the men who were here to start with," Nash clarified.

"My guess is that if that lot are still alive, they'll be in pursuit of the rebels as well."

"My God, in this murk we could end up shooting each other."

"Lieutenant, I know this country well and can see excellently in the dark and thus will be able to prevent such an occurrence, let us cease wasting time and proceed."

My voice had taken on an edge that he recognized and was not ready to contest. He gave some brief orders and indicated that I should lead the way. We left the road in single file, each man within sight of the one before him, the last one in line leading Nash's horse. Though it was obvious they were taking pains to be quiet, the whole parade seemed ludicrously noisy to me. I winced with every careless footstep and snapped twig and fervently hoped that the darkness would provide us the same cover it gave those we hunted.

Free of such limitations, I remained alert to the movement and place of each leaf and branch. It served. Some dozen yards along our rustic path I spied additional tracks heading away from the road. I did not point them out to Nash, as it was unlikely he'd be able to see well enough, but they did confirm my guess that our destination would be somewhere in Suffolk County. Our quarry would be lost for good, then.

Unless we hurried.

I urged Nash to greater speed and damn the noise.

With Elizabeth gone a great portion of my mind that was unoccupied with more immediate concerns had given in to the temptation to think of the events of the last two nights as being a ghastly nightmare from which I might eventually awaken. I did know in my heart that this was nonsense, but as if to confound the facts and confirm the fancy came a near-repetition of what had set everything off.

Ahead, a figure suddenly raised himself from cover and fired at us.

I saw the flash and smoke, heard the crashing report—and froze.

As before, I simply could not take in the idea that anything untoward was taking place. A very foolish assumption, considering what I'd been through, and very selfish, to tarry there like a lout and not consider the welfare of the other men with me. Veterans of battle, they sensibly dropped while I continued to stand and gape. Lieutenant Nash, with a foul curse, knocked a solid arm against the back of my knees and told me to do likewise.

Pitching forward, I threw out my hands and caught myself in time. Nash's blow seemed to jog my head back onto my shoulders, as it were, causing me to start thinking again. I whispered for him to stay put and lifted up just enough for a look around.

The man that had shot at us was quickly bearing himself away.

I shouted something about getting him and sprinted off. Nash yelled after, urging me to use caution, but I was deaf to any objections. The fellow had a good start, but there was no chance that he could match my speed. At best, he could go at a fast walk; unimpeded by the darkness, I was able to run. Dodging by trees and bushes, leaping over roots, I caught up with him like a hound after a crippled hare.

He heard me, glanced back once, and increased his pace. Too little, too late. I bowled into him and brought us both down with a satisfying thud that was more injurious to him than myself. The breath grunted out of him, leaving him too stunned to move. I got up, grabbed away his spent rifle and called for Nash and the others to come ahead. It took them some time to pick their path, but they followed my voice and eventually arrived.

"Who is he?" Nash demanded.

"A damned better man than you, you English bastard," the man snarled back.

Nash, an officer in what was surely the greatest army in the world, had no patience for insults from inferiors. He gave the man a hard kick in the side to encourage him into a more respectful attitude. The fellow had only just recovered his wind and this additional assault once more deprived him of air.

"Do you know him?" he asked of me.

"I've not seen him before," I said truthfully. Having been a regular churchgoer, I knew the faces, if not the names, of just about everyone in the area. "Where are you from?"

"Wouldn't you like to know?" he wheezed back. Nash started to kick him again, but I persuaded him to hold off this time. Though a good beating might serve to satisfy a need for revenge it would also render him unable to speak.

"I think he's from Connecticut," I said, making an educated guess from his clothes and accent.

"I've heard the name," said Nash. "Where does it lie from here?"

"Across the Sound. Put a few stout fellows at the oars of a whale boat and you can row your way across quick as thought."

"Tory traitor," snarled the man in a poisonous tone.

"That, sir, is a contradiction of terms," I informed him. "Now, unless you want these soldiers to hang you on the spot for a murdering spy, you'd better give us your name and business."

"I'm no spy, but a soldier myself, and deserve honorable treatment," he protested.

"Then act with honor, sir. Who are you?"

"Lieutenant Ezra Andrews, and I have the privilege of serving under General Washington, God bless his soul."

"Can you prove that?"

"By God, what proof do I need beyond my own word?"

"Your commission as an officer?" suggested Nash. At a sign from him, two Hessians stepped in to drag Andrews to his feet and turn out his pockets. One of them found a substantial fold of paper, which he passed to Nash. He opened and tried unsuccessfully to read it in the starlight. Andrews cackled.

"Let me," I offered. So as not to startle them, I also made a show of squinting against the dark, then read aloud enough words to confirm that Andrews spoke the truth about himself and his rank. Nash then informed the man that he was his prisoner.

Andrews spat on the ground. Luckily his aim, like his previous shot at us, was just as poor, and missed my shoe by several inches.

Nash took the commission and refolded the paper. "Where are the rest of your men?"

"You can find 'em yourself. I'll not help you."

Yes, you will, I thought. "Andrews...look at me. I want you to listen to me...."

"I'll listen to no one," he snapped back.

"Listen to me, I say."

"The devil I will!"

I stopped cold and blinked. What was the matter with the man? I was staring right at him and nothing I said made any impression at all. As if he were...

Damnation. I gave up in sudden chagrin. I could see him, but unless he could see me, my efforts were futile. It was just too dark for such work.

"Give him over and let's push on," I said to Nash. "His comrades can't be that far ahead of us."

"Mr. Barrett, you have done enough for one night by capturing this man."

"And there's more to be done, sir. Whoever killed Hausmann is still free." I made a point to emphasize Hausmann's name and gesture ahead of us. This was not lost on the Hessians, who looked expectantly at their commander.

Nash could not reasonably back down, not just yet. With ill grace, he ordered someone to bind Andrews' hands behind him and put him in the charge of the tallest and strongest-looking man in our small company. Andrews protested and the soldier told him to be quiet. Andrews did not understand German, but he did get the correct idea, subsiding when his captor drew a slow finger across his own throat while making an appropriate hissing sound. After that Andrews was slightly less truculent.

As we continued forward, I found signs on the ground that others had gone by earlier: trampled plants, broken branches. They'd been in much haste.

"I don't think they're very far ahead," I confided to Nash. Despite his reluctance for this job, he invited me to enlarge upon that opinion. "They must have heard us coming up; the wind's at our backs, you know. I believe Andrews stayed behind to fire a shot to discourage our progress."

"It worked," he admitted. "He bought them a quarter hour, at least. They could be anywhere by now."

That estimation of the time was a gross exaggeration. The man's reluctance was enough for me to accuse him of cowardice, but I held my tongue. "Not if they're waiting for Andrews."

His forward pace wavered. "What do you mean?"

"I believe there's an excellent chance that he was meant to fire, then run after them. They may only be just ahead."

Now Nash completely stopped. "Meaning that those rascals are most certainly lying in ambush for us."

"Possibly, but I rather think they're more likely expecting Andrews, not us."

"I cannot take that chance with my men," he stated. "In the daylight, with sufficient reinforcements we can—"

"Lieutenant, I am not asking you to march them into any ambush, but to allow me to scout ahead."

It must have gone through his mind how bad he would look to his senior officers if a civilian was seen to be doing his duty—and performing it better. "Very well, but no more than one hundred yards."

I intended to travel as far as was necessary, but kept silent to avoid more objections. "Good. If you will instruct your man to give me Andrews' rifle… and now I'll just trade hats with him."

Andrews had listened to this exchange and instantly saw the danger it meant to his companions. He started to raise his voice to shout a warning, but I cut that off quickly enough by clapping a hand over his mouth. He began to vigorously struggle, and his guard and two others found it necessary to wrestle the man to the ground. We made quite a clumsy mob before sorting ourselves out. Only after someone put a fist into Andrews' belly did I dare to remove my smothering hand. He groaned and puffed and by the time he was ready to use his voice again, was efficiently gagged.

I placed his hat on my head, crouched down to minimize my height (Andrews was half a foot shorter), and continued along the path the rebels seemed to have taken. The weight and long barrel of the rifle were awkward. I had to mind where it was pointing lest it catch on something above or to the side.

My much-improved sight was a godsend, though; I covered my hundred-yard limit in very little time.

Other than the signs left on the earth of their late passage, I saw nothing of the rebels. It was safe for Nash and his men to follow to this point, but I didn't want to waste time going back for them. Nor did I want to spend too much time away, or Nash would become more nervous than ever. I could assume he would wait for a little while, then be able to honorably call a retreat. The problem was not knowing just how long he would wait.

I trotted quickly, covering the distance much faster than an ordinary man and marveling at my lack of physical fatigue. My steps were full of spring as though I were fresh and had bottomless reserves to draw upon. I'd felt this before when the chase was up for a hunt or riding Rolly. For a time the sheer joy of movement overcame the goal behind my chase.

The feeling lasted until I saw a blur with a man's shape stirring under some trees just ahead.

"Andrews?"

The voice was pitched to a carrying whisper. Unrecognizable. I slowed, but kept coming.

"Mr. Andrews?"

I gave out with a grunt of affirmation and hoped it would be well received.

"Are you all right?"

Another grunt. I came closer. The shape clarified itself, separating out from the dense shadows where it had been crouching.

Roddy Finch.

I strode forward without thought. A terrible humming seized my brain, or perhaps I was the one humming and was unaware of it. I know that for several seconds I could hear nothing else.

Roddy asked another question. At least, I saw his mouth forming words and the expression on his face suggested he was making an inquiry of me. I was unable to answer.

Andrews? I read the name from his lips.

My continued approach, continued silence alarmed him. He wavered between running and risking another question.

And while he hesitated I bore down upon him like a storm.

I threw away Andrews's rifle. Roddy saw something of the motion and heard its landing, but could make no sense of it. He raised his own weapon, but had left it too late. I plucked it from his hands as one might take a stick from a very young child. He turned to run, but to my eyes he seemed to move exceedingly slow. I caught him by the collar of his coat and lifted him from the ground.

My hearing returned. The screech he gave out went right through me. I did not pause, though. I jerked him right off his feet like a doll and twisted around and let go my grip. He went flying down the path to land in a stunned heap some yards away.

Behind me, someone yelled his name.

I was just turning to look, but instinct had the better part of me now, and I dropped instead.

Once more I was deafened, but from without, not within, as something roared very close overhead. The sweet reek of powder smoke engulfed me, stung my eyes. I was just able to see a young man emerging from the trees, very close. Halfway to my feet, I sprang at him. He was fast. He swung the rifle barrel at my head as hard as he could.

I got my arm up just in time or he'd have smashed my skull. The hard jolt of the heavy iron knocked me right over. I roared from the pain, but lurched to my feet regardless, my blood boiling. He struck again, brutal and cursing, and I had no choice but to use the same arm as a shield. He caught me just below the elbow and the agony was so sudden and so awful that I knew the bones had shattered under the blow.

As I fell away, he dashed past to Roddy and frantically urged him to run. Roddy was too slow and needed help finding his feet.

"Come on, come on!" his rescuer cried desperately.

Like two drunks attempting to support one another, they staggered, then started in the right direction.

No . . . he would *not* get away from me.

My right arm dangling loose and shooting white-hot darts straight to my brain, I reeled over just in time to catch one of them as they passed.

Roddy.

I used my weight and extra height and bore him down. His companion was bowled out of the way by my rush, but recovered and turned on me. Like Roddy before him, he seemed to be moving slowly—that or I was moving just that much faster. This time when he swung at my head with the rifle barrel I was ready and caught it with my left hand. A snarl and a vicious wrench and it was mine.

He was startled, but also of a mind to fight. Doubling over, he butted me in the stomach with his head. It pushed me backward a few paces and hurt, but was nothing compared to my arm. He followed up with two quick fists, but the results were disappointing. I felt them, but they hardly seemed to bother me. Next he tried to take back his rifle, and we played a very uneven tug-of-war for its possession. I held tight.

His breathing was ragged, his poxy face gone red and dripping sweat. I could smell the stink from his bad teeth as his next turn of attack brought us both down and rolling. Now he was biting and kicking like a fury, but I kept hold of the rifle and, by God, I wasn't going to give it up. Had he been thinking, he might have used my bad arm against me by striking at it, but he'd lost his temper and his reason. I got the rifle between us and tried to use it to ward off his fists. This bruised him and slowed him down, then Roddy's unsteady voice rang out.

"They're comin'! Run for your life!"

I heard a confusion of sounds, then the man beating at me was abruptly gone.

"Run for it!" yelled Roddy. He was on his feet now and the other man pelted past him. He shambled forward to follow.

No....

I discarded the rifle as a useless weight and threw myself on him. We came down with a groan. When he attempted to crawl away, I put a knee into his side, stopping him.

"Mr. Barrett! Mr. Barrett!" called Nash. He and his men blundered up, drawn by the shot, but uncertain of the right direction.

I started to speak. There was no air in my lungs. I replaced it, but as I did so the thought occurred that bringing Nash over would seal things forever for Roddy. This boy that I had known all my life would go straight to the gallows. My own death aside, they would certainly hang him for stealing back his father's horses. Though there was probably no direct evidence against him, men had died before for less.

"Mr. Barrett! Where are you, sir?"

We'd played at Rapelji's school, worked there, helped one another. We'd not been especial friends, but he *had* known me. And for all that, he'd still been able to coolly raise his rifle and send me falling into this waking nightmare. He'd put my family through untold grief, put me through hell itself.

But they would *hang* him.

Oliver had once persuaded me to Tyburn to see some murderers pay for their crimes. It hadn't been pretty. The family of one man had hurriedly come forward to seize his legs and pull down as hard as they could to speed the progress of the strangling rope and end his sufferings. The sight had been sickening, though I'd been assured that the fellow more than deserved his punishment. Now I looked down at Roddy Finch and in my mind placed him at those gallows, his feet twitching and his neck stretching and his tongue thrusting from blue lips and his face turning black....

If I called now, it would be out of my hands and the law would run its course. It would be the same as if I'd drawn the rope over Roddy's head myself.

"Mr. Barrett!"

I'd known him all my life ...

"*Mr. Barrett!*"

... and he'd known me.

I stood up. The humming had returned to my brain. "We're here, Lieutenant Nash! I've another prisoner for you."

✦ ✦ ✦

THE WAY WE WERE SEATED on the ground, lined in a row, surrounded by glowering Hessians, anyone would think that we were all prisoners. Andrews and Roddy both had their hands tied, and I was in virtually the same immobile condition because of my injured arm. I was weak and very shaken. It hurt abominably. One of the soldiers had kindly improvised a sling from my neckcloth, and another tried to tempt me with a flask of something that smelled terrible. I thanked him and politely refused. To them, I was the hero of the hour, but their admiration was rather lost on me because of my extreme pain.

Nash made a show of going after the other rebel, but without my help he had no chance of catching up. And I had no need or desire to help. We had Roddy Finch and that was the end of it for me.

The discarded firearms were recovered and one proved to be identical to those that the Hessians carried. They concluded it had been taken from the dead man, along with its accouterments and his meager supply of coin.

"A good night's work," said Nash, when he returned and was informed of this discovery. "You've done the Crown a great favor with your assistance, Mr. Barrett. I'm sure it will not go unrewarded."

Now our positions to aid one another had been reversed, though I had no doubt he would still expect some monetary token from my father later.

Father....

The urge to go home seized me, stronger than ever, now that the chase was past. Elizabeth had been disappointed, but understood; she would not be as charitable over additional delays.

"Thank you, Lieutenant. I would take it as a great kindness if I might be allowed to return to my sister."

He'd only been waiting half the night to hear those words and promptly volunteered his horse for my use. I declined. The effort of getting into the saddle would be too much for my arm. I was able to walk and said as much, preferring my own legs to being jostled around on a horse's back. After trading hats again with the surly Andrews, I set off, slowly leading the way for the rest. Since the object was to reach the road rather than go back on our own tracks, I struck off in a different direction to find it. Once there, they could make their own way back to Glenbriar.

Of the other men who had been at their post with Hausmann, we saw no sign. Andrews and Roddy refused to answer any questions on the subject. Nash was not optimistic.

"Probably murdered as well," he said. "If that's the case, then hanging will be too good for these two."

"Andrews is a soldier," I pointed out.

"More's the pity, he'll probably just be interned as a prisoner of war, which can be worse than hanging from what I'd heard. The other fellow is no soldier, though, which makes him either a spy, a thief, a murderer or all three. He'll hang."

Roddy heard him clearly—Nash made no effort at discretion—went very white, and stumbled as though his legs lost strength. His guard held him up.

"Steady, lad," said Andrews, who had had his gag removed. "You're a proper soldier of Congress, and I'll swear to it in any court they please to call. You'll live to fight another day."

"Ha!" said Nash.

Very likely I would never see Roddy again after this night. He would simply cease to be. I enjoyed no feeling of triumph for his capture. I wanted him punished, but the punishment itself had become distant and abstract. Someone else would handle all the details of prosecution and execution. My only concern was to patch up the damage he had inflicted upon my life.

We might have done better to retrace our steps, for it took us an hour to reach the road again, and even longer to return to the point where we'd left it. I was weary. Those bottomless reserves were turning out to be finite, after all, eaten up by my pain.

In the far distance, as we rounded a long curve, we saw several lanterns bobbing about and many men moving about. The fellow Nash had dispatched for reinforcements had returned, and they were gathered around the spot where Hausmann had fallen.

"That's Da's wagon and team," Roddy exclaimed when we got close enough for them to see details.

True enough, and rather ironic. It was being used to carry Hausmann's body back to Glenbriar. They'd already shrouded him in a blanket. The thing robbed him of face and form. God, I must have looked like *that* as well. I was glad Elizabeth was not here to see it.

Andrews and Roddy were turned over to others to guard and Nash busied himself with issuing orders and receiving news. The missing men had turned up on their own. They'd heard the shot that had killed Hausmann and given futile chase, but lost themselves in the dark.

They'd wandered back sometime earlier, drawn by the lights and noise of the others.

"That's good," Nash concluded. "It seems that you and that lad are the only casualties. If you wish, I'll have them take you back to The Oak and find a doctor for you."

"Thank you, but I'm sure Dr. Beldon, who lives at my home, will see to things."

"Yes, of course. I'd forgotten about him. I imagine he's still out looking for your ... ah ...." Here he trailed off, in sudden doubt over what he should say next.

"For these two," I completed for him, indicating the prisoners. "I hope he hasn't come to harm. Please do tell your men to keep a lookout for him and send him home as quick as may be. He's a lean fellow with popping eyes, favors a black coat and stockings."

"Yes, some of us know him from his visits to The Oak. I'll see to it." Nash recovered from his discomfiture, his altered memory secure once more. He insisted on providing an escort, so I found myself bracketed by two men who were instructed to take me to the door of the Montagu house. Each had a lantern, but our progress was slow. They understood that I was to be given every courtesy and interpreted that to mean setting a regal pace out of consideration for my arm. It pleased me well enough as I didn't feel like going any faster.

The thing had swollen rather badly. The sleeve of the coat I wore was snug around the injury. I was not looking forward to Beldon's ministrations for this. Not that I lacked confidence in his ability as a physician, but it would hurt damnably.

Though thankfully not suffering from fever, my mouth was very dry. I thirsted, and knew that water would not quench it. *I need blood,* I thought without abhorrence or any surprise.

But once the idea jumped into my head that thirst increased tenfold.

My throat constricted and my tongue thickened as it scraped the roof of my mouth. My lips felt like salt and sand. The fingers of my good hand curled and twitched. My very bones seemed to burn with new pain around the break. Much as I wanted to see Father, it would have to wait. I could not tolerate this dreadful need for long.

I walked faster. The soldiers made no comment and kept up. They'd become a sudden inconvenience and would have to go. I tried to recall the words I'd need to dismiss them, but the insistent thirst was too distracting. The phrases that kept coming up in my tumbled mind were either French or Italian or Latin.

As the Montagu house finally came into view, I paused and attempted to tell the men that I no longer required their assistance. My nervous state of mind, combined with my limited German, made it difficult to get the idea across. One of them knew a bit of English, though, so between us things were finally made clear. They looked somewhat worried for me, for I was fidgeting and the longer they lingered, the harder it was to conceal my anxiousness. With many a backward glance, they finally left, their pale lanterns swinging as they went. I managed to remain in one spot just long enough for them to walk a goodly distance, then whirled around to run toward the stables.

The building was unfamiliar to me and much smaller than our own, but the smells and routines were identical. I eased open the door and slipped inside, my eyes eagerly searching the dimness within.

Mrs. Montagu's carriage stood just inside, a lovely bit of work that she kept polished and new-looking for her rides to church and village. She had only the one coachman, who also served as groom, but he'd be asleep in the slave quarters now. The horses, a pair of matched bays out of the same bloodlines as my own Rolly, were quite unguarded.

The animals already sensed my approach, stirring in their boxes. I picked the quieter of the two and moved in next to him. His ears flicked back in doubt and he bobbed his head. I spoke to him soothingly and let him get my scent until he was used to me. It was not easy to stand there calming him while feeling so agitated. The ache in my throat and belly were very great, and I had to suppress an unnaturally powerful urge to dive in and instantly slake that need.

Finally, the animal stood very still and I was able to go on. My earlier experience with Rolly helped. This time my bite was more shallow, my control of the flow more certain. The effect of the blood, however, was the same. I gratefully and rather greedily drank my fill, relishing the warmth and rich taste. It was better than the sweetest water, better than the best wine, more sustaining than any food.

And healing. Some of the grinding agony in my broken arm receded. It was yet far from being whole—the swelling remained—but the promise of recovery was there. I could even move the fingers again, though little more than that.

The small wounds I'd made on the horse clotted over. The blood staining my mouth and chin was minimal; I could easily clean that off if I could just find...

I'd left the stable door open to give me light to work by, and the threshold was no longer vacant. The Hessians stood there, their lanterns raised high. I dropped down, but the movement made noise and they came inside.

Damn the men. Not put off by my dismissal, they'd doggedly returned, whether out of curiosity or a dedicated obedience to their commander to see that his orders were correctly carried out.

I swiped at my mouth. Blood on my hand now. The damned stuff was everywhere. There was no time to brush it away, they were already coming around to look in the box.

They stopped short as the lantern light fell upon me where I crouched in the straw. Each of us gave a start, they with surprise, me with sudden shame and fear. I turned my face from them, but it was too late. They saw the blood and my eyes—which were doubtless flushed scarlet after my feeding. Nora's had always done so.

"*Blutsäuger!*" one of them whispered with awe and horror.

The word had no meaning for me, but I knew the sound of terror. I pushed my own away and raised myself to slowly face them.

The older of the two backed off, making a recognizable witch sign against me with his hand. He invoked God's name in a hasty muttered prayer and kept going. His companion was too shocked yet to move.

"It's all right," I said, but it was hopeless to think I could calm them as I'd calmed the horse. I offered a placating hand, a wasted and foolish gesture. There was blood on it.

The older one recoiled, shouted a warning at his friend, and fled. He crashed against the edge of the doorway in his haste, but did not stop. The noise got through to the other fellow, who started after him.

I rushed up to the opening and watched them retreat in panicked haste across the yard and on toward the beginnings of the lane. They'd probably run straight back to their company and pass along God knows what story. There was absolutely nothing I could do about it, either. I might possibly catch up with them, try to influence them, but what needed to be said to change their memories was beyond my limited German vocabulary.

A black cloud settled about my shoulders, bowing them, sinking into my brain, deadening thought, but not feeling. The impossibility of my situation was too much to bear. While Elizabeth had been with me, I'd been able to take hope from her, but even her support looked to be no more than an illusion...a shadow.

I live in the shadows and make shadows of my own in the minds of others. Shadows and illusions of life and love that fill my nights until something like this happens and shows them up for what they are.

Now as I leaned wearily against the wall of the stable and stared inward to darkness, I knew what Nora had meant. Its exact meaning had been driven into me by those two horrified men with almost the same force as the rifle ball that had killed me. My desire to go back to the life I'd known was never to be fulfilled. I might create an illusion of peace for myself but it would be only that and nothing more. Sooner or later the unnatural aspects of my condition would encroach upon and destroy that peace. This instance was surely the first of many others to come. The weight of such a future was enough to crush me back into the ground again, back into the grave that had rejected me.

Without mind for direction I left the stable and wandered forth into a night that was my illusion of day. A cloud, the color of iron and just as heavy, rolled over my heart and soul, weighed hard upon my spirit, and filled my mind with despair. Even the careless glory of the stars filling the great sky with their light could not pierce or lift it.

I walked and walked, hugging my injured arm. My path took me through fields and across the road. I lost track of time and didn't care. I met no one and was thankful. I wanted no one to see me, not even Father. I was too ashamed of what had happened to me, of what I'd become.

Only when the sky turned unduly bright did I rouse somewhat from the self-pity that had such fast hold of me. I didn't wholly shake it off, merely thrust it aside out of mundane necessity.

My unmindful walk had been in the right general direction. I was on my own land and not too far from the old barn. Elizabeth might even be there. I'd told her about it. Yes. I could bear to see her again, perhaps, but no one else.

The light flooding the sky increased, imparting clear vision to others even as it blinded me. My steps grew clumsy, uncertain, as they'd been the previous dawn. I staggered forward with greater speed, shielding my eyes and looking up only to stay on the path I stumbled over. The barn lay just ahead. I dived beneath the ivy hanging over the entrance and into the comforting shadows beyond with a sob of relief.

Apparently I was not so far gone in my mood as to forsake life just yet. Had I stayed outside, I suspected the sun would burn me down to the bone. A rifle ball was bad enough, but there are worse fates.

My steps dragging in the dust, I returned to the dark shelter of the stall. The only marks there were the ones I'd made earlier. I'd probably be secure enough for the day—at least until Elizabeth came the next evening. I was sorry she wasn't here, but it had only been a faint hope. She was probably still talking to Father, poor girl.

I sat with my back to the wall, trying to ease my aching arm and groaning at the futility of it. This time I would welcome the sleep the day would bring...

◆ ◆ ◆

...BUT THAT WHIPPED BY without any knowledge that I *had* slept.

My eyes had closed and opened. That was all it took and the hot hours of another late summer's day were gone forever. All my future days would be spent like this one, one instant the end of night, the next the beginning of another with no sense of time between. I'd never again see the clouds against the sun, never see its rise and set except as a warning or as an inconvenience that must be endured. No nightmares, but no dreams either, nothing but this unnatural oblivion and its inevitable reminder of death.

Whatever was to become of me?

Did I even care?

After a moment's sluggish thought, I decided the answer was yes. For my body, if not my spirit. Conscious or not, the enforced rest had done me much good. More movement had returned to my arm and the swelling was reduced. The pain was...noticeable, but not as bad as before.

Then I forgot all about it, sharply aware I was not alone. Standing but a few yards away was Elizabeth. Her face bore signs of much fatigue and strain, but happiness as well as she looked at me. She held a lantern and standing next to her was Father.

A hundred years might have gone by since I'd last seen him in the library giving those final instructions to me and Beldon. He'd been so solid and concerned, but confident. And there'd been pride as well, pride for me, and for what I was doing. The kind of pride that always caught at my heart and made me pause and thank God that he was my father.

Sweet heavens, but he's an old man, I thought with dull shock, looking at this near-stranger who stared back, stricken, mirroring my own painful astonishment. His face was so lined, so gray, the lips slack and pale, his eyes so hollow. Even his body seemed to have shrunk, the straight spine bent, the shoulders slumped and the strength of his arms and spirit fled.

I've done this to him.

My sight blurred and swam. I didn't want to look at him. Didn't want to see him like this.

"Forgive me," I pleaded, hardly knowing my voice, hardly knowing why I said it.

He slowly walked over, knelt by me. I could just see that much through the sheeting of tears.

His hands tentatively touched my shoulders. They were steady and strong, making a lie of what I'd seen. Then his arms went around me and he pulled me toward him as he'd done often enough to give solace when I'd been very small.

"Oh, my boy," he whispered, rocking me gently. "My poor, lost child."

I said nothing, did nothing.

He pulled me closer, holding tight, and I felt a great shudder travel through his body.

He was … was *weeping*. I'd *never* known him to …

There came a terrible choking sob from him, and I felt one of his tears splash warm upon my cheek.

"Oh, laddie … thank God, *thank God* …."

My heart and mind began to clear as the realization dawned that he was yet my father, and he loved me still, no matter what had happened or what was to come. All my sorrows, all my hurts were not so great that somehow he could not help me bear them.

"Please, laddie … don't be a dream …."

In a hot flare of shame I cast off my self-pity and surrendered to the love and comfort he wanted so much to give.

CHAPTER
FOURTEEN

ELIZABETH ALLOWED US a decent interval for this precious communion, then put down her lantern. There were tears on her face as well, and she attended to them with a handkerchief before coming over and kneeling on my other side. She patted my head, stroking my hair as though to assure herself that I was indeed solid and not an imagined spirit.

Father looked at her. "I am sorry I doubted you," he said. "Forgive me, daughter."

She touched his arm and smiled wryly. "It's all right."

"What's this?" I asked, straightening a little. Father gave me a last reassuring hug, then stood. From my seat in the dust I once again saw him as the child in me had always perceived him, saw him as he would always ever be to me: a tall, handsome man with strength and energy and honor and wisdom enough to know that he was not all-wise.

Elizabeth said to me, "I did mention that there was no way in the world he would...well, that it would not be easy."

"She told me everything...and I did not believe her." Father regarded me with quiet amazement. "I'm not certain that I even now believe."

I had some difficulty in swallowing. "Told you...*everything?*"

"Yes."

I felt my face go red.

He smiled kindly upon my disconcertion. "Dear child, whoever and whatever this woman was, I'm ready to fall on my knees and thank her for what she shared with you. You've come back to us. I don't care how or by what means. You've come back; that's all I care about."

I started to speak, found my throat had gone thick, and tried swallowing again. This time it worked out a bit better. "It's just that this is still extraordinary to me as well, Father. I've doubts of my own, so many that I can hardly bear them. Sometimes I seem all right and then it overwhelms me and I don't know what to do."

"You've been alone too much with yourself. It's time to come home."

"But I'm afraid."

He looked at me and seemed to see right into my heart. "I know you are, Jonathan," he said gently. "But you've been through all the worst things already, have you not? All on your own, and yet you've acquitted yourself well despite that. Now that we're with you, don't you think it's time to give up your fear?"

With my eyes closed I could almost feel their love beating soft upon me. I welcomed it like the warmth of a fire against the bitterness of a winter night. He was right, and I was being foolish. I opened my eyes, nodded shyly, then he reached down and helped me to my feet. A very bad twinge like the touch of a hot poker shot up through the top of my skull with the movement, making me gasp.

"What's the matter?" he demanded, steadying me.

"It's better than it was," I gritted. "But there's still some work here for Beldon." I cradled my injured arm in its make-shift sling. God, but that had hurt. It had been almost fine until I'd tried to unbend it.

Elizabeth took up her lantern to see better. "What has *happened* to you?"

"Didn't Lieutenant Nash send anyone over to give you the news?"

"He did not. What news?"

"I caught him. I caught Roddy Finch."

In the looks exchanged I marked an astonishing degree of family resemblance between them.

"That's how I was hurt," I added, which did not really explain anything.

This, of course, inspired many, many more questions about my most recent activities. Our slow walk back to the house fully occupied me with the effort to provide answers. It helped to keep my mind off the pain.

"They'll hang him, you know," Father said thoughtfully when I'd finished.

"Yes. I'm sure they will."

After that he said nothing more on the subject.

✦ ✦ ✦

WHILE FATHER AND I WAITED near the stables, Elizabeth went ahead with the lantern to make sure our path to the main house was clear. After that, her task was to send away any servants out of the hall leading from the side door to the library. The other members of the household, Beldon, his sister and Mother, in an outward show of mourning, had forsworn social activities for the time being and could be counted upon to be in their rooms at this early hour of the evening.

Beldon, I learned, had been especially hard-struck over what had happened to me. I'd asked after him and was told he was as well as could be expected. His grief was deep and genuine, and he'd more than once blamed himself for my death, though no one seriously reckoned things in that fashion. Apparently he thought he might have taken more care, somehow prevented it or, had he been a better physician, saved my life. That alone told me how far the extremes of idle thinking his sorrow had carried him. Certainly it was a match to the desolation I'd known last night, and I felt an unaccustomed twinge of sympathy and pity for him.

"He has a great affection for you, you know," Father told me as we waited.

I nodded. "Yes, I'm aware of it, and I'm sorry for him that he does since I cannot return it as he would wish."

"He understands that, I'm sure."

"He's quite a decent fellow, isn't he?"

"He is. It was very bad for him being a doctor and yet unable to help you."

"He did what he could," I said. "I remember that much. It was an awful thing—"

Father went very still. "Did it ... was it ...?"

I instantly guessed what he was getting at and constructed a hasty lie, the only one I'd ever told him, but one he desperately needed to hear. "I felt no pain, sir. It was very strange, that. Very quick. Be at ease in your heart, I did not suffer."

He searched my face.

"Truly, Father. I think it might have been because of Nora's ... gift to me. It seemed no more than a dream while it happened, and then I simply fell asleep."

He at last relaxed. "Thank God."

"What about poor Beldon?" I coaxed, hoping to shift his mind down a different path.

He shook himself. "Perhaps Elizabeth can tell you more. My memory fails me. It was the worst day of my life, and I never want to see its like again. I fear even now that I have succumbed to distraction and this may also be a dream."

"Elizabeth said something like that last night, but I *am* still here."

With that he lay his arm over my shoulders, pulling me close again and kissing the top of my bowed head. "I know not what is to come or how we shall deal with it, but with you here, and with God's grace, we shall weather it. God has been merciful to all of us. Your return is a miracle, it must be."

I felt myself to be the one person least able to offer an opinion on the subject. Once again I thought of Lazarus. Had he suffered this sort of confusion of heart? I was not inclined to think so. Doubtless his faith was greater than mine; besides, there had been people around, including the Lord Himself, to explain exactly what had happened to him. His resurrection *had* been a miracle—mine, I wasn't so sure about, but all the same, it was good to have Father's strong arm to steady me.

Elizabeth's figure appeared in the side door and motioned for us to hurry inside.

The hall was dark—to them. It was merely dim for me. We rushed to the library and Elizabeth swept the door shut behind us. Father guided me to the settee near the dormant fireplace and made me lie upon it.

"Some brandy?" he offered.

I found myself stammering. "No... that is... I mean... I can't."

He swiftly and correctly interpreted the reason behind my distress and shrugged it off. Elizabeth had apparently told him everything. "Light some more candles," he told her. "I'm going to fetch Beldon." Before leaving, he paused by the cabinet that held the house spirits, drawing forth a bottle of brandy. He poured a good quantity into a glass and placed it ready on a table.

"The doctor will need it," Elizabeth explained when he'd gone.

I laughed a little, but with small humor. By God, he certainly would. I felt the need as well, but the scent of it turned my stomach, overriding the desire in my mind. "When did Beldon finally come home?" I asked, to divert myself from the stink.

"Late this afternoon. He was in a dreadful state. He'd been out since the... services... looking for the..."

"The rebels?" I said, hoping that would help. It was an alternative to calling them murderers.

Her mouth twitched with self-mockery. "For the rebels, then. He'd been with a group of soldiers led by Nash's sergeant for most of the time. They went right into Suffolk County, turning out every farm and hayloft along the way. They never found anyone, of course."

"That's hardly surprising. Those uniforms make people very nervous. I should think all rebels, connected to the business or not, ran the moment they clapped eyes on 'em."

"So they did. Beldon came to realize it and decided to strike out on his own."

I was dumbfounded. "But that's appallingly dangerous."

"He seemed not to care. It didn't do him much good, though, and in the end he came to no harm. When he gave up and dragged home at last, he was all done in. He slept the day through. Jericho took a tray up to him earlier, but Beldon sent him away."

"Have you talked to Jericho about me?"

"No. There's been no time yet. I was busy enough talking to Father."

"After I sort things out with Beldon, I must see him next."

"It'll be all right, Jonathan." She'd clearly heard the apprehension creeping back into my voice.

I managed a smile for her. "How were you received when you arrived at Mrs. Montagu's?"

Her back stiffened. "I understood why you had to go off, but I'm not sure I'm ready to forgive you for leaving me adrift like that."

I started to protest or apologize, whichever was required most, but she waved it away.

"Never mind, little brother. You did what you thought right, and that's sufficient reason. I'm still allowed to be exasperated with you, though." She went 'round lighting candles, filling the room with their soft golden light. Though the curtains were drawn, cutting off any outside illumination I might have taken advantage of, this was a token return to normal sight for me and I relished it. No wonder Nora had been so fond of candles.

"How did it go for you?" I ventured again.

"It was not easy. Father was frightfully annoyed and the soldiers with me alarmed him. Under those circumstances I couldn't just blurt out my news. Thank God for Mrs. Montagu. She determined that only something truly important would have drawn me forth at that hour and tucked me under one wing and took me off while Father tried to talk with the soldiers. They didn't make much headway as I think his German isn't much better than yours. By the time he'd finished, I had some tea and biscuits in me, which were a great help. She's such a sensible woman. I could see she was enormously curious, but she most bravely refrained from yielding to it. Heavens, but she doesn't know about you either."

"That will come, in time. What did you say about me to Father?"

She snorted. "I really couldn't say anything. Not about you. I just wasn't ready for it. I was still trying to take it all in myself."

"Elizabeth, I'm sorry. I should not have asked that of you."

Another wave. "It would have been the same whether you'd been there or not. Well, perhaps it might have been noisier. In the end I told him that I couldn't stand to stay in our house alone and decided to walk over to be with them. He was very angry for a time."

Considering the reputation of the Hessians and their commanders with unprotected womenfolk I could see why.

"But then he asked me why I'd really come."

Father wouldn't have taken her story as given. He knew she was too intelligent to leave the house unescorted unless she had a powerful reason to do so.

"I asked Mrs. Montagu to give us some time alone and did my best." Finished with the candles, she took the chair next to the desk. "He tried not to show it, but I'm sure he thought I'd gone quite mad."

"No, I was the mad one to leave you to do that by yourself."

"Mad and selfish and inconsiderate and thoughtless," she added agreeably. "Shall I go on?"

I nodded. "Yes, I deserve it."

"Indeed you do. Perhaps someday I shall laugh about this. I'm much too tired to see that far ahead. It's all done, though. What really helped was when we got home and I took him up to your room to show him the clothes you'd left there. That was a shock, but I could see he was beginning to allow himself to believe me. It was then that he had us sit down and bade me tell him everything all over again."

"How did he take it?"

"He was very quiet. Told me to get some sleep, then he went out. He rode over to the churchyard."

"Dear God, he didn't."

"He most assuredly did. He looked so strange when he came back."

"What? Don't tell me he went to dig up the grave."

That idea horrified her as much as it did me. "No, he did not."

"Then what did he want there?"

"More proof."

"Proof? But what could be there that—"

"Your shroud."

That took the wind out of me.

"He found it all tangled up where you'd left it."

I dropped my head and groaned.

"So you should, little brother. You've been a blister and a boil for doing this to him, you should have stayed with me and not put him through it."

She was right, right, right. "I'm sorry."

"On the other hand…"

I looked up. "What?"

"He did understand why you had to go off last night. But please God, don't you *ever* put him through this kind of situation again."

To be honest, I didn't see how I possibly could, considering the uniqueness of the circumstances, but I made no sport of her feelings and gave her my solemn word to behave myself in the future.

"After showing me that thing he wanted to go straight out to the old barn, but Mother was being difficult about something and Beldon wasn't here to give her any laudanum so he had to stay with her."

Poor Father.

"But the moment he was free he got me and we left. I wasn't sure what to expect when we walked in. You'd told me what Nora had been like, but you were so *still*. It was hard not to think that…"

"That I was dead after all?"

"Yes, exactly. I feared that some cruel mind was at play to give you back to us for a few hours only to take you away again. It was a very bad time for us, standing there, waiting and watching you. Father said that you had no heartbeat, that you were not breathing."

"How did you stand it, then?"

"He noticed that you were warm. He picked up your hand and held it, then made me take it to be sure. After that, the waiting was a little easier, but I don't think he fully believed until you stirred and opened your eyes."

"And your belief, sister?"

"Tested," she said archly. "I'm like you, still trying to make sense of it, to take it all in. I hope I shall get over it soon as I am damned tired of feeling this way."

We looked somberly at one another, then the dark mood suddenly evaporated. She was the one to break first and I followed, the two of us suddenly seized by a fit of humor. Our laughter was by necessity firmly restrained by smothering hands. Necessary, for had we really let ourselves go, we'd have raised the whole house. It passed quickly, though. Elizabeth was half-dropping from exhaustion and the movement aggravated the pain in my arm.

She leaned back in her chair, drowsing, and I wondered what was taking Father so long. Perhaps he was trying to somehow prepare Beldon. Perhaps Beldon had taken a dose of his own laudanum. I hoped not. If drink had interfered with Nora's influence over Warburton, one could logically conclude that a drug might have the same effect. If I could not use my own power of influence to ease Beldon over those first few moments of alarm, things might become very much more difficult, indeed.

Elizabeth's eyes were shut, though I could hear by her breathing that she was not quite asleep. I was perversely alert and listening to the normal sounds of the household. They were distant but strangely clear: the clatter of a pot in the far-off kitchen, the footfall of a passing servant. I found a secret delight in being able to identify each noise, picking it out or discarding it as I chose. I'd adapted rather quickly to this heightened ability; part of me enjoyed it, part shrank away out of a fear for the uncanny.

Then I heard the murmur of Father's voice and the unmistakable sound of them descending the stairs together. Beldon was silent as Father invited him to go on to the library.

"Elizabeth."

She jerked fully awake.

"They're coming. Stand ready with the brandy." She rose and moved to the table.

"You know what I'll have to do?"

"Yes. What you did to calm Lieutenant Nash." Her tone indicated she still disapproved. "I told Father about it."

Good, for then he mightn't be too surprised by what was to come. I nodded my gratitude and we waited. The back of the settee was toward the door. Beldon would not see me right away, which was just as well. I wasn't sure what to expect of him and found myself feeling the same dread and disquiet I'd come to associate with this experience. The reward was great, but the actual passage to that reward arduous.

Father played the servant and held the door for Beldon, firmly closing it as soon as they were inside.

"Your patient's over there, Doctor. Just talk to him and all will be explained," he was saying.

Beldon put down his case of medicines and came around. He

breathed out a quiet greeting to Elizabeth, then turned to confront his patient. His mouth open, he halted in mid-turn to stare, blink and shake his head once, then stare again.

"I don't... Oh, my God. Oh, my..."

"Beldon," I began, "there's nothing to be afraid of; please listen to me."

But Beldon was incapable of hearing anything. His already protuberant eyes bulged out that much more and his skin went so pasty as to make a ghastly match in color to his ever-present wig. Lamenting within that I should be the cause of this, I reached out to him with my good hand, offering words of comfort, while trying to fix upon his mind.

A vain effort. Overcome with the shock, Beldon turned drama into farce by pitching flat onto his face in a dead faint.

Elizabeth said "Oh," Father vented a ripe curse, and as one they dived for the boneless form heaped on the floor. Father turned him over and saw to it that there were no obvious injuries from the fall. Elizabeth gave Father a look of moderate disappointment and straightened Beldon's limbs.

Father was rather sheepish. "I suppose I might have found some better way to ready him for this, but for the life of me I couldn't think of one."

Elizabeth found a cushion and put it under Beldon's head. When he began to show signs of reviving, the brandy was brought into play.

"Not too much," I cautioned. I lurched from the settee and knelt next to him. It seemed important that I be the first one he saw upon awakening.

"Yes," said Father, missing my real motive, which was to keep the man sober. "Don't want to choke the fellow."

Beldon's eyes fluttered. He was calm now, disoriented by his swoon. This was a great help to me, though. I took whole and heartless advantage of his confusion and fixed my gaze and mind full upon him. Taken so unawares, Beldon had no further chance to give in to his fear. His expression went slack and dull. The results—if disturbing to Elizabeth and a wonderment to Father—were gratifying to me. But the moment was brief, for yet again I was about to take on the task of giving lengthy and complicated explanations for my return from the grave.

And in the pause between taking away Beldon's conscious will and the drawing of my next breath, I realized I simply could *not* do it again.

In that instant I knew that if I imparted the least portion of the truth to him and the others who followed there would be absolutely no going back to even an illusion of the life I'd known before. The changes within me were staggering enough; I needed some kind of constancy for the sake of my mind's balance.

And the solution came hard on the heels of this realization: so neat and simple that I could condemn myself for a fool for not having considered it before. I looked up. "Father ... I should like to try something different. ..."

They heard me out. Elizabeth opined that my idea was ridiculous, but admitted she had nothing better to offer. Father shrugged, granting his permission, perhaps for the same reason.

They had the truth, for it mattered much to me that they know it. Nash had the lie, for he did not matter at all. As for the others in between ...

I went to work.

✦ ✦ ✦

BELDON'S EYES CLEARED and his brow wrinkled in honest puzzlement. "Dear me, whatever has happened?"

"We're not sure, Doctor," I said. "You complained of dizziness and the next thing we knew, you went over like a felled tree. Are you all right? Nothing hurt?"

He took confused stock of himself and pronounced that he seemed to be fit. "I remember nothing of this. I was in my room last ... I'd had the most awful dream about you, Mr. Barrett."

"What sort of dream?" I asked innocently.

"It was the most ..." He shook his head. "Oh, never mind. I should not care to speak of it, lest it come true."

I did not press him for more details, since I knew them already. If it worked with Beldon—and it had—it would work with everyone else. One by one I'd speak to them all and convince them that my death and burial had been nothing more than an unpleasant dream. Or nightmare. Either choice, they would be loath to mention it, even if I hadn't given instructions not to. With some unavoidable changes of routine for me, it looked like I might resume the semblance of normal living again. Elizabeth gave me a grudging nod to acknowledge this evidence of my success and asked Beldon if he might not be more comfortable on the settee. He thought he would and she and Father helped him to move.

"I'm terribly sorry for this imposition, please excuse my weakness," he told them. "I'm not normally given to fits of any kind."

"Of course you aren't," said Father, going along with the ruse as if he'd been born an actor. "But it has been exceedingly hot today. The sun's probably caught up with you."

Beldon offered no objection to that conclusion and accepted what remained of the brandy. He made short work of it and then took note of the rest of us, myself in particular.

"Why, Mr. Barrett, something *has* happened to you!"

I sighed and eased into the chair by the desk. "Yes, sir. Father brought you down to have a look at this. When you have sufficiently recovered, I should be most grateful if you would…"

"Great heavens, of course. I shall need my—oh, thank you, Miss Barrett." He accepted his case from Elizabeth and took charge of the situation. Except for my injury, as far as he was concerned absolutely nothing untoward had happened in this house over the last few days. I felt a great surge of joy wash over me. To be looked upon as myself again and not as some ghostly horror come back to trouble the living, to simply be me, as if the terrible event had never been… more and more my burden was becoming lighter. Over Beldon's shoulder, Father caught my eye and smiled, his expression of pleased relief like a mirror of my own feelings.

I was obliged to remove my coat, an exercise which I found most painful. Elizabeth offered to cut open a seam to facilitate things, but we managed to avoid that action. Beldon rolled up my shirtsleeve and clucked over the damage.

"How did this happen?"

"I already told you, Doctor. Don't you—oh, forgive me. It was just before your… ah… fall and you… must have forgotten. I was helping Nash and got into a fight with one of those damned rebels. The fellow tried to crack my skull with his rifle barrel and I found it necessary to thwart the attack with my arm."

"Definitely broken just here below the elbow," he stated. "It must have been a fearsome blow."

"It was," I wheezed. He was being very gentle, but to no avail. "Both of them."

"Yes, it would take more than one to account for this sort of damage. And you received them last night?"

I confirmed that fact with a short grunt.

"But why did you not call for me sooner?" He was accusatory.

"There were delays that could not be avoided," I answered through clenched teeth in a tone that did not invite further comment.

He made none, distracted as he was by his examination. "*Very* odd."

"What is?" asked Father, leaning forward.

"The evidence I see is that this injury's several weeks old."

The blood had done that, I knew. Just as a man's body tells him to take in liquid to ease the pain of thirst, mine had compelled me to take in additional blood to quicken the process of mending itself. Father's face was eaten up with curiosity, but I quietly signaled to him that he should remain silent for the moment.

"The healing is remarkably progressed," Beldon marveled.

"Doesn't feel like it," I muttered.

"That's because the bone was not properly set. See, there's no swelling or bruising, but you can feel here—"

"Softly, Doctor, softly," I cautioned.

"I do beg your pardon, but if you run your finger along here you can feel under the skin where the bone has joined crookedly at the break. Combined with all the other fracturing, well, that explains why you're in such discomfort."

"'Discomfort' is hardly the word that comes to mind," I snarled. "What can you do about it?"

"It will have to be rebroken, of course, then correctly set," he said matter-of-factly.

After all I'd been through, one would think that I could face anything, but the idea of breaking my arm once more in the endeavor to fix it again turned my guts to water. In the heat of battle an injury was one thing, but in the cool reason of the consulting room it's quite another.

"Might I have a little time and think this over?" I asked in a none-too-steady voice.

"Certainly, but I'd advise not delaying for very long or the healing will have gone too far, making the process of breaking more difficult to accomplish."

"It's all right, Jonathan," put in Elizabeth in response to the groan I could not suppress. "Perhaps it can be done during the day while you're unaware of things."

My qualms against this upcoming treatment swiftly vanished. "Heavens, sister, but that's a brilliant idea."

Beldon looked questioningly at her. She and I both suddenly realized her *faux pas*. She generously gestured for me to step in and clarify.

"I am an uncommonly sound sleeper, Doctor," I blandly explained. "I seriously doubt that anything, even having my arm broken again, could rouse me once I set head to pillow."

254 · RED DEATH

He made a noncommittal sound and looked highly dubious. Ah, well, if I had to influence him again, then it would just have to be done. Thinking it through, I could see its looming necessity, otherwise Beldon could not help but become alarmed while treating me during my daytime oblivion.

"In the meanwhile, is there some way in which you can make it more comfortable?"

The soldier's rough-and-ready field dressing was soon replaced by a proper splint and bandage. Beldon's work was practiced and thorough and Elizabeth helped by fashioning a better sling under his directions. I thanked them both and politely refused his offer of a solution of laudanum for the pain. Had I the remotest chance of keeping the stuff down, though, I would have taken it without hesitation.

Beldon announced that he was in need of some solid refreshment and begged leave to be excused so he could see to the inner man. We graciously gave it along with our united thanks for his help and he left.

Father heaved a great sigh and dropped upon the settee in his turn. "That I have lived to see such wonders. You did it, laddie."

"The wonder is that I got through it, sir," I puffed.

"It's enough to persuade one into believing in the power of witchcraft," Elizabeth put in.

"Oh, now, that's hardly fair. You know I only did it because I felt I had to."

"Yes, but that doesn't make it any easier to watch." She hunched her shoulders as though to fight off a shiver. "And you're planning to give that same story about everything having been a bad dream to all the others?"

"It would seem to be the best compromise for my situation.

"Even your mother?" Father asked, leveling his gaze hard upon me.

I could not endure that look for long and let my own gaze drop. "I should like permission to do so, sir, as I seriously question whether she would be comfortable with the truth."

He snorted. "By God, laddie, I can respect that answer."

"You mean I—"

He held up one finger and echoed my earlier caution to Beldon. "Softly, now. We're all aware of what your mother is like; the danger I see is that you might use this—whatever it is—in such a way as to ... well, sweeten her temper."

Genuine surprise flooded me. "Oh, sir, but it never occurred to me—"

"I'm very glad to hear it."

My face was burning. "Father, surely you don't think that I would do such an unworthy thing?"

"No. My purpose was to merely point out the temptations that lie ahead for you. This strange enforcing of your will and thoughts upon others can be a gift or a curse depending on how it's employed. I strongly suggest that in the future you rely upon it as little as possible."

I said nothing for some time, for his words gave me much to think about. I honestly hadn't considered this side of things. For all the use Nora made of it, she'd only done the bare minimum to ensure her own security. When it came to our relationship, she'd discarded it altogether, risking all in the hope that my love for her would overcome my fears. Sadly, though, at the end, she'd tried to make me forget that love.

Perhaps she'd thought it was for my own good.

My eyes stung at the thought. To do something for another's own good must surely be the greatest of all betrayals. It was Mother's favorite tenet, and the one I hated the most, and yet I could not bring myself to hate Nora. In my heart, I felt she'd been sincere and done it out of love for me rather than as a convenience or assertion of power for herself.

"Jonathan?"

I gave a start. "Yes, Father, of course you're right. To do otherwise would be most ungentlemanly and dishonorable."

"Good lad."

"But for what I'm to do tonight...?"

"It is necessary. By this means, yes, make them all think it was but a dream. Beldon took hold of the idea fast enough."

"What about others like Mrs. Montagu and Mr. Rapelji?" asked Elizabeth.

"The same," he said heavily.

She turned on me. "Will you be able to convince the whole Island?"

"Elizabeth, think how hard it was for us both when you first saw me. Now multiply it by every person who knows what's happened. Would you put me through that with them all? Can you trust them to react as well as you have? I can't. I want to come home, and this is the only way I can do it and not be marked out as some sort of grotesque thing fit only to be stared at or avoided. It spares them and it spares me."

She paced up the room and back while a number of ideas and emotions played over her face and made her stride uneven. "Yes," she murmured. "It's just that there are so many. I don't see how you can do it."

"I'll manage somehow," I said. "I must."

"Jericho, too?"

"Ah, well, perhaps not Jericho. It's impossible for a man to hide anything from his valet and in his case it would be pointless to try. I shall give him the truth, but there it must stop or the whole island will be privy to my personal concerns."

"Quite right," Father said. "Are you up to starting now? If you wait much longer they'll all be asleep."

✦ ✦ ✦

As with many projects, the beginning was the most difficult part of the procedure, though there were some rough spots. Elizabeth, with her talent for organization, soon saw that speaking to each servant one after another would take us half the night. Eventually we worked out a faster way to deal with the problem. As each came into the room, I would influence them into a quiet state and ask them to wait. Once together, I could give up to half a dozen of them at a time the same story rather than tell the same story half a dozen times. From Mrs. Nooth to the humblest stable lad, I spoke to the lot of them, and released each back to their duties as they had come with lighter hearts and no worse for wear.

Mother and Mrs. Hardinbrook were the last ones I saw. Perhaps they should have been the most harrowing, but my poor brain was throbbing miserably by then from all my efforts; I was beyond further emotional upsets or excitements. Mother had fortunately slept off the effects of her latest dose of laudanum, making my expenditure of effort on her a success. I confess, though, that in watching her face going blank, I did experience an undeniable thrill. I was very glad to have had Father's advice already in mind, else the temptation to abuse this gift might certainly have proved to be too attractive in my future dealings with her.

Mrs. Hardinbrook was somewhat of a problem, in that she'd indulged herself in the matter of drink not so very long ago. She'd taken just enough to cause me worry, but not so much that I was unable to make an impression upon her. She was quiet when Elizabeth led her away, but I confided my doubts to Father.

"'Tis to be relied upon that she won't be leaving us anytime soon," he said. "I expect that after she's fully sobered you may try again with more certainty on the outcome. How are you feeling?"

"Tired. Much more of this and my head shall split from the work."

But there was only one more left to see and that was Jericho. As with the others, I had to put him in a state where he could readily listen, but unlike the others, I gave him the truth. Still, before releasing him, I instructed—rather than requested—that he believe my story and accept it and myself without fear.

For this liberty upon his will, my only excuse was that I was too weary to do otherwise. Whether the soreness of my head was due to the excessive mental labor or the constant strain of imposing a raw falsehood upon so many didn't matter. What did was my reluctance to face another hour as harrowing as that first one I'd spent with Elizabeth upon my return. No more shocks like that for myself or anyone else, I resolved, and if Elizabeth or Father thought I was being selfish in my decision, neither made mention of it.

Coming back to himself, Jericho welcomed me with the same warmth and joy as if I'd only been away on a lengthy journey and nothing more. This return to normal was what I wanted, what I needed most. I accepted his welcome and submitted meekly to his disapproval at the state of my clothes. He begged permission to see to their improvement. Father and Elizabeth both made haste to agree that I very much needed some restoration and with their good nights floating behind us Jericho all but dragged me up to my room.

"But everything's been moved, Mr. Jonathan," he noted unhappily when he opened the wardrobe.

My shirts and coats and all other manner of clothing had been restored, perhaps not in the right order, but they were more or less back in place again. I came over to touch them and be reassured. With the return of my things it was as if my own person was made more substantial by their presence.

"Thank God. Elizabeth must have retrieved everything for me, bless her."

"Retrieved...?"

"You know."

"Oh," he said, drawing it out with sober understanding. He instantly ceased to be outraged that someone had intruded upon his territory and plunged into straightening some of the more radically misplaced items to their proper areas.

"Is my journal in there?" I asked.

"I do not see it, sir."

"Damn. I wonder who's got it?"

"I shall endeavor to locate it for you as soon as may be."

"Thank you, though I can't write much in it with my arm all trussed up.

"It pains you?"

"A great deal, but I've been through worse."

He chose not to comment on that truth and concentrated on getting me in the same kind of order that he imposed upon the contents of the wardrobe. It was only when he was scraping away at my stubbled chin that he finally gave in to a reaction to the impossibility of my presence. He caught his breath and turned away suddenly.

"What is it? Jericho?"

His self-possession deserted him for a few moments and it was a struggle for him to wrest it back. The expression on his face kept shifting alarmingly back and forth between calmness and distress.

"I'm sorry. It's just that the last time I shaved you was after they brought you ... it was ...."

My poor friend. "I know. It's all right. This is going to be strange for all of us for a time until we're used to things."

He nodded once or twice, rather forcefully. "I expect so, sir."

"But there's nothing to be afraid of; I'm still myself."

His nod was less abrupt, and I looked elsewhere while he swiped impatiently at his eyes. When his hand was steady once more, he resumed and completed the job of shaving me.

As it was much too late and too much work to prepare a bath, we made do with a wet towel to refresh my grubby skin. A change of linen completed my toilet. Relaxing back on the bed with my dressing gown half on (out of deference to my arm), I felt more like my old self and better able to consider some of the grim practicalities of my changed condition.

"Something will have to be done about that window," I said. "I suggest that you close and lock the shutters and then find something to stop up the chinks."

"It will be like a sickroom, sir, with no air or light."

"In truth, that's the whole point. I don't seem to need air, and I've found the latter to be highly inimical to my continued well-being. Please trust me on this, Jericho. I don't want a single ray of light coming in here tomorrow. And it will probably be best that my door remain locked. I shouldn't care for one of the maids to walk in while I'm ... resting."

"Will it always be so for you?"

"I don't know. Perhaps later I can ask Dr. Beldon to suggest a way to help me improve the situation, but this is how it must be for now."

"And you say you are completely unconscious while the sun is up?"

"Yes, unfortunately. I can already see that it's going to be a deuced nuisance."

"More than a nuisance, sir."

"What do you mean?"

"Have you considered what could happen to you should the house— God forbid—catch fire?"

The horror of his idea went all over me in an instant, and I sat with my mouth hanging wide as imagination supplied such details as would have better been left unimagined. Out of necessity, we were all very careful in regard to fire and candles, but accidents happened, and if one occurred during the day while I lay helpless....

"By God, I'll have to go back to that damned barn to get any rest!"

"I think you should remain here, Mr. Jonathan, where you can be watched and otherwise protected. It really is much more secure."

"But not as fireproof. I suppose I could sleep in the root cellar, though that might vex Mrs. Nooth and alarm the rest of the kitchen."

"Actually, I was going to recommend some additional changes be made to the buttery," he said.

"The buttery?"

"There was some discussion before your...accident about enlarging it to accommodate hidden stores against the commissary men. It won't be too much extra work to make it larger than planned and fit it with such comforts as you might require."

"And live like a rabbit in a hole in the ground?"

"Rabbits have no fear of being burned alive while in their holes," he pointed out.

I laughed once and shook my head. "Yes, I suppose so. I'll talk to Elizabeth about it. Think she's still up?"

"Miss Elizabeth retired some time ago. Mr. Barrett as well."

Yes. They'd both been worn out, and it was well past their normal bedtime, but I still felt a stab of loneliness for all that. It was as I'd anticipated and I would just have to get used to spending the greater bulk of the night hours on my own. Oh, but there were many, many worse things in the world, though I felt to have been through a goodly number of them already.

"Very well. Hand me that volume of Gibbon from the shelf, would you?"

Jericho selected the correct book and placed a candle on my bedside table. With the shutters closed, I found I needed it. I cannot say that the conflicts of the late Roman empire held my whole attention while he worked to seal up the room from the sun's intrusion, but it helped. When Jericho had finished and I bade him to go off for some well-earned sleep, my study was even less successful. In the end, I left off with Gibbon in mid-word to search out and open my Bible.

I was seized with an uncommonly strong urge to read the eleventh chapter of John again.

CHAPTER
FIFTEEN

EYES WIDE, I FRANTICALLY CLAWED up from my internal prison, drew in a shuddering breath, and rolled out of bed to slam against the floor. The impact jarred my maimed arm, sending me instantly awake and aware of its every insulted nerve.

"Mr. Jonathan?" Jericho's voice, alarmed.

I shook my head and would have waved him away if I hadn't been busy biting back the pain. He must have read something of it in my posture, and held off, only stepping forward when I was ready. It took some minutes before I extended my good arm and allowed him to help me to my feet.

"More bad dreams?" he asked.

Nodding, I sought out the chair by my study table. I had no wish to return to that bed. Good elbow on the table and forehead resting against the heel of my hand, I breathed deeply of the stale air of my room and tried to collect myself. Jericho pulled down the quilts he'd draped over the window and opened the shutters. It was just past sunset, but my room faced east, so the remaining sky-glow flooding in was bearable to my sensitive eyes.

"Will you speak to Dr. Beldon?" he asked. His tone was not quite reproachful yet leaning in that direction. He'd made the suggestion yesterday evening and I'd summarily dismissed it.

Time to give in. "Yes, I'll see him, though God knows what good he'll be able to do me for this."

"Perhaps he can determine whether it is, at root, a physical or a spiritual problem."

Or both, I thought unhappily. In the three days since my return, I had gotten no rest to speak of while the sun was up. Cleaned and groomed and tucked away in the comfort of my own bed, my family life resumed with hardly a ripple, one would think that my troubles were abated, but not so. The utter oblivion that I'd known before, that had caused the day to flash by without notice, was gone. Now I was aware of every excruciating second of the slow-passing time.

When the light came and my body froze inert where it lay, so came the dreams, sinuous things that wound through my mind like poisonous snakes. Striking at my most tender thoughts and feelings, I was helpless to escape from them by waking and yet could not fully sleep. All the memories of my life were drawn forth to play before me or worse—directly involve me. If pleasant, an experience was twisted to something ugly and grotesque, if not, then I lived and relived the horror without mercy. After three days of it I'd lost count of the times Tony Warburton had tried to kill me—sometimes succeeding—or the times I'd found myself back in that damned coffin screaming away my sanity.

After the first day of this private hell, I'd asked Jericho to stay and watch for signs of inner disturbances and to wake me should he see them. He saw nothing more than my still and unresponsive outer shell. The next day his instructions were to try waking me at intervals, in hopes that that might help. Though I was aware of his presence and his efforts, it was ultimately useless. The dreams, worthy of the darkest fantasies of the maddest opium eater, continued unabated.

More weary now than when I'd retired that morning, I had to force myself to dress. Jericho managed to get me properly turned out except my coat. For that, I could only slip on the left sleeve and drape the rest over my right shoulder. Previous attempts to straighten my arm had proved to be too agonizing to complete and the constant inconvenience was such that I would have to see Beldon, anyway. Loath as I was to have him rebreak it to put things right, it was rapidly coming to that point.

Leaving Jericho to continue his duties, I walked downstairs to the drawing room. Elizabeth was practicing something new on her spinet and having trouble with a particular phrase, but the sounds were a fresh delight to my ear. She paused when I walked in, smiled, then went on.

Mother, Mrs. Hardinbrook, Beldon and—I was surprised to see—Father were playing at cards. He usually had no patience for them, preferring his books, so I could guess that Mother had nagged him into joining their game. They also looked up and nodded at me.

Everything was so unutterably, wonderfully normal. I wanted to embrace them all for just being there. Until faced with its loss, I'd never truly valued all that I'd had.

"So you're finally up," said Mother.

"Yes, madam." Even she could not dampen my goodwill.

"You've missed the entire day, you know. How can you help your father with his work if you play the sluggard?"

If she had a talent for anything it was for asking impossible questions. It was also interesting to me that though possessed of an active contempt for Father's law practice she found it useful enough now to point out my apparent laziness.

I bowed toward Father. "My apologies, sir."

He restrained a smile. "Never mind. Just get that arm well, then I'll find work for you."

"You're too soft on the boy, Samuel," she sniffed.

"Perhaps, but he's the only one we have," he smoothly returned.

Beldon and his sister maintained a diplomatic silence during this exchange. Elizabeth paused again in her play to glance at me. My mouth twitched and I jerked my chin down once to let her know that everything was all right. It was becoming easier to find amusement, rather than resentment, in Mother's shortcomings. The three of us had passed through the fire and with that shared encounter, we'd discovered that the irritations Mother had to offer were very minor, indeed.

I drifted over to the spinet to watch Elizabeth. "How you can read that is beyond me," I said, indicating her music.

"It's just like learning another language for you. One day it suddenly all makes sense."

"But to translate it with your eyes to your hands and thus to the ear…"

"Jonathan!" Mother's voice cut between us like an axe blade. Elizabeth missed her notes and ceased play altogether. Mother glared at us with disturbing malevolence, recalling that awful night more than three years past and her obscene accusation. "Have you nothing better to do with yourself than disrupt your sister's practice?"

Her lips quivering, Elizabeth was about to say something we might all regret. I quickly stepped in first. "Quite right, madam. I am being most inconsiderate. Please excuse me."

She made no reply, but some of the tension in her body eased back just a little. This was the only sign that I'd received her pardon. Her gaze flicked to her cards. "Find something to do, then. Your wandering about the place is most aggravating."

"Yes, madam. I only came down to ask when Dr. Beldon might have a free moment."

"Then you should have said so in the first place. The doctor is, as you can see, occupied."

Beldon raised his head. "Your arm?" he asked.

"Partly. But as you are busy, it can wait. I'll be in the library when you're free."

Beldon read enough from my manner to know that this medical call was not urgent, so he had no need to risk Mother's ire by immediately responding. He returned his attention to his hand, and I left the room.

My feet took me to the hall, past the library, and out the side door, leaving the flagged path to wander in the yard. It was better out here, the air more free, the scents it carried of earth and grass and flowers more pure. I wanted to roll in it like a mongrel dog, free and easy. I settled for sitting beneath a tree and stretching out my legs. Here was peace and a kind of rest. I was so very, very tired. In days past, I napped here in the summer heat. No more. While the sun was down, sleep obstinately eluded me, even when I tried to find it.

But I closed my eyes in another hopeful attempt. My other senses leaped in to take up the slack. I heard the rustle of every leaf and night creature, the sweet tones of the spinet, felt the cool ground and each tuft of grass under me, smelled the hundred messages on the wind, tasted the first dry swallow of thirst.

That would be tended to later, though, while everyone slept.

Upon my return to the hearth, Mrs. Nooth's first instinct had been to provide food for me and thus she required further influencing on the subject. Now she and all the rest of the household simply ignored the fact that I did not eat with the family anymore, indeed, that I seemed not to eat, period. No one questioned it, no one remarked upon it. It was quite the best for all concerned.

As for the stable lads, I had them well-schooled to completely ignore me should I be seen in the stalls at any hour of the night. As the young master of the house it was certainly within my duties to check on the horses at a time of my choosing. So far, all was well. If any of the lads glimpsed my true purpose for being there, none seemed to consider it worth mentioning.

Elizabeth's playing ceased again, and I saw movement against the curtains of the drawing room. The card game must ended. I heaved up and stalked back to the house, feeling considerably better for the respite outside. As much as I desired and cherished the company of my family, getting away from them now and then was also necessary.

Beldon was in the library, and I apologized for not being here as promised. He bowed slightly to dismiss the issue, and I inquired if he would like some sherry, which he declined.

"I am still astonished at how quickly it healed after the injury," he remarked, nodding at my arm. "How is it for you?"

"The same. I still cannot straighten it."

"I feared as much. I saw something similar once, a man with his elbow shattered by a rifle ball. It healed, but remained frozen at a right angle. Unless you want to risk the same permanence of condition, I fear we shall soon have to—"

"Yes, I know that, but I wanted to consult you about something else."

"Indeed?"

We seated ourselves and I explained my problem to him.

"You're getting no rest at all?" he asked.

"None. I seem to fall into a kind of waking doze, a halfway state, and can neither rouse from it or sink into true sleep. During this, I'm subject to endless dreaming, so even if my body rests, my mind does not, and that's what leaves me so fatigued all the time."

"And yet but a few days ago you assured me that you were a very sound sleeper."

"So I was—a few days ago."

"Has there been any change in your usual habits?"

More than I can begin to number, I thought.

"Any change in your room, bedding or night clothes?"

"No, nothing like that."

"Does the pain from your arm keep you awake?"

"It only hurts when I try to move it and I take care not to do so."

"I can prescribe something to make you sleep," he said reluctantly.

Laudanum, or some other preparation, no doubt. I shook my head. "If else is available, I should prefer some other treatment, Doctor."

He sat back and crossed his arms, studying me from top to toe. "There are always many reasons why a man cannot sleep. Has anything been troubling you lately? Any problem, no matter how minor, can prick at the mind like a thorn just at the moment when one most wants to forget it."

"Perhaps it's this business with Roddy Finch," I offered lightly, after a moment's consideration. "There's been some protest, but there's no doubt they'll soon be hanging him."

"And you were the one who turned him in. Yes, a burden like that can't be easy for a young mind like yours to bear. It's well out of your hands, though. Like it or not, justice will be served," he said grimly.

Justice or the law? I well knew there was often a wide difference between the two.

"The best thing for you is to try and forget about it."

My belly gave a sharp twist at these words. The knowledge flamed up in my mind that the one thing I could *not* do was to forget.

Knowing what his fate would be, I'd turned Roddy over to the soldiers without a qualm. Now the doubts were creeping in. I'd had many, many dreams about him, about what his hanging would be like. I kept seeing his father rushing forward to drag on his son's heels to hurry the work of strangulation. After what my own family had experienced, would it do any good to put Roddy's through the same anguish and grief? How could that serve justice?

But it was the law that murderers and thieves and now spies should be executed, and Roddy was guilty of all three crimes as far as the courts-martial were concerned. It was out of my hands, but not my heart. Beldon thought I should forget it, but Father had always taught us to face our problems, not run from them.

"When you come to a fence either jump it or go through the gate, but don't let it hold you in," he'd said.

"Thank you, Doctor," I heard myself saying. "You've given me some ideas that want turning over." I excused myself and left before he could raise further questions or the topic of re-breaking my arm. On the way up the stairs, I hailed Jericho and kept going.

"What is it, sir?" he asked, rushing into my room.

"Get my riding boots out. I want some exercise."

"At this hour, sir? The soldiers have been most discouraging to travelers out after curfew."

"To the devil with them."

He correctly read my mood, fell in with it, and found my boots. Before a quarter hour had passed, Belle was saddled and one of the stable lads gave me a leg up onto her back. I took the reins with my good hand and swung her around toward the front lane leading to the main road. Not sure how good her eyes were at night, I didn't ask for an impossible pace, especially along areas steeped in shadows, but once on the road, the way was fairly clear and I kicked her into a decent canter for as long as my abused arm could stand the motion.

Not very long.

She never really worked up a sweat, though if she had the remaining walk would have cooled her down. Despite the curfew, we met no one along the way, not a single soldier until we reached Glenbriar and The Oak came into view. There I was challenged quickly enough, but after giving my name and a formal request for an audience with Lieutenant Nash, I was immediately escorted in to see him. Apparently the guards presently on duty hadn't heard any strange rumors from their fellows about my blood-drinking.

"This makes a fine change from having to shout at you from the street," I said after greetings had been exchanged.

"Aye," said Nash. "You're still the hero with the men for all that you've done. That's a night I shall not soon forget myself. Your sister is in good health, I hope?"

"Very well, thank you."

"And I trust your arm is mending?"

"Middling fine, sir."

Nash took note of all the curious eyes trained on us and invited me to a more private room. It was the same one as we'd used before, but his manner indicated that it held no inconvenient memories. He inquired after the purpose of my visit.

"I wish to see the prisoner, Roddy Finch."

"May I ask why?"

There was more than sufficient candlelight to work with. "You may not," I said evenly, fixing my gaze hard upon him.

He blinked only once and with no alteration of his expression, stood. "Very well, then, Mr. Barrett. I should be pleased to take you to him. You'll want that candle, as it's very dark."

"He's in the cellar?"

"There was no other place to put him. This village is too small to have a proper lockup."

Until the soldiers came we'd had no need of one, but I held my peace and picked up the candle. Nash led the way through the common room, where we were both—and I imagined myself in particular—subject to more staring. I caught a glimpse of the landlord, but he ducked from sight when I turned for a better look. Elizabeth's fear that I'd have to have a "talk" with the whole island had some substance to it. Well, Mr. Farr and the rest would just have to wait.

We reached a back passage near the kitchen, where a man with a sword and rifle came to attention when he saw Nash. He moved from off the trapdoor where he'd been standing and slid back a bolt that looked to have been recently attached. Lifting the door, he took a ladder from the wall and lowered it into the darkness, then went down ahead of us. Nash took charge of the candle, and I followed the guard as best I could, hindered as I was with my arm in its sling.

The place had a nauseating smell of food stores, damp, human sweat and unemptied chamber pots. The roof was low; Nash and his man were all right, but I had to stoop quite a bit to keep from bumping my head.

"Over there," said Nash, pointing to a far corner.

I took the candle back and peered, needing every ray of its feeble light in this awful place. I could just make out two hunched shapes huddled close by a supporting pillar of wood. Drawing closer, they took on form and identity and became Roddy Finch and Ezra Andrews. Both stirred sluggishly and winced against the tiny flame. There were chains on their wrists, the links solidly fixed to the pillar with huge staples. Neither of them had much freedom of movement and they reeked from their confinement.

Turning toward Nash, I thanked him and made it very clear that he and the guard need not remain. As before, he gave no outer sign, but instantly obeyed my request. The two of them went up the ladder. The trap was left open, but I didn't mind.

"What do ye want?" Andrews demanded when I returned to them.

An excellent question and not one that could be answered while he was listening in. I knelt close so he could see me. "I want you to sit back and go to sleep."

I knew I'd reached him, but it was still a little startling to witness how quickly he complied. He gaped at me empty-eyed for a few seconds, then did just as I said, just like that. Oh, but I could see that Father was very wise in advising me to be sparing with this ability.

Roddy was also gaping, albeit for a different reason. "Jonathan? What—?"

"Never mind him, I came to talk to you."

He raised himself up, his chains clinking softly. There were raw patches on his wrists and his face was dirty and drawn. His own eyes were nearly as empty as Andrews's, but, again, from a different cause. Beneath the sweat and grime and the heavy miasma of night soil, I could smell the thick sour stench of his fear.

"Talk about what?" he asked. There was a lost and listless tone to his voice.

"About what happened to me."

He shook his head, not understanding. "I didn't do it; 'twere Nathan. An' I'm that sorry about it, though." He nodded at my arm.

"Not this, about what happened at the kettle when the soldiers were after you for the horses."

"They was our hosses. It weren't right as the soldiers should take 'em the way they did. I were only tryin' to get 'em back for Da."

"Yes, and you ... killed a man doing it."

"What? I didn't kill nobody."

His protest was so genuine that it set me back a step, until I realized that under these circumstances he would certainly deny any accusation against him, especially one of murder.

"But you did, Roddy. I know. All I want to know now is why."

"You're daft," he stated, looking mulish enough to pass for his younger brother.

We could go around all night on this, but I saw no advantage to it. "Look at me, Roddy, and listen to me .... Do you remember the day you took back the horses from the soldiers?"

"Yes," he said in a voice as flat and lifeless as his expression.

"You were standing above the kettle and you looked across, and you must have seen me."

"No."

"You saw me and raised your rifle and shot me."

"No."

"You did, I saw you do it, Roddy."

"No."

Damnation. How could he *not* speak the truth while in this state? He was so far separated from his own will he couldn't possibly do otherwise. I was frustrated to the point of trying to shake it out of him, until a simple little thought dropped into my mind like a flash of summer lightning on the horizon. Since waking up in that damned box, I'd had a thousand distractions keeping me busy, keeping me exhausted, keeping me from seeing that which should have been obvious. In all the time since his capture I'd never once questioned why Roddy, of all people, had expressed no surprise at my miraculous return from the dead. I'd looked across the kettle and recognized him and his eye was sharp enough for him to know me in turn.

Or rather, I *thought* I'd recognized Roddy. But if I was wrong...then the young man who had ...

Nathan Finch?

I had not seen him in three years. He'd have grown up in that time and at a distance...I'd taken him for his brother. "Nathan shot that man, didn't he, Roddy?" I asked tiredly.

"Told 'im he shouldn'ta done it," he replied.

I lowered my head and groaned and wished myself someplace that didn't have soldiers or prisons or scaffolds.

"*Why?* Why did he do it?"

"They were comin' for us an' Nathan said as that fellow in the coat must be their general, shootin' 'im would solve our problems. They'd leave off chasin' us and see to 'im, instead, and they did."

"Coat?"

"A fine red coat with braid, 'e said, which meant 'e were like to be General Howe. So Nathan got 'im. Said 'e couldn't hardly miss. Our Nate ain't so clever on some things, but 'e's the best shot in the family. We never want fer a bit of coney 'r squirrel when 'e's on the hunt."

Just as I'd mistaken him for another, Nathan had returned the favor, doing his patriotic duty by killing an enemy general. The fool. The bloody, bloody *stupid* fool. As if a general would be on a hunt for stolen commissary stock. I found I could not speak for a very long time. It was absurd and awful and idiotic and unutterably sad.

It was the truth.

✦ ✦ ✦

THE WHOLE NIGHT MIGHT have slipped past with me staring at nothing and trying not to think and failing if not for Roddy. He eventually woke up to regard me with both wariness and curiosity. He also seemed to have some vague memory of the questions I'd put to him.

"You goin' to tell on Nathan?" he asked.

"He killed that man, didn't he?" I returned. I still had enough wit to try maintaining the fiction of another's death.

"Well, it's war, ain't it? People get killed in wars."

There was no point in gainsaying him on that grim fact. "And what if it had been you? Would you care to have someone shoot you down just because there's a war?"

He shook his head, not for an answer, but in puzzlement. Apparently he'd never before considered himself as ever becoming a target.

"Did Nathan kill that Hessian boy as well?"

Roddy's gaze dropped in reply.

"Then I suppose they'll hang you for that, too."

"But Ezra here said—"

"They know you're no soldier. He can take any oath he likes on your behalf, but they won't believe him. They'll hang you for a horse thief or a murdering spy no matter what."

"But I'm no spy, an' how can I be a hoss thief when it was our own hosses we were takin' back?"

Oh, but there was such a terrible difference between the law and justice in some circumstances. Father often discussed that conundrum of right and wrong with Rapelji. There was nothing right about this situation. Roddy should not suffer for a murder he did not commit or be hanged for taking his horses back from thieves operating within the law. He was guilty, but innocent…and thinking too much on that just made my head hurt.

What if Nathan had been here instead, and I'd learned the truth, learned from his own lips, that he had been the shooter? My murderer. He wasn't as likeable as Roddy, and certainly guilty. But though he'd killed me, *I wasn't dead.*

"Jonathan?" Roddy was giving me a strange look. "What are you laughin' about? Nothin' funny 'ere."

Eventually I hiccupped my fit of misplaced mirth to a halt and took stock. Before me were two dead men. Neither of *them* would return from the grave. One innocent of murder at least, the other carrying out what he thought to be his duty. How could I leave them to be hanged?

That question spun through my mind, followed by the unavoidable answer that I couldn't.

"There's been enough death…" I began, wiping my eyes.

"Eh?"

"Roddy, if I get you out of here, can you find a way off the island?"

"What d'you mean?"

"If you escape you'll have to get as far from here as you can. That means not going home or even to Suffolk County, as those will be the first places they'll look."

"I don't see as how it can be done, but Ezra here said as he knew where we could lay hands on a boat and row across to Connecticut to join up with his regiment. Nate was to do that if we got separated."

"Where's this boat?"

"Five miles, maybe less from here."

"Think you can make it there before light?"

"Easy. But how can—"

"Never mind how. I'll be back in a few minutes. Wake up your friend and tell him to keep his mouth shut when I come."

I left the candle with them and, bending low, made my way back to the ladder. Nash had gone but the guard was still at his station as I emerged.

"*All is well?*" he asked.

"*Ja.* Are you sleepy?" I added in English. I couldn't recall the right words in German.

"*Was?*"

"Sleepy?" I pantomimed a yawn, lay my head to one side with my eyes shut for a moment, then pointed questioningly at him. He grinned and shook his head.

The idiot.

"*What is the German for ...?*" I repeated my pantomime.

Puzzled that I should want a language lesson, but flattered by my interest, he promptly supplied me with the weapon I sought. "*Schlafen.*"

"Yes, *schlafen, mein Freund. Schlafen. Schlafen ...*"

I caught him as he dropped forward, not an easy task with only one arm. A dead weight and unwieldy, I just managed to lay him out without making too much row. His rifle and sword caused a little clatter, but there were stout doors between us and the rest of the inn. I had to hurry, for Nash might return or someone else could blunder in and disturb me while I was clawing through the man's pockets. Snuffbox, a few coins—where did the fool keep it?

There. A ring heavy with keys. I grabbed it and dived down the ladder. Andrews was awake and looking belligerent.

"What d'ye plan for us? That we should be shot while escaping? Is that what yer up to?"

"Don't be such a fool, Mr. Andrews—"

"That's Lieutenant to you, ye lyin' Tory."

"Lieutenant fool, then." I sorted through the keys, trying to find the right one to fit the locks on their chains. "Think what you like, but keep your mouth shut. If you get caught again, then we're *all* for the gallows, and I've no wish to hang for the likes of you."

"He's tryin' to help us, Ezra," put in Roddy. As if to confirm his statement the next key worked and his hand was free. I gave him the ring and told him to finish the job while I kept watch.

The guard was as I'd left him, safe for us, but highly noticeable should anyone come in. My stomach turned over and over. If we were caught now—it still wasn't too late to put things back—it was too much to hope to get Roddy and Andrews away ... there were too many soldiers about.

Turn and turn again.

Roddy's head appeared above the trap's opening. He looked feverish with his sweat-smeared face and frightened and overly-bright eyes. He goggled at the sleeping soldier, but sensibly nodded when I put a finger to my lips. He crept out and made room for Andrews.

"Keys?" I whispered.

"I left 'em down there," he said unhappily.

Oh, well, I'd have to go back for the candle, anyway. "Through there," I said, pointing to a passage behind them. "It should take you outside and as you value your lives don't make a sound and don't be seen."

By now it had finally penetrated Andrews's hard skull that I'd had either a change of heart or of loyalties. He grabbed Roddy's arm and they were gone.

Stomach still spinning, I made one more trip down the ladder, painfully jarring my arm when my footing slipped on the last rung. I bit back a grunt and kept moving, retrieving the keys and candle from where they lay on the earthen floor. When discovered, the abandoned chains would be a considerable mystery to Nash.

A final clumsy climb up and I was stuffing the keys back in the guard's pocket with trembling hands. Looking at his guilelessly peaceful face, I realized I couldn't leave him like this. Any hint of irregularity and the first course of action would be to check on the prisoners. They needed time to get away, and I needed to put some distance between myself and my crime.

Good arm under his shoulders, I heaved the man to his feet, shaking him. The activity brought him awake and left him somewhat confused. Giving him what I hoped would seem a smile of friendly concern, I helped him pull himself together, dusting his clothes and hoping to confound him more with swift, incomprehensible speech.

"Dear me, but I thought you might have hurt yourself, everything all right now? Bumped our heads together, don't you know, when I'm came up, you went down, and bang! There you are, but accidents do happen. All's well now, eh, what?"

"Was?"

"Ah... der Kopf..." I tapped first my forehead, then his, and said "Ow!" while giving an indication that he'd fallen. For all my acting, I received a deservedly strange look from him, which I pretended not to notice. He picked up his rifle, straightened his sword and scabbard, and tried to resume a dignified attitude. I indicated that he should close the trap and shoot the bolt.

"I'll just be off to see Lieutenant Nash. Vielen Danke und gute Nacht."

The mention of Nash's name reminded him that I had some kind of special status. I gave him a couple of pennies for his trouble and left. Now, if he'd just leave his charges undisturbed for a while. A pity I didn't know much of the language or I could have arranged something more to my advantage. On the way back, I vowed to take some positive steps toward enlarging my German vocabulary before another week had passed.

Nash welcomed me and asked if my interview had gone well.

"Very well, indeed, sir. I am most grateful for your kindness. Just wanted to see the wretch one more time and to ask if you would be so good as to find a use for this." I produced a small purse and lay it on the table between us.

He pretended surprise. "But what is this, Mr. Barrett?"

"Let's just call it a contribution toward His Majesty's victory. I'm sure that you can find some way to make life a bit easier for your soldiers."

Peering into it, Nash looked quite gratified. He must have been worried that the bribe I'd promised would be unduly delayed. It was my own and not Father's money, though, a fraction of what I'd managed to bring back from England. He'd written that good coin was becoming rare and the paper money in circulation was hardly more than a grim joke. It seemed to me that a ready supply of silver and gold would be a very handy thing to have around and so it was now proved.

Nash gave warm thanks for my generosity and offered to stand me to the best the house could offer in the way of drink. He could well afford it, but I politely declined.

"I must head home before it gets too late…"

Someone began pounding on the door. *"Herr Oberleutnant!"* Oh, good God.

But the man who rushed in was not the guard I'd left; however, his news was just as calamitous. Some eagle-eyed sentry had spotted two men haring out of town, recognized them as being the prisoners, and given the alarm.

"How the devil did they escape? You don't know? Then find out! Never a moment's peace," Nash complained. "I'd ask you to come, sir, as you might enjoy another hunt, but with your arm…."

Feeling that my face might crack under the strain of looking calm and brightly interested, I waved down his objections. "But I wouldn't miss this for the world, Lieutenant. I would be singularly honored if you allowed me to render such limited service as I might be capable of offering."

"Well, you do know the land, and I was highly impressed with the sharpness of your vision the other night. One of the men said that you'd be like to find a black cat in a root cellar."

I laughed deprecatingly, wishing to high heaven that he'd not mentioned cellars.

✦ ✦ ✦

"LAUDER REPORTS THAT he believes they are only just ahead of us, sir," said Nash's sergeant.

"He believes?" Nash sneered. "Go back and inform him that I am not interested in what he believes but what he *knows*." The sergeant whipped off.

Nash had been optimistic when we'd started the expedition but as the night grew old and he and the men more tired, his high spirits had taken a sharp turn in the other direction. His faith in my ability to see well in the dark had also suffered a decided setback. At the first opportunity, I'd done what I could to lead them in the wrong direction, but it hadn't been very successful, largely due to the tracking efforts of one Hessian corporal.

The man must have been part hunting hound, and indeed, some few of the hapless serfs sold by their greedy princes into the service of King George were *Jägers* in their homelands. They went for double the price of regular soldiers because of their hunting and shooting skills. If his majesty's generals here matched a few thousand such men to the new Ferguson rifles—while in England I'd seen one of the newest of those beauties demonstrated—they would make short work of the Congress's rabble and possibly end this wretched rebellion before winter.

For now, though, this specimen from Hessen-Kassel or Württemberg or wherever was a damned inconvenience to my objective. Each time I managed to take a misleading course, he invariably brought us back on the right trail again. I was forced to hold myself in check, lest Nash become suspicious.

We moved after the sergeant, Nash on his horse, I on Belle and a dozen soldiers at our backs doing their best to keep up over the uneven ground. Some carried lanterns like the two fellows trotting before us and the lot of them made enough noise to wake all this half of the island. Whenever we passed a house, the shutters would either open with curiosity or close in fear, depending on the boldness of its residents. If anyone deigned to call out a question, Nash's answer was that we were on the king's business and not to hinder us. No one did.

I stood up in the stirrups to get a look at things. Half a mile ahead was Lauder and his party, which included the German corporal. The sergeant was almost to them, bearing Nash's impatient message. Another half-mile beyond, I made out two struggling figures against the clean background of an empty field. Had it been full daylight, Lauder would have been upon them in very short order.

Couldn't those fools move any faster? One of them seemed spry enough, but the other was having trouble of some sort, limping, perhaps. Damnation, at this rate they would be caught.

"See anything?" Nash asked hopefully.

I started to say no and changed it at the last second. "I'm not sure. I think I shall ride ahead with the advance party."

"It could be dangerous, Mr. Barrett."

"I doubt that; the prisoners are unarmed, after all." Before he could oppose it, I put my heels into Belle's sides, and she obediently shot forward at a fast canter. Oh, how that shook and tore at my arm. I clamped my jaw shut and concentrated on getting to my goal. We passed the sergeant without a word and I reined in Belle at the last second. A canter was bad enough, but the change in gait from it to a walk required some trotting in between and I wanted to keep that to a minimum and thus spare my arm.

"Any luck, Sergeant Lauder?" I asked. I brought Belle to a full stop across their path, causing Lauder's party to halt as well. Anything to give Roddy and Andrews a little more of a lead.

"The tracks are very fresh," he replied. His manner was polite, but very cool, as he hadn't forgotten our fight in front of The Oak earlier that week. I was relieved to note that he was walking normally again, though. His *Jäger* corporal, who had a lantern, pointed at the ground where some grass had been crushed and spoke in German. "We will soon have them," Lauder translated.

"You're sure? It doesn't look like much to me."

The corporal picked up on my disparaging tone and made a vigorous argument to the contrary.

"He says that they are here."

I obstinately continued with my pose of disbelief. "Perhaps, though I don't know how you can sort anything sensible out of that muddle."

Just as stubborn, Lauder repeated his previous statement and made indications that he would like to proceed. Just then, Nash's sergeant caught up and delivered his caustic message. Lauder maintained a phlegmatic face, but we could tell he was hardly amused at this questioning of his efficiency. He vented it upon the corporal and ordered him to proceed as speedily as possible.

I looked past them toward Roddy and Andrews. They seemed to be going slower than ever. Their three days of confinement in the cellar must have taken all the strength out of them. They'd never make it.

"Sergeant Lauder, I shall run ahead and see if I can't properly spot 'em. You go on with what you're doing."

I gave Belle another kick and—quite stupidly from their point of view—charged over the tracks the corporal was trying so diligently to follow. About fifty yards on, I veered off to the left so I was riding parallel to the trail.

Roddy was the one limping; Andrews supported him, but they hadn't a hope of breaking away at this pace. I drew up even with them, but some twenty yards to their left, and gave a soft hail.

"Roddy, it's me. I've come to help."

"More like to lead 'em to us," said the ever-mistrustful Andrews.

"Please be so good as to keep your voice down, Lieutenant, or we'll all be chained in the cellar."

"What do ye want, then?" he demanded in a gruff, but somewhat softer tone.

"The Hessians are catching you up."

"Tell us something we don't know. Of course they're comin'."

"Good, then you know you'll need to go faster."

"Aren't we doin' the best we can? The poor lad all but twisted his ankle off gettin' away."

"I'm ready to loan you my horse, but we'll have to be careful—"

"Then bring 'im over here an' we'll get the lad—"

"Do that and a certain tracker back there will read the signs we leave like a book. There's a stony patch not far ahead. You'll have to make it that far first."

Andrews was for wasting time by asking more questions. I moved past and guided Belle down a slight slope to a wide place between the fields where the earth had been scraped away by some ancient and long-departed glacier. That's what Rapelji had taught us, anyway, when he'd once led our class out here to study geological oddities. I never thought then that his science lesson would have ever proved to be of any practical use to me in life. Blessings to the man for his thoroughness in pounding such diverse knowledge into our heads.

Roddy and Andrews finally caught up with me. I dismounted from Belle and took her over to them. They'd both need to ride her, but Andrews insisted he could do well enough on foot.

"As long as the hoss is carryin' 'im an' not me, I'll be quick enough."

"Yes, and leaving your tracks as well. When we go I want that man to find only mine and Belle's, yours are to disappear completely."

The dawn finally broke for him. "Oh, I see what yer about. That's good brain-work, young fella."

"If my brain were properly working, I wouldn't be out here. Get Roddy into the saddle and shift yourself up behind him. I'll lead the horse."

"Thank you, Jonathan," Roddy gasped.

"Later," I said. "When we know you're safe."

Both of them mounted. I took hold of the reins and led Belle away from the spot, resuming the path I'd been on earlier. Hopefully, the corporal would interpret things to mean that I was afoot for some reason other than the real one. If questioned later, I could always say that I'd wanted to give the horse a rest.

The boat that Andrews had been making for was still a mile ahead. Roddy's mere five-mile jaunt had been almost twice the distance because of the character of the land and their need to avoid the soldiers. They made better time now, but our speed was still limited to a walk. On the other hand, we knew where we were going and the Hessian tracker did not.

Before too long I heard the measured rush of sea waves carried on the fresh wind. Following Andrews's directions, we slipped quietly by some farmhouses, rousing only a barking dog or two along the way. I didn't care much for that row, but the animals were too distant to do us any real harm; there were worse dangers waiting for us.

Nash had boasted that you couldn't toss a rock into a field without striking one of His Majesty's soldiers, and now as we passed an old unused church I spied several of them walking over its grounds toward us. The church was occupied, after all, quartered with British troops. One of the men saw our figures moving against the general darkness, correctly assumed that we were up to no good, and gave a loud challenge.

I flipped the reins over Belle's head and pressed them into Roddy's hands. "Ride like the devil. I'll lead them off!"

"But—"

Andrews sensibly gave Belle a kick and away they went, heading for the sea. I yelled to encourage the horse to go faster and to draw the soldiers' attention to me. It worked far better than I would have liked. Calling for help from their companions in the old church, they started my way with all speed. I took to my heels, heading south, trusting my improved vision would give me sufficient advantage over them to escape. On the other hand, I still had to keep them close enough on my track to give Roddy his chance to get away.

"Over there!" someone shouted in good king's English this time. So far they'd likely seen me only as a murky figure; they couldn't be allowed a better look lest I end up taking Roddy's place at the gallows. I dodged under the shadows of a small orchard, threaded between the trees, went over a fence, and charged through a sheep pasture. The sheep (apparently this lot had been overlooked by the commissaries) scattered madly, bleating in protest. They made a fine confusion for the soldiers in my wake. God but this was sport, indeed. As I raced along, I laughed aloud to think what Jericho would have to say about this abuse of my riding boots.

I was still laughing when I made it to the top of a rise and paused for a glance back to see where my pursuers were. A foolish thing to do, for I'd underestimated their speed, overestimated my own, and silhouetted myself against the sky. In that instant one of the men raised his rifle and used it.

A puff of powder smoke obscured the shooter—just as it had that morning by the kettle. Whether a Hessian *Jäger* or Nathan Finch himself returned to finish me off for good and all, the awful image quite froze me.

He was a skillful shot—that, or uncommonly lucky.

It would have made no difference had I sensibly dodged; to hear the report meant it was too late to save myself.

And—just as it had that morning by the kettle—time ceased its normal progress; the world was engulfed by my illusion of everything slowing to a halt.

The devastating impact of the rifle ball slammed me flat as though my legs had been scythed away. My was chest on fire...no, my back...my whole body....

Oh, sweet God, *not again.*

Above, the glowing stars flowed and spun like water in a bright stream, swirling into glittering whirlpools and splashing up into self-made fountains of light.

Below, the black land twisted, exchanging places with the heavens. They merged wildly, broke apart, merged again.

Crying out, I tumbled helplessly, dizzily down the other side of the rise.

Even as I fell, my voice died away, breath gone, crushed from me by the hideous burden of the pain. It completely overwhelmed me, heavier and more horrible than the other time, for I *knew* what lay ahead—

No, I can't go through THAT *again.... No!*

The sounds of the night, the soldiers, the sheep, the rush of the sea, the unspeakable pain itself, abruptly ceased, like the snuffing of a candle. One second I could see, the next all was gone, consumed by a thick, dark gray fog.

The change was so sudden and swift that I couldn't sort it out at first. I was beyond thought for the longest time, unable to grasp what had happened. I seemed to drift like a feather on the wind. No, not a feather. The lightest bit of down was yet too weighty compared to me. I was more like smoke, rising and floating carelessly, too faint to have a shadow to mark my passage.

I was floating; I was falling.

Then came the answer: instinct and memory told me I must again be caught up by whatever force it was that had magically seized and hurtled me from my coffin without disturbing one clod of dirt in between.

But that was *quite* mad.

Quite....

Ah. *That* was it.

I understood now. The poisons of my Fonteyn blood had finally corrupted my brain. I was as mad as Mother. More so. On the day of the shooting I'd simply taken too much sun and collapsed in this nightmarish fit. The business about me dying and escaping from the grave, drinking blood, it was all nonsense, no more than a dream. When next I woke I'd be in my own bed, wrapped immobile in sheets like a newborn in swaddling. That would be good, for it would keep me from hurting myself or others in my ravings. During quiet interludes Jericho would feed me porridge a spoonful at a time and wipe my mouth when I drooled and good Doctor Beldon would see to it I had plenty of laudanum so my screams would not disturb the rest of the house.

Yes, that was it. *Had* to be.

Reason slept. Reason itself was an absurdity when measured against this. Instinct told me to be calm and not to struggle, and I listened to it. I was beyond argument, beyond fear. I felt safe, like a tired swimmer who finally ceases to fight the water and gives in to its embrace only to discover his own buoyancy is saving him. So insanity was saving me from ... well ... something too strange and awesome to be borne.

After what must have been a great while, my mind eventually began to work again, sluggishly attempting to form questions and find answers. Just because I'd gone mad didn't mean I was totally bereft of moments of clarity.

I tried to be orderly about it, taking one sensation—or lack thereof—at a time.

The fog, for example. I seemed surrounded by fog, yet felt no evidence of its damp presence. What sensation remained came from outside my body: the pressure of the wind, the rough kiss of grass and ground flowing by.

Of my own body—I knew I *must* still possess one—I'd lost awareness of weight and form, if not the memory, of it. No arms or legs, no head to hold my thoughts, no mouth to express them. I could hear things, but only in a vague way as though my ears—if I'd had any—had been swathed in a soft blanket.

Perhaps that rifle ball had finished me off and the fog I drifted in was part of the process of dying. Perhaps I was already a ghost....

Then it struck me how absolutely, utterly *ridiculous* it all was.

I gave myself a kind of internal shake, half in my mind and half in the body I knew *had* to exist.

Of course I was not dying or dead or gone mad.

Not dead. Not a ghost.

Ghost-*like*, perhaps...?

I felt the beginnings of gravity tugging upon my limbs, upon what *should* be my limbs....

And then I was myself again, sitting on the bare earth as if I'd always been there and with everything returned to its proper place in the universe: stars above, land below, and me in the middle. There was no sign of the soldiers, and if I read things right, I was a good half mile or more from where I'd been before.

How...?

I'd traveled downwind. I'd traveled *on* the north wind coming from the Sound.

Falling and floating, or in this case, floating and drifting.

"Ridiculous."

But giving thin voice to my first reaction to an unlikely conclusion was no help to my bewildered brain, for my thoughts could only return to the question: how *else* could I have gotten here so quickly?

And...how else could I have escaped the prison of my coffin that first night? The answer, however impossible, was undeniable.

No. I shook my head. It was far too fanciful. Frightening, too.

But how else?

The answer, the impossible answer, lay within me. Brought forth by panic or pain, I had somehow ceased to be part of the corporeal world.

Perhaps I was able, without conscious effort, to slip through some invisible doorway into an equally invisible sphere of existence and walk there—float—until such time as I was evicted back to my own land again. Maybe that's the place where ghosts resided, and I was but a visitor to their realm even as they visited ours....

That seemed awfully complicated, though. Ghosts? I could almost hear my sister's snort of derision.

The simpler explanation might have to do with my own body changing form, ceasing to be solid, like water boiling away to steam—but the process being instantaneously fast.

Nora had *never* mentioned it. Either she knew nothing about it, or had correctly concluded it too preposterous for me to believe even with her influence to convince me otherwise.

Well-a-day. Apparently she was right. I'd obviously plunged into something most extraordinary, and even after going through it my credence for its truth was shaky at best.

Could I—dare I—try to achieve that state on purpose? That would be the proof I wanted.

Best to try it now before I over-thought things and allowed reason to talk me out of the possibility.

I recalled what that strangeness had felt like. My most intense memory was of a fierce desire to not *be* where I'd been.

As if a great gray shadow had enveloped the world, my vision clouded over. The wide hum of night noises faded. I raised my hand. It gradually became almost as transparent as glass. The more ethereal it was, the less clearly I could see. Then the grayness took everything, leaving me sightless. That's when the constraint of gravity ceased its constant and familiar hold and I was *floating.*

The earth that once supported me was not really solid at all, but porous. Then, as I began to sink in a little past its surface, came the thought that it was I, and not the ground, that was no longer substantial. I gave a kick like a swimmer and felt myself rising until I sensed myself hovering a foot or so above the grass. There I was able to hold in place against the wind.

Sweet God, what had I *become?* What was this...ability?

My concentration wavered. The night crashed back upon me. The earth's pull resumed soverignity in a most vigorous way. My arms jerked outward to regain lost balance, and I only just managed to land on my feet. As before, I'd moved some distance from where I'd been.

I gaped about me, torn between shock and fascination.

Ghostlike, I had escaped the grave. I'd ceased to be solid and passed through the intervening ground to freedom. Just now I had virtually flown over the ground like a wraith on the wind to escape the soldiers.

And the pain of being shot.

That was gone. There was no sign of any wound on my flesh, though it was upsetting to find a hole larger than my thumb torn through my bloodied clothes. The rifle's ball had gone in and out, leaving behind this evidence only of its passage, the same effect the sword blade had had on Nora's clothes. She'd bled, but had somehow recovered. This must have been how she—

My arm. My right arm, shattered and useless for nearly a week...

Restored. Completely healed. *Free* of pain. I could bend and straighten my elbow with ease, as though it had never suffered injury.

Despite this astounding turn, I felt a thick queasiness trying to manifest and ooze up from within. In the absence of a fast-beating heart, I could interpret it to be a symptom of my near-paralyzing fear of this, my changed state, a fear that I'd pushed away so often before. As entitled as I must be to surrendering to it, I must not give in to the temptation. True, my situation was monumentally strange, but beyond the strangeness, beyond the changes, I was still the same man, still Jonathan Barrett, and I had no need to be afraid of myself.

Accept it, Nora had said whenever I'd witnessed anything supernormal about her. She had only to hold my gaze to make me do so, but always she'd given me the opportunity to abandon the confines of the mundane first. I usually failed her, requiring artificial urging in the right direction. Whether because of her influence on me or my own temper, I could forgive her, for her gentle coercion had been in a good cause, soothing soothed away all unease between us.

"Accept it," I said aloud.

Accept your new self...for the only other alternative must surely be madness.

Accept without fear, without expectation, and with hope for the best. With God's grace and guidance I'd be able to triumph over whatever future lay before me.

Accept....

◆ ◆ ◆

THE SEA SOUND ROARED IN MY EARS and seemed to bestow a kind of movement to my forever-stilled heart. The shifting water was so beautiful, a living, glittering thing, restless and untamed under the calm luminescence of thousands of minute suns. It stole their silver light, tossed it in the waves, and playfully threw it back again. I could have stood on the bluff and watched for hours, but the night was beginning to turn and I had a long road ahead.

Below, in the shelter of a tiny cove, was Belle, her reins dragging on the ground. I was glad to finally find her. I'd been walking along the edge of the coast for a very long time, looking. She appeared to be no worse for wear and occasionally dropped her head to graze on a patch of grass.

There was no sign of Roddy Finch or Ezra Andrews. If their boat had been stored here, it was long gone. I wished them a safe journey.

I made my way down to Belle, took up the reins, and mounted her. Perhaps she sensed that we were going back to her stable. I didn't have to guide her in the right direction; she took it for herself and set a good pace. As we moved up onto a clear and well-marked road, I gave her the signal to go faster, and she readily obeyed. Trot, canter and finally gallop. She would never match Rolly's speed, but she made her gait smoother and more graceful. I crouched over her, one hand on the reins, the other stretched before me as though to taste the streaming wind.

Accept....

Accept the wind and the sky and the earth and the joy and the sorrow.

Accept this new chance at life.

Live and laugh again.

And I did laugh.

It grew distant and hollow as my solid hand began to fade and vanish along with the rest of the world.

I stopped the fading at a point where I could just see through my flesh to the horse's bobbing neck below. The wind tugged at me, but not as hard as before, and I knew I could move against it or with it as I chose.

I'd had much time to practice during that long walk, looking.

Now my hand was only just visible. The world was nearly lost in gray fog, but I was able to hold it like this if I concentrated. I could only just sense the horse's strong movement beneath me.

And then I shot free of her. My booted feet lifted clear of the stirrups. I was above her now, arms thrown wide like wings, but carried along by my will alone. I pressed against the wind, matching Belle's speed for a moment until, with an unvoiced cry, I broke away.

Ten feet, twenty, thirty. Higher and higher.

I soared and turned and rolled like a nighthawk, pushing ahead of Belle or falling behind, but always keeping her within safe sight.

I soared high over the rushing earth, caught up in my own soundless laughter as I embraced the dancing sky.

We were going home.